The Architect

A NOVEL

James Williamson

For Nancy,
With appreciation.
Here's a little touch
of Memphis.
Enjoy!
Jim Williamson
AIA Memphis
2·11·11

Library of Congress Control Number: 2007939813

Printed in the United States of America
ISBN 978-1-58385-205-7

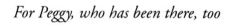

For Peggy, who has been there, too

The fate of the architect is the strangest of all. How often he expends his whole soul, his whole heart and passion, to produce buildings into which he himself may never enter.

—*Johann Wolfgang Von Goethe*

Art hath an enemy called Ignorance.

—*Ben Jonson*

The Architect

A NOVEL

James Williamson

Chapter One

It was sweltering, a day for seersucker. The tall man in the rumpled suit glanced at his watch and shifted restlessly in his seat. He tugged once more at his old polka dot bow tie. The knot was a little too perfect; it lacked the loose, slightly disheveled air of nonchalance he cultivated.

By contrast, the shorter, older man marching down the aisle toward him was tanned and sleek, tastefully attired in a crisp poplin suit set off by an Hermès tie. He was accompanied by an attractive but matronly woman in an expensive silk blouse.

Instinctively, the man in the bow tie rose.

The other caught his eye and paused in the aisle, eyeing the wrinkled seersucker with a faint air of disapproval. He did not smile, and he hesitated a fraction of a second before offering his hand. When he spoke, his tone was cool and superior. "Afternoon, Ethan, so glad you could join us." He turned to his companion.

"Roberta, surely you and Ethan Cotham know each other?"

"Do I know him?" she gushed. "Why, I've kissed him!" She was about to say more but the man in the Hermès tie interrupted.

"Excuse me, Roberta, but it's already past one o'clock and we have a full agenda. Come along; we must get started. I believe you're number two, Ethan? I'm sure we're all anxious to hear your presentation on the Center for Southern Culture. It's quite a large project for a small firm like yours." He turned abruptly and headed for the long table at the front of the room.

The conference room of the public library on Front Street was beginning to fill for the monthly meeting of the Memphis Board of Design Review. The location struck Cotham as a profoundly ironic choice for an agency charged with the preservation of the city's historic architecture. Built in the sixties, the library was a long, low, steel and glass Modernist box boasting a metal sunscreen, a *brise soleil,* stretched across the façade. On the same site had once stood the remarkable red sandstone Romanesque-revival Cossitt Library. Demolished in the name of progress and functionalism to make way for the new box, the loss of the old library symbolized for him the triumph of Philistinism that had characterized too much of the city's past.

Cotham cherished vivid childhood memories of its bulging bay windows, crenelated parapets, and the swelling rotunda with its soaring tower. Wingback lounge chairs flanked a yawning, cave-like fireplace, its mantle inscribed with aphorisms in praise of the life of the mind. He could see himself ensconced there, a precocious nine-year-old entranced by the adventures of Huckleberry Finn, awaiting the return of his mother from her shopping expedition at Gerber's Department Store.

Outside the new building a shallow concrete pond scooped out a half level below the sidewalk had replaced the rotunda. Intended by its designers as a reflecting pool, the basin was empty, littered with tattered bus timetables, styrofoam cups, dead leaves, and a discarded condom. An abstract marble sculpture in the pool had once depicted citizens absorbed in the books balanced in their laps.

That was before vandals had decapitated their heads.

Cotham surveyed the conference room. A grandmotherly lady was seated directly in front of him. He recognized a reporter from *The Commercial Appeal* and a couple of other architects, presumably present to represent the other projects on the afternoon's agenda. The members of the Board were taking their places. At the head of the table, Richard Brisbane Astor, the chairman, the man in the poplin suit, the self-appointed dean of Memphis architects, began shuffling through a sheath of notes. To Astor's left sat Roberta Quonset. Next to her Cotham recognized Mabel Meriwether Malone, the vice-chair and a past president of the Victorian Society. She wore sensible shoes, and her thin mouth was set in a permanent look of disapproval. Stuffed into the chair on her left was the Reverend Thelonious Calhoun, pastor of the Vance Avenue Church of God in Christ and the only African-American member of the Board. Next came an overweight man in a polyester suit whom he did not recognize—apparently the dentist listed on the Board's letterhead. Across the table sat the new executive director, Evelyn Penobscot, an immaculately groomed young woman in a navy blue suit and white blouse. With her freshly minted Master of Historic Preservation degree, she wore the self-assured confidence of the graduate student to whom all has been revealed.

Astor opened the leather portfolio that lay before him, glanced at the agenda, and rapped the table with a wooden gavel. Roberta glanced across the room and smiled at Cotham. Astor caught the exchange and frowned. "The meeting will come to order," he intoned. *A powdered wig would become him,* Cotham mused.

Evelyn Penobscot walked to a PowerPoint projector at the end of the table. "Good afternoon, Mr. Chairman, ladies and gentlemen.

Our first case involves proposed alterations to 1256 Lee Avenue. The applicant, Miss Hattie Mae Prewitt, has requested permission to demolish and replace an existing garage. The house, constructed in 1910, is an intact example of the four-square style that is characteristic of the Annesdale-Snowden Historic District."

The projector showed a two-story house with a wide front porch shaded by magnolias. In the shadows of the porch huddled a matched set of ancient wicker armchairs and a sofa painted that shade of dark green virtually indistinguishable from black. To the left of the house, a driveway extended to a diminutive garage with a sagging roofline, barely visible in the backyard.

"Staff has reviewed the application and finds that demolition of the garage, which can be clearly seen from the street, will exert a negative impact on the district. The garage is covered in cedar shake siding, a material that is characteristic of the district. The hipped roof is also typical. The applicant proposes to build a new two-car porte cochere. Staff finds that the new carport will interfere with the scale of the house and the neighborhood. We recommend disapproval." She resumed her seat with an air of efficiency and decisiveness that proclaimed, "End of discussion."

"Is Miss Prewitt here?" asked Astor, peering about the room until he spied the frail little lady seated in front of Cotham. "Ah, Miss Prewitt, would you care to address the Board?"

"Why, yes, I would, sir." She stood and faced the table, leaning on a cane for balance. "When I moved to Lee Street in 1921 with my family, we had just one car, a Packard." Cotham recognized the lilting, old Memphis accent he associated with his mother. He had heard of the Prewitts; perhaps they had even been friends of his parents.

"Many of our neighbors had no car at all, don't you know, and my Daddy was proud of that Packard. So he had this garage built. But time went by, and cars got bigger. I remember trying to squeeze our 1957 Chrysler into it. The back end stuck out about three feet, and the old garage was so narrow I couldn't get the car door open enough to get out. Why, I distinctly remember that another lady in our neighborhood had the same thing happen, except she couldn't get her car's motor started again. It was winter, very cold with snow on the ground, and she lived alone. She was trapped in that car, and when they finally found her a week later, she had frozen to death.

"So I stopped using my garage, and it began to get in bad shape. It's full of termites now, and the contractor says it would cost as much to rebuild it as to start over. So I had him draw a plan for a new two-car porte cochere with a covered walk to the back door. That way when I come home from bridge at the Nineteenth Century Club on Monday nights I can park under cover and then go straight inside. All I want to do is build a nice new place for my car in my own backyard just like Daddy did."

"Mr. Chairman," responded Mabel Meriwether Malone in an authoritative tone, "the original structure is typical of many other outbuildings in this historic district. In my opinion, if we begin to allow them to be demolished, it won't be long until they've all been lost." *So now we have the Domino Theory of Preservation,* thought Cotham to himself.

"I agree with Mrs. Malone's excellent analysis," chimed in the dentist in the polyester suit. "It is our responsibility to maintain the character of this neighborhood. Has Miss Prewitt considered having her garage moved to another site in the district? We might be able to permit that if it were to be relocated behind another house nearby."

Astor peered around the table waiting for others to speak.

Roberta Quonset cleared her throat. "Mr. Chairman, I don't believe the preservation of the district will be negatively affected by the demolition of this old garage. It's virtually invisible from the street, and as you can see, it's in poor condition. After all, Miss Prewitt is the sort of civic-spirited, long-time resident who is responsible for the district having survived for the better part of a century without the protection of this Board. We should temper our inclination to be purists with realism."

"Thank you, Roberta," replied Astor. "I must say, however, that I feel it is our responsibility to be purists when it comes to historic preservation."

"Perhaps, Richard, but we should also bear in mind that there are such things as property rights."

"Yes, well, thank you for that helpful reminder, Roberta," replied Astor. "Now, if there are no further comments from the Board, I'd like to ask Evelyn if the staff would be willing to support a requirement that the garage be moved to another site."

"As you know, Mr. Chairman, there are precedents for this. I believe staff could support a requirement that Miss Prewitt advertise for a buyer who would agree to have the garage moved to an appropriate location. Perhaps she could reappear in six months to report to the Board on the results of her efforts." Roberta rolled her eyes.

"Very well, then. Without further comment, the Board tables final action on Miss Prewitt's application with the understanding that she will make every effort to move her garage to another suitable location as approved by the Board."

"But, Mr. Chairman," exclaimed Miss Prewitt in dismay, "the old thing's about to fall down. Who would want it? Surely there's some other way!"

"Call the next case please, Ms. Penobscot."

"Mr. Chairman," said the executive director, "our second case involves a special request from the Center for Southern Culture to evaluate the winning entry in their design competition for the proposed complex to be built on Riverside Drive at Beale Street. I believe the architect, Mr. Ethan Cotham, is in the audience and has agreed to answer any questions from the Board."

"Very well," replied Astor. "Perhaps we could begin with the staff's presentation and then open the floor to discussion."

Evelyn Penobscot resumed her place at the projector, and onto the screen flashed a photograph of a model of Cotham's dramatic winning design. "As you know, Mr. Chairman, technically the Center for Southern Culture, the CSC, is not within the bounds of an historic district. Nevertheless, I'm sure all of us realize the danger posed by inappropriate modern buildings on prominent downtown sites, such as the banks of the Mississippi River at the foot of historic Beale Street. That is why the Board of the CSC seeks our blessing in order to reassure the City Council, who must agree to make the site available, that the project will be architecturally suitable."

As Penobscot proceeded through the photographs of the model and then the drawings, Cotham shifted uneasily in his seat, listening carefully not only to the content of her remarks, but the choice of words as well.

"Staff has reviewed the plans and finds that they contain many commendable features. We are particularly impressed by the way the architect has oriented the buildings so as to take maximum advantage of the views downstream along the Mississippi River. Staff also commends the brick paving and the alignment of the main plaza with the axis of Beale Street as a way of creating a link between the river and the street grid of downtown." Her tone fairly dripped with condescension.

"On the other hand," Penobscot continued, "staff finds certain aspects of the design concept troubling. The most significant of these is the architectural imagery. The curving facades, the patterned masonry, the non-traditional composition of both large and small windows, and the asymmetrical placement of the main entrance appear too unconventional, too *contemporary.*" She pronounced the word with contempt.

"And that huge sign across the front!" interrupted Mabel Meriwether Malone. "I'm sorry, Evelyn, but it's positively *vulgar!* We would never allow that in Germantown."

Penobscot gave Malone a small, knowing glance before continuing. "In their totality, these elements fail to relate to the nineteenth century architecture of the upper Mississippi Delta region. Staff would have preferred, for instance, that the architects look to the traditional vocabulary of Front Street or Beale Street for inspiration.

"In short, we believe the design would be more acceptable if the forms were softened. Perhaps the massing could become more symmetrical so as to be more visually appealing to the ordinary citizen. Perhaps the entrance could be relocated and a simple red brick veneer substituted for the overly complicated masonry pattern. And, of course, the signage needs to be completely redesigned, if not eliminated altogether." Cotham winced.

"Pitched roofs and a neoclassical vocabulary, a columned portico, for instance, would create a bridge between the past and present. While staff recognizes that the accommodation of the curvilinear elements of the floor plans to a neoclassical vocabulary could prove problematic, we see little basis for these forms in either function or esthetics. We feel that their loss would not endanger the architect's underlying concept."

"Hey, good idea! I like columns," offered the dentist.

As Penobscot took her seat, Mabel Meriwether Malone nodded in agreement. "Mr. Chairman, I must agree with our executive director. Memphis is not Chicago. We should honor our Southern architectural heritage."

Astor gave her a brief approving glance before turning to Cotham. "If the architect would care to make any remarks in response to the staff report, the Board would appreciate hearing from him. Mr. Cotham?"

Cotham rose and faced the table. "Thank you, Richard. I've listened to these proceedings with interest. I will try to be brief.

"As you know, my firm was named the winner of the competition to design the Center for Southern Culture. When I agreed to undertake this competition, it was with the understanding that the winner would be selected by an independent jury. Nothing was said about an additional requirement to satisfy this Board.

"I am familiar with the history of censor boards." Astor looked up sharply from his note pad. "Years ago the Chairman of the Memphis Board of Censors routinely axed all films that portrayed African-Americans in any roles other than servants or minstrels. He refused to allow Charlie Chaplin to perform on stage because of Chaplin's leftist sympathies. He refused to approve any film depicting a bank robbery because he himself had once been robbed by Jesse James.

"This afternoon I have seen our new censor board in action, refusing in the name of 'purity' to allow a citizen to replace her own garage behind a house she occupied before any of us were born.

"We have heard it said that we are not Chicago and that we should honor our Southern architectural heritage. We are not Charleston or Natchez, either. The alleged purity of our historic districts in Memphis is mixed at best. Instead, diversity and eclecticism are the rule, and it is this mixture of old and new, of classical styles and naive mongrelizations, that is at the root of their charm. In its insistence on purism this board is attempting to recreate a past that never was.

"You have invited me here to defend my ideas and to explain why your criticisms are without merit. I will not do so. To defend myself would be to acknowledge their validity. Your staff finds my design lacking. I find your staff, like all censor boards, to be blissfully unburdened by the prospect of its own fallibility. Certainly Ms. Penobscot is well versed in history, but what is her design background? If any of you can explain how she has become qualified to tell me how my building should be designed, I will apologize and reconsider her recommendations."

"Excuse me, Mr. Cotham," interrupted Astor. "You were invited here to explain your ideas, not to attack the qualifications of the Board or its staff!"

"I beg your pardon, Richard, if what I say offends you. But it is Ms. Penobscot who has attacked me. Can you tell me why any architect who has lain awake grappling with an idea that day after day resists being born, who has wrestled with every conceivable design alternative, should defer to the quick, easy judgment of the dilettante?

"Ms. Penobscot's training in art history has taught her to recognize the stylistic details—classical orders, roof slopes, cornice profiles, whether the brick is laid in Flemish bond, and so forth. But in a work of architecture, the details derive from larger, more significant ideas. When I designed this roofline, I was thinking of the sweeping horizon of the Delta, not only how to shed rainwater. When I designed the windows, I was thinking of framing the views of the Mississippi, not of faux divided lights or our precious 'Southern architectural heritage.' In my opinion, those who cannot perceive these relationships between the whole and its parts are unqualified to judge the work of those who can."

"Mr. Cotham, I must insist that you not disparage…."

"A wise man once said, 'The good is ever the enemy of the best.' I recommend that thought to you today as you presume to redesign my project for me. Consider that in your conviction, common to all censor boards, that you have been granted special insights and unique access to the truth, you may, in fact, see through a glass darkly. Ask whether in your confidence that the unfamiliar is synonymous with the undesirable you are not merely reducing the excellent to the good." Cotham abruptly took his seat.

The Board members glanced uneasily around the table. Behind his heavy, black Le Corbusier spectacles, Astor's face was crimson, and the color had risen to the crown of his bald head. A long silence hovered over the conference room. At last he cleared his throat.

"Well, er, thank you, Mr. Cotham, for that enlightening treatise. I'm sure we will give your remarks the consideration they deserve. If there are no further comments from the Board, I think it might be best if we ask everyone to excuse us while we vote on whether to approve the plans for this project. We will adjourn for fifteen minutes."

"Mr. Chairman, I would like to add one last comment." It was

Roberta Quonset, who had sat listening in silence. "I think Mr. Cotham has made some valid points, and I am concerned that this Board may be overstepping its bounds.

"We need to bear in mind that our overworked staff consists solely of Ms. Penobscot and our new intern. I'm getting the impression through these repeated references to 'the staff' that we command a legion of experts.

"I don't know how Mr. Cotham, one of the most respected architects in our city, can bear to sit here while non-professionals scrutinize his work! None of us, with the exception of our Chairman, of course, has ever had to grapple with the task of designing even a small building, much less a project as complicated as the Center for Southern Culture. Have any of us studied structures or seismic theory? Have we any experience in the concepts architects spend years mastering? It's one thing for us to try to guide Miss Prewitt on the design of her new porte cochere. But I have real questions about our trying to second guess Mr. Cotham."

"Thank you, Roberta," Astor said, a bit testily. "However, we were appointed by the Mayor because of our interest in this community and our wide-ranging diversity of life experiences—not necessarily for technical expertise. Now may we call a recess while we vote?"

As the room began to empty, Cotham made his way to the table at the front where Astor stood gathering his papers. Astor glanced up. "Yes, what is it, Ethan?"

"You entered the competition as well, Richard. Everyone knows you lost. You will recuse yourself from the vote, won't you?" Astor glared at Cotham in silence. Cotham returned the stare, turned, and walked away.

The vote did not take long. Evelyn Penobscot stepped out of the conference room into the hall where a few spectators lingered and where Cotham stood at the window, contemplating the headless sculpture in the reflecting pool. She wore a look of thinly concealed triumph. "Mr. Cotham, I'm sorry to have to tell you that Design Review has voted not to recommend your design to the Board of the Center for Southern Culture. Staff will now draw up a list of recommended changes that will make the project more acceptable. These will be forwarded to you within a week with a copy sent to the CSC Board."

"I see," replied Cotham, his voice cold. "May I ask how the vote ran?"

"I regret it is our policy that votes of the Board remain confidential," she replied evenly.

"I can tell, you, however, that there was near-unanimous agreement that the plans as drawn are unacceptable. I suppose you'll just have to start over, won't you?"

Cotham made his way down Front Street back toward his office, head down, lost in thought. People passed him on the sidewalk and one of his old clients spoke to him, but he ignored them, oblivious to his surroundings.

DeMarco Johnson was not having a good day. He had already been late for his morning deliveries, and now his ex-girlfriend was chewing him out on the cell phone. He stepped on the gas and the FedEx delivery truck careened down Madison Avenue and around the corner onto Front Street. Just ahead he spied a young woman in a tight red dress, hips swaying as she sashayed down the sidewalk.

He leaned out the open door, grinned broadly, and waved. "Hey, Baby, how 'bout a little bit for DeMarco?"

At that moment, a tall man in a seersucker suit stepped off the curb and into his path.

Chapter Two

Months earlier, in the wee hours of a cold winter night, Cotham could have been a monk illuminating a medieval manuscript as he sat hunched over his drawing board. He took no notice as the rising sun broke through a tear in the stratus clouds and spilled over the Mississippi River, where a ghostly fleet of ice floes from Minnesota, Wisconsin, and Iowa drifted downstream. The watery light boiled over the far bank, inundated the Arkansas flood plain, and swept west to engulf the levees. Far below on the deserted street the blue needle of shadow cast by the old skyscraper contracted as the sun inched higher.

Under the fluorescent pall the small office appeared to have been decorated by some manic paperhanger. Sheets of the tracing paper they called "yellow trash" festooned the walls, and crumpled wads littered the floor around the drafting table. On the CD player the last notes of Schubert's *Trout* Quintet reverberated through the studio and died away.

The idea had been born only after a prolonged labor. Now that he had the concept, the real work had begun, the struggle to make a building out of what had begun as an inspired doodle on the back of an envelope.

Cotham spread a fresh roll of tracing paper over the seven layers already taped to the surface. With the stub of charcoal he drew again, for the eighth time, a series of interlocking convex curves, nearly duplicating those on the sheet immediately beneath. This time, however, as his hand swept to the lower corner of the sheet, it veered, and the curve was transformed into a straight line. Another abrupt reversal of course, and the line swerved at a sixty-degree angle, following the outline of a street grid on the first sheet of paper faintly visible below.

He stared at his work and groaned with fatigue. It had been a long night, but perhaps the effort had not been in vain. He could not yet tell; he was too close to his own vision. Relying on years of discipline in which he had learned to clear his mind of preconceptions and prejudices, he noted with cautious satisfaction the sense of order that had at last begun to emerge in the drawings. It seemed to him now that the order had always been there, waiting to be revealed through some hermetic process that he himself only dimly understood. It had almost grown out of the fibers of the paper, out of the Schubert perhaps and the crackling fire he always built for himself when he worked through a winter night alone.

The drawings had gradually become more assured, more graceful, less tortured. While skeptical at first, over the last hour he could not deny that something lyrical had begun to stir in the floor plan. The voluminous curves now seemed to play against each other just as the Schubert piano played against the violins. The final unexpected twist was the sixty-degree angle. It was what he had been searching for, a bold violation of the rules he himself had decreed. In an almost mystical way their violation had brought the rules to life. The drawing had begun to sing.

He scribbled a note to Tensing, his intern, who would no doubt arrive an hour later at precisely eight o'clock. "Draw this up," it said, rather curtly. "Don't sweat the details. Keep the spirit."

He stepped out of the tiny marble lobby onto the deserted Main Street Mall, formerly Main Street. It had been closed to traffic in the 70's in order to "enliven the downtown." A wind from the river struck him, ragged as the ice floes, and he turned up the collar of the ancient naval officer's bridge coat he had bought as an ensign the year the mall was finished. He was secretly proud that it still fit until he remembered that it had been let out the year before by his tailor. He was no longer "lanky," as his high school basketball coach had dubbed him. He frequently berated himself for lacking the willpower to cut back on the Bordeaux he favored and tried not to notice the undeniable paunch he was developing. He limped slightly, the dull ache in his leg flaring up as it often did when the weather was cold and damp. It was another reminder of his brief naval career and the night he had taken the Vietcong bullet during the "special op" that had gone so terribly wrong.

He turned the corner into Court Square, his favorite spot in downtown Memphis. The shapeless lump of a homeless man huddled on a bench, its cast iron supports decorated to resemble rollicking Mississippi River catfish. The once-elegant urban park was one of the four original squares laid out by Andrew Jackson and his business partners in 1819. Dignified stone and terra cotta façades dating from the nineteenth and early twentieth centuries framed a grove of mature oaks, a bandstand, and a fountain—the latter presided over by a sculpture of Hebe, the ancient water bearer to the gods. As a small boy a half-century before, he had perched on his father's shoulders at this very spot to watch the floats and the marching bands in the Christmas parade as it wound its way down Main Street, along the west edge of the square. Despite a number of decrepit buildings and the scruffy pigeons, it still possessed a shabby civility and an intimacy that appealed to him in a way that no sanitized suburban shopping mall ever would.

He glanced back up toward the sunlit spire of the twenty-one story Lincoln American Tower to the row of three windows at the very top that marked his office. From his tiny aerie he enjoyed a 360-degree panoramic vista of the city and the river. At the pinnacle of the tower, a flag danced above the tiny cupola, where there had once flashed a rotating beacon for the city's first airliners. Originally known as the Columbian Mutual Tower, the building was a diminutive copy of Cass Gilbert's 1913 Woolworth Building and was one of Memphis' first skyscrapers, built a decade or so after the New York prototype. Its elegant proportions gave it a cool, feminine character that belied the muscular steel skeleton that lay beneath the cladding of gleaming white terra cotta. Colonel Isaac Bucksnort, the tyrannical city censor who had imposed his small-minded morality on the community for thirty years, had built this chaste structure as a display of personal vanity. Ironically, the man was said to have been a notorious womanizer. In the alley at the base of the tower, the censor and his secretary had been surprised *in flagrante delicto* by Jesse, the wizened custodian of the Lincoln American Tower who still repaired the steam radiators and changed the light bulbs.

These days the building contained much empty space. On the ground floor a restaurant poured grease-laden exhaust, heavy with the aroma of homemade biscuits, over Court Square. The other tenants included a tanning salon, a bonding outfit, a private detective agency, an insurance company, and the Odd Fellows lodge that occupied the entire fifth floor. The Odd Fellows owned the land beneath the Lincoln American Tower, and it was said that the lease stipulated payments in gold. On Sunday evenings Cotham would sometimes encounter a handful of the curmudgeonly Odd Fellows, none of whom he judged to be less than eighty years old, in the elevator bound for their well-appointed pool room overlooking Court Square. He had once been led on an unauthorized tour of the clubhouse by Jesse and was astonished to discover hidden in the center of the building a dramatic two-story chapter room hung with medieval banners, surrounded on all sides by ornately carved, high-backed thrones. In an adjacent storeroom was stashed a veritable armory of swords, lances, armor, and shields. The members made for an odd group, indeed.

Despite the building's checkered history and its reputation for sleaze, however, he had been thrilled to find the vacant space at an amazingly low rent when he had made the risky decision to hang out his shingle. The censor's old penthouse was now his. Visitors stepped out of the elevator directly into his office where they were greeted by the gleaming bronze letters on the wall proclaiming "Ethan Cotham, Architect."

———

The nineteenth century architect Henry Hobson Richardson, asked to name the most important part of practicing architecture, was said to have replied, "Get the job." Even though it was sound advice as Cotham could admit, when opportunity had tapped at his door on an evening two weeks earlier, he had struggled to overcome his introspective inclinations and his natural reluctance to aggressively chase new work.

Opportunity had taken the guise of a chance encounter at the Christmas party and opening of the Giuliani show at the Brooks Museum. Had Pallie not invited him to be her escort, or had his distaste for large social events prevailed, he would not now be preoccupied with the largest potential commission ever to come his way. Pallie had been insistent, however, and in the end it had been easier to give in to her infallible judgment about such things.

It had been some time since Cotham had last worn his tuxedo, and the trousers had grown sufficiently tight that suspenders were no longer necessary. His housekeeper had laid out the full set of accoutrements on his bed, including both the cummerbund and the black silk waistcoat. He deliberated a moment and chose the waistcoat. It seemed a bit more rakish somehow, and he liked to wear his grandfather's gold watch in its vest pocket. The watch had not actually run in years, but he liked the look and its satisfying heft, the weight of an authentic artifact of substance, full of gears and sprockets instead of microchips.

He finished knotting the black bow tie, taking care that the knot was not too perfect. Then he critically appraised himself in the mirror. Somewhere he had read that a tuxedo made any man appear slightly dangerous. As much as he might have wished it to be so, the image that confronted him through his horn-rimmed glasses was more that of a well-worn college professor. *So, I too am getting old,* he thought. His face was rounder now than it had once been though his cheeks still bore the scars and pockmarks of acne that had tormented him as a teenager. The dark hair was closely cropped, and silver showed at the temples. The nose was hawkish, overly large and slightly off center in its placement, which gave the features a certain tension. His pale blue eyes were the most youthful aspect of the face—frank, restless, and inquisitive, although their true brightness was somewhat obscured by the thick lenses necessitated by a severe myopia, a condition Cotham attributed to years of scrutinizing construction drawings.

Cotham would always be haunted by the conviction that he was physically ugly. It was not until he had read that many of the great artists of the Renaissance, including Brunelleschi, Vasari, and Michelangelo, were unattractive and that artistic genius had been associated with lack of physical beauty that he had made some peace with what he believed to be a fact. He took comfort in Boccaccio's observation that "nature has frequently planted astonishing genius in men of monstrously ugly appearance." Having recognized this reality concerning his physiognomy, Cotham was always at a complete loss to explain why women often seemed attracted to him. Buttoning the waistcoat and sucking in the paunch, he resolved to venture back onto the squash court as soon as the holidays were past.

Pallie's sprawling Italianate house on Central Avenue with the broad, bracketed eaves and shadowy front porch could only be glimpsed from the street, obscured as it was by the magnolia grandiflora trees, their mass almost black now in the fading light. The house had once been fully occupied by her family of six, and a wooden swing still hung from a branch of the oak in the side yard. A smaller screened porch, furnished with ancient wicker chairs and sofas, overlooked a neglected rose garden, centered around a mirrored gazing ball. Now the family was gone except for Pallie, the only sibling who had remained in Memphis. Her father, a prominent lawyer, and her mother, the daughter of a Greek immigrant who had founded a local line of grocery stores, had died ten and eleven years ago, respectively. Pallie had refused to agree to the sale of the house to the consternation of her three brothers and now lived there alone. Although she had received a sizable inheritance that would have easily allowed her to hire a gardener, she preferred to allow the giant azaleas and nandinas to sprawl in undisciplined profusion around the foundation.

Cotham pulled his battered Rover into the curving driveway and parked outside the porte cochere behind the dark green Mercedes Benz sedan. He crossed the front porch and lifted the solid brass doorknocker with its two-headed image of Janus. Through the single beveled-glass light of the oak door he could see the entrance hall and the curving stairway illuminated by what was almost certainly a Tiffany chandelier. To the right was visible a set of tubular steel dining room chairs designed by Marcel Breuer. On the Chippendale sideboard gleamed a Gorham silver service.

As usual Pallie was ready on time, as though she had sensed him turning into the driveway and would have come to the door even had he not knocked. Cotham made a note to test his hypothesis the next time he came to call.

The lithe figure descended the stair, wearing a simple black cocktail dress. Her dark hair, showing a trace of gray, was piled high like that of women in photographs taken in the 1920s. She wore only two pieces of jewelry, a simple silver bracelet and around her neck a small silver head of the Medusa. Pallas Athena Pelham was a striking woman, and the air of authority she exuded resonated perfectly with the dignity of the house. It would not be difficult to imagine her presiding with serene majesty over a crew of servants, children, and guests.

"Hello, Pallie. You look ravishing, as usual." Cotham greeted her with a kiss on the cheek. She smiled, and in her calm gray eyes he thought he detected a momentary flash of green.

"And you, Ethan, look positively lethal." Cotham, convinced that he looked every bit as lethal as a day-old cream puff, could not suppress a tingle of pride. "You'll need all your charm tonight. You know the entire local art world will be there, falling all over each other trying to see and be seen."

"I am grateful you invited me to be your escort," he replied. "I would hate the thought of your having asked Richard Astor instead."

She laughed, "I'll admit Astor's new Jaguar would make a grander entrance pulling up in front of the museum than that old piece of junk you call a car, but then I'd have to listen to him talk about himself all night. I'd prefer your scintillating repartee anytime."

Was there a touch of irony in her remark? He regarded himself as anything but a brilliant conversationalist, but somehow this never seemed to bother Pallie. "If that's the way you feel about my immaculately maintained automobile, let's take yours instead. You'll make a more fitting impression emerging from a respectable vehicle."

"But, Ethan, what makes you think I want to make a respectable impression?"

During the short drive across McLean Avenue to Overton Park, the conversation lagged. Though far more outgoing than he was, Pallie was no extrovert. As they pulled up in front of the Brooks Museum, its white marble glowing in the floodlights, she seemed unusually quiet.

Cotham turned to her. "You seem a little preoccupied. Not

thinking about having to see Lucretia, are you?"

"I can do just fine without ever seeing her again, as you know perfectly well. But I don't think about her."

"Well, something's bothering you," he persisted.

"I don't know what it is, Ethan, but I've been having another of my intuitions all day. I just feel a bit uneasy, as though something is coming."

Cotham reflected on this in silence. Ordinarily he was a skeptic when it came to the paranormal, but with Pallie it was different. At times she did seem to possess an uncanny ability to know things that she had no way of knowing, as on their first date a year ago. He had taken her to dinner at the University Club. They had been met by Amos, the headwaiter, who informed Cotham he had a telephone call in the bar. He had asked Amos to seat her and take her drink order while he excused himself to take the call. When he returned, she was sipping a sherry. A Tanqueray and tonic awaited him.

"How did you know this is my favorite?" he asked. "I usually order a glass of Bordeaux since they say it's healthier, but in a perfect world I'd drink nothing but G and T!"

The bottomless gray eyes gazed steadily at him, questioning. "Why, isn't that what you asked for?"

"Well, no, I'm sure I didn't specify."

"That's funny; I was certain that was what you wanted."

Amos was busy seating another couple across the dining room. She might have asked Amos about Cotham's favorite, of course. Since he rarely actually ordered gin and tonic, however, it was unlikely that the drink would have come to Amos' mind. The incident had left him vaguely uneasy.

"Am I in the company of a witch?" he had asked wryly.

Pallie had not smiled, and he immediately regretted the comment. After all, after a year he still hardly knew this intriguing woman. "When I was little," she said slowly, "my grandmother used to say I had second sight. I was born with a caul over my face and that was taken as a sure sign. I think it explains my name too—that along with the fact that my mother's family was Greek. Actually, I don't think I have any special ability that others lack. Everyone has intuitions. It just seems that mine are stronger and sometimes it's hard for me to separate them from what I've actually read or heard."

They made their way past the arched beaux-arts entrance portico of the original museum to the graceful rotunda of the contemporary addition. Designed in 1910 by James Gamble Rogers, the architect of the fine Harkness Quadrangle at Yale as well as the Shelby County Courthouse, the Brooks Museum was among the city's most distinguished works of architecture. The evening was cloudy, cold, and strangely calm with a hint of snow in the air. Pallie shivered slightly, even though she wore a full-length black mink. As they approached, a midnight blue Jaguar sedan pulled away, a teenage valet at the wheel. They heard the engine roar and the tires screech as it disappeared behind the building. Just ahead of them, visible through the open front door, a short, stocky, balding man in his early sixties, wearing the same owlish glasses made famous by Le Corbusier, was handing his fur coat to the attendant.

Richard Brisbane Astor was nothing if not elegant. Tonight he was sporting a silver silk waistcoat with matching bow tie—knotted with perfect symmetry, Cotham noticed. The wing collar of his dress shirt, strangely incongruous on a man of his age, sank into the folds of his heavy jowls. He stood carefully poised like an eighteenth century cavalier. Shiny patent leather evening slippers adorned his tiny feet.

"As I live and breathe! If it isn't Pallie and Ethan!" he exclaimed jovially, rising slightly on tiptoes to deliver a kiss to Pallie's pale cheek. "I'm delighted to see the two of you together these days. How did the poet put it? 'She's beautiful and therefore to be wooed, she is a woman, therefore to be won.'"

Cotham, suddenly irritated by Astor's familiarity, wondered how long he had known Pallie. He fought to banish the ironic chill from his voice. "Good evening, Richard, how's Pembroke Place shaping up? That was a nice article in the real estate section on Sunday."

Pembroke Place was the largest shopping mall yet to be built on the city's perimeter. Judging from the rendering in last Sunday's edition of *The Commercial Appeal,* it was to be a hideous Disneyesque pastiche of styles ranging the gamut from medieval to art deco.

Astor beamed. "Yes, and it was nice of Gertrude Philpot to mention us. I'll admit the design's a bit eclectic, but that seems to be what people like. You know, Ethan, I find that there's a real resurgence of popular interest in architecture these days."

It was hard for Cotham to believe that he had worked in the pompous Astor's office some thirty years ago. But then, Astor's work had been more serious and less lucrative in those days. Now it seemed all he cared about was getting larger and larger projects built more and more quickly at less and less cost. Of course his practice was booming, and his staff had grown to almost a hundred at last report. That was an onerous payroll to make every month, and Cotham shuddered at the thought.

"I expect Pappas was very pleased with the article, too," Cotham replied, pushing his feelings aside.

"Oh, yes. Nikos and I have had some very lengthy conversations about the revival of historic styles as a way of counteracting the cookie-cutter sameness of the suburbs. Bringing a little sophistication to the hinterlands. For a developer, he is unusually interested in these issues, I find. The other day he even referred to Jane Jacobs' *The Death and Life of Great American Cities.*"

Cotham almost rolled his eyes at the thought of this most urbanistic of treatises cited in defense of yet another suburban development in what a critic had christened "edge city." Because of projects such as this, the rural countryside of eastern Shelby County, which as a young man he had loved to explore in his old Austin Healy roadster, was being rapidly despoiled. It was a subject he felt strongly about, and he sensed his irritation rising. Now that Astor had been appointed Chairman of the Memphis Board of Design Review, he had assumed intellectual pretensions that made his shortcomings as a designer even more difficult for Cotham to bear. One day Astor's pomposity was going to push him too far.

Pallie must have sensed Cotham's feelings, for she took his arm rather firmly, effortlessly assuming the role of the Southern Belle, a guise she could adopt on a moment's notice when called for in a social emergency. "Now, Ethan, you and Richard can jabber on about architecture some other time. There are more important things in life, you know, such as which one of you is going to offer me a glass of champagne?" She deftly tugged at Cotham's arm, forcing him to disengage from Astor and allowing them to melt into the growing crowd.

Cotham reflected that when he was younger an opening at the Brooks would have been a strictly Old Memphis affair, perhaps with a sprinkling of faculty from the Art Department of Southwestern

College and the Academy of Art. The majority would have been matronly women, members of the Brooks League, and their husbands, the bankers, lawyers, and cotton merchants who would have prefererered to spend the evening in the grills of the Memphis Country Club or the University Club. While an adventurous handful of the women might have been defenders of abstract expressionism, the majority would have been partial to the better-known Impressionists. Many of the men would have been utterly indifferent to all art forms, with the possible exception of the scenes of duck and quail hunts that decorated their paneled dens. In those days Cotham would have recognized most of them and known many as friends of his parents.

These days the mix had become decidedly more pluralistic. There were a few artists, men and women with short haircuts dressed head to toe in their *de rigueur* uniforms of black. Old-monied bluebloods were outnumbered by transplanted corporate executives from Federal Express, Autozone, and International Paper. Instead of the soft murmur of cultured Southern accents that had filled this room in the past, the louder, harsher speech of the newcomers reverberated through the space. Many of the voices were midwestern or northern, or simply the ubiquitous "standard American" that was replacing regional speech patterns in the same way urban sprawl was replacing the gently rolling landscape of the Mid-South. Although the majority of the guests were in their late forties and fifties, people of Cotham's generation, there were a great many that he did not know. The corporate types supported the Brooks Museum financially with their personal and business donations, and he had met some who were well educated and genuinely passionate about the museum's collections. As far as he could tell, however, others cared no more about serious artistic issues than had many of the Old Memphis aristocracy.

He turned to Pallie, ready to make some pointed comment about Astor. She looked at him knowingly from beneath dark eyebrows that reminded him of some fey enchantress from a Viennese Secession painting by Gustav Klimt, and he knew that she had read his thoughts. Eyeing the crowd that separated them from the bar, he smiled wryly and said, "Wait here. I'll be back with something to drink. You mentioned champagne?"

Presiding over the bar in his trademark silver suspenders decorated with little crescent moons, stood none other than Amos. Cotham wondered if the decorations were a whimsical comment on Amos' moonlighting jobs at society gatherings all over town when he was not on duty at the University Club. "What'll it be, Mr. Cotham, a nice glass of Bordeaux?" Amos seldom missed a trick.

"Yes, and a champagne, please, Amos." He was suddenly conscious of someone standing very close at his side and the scent of magnolia in the air. He turned and stared into a pair of dark brown eyes. They bored into his skull, and Cotham felt like a deer trapped in the headlights of an oncoming car.

"How sweet of you to get me a drink, Ethan," breathed Lucretia Silvetti as she appropriated Pallie's glass from Amos. The director of the Brooks, Lucretia had been hired away from the Kimball Museum in Fort Worth and had quickly established a reputation as a brilliant iconoclast. In the minds of some of the Memphis art establishment she was a threat to the venerable traditions of the Brooks, while to others she was a much needed breath of fresh air. Characteristically she had crept up on him like a panther stalking its prey. She frequently did this to him at parties, and it was always unnerving. Also like a panther she was in black, and it seemed to Cotham that she looked rather hungry. "Have you seen the Giulianis yet? They're spectacular. Come let me show you my favorite."

He began to protest, remembering Pallie somewhere in the crowd behind them, but Lucretia was already slinking toward the main gallery. Cotham rationalized that it would be rude not to follow the director of the museum who wanted to discuss art with a guest. He caught up with her as she moved through the mass of faces, smiling, calling patrons by name. He noted the delighted grins of the men and the tight half-smiles of the women she encountered.

Across the room a rotund, bearded man with a dark complexion and teeth like piano keys seemed to be holding court, surrounded by admiring patrons. He heard one of the women give an embarrassed little shriek and saw the man leer at her, his teeth flashing.

Lucretia paused at the entrance of the gallery and gestured toward the first work, a gigantic black and white photograph of a bearded man in a dark turtleneck shirt. It was the same man who was now holding the crowd spellbound on the far side of the gallery. In his left eye gleamed a small fleck of red.

"Look closer," whispered Lucretia excitedly.

Cotham stepped up to within three feet of the photograph. At first he could make out nothing except that the image had dissolved into a pattern of black and gray half tone dots, each about the diameter of a pencil. He moved a little closer, and suddenly he got it. Each of the dots was itself a miniature photograph of male genitalia in varying states of arousal. At first he thought the dot of red was a bow on a tiny candy cane, which seemed strange. Then he realized that the bow was not tied around a candy cane. Stepping back rather quickly, he bumped into Lucretia, standing close enough behind him to breathe down the neck of his starched formal shirt.

"Well, what do you think?" She smiled lasciviously. "Old Giuliani's a bit of a satyr. I can't wait to watch some of these old biddies when they see this. Not exactly an exhibition of Degas ballerinas, is it?"

Cotham did not want to appear speechless. He wanted to say something worldly and sophisticated to show that he was a member of the cognoscenti and no provincial stick-in-the-mud. But his mind was blank, and Lucretia's headlights were again boring into his cranium. "You know, Lucretia, I'm just sort of an ordinary guy when it comes to art. I like artists who can draw." He was immediately overcome with self-loathing. *What an inane comeback!* This extremely attractive woman was coming on to him, and he was as flustered as Oliver Hardy in an old film. He had a momentary vision of the embarrassed Hardy, rolling his necktie up and down on his chest.

"Come on, Ethan, you can't tell me there's no place for the erotic in art. We all have our kinky side, even if we don't ordinarily let it show. Why, I'll bet that even the imperturbable Cotham...."

"What Ethan is too polite to say is that this stuff is rubbish!"

Ethan whirled around to see Pallie glaring at Lucretia. She took a menacing step toward the director like a mongoose closing in on a cornered cobra. Why did he never notice these women sneaking up on him? For a moment he thought he might have to step between them.

Instantly, though, Lucretia was in full control of herself, replacing the seductive manner with the icy hauteur of the art professional. Pallie was a member of the Board of the Brooks and as such was one of Lucretia's bosses. The director, he realized, could ill afford to engage in a public row with one of the principal donors to the museum who had a voice in funding her various projects and ultimately in her job security.

"I'm so sorry you don't approve, Pallie. But we do have an obligation to educate our public with a variety of esthetic viewpoints. I've been trying to get this show ever since it premiered at the MOCA in Los Angeles last year. You'll recall the write-up it got in *Time* magazine."

"You know, Lucretia, one of these days our public is going to wake up to the fact that the Emperor has no clothes. I hope the show is a financial success, but we'll want to discuss how these sorts of decisions are made at the next Board meeting. It's been wonderful seeing you again. I'm so sorry to interrupt your conversation; I was just coming to ask Ethan what happened to my champagne."

They made their way back to the lobby, and Cotham was acutely aware that Pallie had grown silent. Was he being reproached for a scene over which he had had no control? And why was he now feeling slightly guilty? Wasn't he a bachelor without obligations to any woman?

He was greatly relieved to encounter his old friends, Roberta and Thurston Quonset. Cotham had known them both since grade school.

"Why, Ethan," she beamed, "where have you been keeping yourself? I was hoping Pallie would be successful in dragging you along tonight. There's something I've wanted to ask my favorite architect, and somebody I want you to meet, too!"

"Hey, Pallie! Ethan!" Even though Thurston was in his cups, as usual, he never failed to greet a lady before her male companion, and Cotham liked that about him. Thurston planted a wet kiss on Pallie's cheek then grabbed Ethan's hand with both of his, shaking it hard and refusing to release it.

"What did you think about the last play of that game Saturday? You think it's gonna come down to either the Vols and Rebels in the Sugar Bowl again this year? Hot damn, I hope so; those U.T. hill-billies need their comeuppance!" Despite his excitement, he finally let go of Cotham's hand. Cotham sighed as they became helplessly enmeshed in Thurston's seemingly unending take on the upcoming bowl games. At least it freed him from the task of trying to break the ice with Pallie, and Thurston was so taken with his own analysis that Cotham was required to do nothing but nod occasionally.

"I was just about to ask Ethan if he ever does houses." Roberta finally interrupted her husband's monologue. "Thurston and I would love to come and talk to you about an idea we've been mulling over. You know we've bought the most gorgeous lot in BluffTown, right on the edge of the river. It has a view to die for!"

"Of course, I'd love to hear about it, Roberta," Cotham replied, smiling. "Give me a call Monday and let's set a time." He was about to ask her more, but Roberta had turned away slightly and was gazing over his left shoulder. She firmly grasped both his arm and Pallie's and spun them around to face a short, white-haired man in a blood-red bow tie and a red carnation boutonniere in his black silk lapel.

"Nikos, have you met Ethan Cotham, the architect? You know Pallie Pelham, of course. Ethan, this is Nikos Pappas." Roberta gave Cotham a significant glance.

Pappas gave a little, courtly bow. "Of course, I know Ms. Pelham. I have the honor of serving with her on the Board and we share an interest in all things Hellenic. And I've admired your work, Mr. Cotham, especially the Athenaeum Society Library." The gem-like little private library had been Cotham's first major project. That he was on the map professionally (and it was certainly debatable whether his small practice registered more than a blip) was due to the Athenaeum. The library was the home of a venerable salon that counted the city's liberal intellectual elite, including Pappas, among its membership. The adventurous design had shocked some, but after it had received several Honor Awards from the American Institute of Architects, the furor had subsided. The passage of time had also helped and now, ten years later, it seemed quite tame.

"And I admire your new interest in urbanism, Mr. Pappas. In fact, Richard Astor was telling us about it a just a few minutes ago."

Pappas was something of a legend in Memphis business circles. He had been born into one of the handful of wealthy Greek families with roots extending back beyond the Yellow Fever epidemics of the 1870s, when many of the other wealthy Greek, Italian, Irish, and Jewish families had fled to St. Louis. He was a Phi Beta Kappa graduate of the University of Pennsylvania, a contributor to liberal political campaigns, and a benefactor of the arts.

He was also an astute real estate developer who had foreseen the exodus to the eastern suburbs before it became a stampede following the assassination of Dr. Martin Luther King Jr. in 1968. He had begun buying up rural acreage at low agricultural rates, and when the rush came, he was ready. To Cotham's knowledge Pappas had never invested a dollar inside the perimeter of Interstate 240, the circumferential expressway that marked the unofficial border between the city and the outer suburbs of Germantown, Bartlett, and Cordova.

"I'm interested to hear you refer to my interest in cities as 'new,'" said Pappas, smiling. "You know we've been helping build Memphis for over forty years now." Cotham wondered if he were being lured into a debate.

"With all due respect you've been building suburbia, not the city," Cotham replied evenly. "Astor tells me you've been reading Jane Jacobs. Surely you know Jacobs was a proponent of revitalizing the inner city, not luring people away from it with more expressways, subdivisions, and shopping centers."

"Great cities have always expanded, Mr. Cotham. Look at Paris and London. Time and again they outgrew the confines of their walled fortifications and spread out into the countryside."

"And look at where we Americans go when we visit Europe," retorted Cotham. "We visit the old centers of those cities. We want to walk the streets of the Left Bank and Montmartre, not La Défense. A real city is a good place to be, not a place to escape from. It's one thing to evolve organically, slowly over hundreds of years, like Paris. It's quite another to gobble up farmland and bulldoze forests at the rate of thousands of acres a year and then cut the new suburbs off from the old city by expressways."

Pappas was beginning to flush slightly, but his voice remained calm. "I know about life in the inner city, Mr. Cotham. It's overrated by romantics. I grew up in the Pinch district north of Downtown. That's short for Pinch-Gut, so named because most of the people in my neighborhood lived in poverty. My family was lucky. We weren't poor, and we couldn't wait to get out. I'm not talking about living in a gentrified neighborhood in Midtown where diversity takes the form of a single well-to-do African-American doctor on the block. I'm talking about living in the real inner city, always on the lookout for whores and panhandlers, not knowing when your wife is going to be mugged in front of your house or when your children are going to be offered dope on the school playground.

"The worst thing that ever happened to Memphis was when they stopped I-40 through Overton Park. It would have kept Downtown alive by letting people drive straight to and from Germantown."

Cotham remembered how, over thirty years ago, the grassroots effort to stop the expressway from bisecting the very park in which they now stood arguing had torn the city apart. The vast park covered over three hundred acres, half of which was old-growth hardwood forest with some trees estimated to be over two hundred years old. It had been set aside as parkland on the recommendation of Frederick Law Olmstead, the designer of Central Park, and was one of the city's greatest treasures. The suit to force the abandonment of the expressway plans had ultimately been decided in the Supreme Court.

Before Cotham could reply, Pappas continued. "Let me ask you something, Mr. Cotham. Suppose you were a wealthy, benevolent despot, the Lorenzo de Medici of Memphis, let us say, and you could spend a very large sum of money on some civic project that would make the inner city a place where everyone would want to live. What would you do?"

Cotham was taken aback by this sudden change of tactics. It was a skillful way of placing him on the defensive, since it was certainly easier to criticize how Pappas exerted his power and wealth than it was to propose a constructive alternative. He took a rather large sip of his wine and slowly withdrew his pocket watch, consulting it thoughtfully. Perhaps Pappas would not notice that it was permanently frozen at ten minutes until 1:00. As he did so, he was aware of Pallie and Roberta watching him. Thurston had disappeared, probably to the bar. Pallie looked pale, as though she were not feeling well.

"It seems to me," he began, carefully, "that Memphis will never be a city in the best sense of the word until we heal the racial wounds that divide us into two cities, black and white. When Martin Luther King was killed here, it accelerated the white retreat to the suburbs. But, of course, that was only the culmination of a century of segregation, and a half-century of slavery before that. I think Faulkner was right when he said 'the past is not over; it's not even the past.'

"If I were one of the Medici of Memphis, as you suggest, I suppose I would try to come up with a project that would take a meaningful step toward the healing of those wounds and to let whites and blacks discover what they have in common, instead of what divides them. And since I am an architect, that project would probably be a building of some sort."

Pappas eyed Cotham sharply, but before he could reply, Thurston reappeared, teetering slightly, "Hey, Nikos," he interrupted, a bit too loudly, "how 'bout them Rebels last weekend?" Thurston despised the Ole Miss Rebels, except when they defeated the University of Tennessee Volunteers, whom he hated with sincerity and profound passion.

"Yes, and how 'bout them Quakers?" replied Pappas with just a trace of irony. Thurston looked blank. "Surely you follow the Ivy League as well as the Southeast Conference. It's not every year that Penn trounces Yale 20-3."

Turning back to Cotham, he gave another of his little bows. "I've enjoyed our discussion, Mr. Cotham, even though I see you are misguided on several points. I suppose I had better be heading home, back out to the suburban wastelands, you might say. Good night, ladies, Thurston."

"Perhaps we should be going as well," said Cotham. "I look forward to hearing more about your new house, Roberta."

As he and Pallie made their way toward the door, she grasped his arm. "I'm sorry, Ethan, I'm suddenly feeling a little woozy. Can we sit down a moment?" Cotham steered her toward a bench next to the wall, and they passed a waiter carrying a tray of champagne glasses. Cotham caught his eye, and the waiter held the tray toward them. Pallie reached for a glass.

As she did so, the tray began to vibrate with a low hum, and little ripples appeared on the surface of the champagne. A distant rumbling sound, like an approaching freight train, engulfed the room as the floor gave a sharp jolt. The tray crashed to the floor, the lights went out, and muffled gasps filled the darkness around them. Cotham felt Pallie slump against his shoulder.

Suddenly the room was illuminated again. The rumbling faded away, and all was unnaturally quiet. The guests stared at one another.

"A little temblor," said Cotham, to no one in particular. He looked at Pallie. Her face was white, and she was trembling. "It's over now. There's nothing to worry about. Just the New Madrid Fault realigning itself a bit, I expect."

Around them people were smiling with relief and there were a few uneasy jokes about a truly earthshaking opening, but they were all discreetly streaming toward the exits. He and Pallie joined the crowd, Cotham making an effort to walk slowly, as though earthquakes were just another of life's little annoyances.

Outside they stood in relieved silence for several minutes until Pallie turned to him. "Ethan, I knew something was coming; I just didn't know what." He looked into her eyes, wondering whether she had truly foreseen the future. He had heard that some animals could sense an approaching earthquake; why not a sensitive human?

The wind must have shifted direction, for in the distance they could hear a cacophony of animals in distress—what was surely the bass roar of a lion or tiger, followed by the treble bleating of some hoofed creature. These were in turn followed by the eerie howling of wolves and then by almost human screams of alarm from some form of primate. It was as though Noah and his ark were aground and breaking up somewhere across the dark sea of the park. Then the source of the bedlam dawned on them. Pandemonium reigned in the Overton Park Zoo, a quarter mile or so through the trees to the north.

Chapter Three

The next morning the Hebe fountain stood frozen and Cotham idly wondered if the unfortunate bronze maiden, clad only in her gauzy tunic, longed for the olive groves and ambrosia of sunny Olympus. Icicles, a rare sight in Memphis, hung from the eaves of the Tennessee Club as he hurried through Court Square, *The Commercial Appeal* under his arm, coffee sloshing in a Styrofoam cup. In the other hand, he gripped the old leather briefcase that looked as though it might have been run over by a bus. Straining against the stinging wind, he managed to pry open the door and stagger into the lobby of the Lincoln American Tower. He pressed the button for the express elevator that traveled all the way to the top floors and thirty seconds later stepped out into his tiny office.

Paul Dole, his senior assistant, greeted him. Everything about Dole was gray. He had gray hair, wore gray suits, and the cigarette smoke that permeated his clothes gave his hands a gray pallor. His one passion in life seemed to be art films, of which he was an enthusiastic connoisseur.

"Morning, Ethan, you just missed the courier. He left this for you." He handed Cotham a buff-colored envelope that bore no return address. Cotham stuffed it into a fold in his newspaper.

"Thanks, Paul. How was your weekend?"

"Not bad," Paul replied. "Saw a couple of interesting new independent films at the Brooks on Sunday. Reminded me of the old Guild Theatre on Poplar. You remember the Guild, don't you, Ethan?"

"Sure do. *Black Orpheus, Knife in the Water, Phaedra*...they don't make them like that, anymore."

"Oh," continued Dole, "and I came in Saturday to check the millwork shop drawings on St. Mary Magdalene Church. They're mostly okay, but they don't show any kneelers on the pews. Catholics will want kneelers, won't they?"

"Indeed they will. And we'll both end up in hair shirts if they deliver thirty pews without them. Let's get together in about an hour and have a look. And we can see what's on for the week."

Cotham threw his coat over the drawing board in his office and opened the morning's paper, attracted to a page two story that dealt with the details of yet another long-range plan for the development of the Memphis riverfront. The last plan had been an enlightened effort to tie Downtown to the riverfront more strongly. The mayor, pressured by a coalition who opposed spending public money on Downtown planning boondoggles, had ultimately ignored it. Now, years later, this same coalition, including many of those who had pushed for an expressway through Overton Park, was advocating the widening of Riverside Drive to handle more traffic during rush hour. No one seemed to notice or care that doing so would make the riverfront even more inaccessible than it already was, requiring pedestrians to cross six lanes of traffic. Cotham sighed and shook his head. At the bottom of the page he noticed a small article:

EARTHQUAKE RATTLES BLUFF CITY

A small earthquake rattled windows across Memphis at 9:03 p.m. last night. According to the University of Memphis Center for Earthquake Research and Information, the temblor was measured at a magnitude of 3.1 on the Richter Scale. Its epicenter was estimated to be near Marked Tree, Arkansas, some thirty-five miles north of Memphis. Minor damage, but no injuries, was reported in Marked Tree, which lies near the southern end of the New Madrid Fault, said to be one of the least stable seismic zones in the nation.

The great earthquakes of 1811 and 1812 occurred along the New Madrid Fault. According to eyewitnesses, the Mississippi River briefly reversed its course, flowing north. The quakes created Reelfoot Lake in northwest Tennessee.

In 1990 Memphians were alarmed when California geologist Hiram Buckley predicted that a major earthquake would decimate the city in December, prompting near panic in some quarters. The date passed with no disturbance, and Buckley's theories of earthquake prediction have since been discredited by most seismologists, although most agree that Memphis remains vulnerable to a large quake.

Cotham remembered the Buckley debacle. The city had been on the brink of panic as the predicted date approached. Entire families left town. Those who stayed prepared earthquake kits consisting of camping equipment, first aid supplies, food, and cases of toilet paper. At his niece's private school, earthquake drills were instituted, reminiscent of the "duck and cover" nuclear attack exercises held in the fifties. The faculty was issued black felt-tip pens for marking the foreheads of the dead with a large "X." When no quake materialized, Buckley faded into obscurity. No doubt the thousands of forgotten emergency kits stashed in closets all over town were now full of foul water and rotting peanut butter.

Still, as an architect, Cotham recognized that Memphis' proximity to the New Madrid Fault was a legitimate concern. He had supported the effort by local structural engineers to strengthen the seismic design requirements of the local building code so that the likelihood of new structures suffering collapse would be decreased should "the big one" ever strike. Of course, the code applied only to new buildings, while the overwhelming majority of Downtown structures, including the Lincoln American Tower, were as vulnerable as they had ever been.

Cotham finished the first section of the paper, read through the Local News section, the movie ads, the comics, and finally arrived at the sports section. He disciplined himself by scanning the sports headlines every day so that when trapped in conversation he would not appear totally oblivious to the fate of the Grizzlies or Tigers. As he unfolded the section, the envelope handed to him by Paul Dole fell to the desktop. It contained a single sheet of stationery embossed with the letterhead of Pappas Investment Corporation. The note was typed.

Dear Mr. Cotham,

You are invited to meet with Mr. Nikos Pappas to discuss a matter of mutual interest. Please call me to confirm your availability for luncheon at noon, tomorrow, at the offices of Pappas Investment Corporation.

Sincerely yours,
Kimberly Craft
Assistant to Mr. Pappas

Cotham glanced at his calendar. Although he had no lunch plans the following day, he momentarily considered declining the invitation. He could think of no topic of mutual interest he shared with Pappas after the conversation of the previous evening, and he was faintly annoyed that the man had assigned his secretary to contact him, rather than picking up the telephone himself.

In the end he decided to ask his assistant, Jean Sergeant, to call to accept for him.

"My, my...Nikos Pappas. Moving up in the world of high finance, I see," she commented, smiling wryly. Cotham rolled his eyes and retreated down the spiral stair to the studio on the floor below.

———————

The drive from Downtown to Germantown along the southern leg of the circumferential expressway always slightly depressed Cotham. It reminded him that Downtown and Midtown, the parts of the city he considered the real Memphis, were now only a tiny part of a sprawling metropolitan area. Like the rest of America, the outer reaches of the city were quickly degenerating into mile after mile of low-rise office parks, fast-food joints, and soulless subdivisions, hunkered beneath oversized billboards hyping topless clubs and casinos in Tunica. On one of these an apocalyptic message ominously warned:

Don't make me come down there.

—God

By the time he reached the headquarters of Pappas Investment Corporation he was hungry and in a bad mood.

"Please have a seat, and I'll tell Mr. Pappas you're here," chirped the receptionist seated behind the oversized rosewood desk on the twenty-eighth floor. The size of the room was impressive, but Cotham found it slightly vulgar in its appointments. A crystal chandelier hung from the acoustical tile ceiling. The furniture was overstuffed and covered with black leather, and a large Persian rug was laid over the wall to wall carpet. On the coffee table lay current issues of *Town and Country, Architectural Digest,* and *Mid-South Development.* One wall was entirely glass with a superb view to the east. Cotham crossed the room and stood at the window. Here and there in the distance a pasture was visible, and he could pick out the church steeples of old Germantown. The rest of the landscape was dominated by gated subdivisions clustered around cul-de-sacs, the roofs of their expensive pseudo-chateaux styled houses peeping above the treetops. In the middle distance to the northeast gaped a huge clear-cut area of forest, where clouds of dust raised by earthmoving equipment billowed into the sky.

"Good morning, Ethan. Admiring our progress on Pembroke Place, I see." Nikos Pappas, immaculate in a black suit, stood at Cotham's elbow smiling broadly and offering his hand.

"Morning, Nikos. Good of you to invite me. Every time I come out here there's more construction under way." Although it felt awkward, Cotham made a conscious effort to use Pappas's first name. Upon turning thirty he had resolved that when anyone called him "Ethan," he would respond in kind, regardless of age or social status.

"Let's step into the board room, if you don't mind. I think we've got a light lunch waiting for us, and I have something to show you."

Pappas led the way down a short corridor and through the double doors into the large room, dominated by a mahogany conference table surrounded by at least twenty black leather Knoll armchairs. Three walls were covered with paintings. Cotham thought he recognized one as a Corot and, judging by their styles, a Van Gogh landscape and a Monet seascape. A small sculpture, apparently a Giacometti, stood on a sideboard, guarding a huge bowl of chicken salad. In one corner was a larger bronze, which looked like a Lipchitz.

Despite the presence of works by these modern luminaries, it was another piece that dominated the room. Cotham stared in amazement at the sculpture of Poseidon, lithe and bearded, trident cocked in the throwing position, its bronze patina green with age. It was similar, although not identical, to the famous heroically-scaled version he had seen in the National Museum in Athens. Could it possibly be authentic? As in answer, Pappas spoke quietly at his side, "Yes, Ethan, it's real. It dates from the mid-fifth century BCE. I could never acquire such a work today with the ban on the import of Greek antiquities, but as you know, the British 'liberated' a number of such artifacts in the eighteenth and nineteenth centuries, and some are still in the hands of private collectors. Until recently a few were still available, for a price. I'm thinking of returning it to Greece, but so far I've not been able to bring myself to part with it."

Poseidon: brother of Zeus, Ulysses' inveterate enemy, the remorseless god of the sea, protector of horses, and of...what else? Something else lay buried just beyond the grasp of Cotham's memory, some further detail of mythology, but it eluded him. Still in thought, he stepped to the curtain of glass facing west toward the city. In the far corner of the room, pointing toward the hazy downtown skyline stood an antique brass astronomical telescope, complete with setting circles, on a wooden tripod.

"Welcome to our 'war room,'" smiled Pappas. "This is where we make our most important decisions, and so I thought it would be a good place for us to talk. Will you have some chicken salad? And how about iced tea or coffee?" They helped themselves at the sideboard and returned to the table. Pappas took a seat at the end, motioning to Cotham to take the chair to his left facing the windows. He fixed Cotham with his gaze.

"I'll come right to the point, Ethan. I know what you think about Pappas Investment. You believe we are all an insensitive group of money-grubbers with no sense of social responsibility. You think we care only about raping and paving the countryside and that we have no interest in the older neighborhoods of Memphis. You think we care nothing about architecture."

Pappas paused and looked searchingly at Cotham. Cotham said nothing, but Pappas noted the slightly arched eyebrow. "I will admit that some of our developments fall short in architectural merit. And if it is a crime to provide what people want, then I plead guilty. But you are wrong to think that I don't care about the inner city. As I told you the other night, I grew up there. Yes, I'm bitter about some of my memories of life in the Pinch district. But there are other things I remember, too.

"On Saturday mornings when I was ten or eleven, my best friend and I would take the dollar or two we had earned during the week and ride a bus to Court Square. We would spend the whole day exploring Downtown, which in those days was where all the action was. First we strolled down Main Street. The sidewalks were crowded with blacks and whites, poor folks and businessmen, city slickers and sharecroppers. Well-dressed ladies were shopping at the department stores, Goldsmith's, Levy's, Lowenstein's, and Gerber's. Whores leaned against the walls in the alleys and outside the pool halls and juke joints. There were shoeshine stands, and newspaper stalls were hawking the old *Press-Scimitar, Ebony,* and *Esquire.* Sure, there were the separate drinking fountains for 'white' and 'colored,' and blacks had their own side doors leading to the balconies of the movie theatres. But everyone was there, on the same street, rubbing shoulders, jostling each other, enjoying their Saturday.

"There were four or five movie palaces on Main and on Union, the Loew's State and Loew's Palace, the Warner, the Strand, and the Malco. We would check them all out, and maybe decide to blow part of our dollar on the latest Steve Reeves sword and sandal classic or maybe Victor Mature or Charlton Heston in some Biblical epic. Between the Warner and the building next door was shoehorned a tiny shop that sold stamps for collectors, called Herron-Hill. It was not much larger than a telephone booth, with stools arranged along a green felt-covered counter for the customers. The owners, a married couple, would let us sit at that counter as long as we wanted while they pulled out album after album of exotic stamps for us to look at, none of which we could afford. After an hour, we might buy fifty cents' worth of garden-variety commemoratives for two or three cents each, which they tucked into little glassine envelopes for us as carefully as if they had been a complete mint set of the 1892 Columbian Exposition.

"If we were feeling brave we'd stroll down Beale Street, where most of the people were black. Beale Street was dirty, unsavory, and totally entrancing. It was also perfectly safe, although it felt dangerous. In those days, we did not run into gambling, prostitution, or even much music on Beale, though I suspect we just didn't know where to look. But there were lots of pool halls and pawnshops with the three brass balls hanging over the door, mostly owned by Jews like Nathan Novick. The shops were crammed with fascinating objects from pistols to electric guitars to magic potions in colored glass bottles and decks of cards with naked women on them. You could, of course, haggle with the owner. If Novick didn't like your offer, he would spit on the bare dirt floor, right at your feet, raising a little cloud of dust. I remember the day I bought a rosewood Martin guitar from him for fifteen dollars. I had worked him down from the original eighteen he was asking."

"Yes," remarked Cotham thoughtfully, "one of my professors in architecture school used to say that a city is a place where a small boy can walk down the street and discover something he will want to do for the rest of his life."

"Much of that changed after the King assassination and the riots of '68," Pappas continued. "Father Demetrios Karos was a family friend, and during the sanitation workers' strike that brought King to Memphis, I drove Father Karos Downtown to urge Mayor Loeb to bargain with the strikers. The strikers were all black, and were clearly exploited by the administration. A decent living was impossible on their meager wages. There had already been some disturbances and marches, and Main Street was lined by National Guard troops in riot gear. Parked a short way down every side street were tanks and armored personnel carriers. Father Karos came back to the car shaking his head. 'The mayor has hardened his heart,' he said sadly. The next day Dr. King was killed at the Lorraine Motel."

Cotham nodded. "Yes, Nikos, I remember. On the night of the assassination all the neighbors on my family's block stayed awake the entire night, the houses ablaze with lights. Old Dr. Reynolds next door to us was the quietest, gentlest soul you could imagine. But that night he sat up on his front porch with a radio and a loaded shotgun, ready to defend his home against the marauders he believed were on the way. Fear and panic were in the air, bordering on mass hysteria. I remember the hostility and distrust that sprang up overnight between blacks and whites. *Time* magazine came out with an article that referred to Memphis as a 'decaying backwater river town.' It made me angry, but I suppose in some ways it was an accurate observation. A lot of people think the strike and the assassination held the city back for three decades."

"I think it probably did hold us back," mused Pappas. "Certainly Downtown was never the same. White people became afraid to come Downtown after dark, and many were afraid in the daytime. The major department stores and movie theatres began drying up for lack of customers, along with the small shops like Herron-Hill. Instead of joining together to address the underlying causes of the riots, poverty, racism, and injustice, whites moved out east, led by several of the largest corporations and banks. The result was that Downtown became increasingly black, and the city became more segregated in many ways than it had ever been before."

"And wasn't Pappas Investments one of those companies that left? It seems to me I remember when you were on Union at Second."

Pappas looked away momentarily. "Yes, Ethan, I'm afraid that's true. But our staff was threatening to quit. The secretaries all wanted to leave early every afternoon so they wouldn't have to walk to their cars in the dark. As prudent businessmen we had little choice.

"Look, I'll grant you our company capitalized on the migration to the suburbs, but it would have happened without us. I only remind you of all this, Ethan, to put what I want to discuss with you in its proper context. In those days I did not have the resources to make a difference. You may be thinking that I lacked the courage, as well. Perhaps."

"I'm not here to judge you, Nikos," replied Cotham. "Racism is in our bones, I guess. I went to an all white high school—never even met a black kid who wasn't the child of a maid or a janitor until I was in the Navy. Suddenly I shared a cabin with a black officer with a chemical engineering degree from M.I.T. It took me a while to adjust, I can tell you."

"Ethan, it's been almost forty years now since the assassination. Maybe the time has finally come for putting all that behind us. Maybe we can recreate some of that sense of vitality that I used to love about Downtown as a kid, but without the racism that went with it. Maybe we can finally heal some of the wounds that divide us into two separate worlds, black and white, and become one city again."

"So, what does this have to do with me?" asked Cotham.

"When I met you the other night at the Brooks Museum, I was shocked to hear what you said about how a building could help accomplish this. I was shocked because I have been thinking the same thing. Only a few other people know about it. Come here, I want to show you something."

Pappas stood and crossed the room to the sideboard. He opened the lower doors, withdrew a roll of what appeared to be architectural drawings, and returned to the table. With Cotham at his side, he unrolled the plans. Cotham recognized the first sheet as a site plan of the south half of Downtown. There was Main Street with Beale Street intersecting it. Three blocks to the west, Beale descended the bluffs and terminated at Riverside Drive. No more than a hundred yards away, separated from Riverside Drive by a strip of vacant land, were the banks of the Mississippi River. On this parcel was superimposed a bright orange circle with a label in capital Helvetica letters proclaiming, "Center for Southern Culture." In the lower right-hand corner of the sheet a title block was emblazoned, "Astor Architects."

"These drawings are strictly preliminary, Ethan—and very confidential, but I think they show the scope and promise of what I have in mind. I believe, and apparently we agree on this, that because of the uniqueness of the Southern condition, blacks and whites are actually more alike than they are different. The Center for Southern Culture is intended to be a place that celebrates that common ground and that attempts to bridge the cultural gap between the races.

"We have proposed a site that is symbolically significant. The Mississippi is the most fabled river in the country. Less than a hundred years ago steamboats still docked here, bringing cotton, gamblers, and planters. It was the focus of business for the white community."

"Yes," interjected Cotham, "but before the Civil War those riverboats also transported slaves...."

"You're correct, of course. They brought slaves to Memphis, but also the blues from down in the Delta. Those slaves were bought and sold on this very site, as well as in Auction Square. Beale Street, of course, became the Main Street of black America until it was razed by Urban Renewal in the sixties. W.C. Handy wrote his blues there. Martin Luther King gave his most important speech nearby and was killed a few blocks away.

"And what was it, Ethan, that, despite their differences, these blacks and whites had in common? I think it was a shared culture of suffering and adversity. Certainly, it goes without saying that as slaves, blacks suffered more than whites. But whites suffered as well. Most of the first settlers were very poor. They had come to Mississippi and West Tennessee when this was still the frontier, one great, unbroken expanse of forest to be cleared. Contrary to the popular mythology, most of these whites were not slave owners, and of those who did own slaves, most owned only a small handful. You see, except on the large plantations, blacks and whites cleared the forests and worked in the fields together. The Civil War crippled the economy and the infrastructure that everyone depended on. The same was true for the Depression, which hit the South harder than most other parts of the country. In Memphis, the effects of poverty, floods, war, Yellow Fever, ignorance, prejudice, and isolation have devastated blacks and whites alike."

"Yes, I expect most Memphians tend to forget this," commented Cotham, trying to conceal his curiosity about the drawings that lay before him.

"Forgive me if I'm lecturing, Ethan. But it's important that you know the basis for my idea. My main point is that the need to rise above adversity resulted in the evolution of a common culture. And I think that culture was built around the arts, principally music and storytelling. Certainly the blues and gospel music had their origins in slavery, and before that, in African traditions. But non-Southerners are often surprised to find how deeply whites feel about this music too.

"Listen, I know more than one Memphis native who has settled in New York. When I ask them what they miss most about Memphis, they say the same thing—they miss the black people and the music. And if you visit a fraternity house at Ole Miss on a Friday night, for instance, you'll hear a black combo playing primarily for white boys and girls. Except for the raunchy lyrics, the music is virtually identical to what you'll hear in a black church on Sunday. And upstairs in the fraternity living room, it's not unusual to see a white boy from a prominent Delta family playing and singing the blues on the piano.

"Or go on a duck hunt in the flooded bottoms along the river. Shooting ducks is almost beside the point. The real serious business is storytelling."

"You're right about that, Nikos," replied Cotham. "The subject doesn't matter. It can be anything from how you outsmarted somebody in a business deal, to some famous football game, to the first time you had a drink of moonshine." He had to admit there was something contagious about Pappas' enthusiasm.

"That's it," continued Pappas. "What matters is how you tell the story, how you set up the listener for the climax. It's a tradition handed down from countless evenings spent on front porches where people had to entertain themselves. And it's a way of life blacks and whites share.

"So it occurred to me to make a place where this common ground is studied, documented, and, as I said, celebrated. As I see it, the Center for Southern Culture will become a national treasure, a destination point for people all over the country. It will include a museum, a theatre, classrooms, a place for outdoor assemblies, important works of art, and perhaps most important, a 1000-seat concert hall where people can hear the music of the South. Blues and gospel, rockabilly, rock 'n roll, bluegrass and rap. It will all be there.

"There's one other message it should send, as well. This is a very prominent site, a site of national importance, even. What we do here will be highly visible; it will set an example for others. So we want the Center to reflect the most advanced thinking in seismic design. We've ignored the risk of a serious earthquake too long in this town. One of these days we are going to have a major seismic event—more than a little jolt that simply puts the lights out and runs people away from a party. Despite the false alarm of the Buckley scare, we are all sitting on a time bomb.

"In order for it to do all this, the Center for Southern Culture must also be a truly distinguished work of architecture. And that's where you may come in, Ethan."

Cotham looked down at the drawings. "Nikos, I'm flattered; I truly am. I appreciate all you're saying and agree with most of it. And the site is certainly spectacular. I'd love to be involved, but I see you already have an architect." He pointed to the title block.

"Oh, that. It's no secret that Richard Astor does a lot of work for us. So I asked him to sketch up some preliminary ideas. But it's also no secret that his vision is, how shall I put it, somewhat limited. His firm is skilled at turning out commercial work fast. They've got it down to a formula. Contractors can build it with no problems. People like it when it's finished, and their fees are more than reasonable.

"But for the CSC, I'm looking for something else. I want a unique work of architecture, one that speaks to a sense of history and to what makes the South special. But it must speak without sentimentality.

56

No moonlight and magnolias. It must speak to that shared sense of suffering, to the dignity that grows out of enduring adversity.

"Of course, we'll have to consider Astor for the job; he's worked for us too long not to do that. But what I'm proposing is a competition. I'd like to invite a handful of our best architects to show what they can do. We'll put together a blue ribbon jury to decide which plan is the best, and the one they pick is the one we'll build. Are you interested?"

Cotham gazed past Pappas, through the window, toward the distant Downtown skyline. He felt the grip of conflicting emotions. On one hand, the project sounded truly exciting, the sort of commission every architect dreams of, the chance to create a masterpiece, even. He hesitated.

"Nikos, may I speak freely? You may not like everything I'm about to say."

Pappas nodded.

"A competition could be very exciting, not only for the architects involved, but for the whole city. As I'm sure you know, a number of the most famous projects of the last two hundred years began as competitions, including the Sydney Opera House and the Vietnam Memorial.

"From a selfish perspective there's no doubt in my mind that we would stand a good chance in any local competition based solely on design merit. But there's the rub, Nikos. Architectural competitions have a reputation for being notoriously unfair, both to the winner and the losers. I can tell you countless stories of biased or unqualified juries who arrived at their decision based on political favoritism, fashion, sentimentality, picturesqueness, or as a compromise among jurors unable to agree on a controversial entry. With most juries the odds are stacked against the unusual or the original. Frank Lloyd Wright once referred to architectural competition winners as 'an average of the average by the average.'"

"Well, I've read a bit about the one held for the Chicago Tribune Building. Around 1922, wasn't it?" asked Pappas.

"A case in point," continued Cotham. "It attracted many of the world's most eminent young architects, including Walter Gropius, Eliel Saarinen, and the radical Adolph Loos. Their designs were all bold, striking, and original, and the selection of the Gropius or Saarinen schemes would have amounted to a vote of confidence in the new Modernism that had begun to excite the younger generation of American architects. Instead, the jury selected the entry by a well-connected but utterly conventional local firm, a reactionary fantasy that disguised the muscular new steel technology of the skyscraper with the trappings of medievalism. The completed Tribune Building has a grotesque Gothic spire complete with flying buttresses."

"Go on, Ethan. I'm listening."

"Competitions carry other baggage, too. A great work of architecture usually requires a healthy give-and-take between the architect and the client. It should be a collaboration. The nature of a competition rules this out; it forces the architect to work in isolation, making guesses about all sorts of crucial issues, not the least of which is the cost. In the end the design may be spectacular, but without meeting the client's needs.

"Have you established a budget?"

"No, not yet. As I said, we are looking for a truly distinguished work of architecture. The competition rules specify that a budget recommendation be made by the architect."

Although Pappas seemed to be listening to Cotham's concerns, he was silently tapping a finger on the table.

"Well, Ethan?" he finally asked. "Are you interested?"

"Who are you thinking of for the jury?"

"We haven't made a final determination," Pappas evasively replied. "But they will be people you know and respect."

"A local group?"

"Most likely. We want jurors who understand the cultural context of Memphis and who will be able to evaluate the proposals in terms of local values."

Somewhere in the recesses of Cotham's mind a series of tiny alarm bells were ringing. Pappas's answers were far too vague. Cotham was worried about the lack of a budget. And the fairness of the selection process would hinge on the background of the jurors and these so-called local values.

"Who else will you invite to compete?"

"Other than you and Astor, we intend to invite Seth Gerber. He's younger than you and Richard, but his new library in Orange Mound is impressive, and we believe in recognizing African-American talent in the community whenever we can."

So now the little circle was complete. Just as Cotham had once worked in Astor's office, Gerber had once served as Cotham's intern. There was no doubt that Gerber was a gifted designer, and after he passed the registration examination, Cotham had considered offering him a partnership in his firm. He had been sorry to see Gerber leave to open his own office, but had encouraged him once it became clear that his mind was made up.

Cotham could think of no way to raise his next question obliquely, but since Pappas had made no mention of it, he had to ask. "Nikos, the design of a project of this size could require a great deal of time and effort for the architects you invite. Will there be any compensation?"

Pappas raised his eyebrows. "We have assumed that the chance to be considered for such a project would be its own reward, Ethan," he replied in a slightly condescending tone, "and it is our intent to award the commission and a full fee to the winner."

He crossed his arms over his chest. "Ethan, you seem to have a great many questions. I need to know whether you will be competing. If so, I have a package of information for you. In it you will find a site plan, our program of requirements, and the submission guidelines. The deadline is three weeks from tomorrow, so I must have your answer immediately. If you are not interested, I need to contact the next firm on our short list."

Cotham did not take kindly to pressure, especially from those whose power was derived from their net worth, and for a moment he considered declining the invitation on the spot. Why the rush? Why was no compensation being offered, even if it were simply a token honorarium? And why was the identity of the jury such a secret? He felt manipulated by Pappas, who no doubt understood that he could get the participation of almost any architect in town without having to offer any of these things. Cotham stood and walked slowly to the glass wall where the telescope stood.

He tried to imagine Pappas asking the same of a lawyer or a physician. *Tell me in advance how you plan to handle my defense in court or what drugs you intend to prescribe, and I'll let you know whether you'll get me as a client or a patient.* At one level it was insulting. But architects had created the problem for themselves. The good ones were ambitious and wanted too badly to create great buildings, and there were not enough prestigious commissions to go around in a city the size of Memphis. No sensible architect was in the profession primarily for the money; anyone who was would be a fool. The Pappases of the world understood this and used it against them. All the doctors and lawyers Cotham knew would have been out the door already, yet here he stood debating an answer.

In Pappas's defense it was clear, as well, that if he were to choose his architect in the same way he selected his lawyer or doctor, Cotham would not have been summoned to this meeting. Astor would have gotten the job as a matter of course. The fact that a competition was being held at all was recognition of the fact that in architecture, as opposed to law and medicine, individual creativity mattered. The public assumed that when faced with a given legal or medical problem, there was only one correct course of action, and that all competent professionals would take the same approach. In a sense, it was a compliment to his profession that people valued the fact that architects did not all design in the same way.

There was another problem: a three-week deadline meant that he would have to put his meager handful of other projects on the back burner in order to throw himself and his staff into the Center for Southern Culture. This meant he would not be able to bill his other clients and that he might even have to reach into his own pocket to make payroll. He tried to imagine any of the businessmen he knew agreeing to take a similar risk.

Cotham bent and peered through the eyepiece of the telescope. The image was inverted as in all astronomical telescopes, and he was momentarily disoriented. He twisted the focusing knob and the blurred skyline became sharp and distinct. There in the center of the field of view he saw the spire of the Lincoln American Tower.

He could easily distinguish the flag flying from the cupola and the windows of his own little office. How strange that a telescope in a tower here in this suburban nether world was already aimed directly at his office.

He turned to face the developer across the room. It was important to sound more decisive than he felt. He took a breath. "Very well, Nikos, count me in."

Chapter Four

It was a relief to escape the city and the mounting pressures of the competition. Cotham looked forward to inspecting the progress of construction at St. Mary Magdalene Church. The hard realities of building were always a welcome relief from the mundane tasks of managing an office that normally consumed his attention.

The angular silhouette of the incomplete structure loomed above the shoulder of the hill. Its broad gables suggested the weathered barns that hovered like nesting hens, their wings spread protectively over the rolling countryside of north Mississippi. Cotham smiled to himself as he recalled the first time he had pointed this out to the Building Committee. They had looked at him searchingly, as though this architect from the city might perhaps be making a joke at their expense. Most were either yeomen farmers or small business people removed from life in the country by only a single generation, and Cotham soon realized that some possessed a self-conscious fear of being seen by him as unsophisticated rustics.

In fact, he had meant the exact opposite. He was a great admirer of "vernacular" architecture, as architects referred to the old rural buildings of the South. He loved the way they had been gently tucked into groves of oaks and magnolias or nestled against the south side of a hill, just below the top, to catch the precious southerly breezes of summer. He had told himself that he would be satisfied if he could do half as well in the placement of this church.

As the Rover rounded the curve at the base of the hill, the building was blocked from view by the grove of mature red oaks that Cotham had ordered the bulldozers to spare. He remembered the resistance advanced by Don Childers, the contractor's superintendent, when Cotham had first emphasized the importance of protecting the trees.

"Don, be sure to remind your guys that the oaks are to stay. We need to get some batter boards up around them, don't you think?"

"You know, Mr. Ethan, I been thinkin'. We could pick up probably fifty parking spaces if we get rid of them trees. They ain't hardly got a chance of makin' it anyhow, onest we grade around 'em and pour all that asphalt."

As they had debated the question, Cotham trying to think of a practical rather than an esthetic argument that would make sense to Childers, a deer had emerged from the threatened grove, no more than thirty yards away. It stopped at the edge of the tree line and gazed at them with solemnity. Cotham felt a prickly sensation at the back of his neck. It was as though they had been confronted by an emissary from some primordial realm, sent in silent protest against the modern age and its disregard for the natural world. Childers, an ardent hunter, saw it too and grew still. After a long silence between them and without turning toward Cotham he said quietly, "Well, I 'spect we could live without a few of them parking spaces, if you don't think they'll miss 'em." As though it had heard, the animal melted back into the dappled shadows and was gone.

Turning into the driveway of the parking lot, he saw the structure suddenly reappear directly ahead of him, closer now, and higher, the skeletal frame of the bell tower rising above the ridge of the roof, solidly anchoring the composition to the earth.

The design had not been without controversy, but with the help of Sophie Leland, the farsighted and persuasive chair of the Building Committee, they had managed to reach a consensus on the issues that had arisen. One by one, each decision had been dissected and debated before everyone agreed to move ahead. Cotham reminded himself that their uncertainty was understandable. Most had never planned a building before and found themselves in unfamiliar territory, forced to rely on his judgment. Everyone had seemed to settle down once ground was broken, and now Cotham sensed signs of real anticipation from most of the committee that the project would soon be finished. With the design decisions mostly behind, he was relieved to finally be able to concentrate on the purely technical concerns of construction.

Although far from complete, the walls and vaulted steel roof structure were now sufficiently intact to suggest the breathtaking volume of the main worship space, or nave, as Cotham liked to call it. The word originated from the Latin word for "ship" and referred to its ribbed roof structure, which did, in fact, resemble the inverted hull of a boat. It was exhilarating to finally step into the three-dimensional reality of a space he had designed and that had existed for so long only in his mind. Cotham recalled the seemingly endless debates in the committee meetings over the height of the roof. He had held out, refusing to give in to those who argued that his concept was too extravagant and not worth the additional cost. Cotham had insisted that to create a sense of transcendence the key was space and light and that this was as true now as it had been in the age of the great cathedrals. Sophie had stood by him, skillfully working to bring the recalcitrant members around until at last they had all agreed. The exposed bones of the spacious room gave it something of the timeless character of an ancient ruin.

"Hey, Mr. Ethan!" came a familiar voice from behind, and Cotham turned to see Childers striding toward him in muddy boots, army surplus pants, and a camouflage jacket, the hood pulled up beneath his hardhat. Under his arm was a tattered roll of drawings and on the right cuff of the jacket sleeve was a dark stain. From the beard stubble and bleary eyes it looked as if he might have been up all night.

"Morning, Don. You look as though you were up early."

"I been huntin'," he grinned. "First time this season. Me an' a buddy spent the night up there in that bell tower of yours. Makes a damn fine deer stand!"

Cotham thought of the deer in the grove. But since he was not sure whether or not to take Childers seriously and could think of no rejoinder that would make him seem neither gullible nor judgmental, he quickly changed the subject. "What about those brick samples for the mock-up panel?"

"We got 'em in and the panel is ready for you to look at."

They trudged across the muddy site where a handsome slate plaza would eventually mark the main entrance to the church. At the contractor's job trailer, they stopped to look at the masonry sample that had been erected just outside. As detailed in the drawings, the brick was arranged in a three-color diagonal diaper pattern. It was a complex design; Cotham wanted to be sure that the masonry subcontractor could execute it flawlessly before beginning the façade of the church. He was irritated but not surprised to find an error.

"It looks like your mason needs to study this pattern a little closer," he said to Childers. "See here, where the tan bricks touch the red ones? There is supposed to be a black brick inserted between them."

Childers unrolled the drawings, and they studied the pattern painstakingly laid out by Tensing, showing every individual brick. There was no room for any claim that the intent was ambiguous. The masonry subcontractor had simply failed to pay attention to the details. In Cotham's eyes, few sins were more serious, and he was about to reprimand Childers for his lack of supervision.

"You shoulda heard them mason-ary guys cussin' when they seen this drawing," drawled Childers. "They wanted to know what had that architect been smokin'."

"Well, Don, I grant you the architect may have gone round the bend, but he knows what he wants. I need to ask you to tell them that we've got to have this sample done over until they get it right."

They were interrupted by the sound of crunching gravel as a red Volvo station wagon swung up the driveway and pulled to a stop in the unpaved parking lot. Two figures emerged. The driver, a heavy-set woman in her mid-fifties wearing a canvas barn jacket and muddy green rubber boots, was accompanied by a short, slightly overweight man attired in black suit and white clerical collar. He was munching on a doughnut; as they approached, he waved. Cotham noted the ruddy complexion, speculating that it was explained only in part by the cold.

"Peace be with you, my architectonic sons!" he exclaimed in an outrageously incongruous Boston accent.

"Welcome to Mississippi, you carpet-bagging ecclesiastical troublemaker!" retorted Cotham. "And, Sophie, my condolences to you, although I see you had the foresight to stock up on doughnuts before you picked up the good cleric at the airport.

"Father Tom Cellini, this is Don Childers, construction superintendent and deer hunter extraordinaire. Sophie knows Don, of course."

"How do you do, Don?" said Cellini. "Take me with you some time. I've wanted to go hunting in Mississippi ever since I read Faulkner in high school."

Childers's expression was blank as he wiped his hand on his trousers and clasped the priest's extended hand.

"How was the flight?" Cotham inquired, changing the subject.

"The flight was par for the course on 'Northworst,' three hours with no sustenance but a bag of peanuts and a couple of Bloody Marys. And I've got to remember to stop wearing this damned collar on airplanes. Every time I do I sit next to some recovering Catholic who wants to tell me how the church ruined his life. Either that or someone who thinks I can tell her how to save her marriage. Hell, I'm an art historian, not a parish priest!"

Cotham, Tom Cellini, and Sophie Leland had come to know each other well over the three years since Cotham had been selected to design St. Mary Magdalene Church. Cotham felt sure he owed his selection to them. He had sensed an immediate affinity with both the priest and the committee chair ever since the interview. Cellini had posed the right questions, giving Cotham the opportunity to speak sincerely about his design philosophy, and tying it neatly to his knowledge of the history of ecclesiastical architecture and the sweeping reforms of the Second Vatican Council. Sophie had drawn him out about his approach to working with a committee, and Cotham had explained the importance of having an architect

who would listen to their concerns. It seemed to make no difference to either of them that Cotham was neither a Roman Catholic
nor a Mississippian, although he did assume that his indeterminate
religious background had been discussed among the members of
the Building Committee. Without their intercession on his behalf,
Cotham suspected that a local Catholic architect might have been
given the inside track.

As though he had suddenly been reminded, Childers piped up,
"You jus missed that Bishop again. He drove up in that big Lincoln
and then walked across here in his dress shoes, right through all this
mud. It's the third day in a row he been out here, jus walkin' around,
lookin'. Won't talk to nobody. Don't look too happy, neither. Left
right before you got here, Mr. Ethan."

By reputation, Hervey Coltharp, Bishop of the Diocese of
North Mississippi, was not one to indulge in idle conversation with
construction workers. Or architects for that matter. On the one
and only occasion that he and Cotham had met, the Bishop had
been polite but cool, and Cotham suspected that he had not been
the Bishop's first choice as architect for the project. Coltharp was a
complex figure. The first African-American bishop in Mississippi and a social liberal, he was also a liturgical conservative who
privately opposed many of the changes that had swept the church
following Vatican II in the early sixties. He was known to feel little
empathy for northern theologians in general and in particular for
the liturgical advisor from Boston invited into his diocese by a
predominantly progressive parish like St. Mary Magdalene.

At the entrance of the nave a two-foot deep octagonal pit about
seven feet in diameter had been sunk into the concrete floor slab.
Here in predominantly Baptist north Mississippi, it had been a

major topic of conversation among the construction crew that the Catholics were building a church where baptisms would involve immersion. There had been more than one joke behind Cotham's back about the new church with the big Jacuzzi.

Cellini examined the baptismal font with professional interest. "I hope it's going to be big enough, Ethan. You know there has to be room for both the priest and the candidate for baptism. And there will be steps down, I assume?"

"Right on both accounts, Tom. I understand you decided to pour the steps later after the granite arrives, didn't you, Don? And remember, we decided to reduce the width by a couple of feet in order to allow more people to gather around it."

As they reached the center of the nave, outside the clouds parted and a shaft of sunlight sliced through the circular opening in the south gable where the rose window would eventually be installed. It fell at the foot of the raised concrete platform directly ahead of them.

"Oh, my!" gasped Sophie. Cotham glanced at his watch and noted with satisfaction that the time was ten minutes until noon. He had taken care to orient the building directly toward the south so that in the winter months this long shaft of light would illuminate the room as the Sunday morning mass was in progress.

Cellini glanced at him but said nothing. They climbed the three steps that surrounded the platform. In its center below the location of the future altar, a cavity some twelve inches square and of equal depth had been formed into the concrete slab. Shortly prior to the dedication of the completed church, a relic furnished by Rome would be sealed into this cavity—perhaps a lock of hair or some other personal artifact associated with a saint.

The location of the altar had become one of the controversial aspects of the design. Ever since the Middle Ages, traditional Catholic practice had dictated that the altar be placed at the far end of an elongated nave, its remoteness accentuated by a railing that separated the clergy from the congregation during the mass. The sanctuary, the space beyond the altar rail, had even been off-limits to women, a fact that Sophie had indignantly pointed out to the rest of the Building Committee.

The Second Vatican Council, however, had decreed that this practice be abandoned. Along with celebration of the mass in the vernacular instead of Latin, the guidelines suggested that the altar was now to be positioned nearer the center of the worship space with seating arranged around it in an arc. The objective was to create a stronger sense of community by allowing the worshippers to face each other across the space.

Led by Sophie, most of the younger members of the Building Committee had concurred with the centralized plan, but there were others, including several of the older members, who resisted. This issue had threatened to split the committee into factions until Cellini delivered a powerful and persuasive homily explaining that St. John Chrysostom and other fathers of the early church had taught that the presence of Christ was best experienced through a sense of community shared by the congregation. The new configuration fostered this sense while the traditional layout emphasized the separateness of individual worshippers and isolated the clergy. Sophie had followed up with a reminder that both the liturgical advisor and the architect were in agreement and that the committee would be foolish to ignore this combined expertise.

There was also the matter of the Eucharistic Reservation Chapel. In pre-Vatican Council times, a portion of the Host, the consecrated bread of the Eucharist, was set aside following the mass and sealed in the Tabernacle, a ceremonial container placed on the altar. In perhaps its most emotionally volatile pronouncement, the Council had decreed that henceforth, the Reserved Sacrament would be kept in a separate place away from the altar, so as not to compete with the primary symbol of the presence of Christ, the altar itself. Cotham had designed a chapel for the Tabernacle in the base of the bell tower where it was intended to occupy a special place of honor. Even so, the decision had provoked much heated discussion from those who saw its removal from the altar as a sign of modern irreverence bordering on blasphemy. There had even been rumors that some of the wealthiest families might withdraw their substantial pledges to the building fund.

When word had first reached Bishop Hervey Coltharp of the controversies swirling at the largest and wealthiest church in his diocese, it was said that he became so agitated that his Chancellor had feared he was experiencing a second heart attack. A glass of sherry had been required to enable him to regain his equanimity.

"Ah, yes, the Bishop," mused Cellini as though he had read Cotham's thoughts. "Perhaps we could have dinner tonight and discuss the situation. Will you join us, Sophie?"

"Unfortunately, I can't. I promised my daughter I'd be there for her middle school play, and I'm covered with mud from the stable. But since it's the two of you on the hot seat, why don't you go ahead without me? You're staying at the Peabody, aren't you, Father? I'm sure Ethan wouldn't mind giving you a ride back to Memphis."

Comfortable in each other's company, neither Cotham nor Cellini felt compelled to carry on a continuous conversation as they headed north up Interstate-55 on the trip back to Memphis.

Perhaps the priest was tired, and Cotham was content to drive in silence, admiring as he always did the sad, sweet Mississippi landscape in winter. It was as though it had imprinted itself into some unconscious recess of his brain during the duck hunting expeditions that were a part of growing up in Memphis. Those trips would unexpectedly flood back into his consciousness at times like this, triggered by the muted sienna browns, moss-greens, warm grays, yellow ochres and olives of the pastures and pine forests that rolled past the windshield.

Like many Southerners, Cotham was well versed in his family's history. As a child, he had heard the stories of how the Cothams had first migrated to Mississippi in 1837 from Davidson County in Middle Tennessee to settle on the cheap, rich land that ten years earlier had belonged to the Chickasaws. While these pioneers and their slaves had cleared the ancient hardwood forests and planted cotton, the Chickasaws had been marched to Oklahoma along the infamous Trail of Tears, prodded by the bayonets of Andrew Jackson's troops. His mother's great grandfather had also arrived in Calhoun County from North Carolina about the same time. Cotham knew of four direct ancestors, three on his mother's side, who had fought for the Confederacy, including one who had ridden in Bedford Forrest's cavalry and who had taken a Federal bullet through the hip at the Battle of Franklin. The amputation of his leg had been unsuccessful, and he lay buried in the Lafayette cemetery in a plot not far from Faulkner's family. Like many others, his grave was commemorated by the cast iron Maltese cross inscribed with the defiant motto *Deo Vindice,* placed there by the United Daughters of the Confederacy.

They drove on past the exits to the small towns of Sardis, Como, and Senatobia. As they crossed the Coldwater River the cypress trees, stark white against the blackness of the swampy shallows, stood at attention like the ghosts of Forrest's troopers who had once galloped across the forlorn and tragic countryside.

Hernando, Horn Lake, and Nesbit slipped past and Cotham's thoughts turned back to St. Mary Magdalene and the odd thing that had happened as he and Cellini walked to the parking lot. Cotham had glanced back toward the grove of red oaks and was almost positive that he caught a glimpse of a tall black man in a dark suit and clerical collar standing in the trees not far from where the deer had appeared.

Chapter Five

Cotham and Cellini met at eight o'clock that evening in the lobby of the Peabody Hotel in Downtown Memphis, which better suited Cellini's refined tastes than the Hampton Inns in which he was usually forced to stay on his consulting trips. In one corner of the ornate, high-ceilinged space, next to a twenty-foot Christmas tree, a player piano cranked out a jaunty version of "Jingle Bells" followed immediately by a reverently slow-paced rendition of "Dixie." At the railing of the mezzanine above, debutantes in satin evening gowns, drinks in hand, accompanied by dates turned out in tuxedos and winged collars, surveyed the comings and goings of the tourists, businessmen, and the black gospel choir now forming to begin a concert. The mallard ducks, which had inhabited the Carrera marble fountain in the center of the lobby since the 1930s, cruised nonchalantly in circles, oblivious to the hubbub and the occasional flash bulb. From the ballroom on the mezzanine floated the syncopated beat of a rock band grinding out "Hot Nuts."

Cellini had shed his priestly garb. In his tweed sport coat he now looked more the professor of art history. In addition to his free-lance position as a liturgical advisor to churches, he was adjunct professor at the Harvard Graduate School of Design, where he had earned his doctorate. Cotham had read and been impressed by his thesis, entitled "Aspects of Sacred Space in the Architecture of Le Corbusier."

Cotham and Cellini walked the half block to the Rendezvous, across Union Avenue and down an alley, following the heavy perfume of barbecue and smoke on the crisp night air. In Memphis, barbecue was a noun rather than a verb, and it was redundant to mention the species of meat. Barbecue meant pork, and it was only necessary to specify whether one preferred ribs or a sandwich, served with sweet or hot sauce, and at the Rendezvous, either the "dry" or "wet" recipe. They asked for a remote table in the rear. Cotham ordered a Rendezvous Special for two: smoked sausage, cheddar cheese, hot peppers and soda crackers. Cellini nodded his approval when Cotham, in deference to his guest, asked for Samuel Adams beer.

"I thought you should see this letter from the Bishop," began Cellini, blotting away a tiny speck of pepper juice and handing Cotham a sheet of heavy buff-colored stationery bearing the coat of arms of the Roman Catholic Diocese of North Mississippi.

Dear Father Cellini:

It has come to my attention that certain decisions of major importance with regard to the design of St. Mary Magdalene Church, located within this Diocese, have been and are being made in the absence of adequate consultation with Diocesan officials. As a result, the seeds of dissension and unrest have needlessly been planted within the parish family.

*Please be reminded that as Bishop I am the Owner of this prop-
erty, and, as such, expect to be kept fully informed and involved.
You are hereby requested and directed to appear at my office at
2:00 p.m. on Monday, December 20, to discuss these issues.*

*You are further directed to request the presence of the
architect, Mr. Ethan Cotham.*

Yours in Christ,
Hervey Coltharp, Bishop, O.B.

Following the bold signature in heavy black ink was scrawled a
small cross.

Cellini returned the letter to his inside jacket pocket and took
a deep pull from his beer. "I'm hearing from some friends in the
Bishop's office that the real issue for Coltharp is not the design,"
began Cellini. "He cares little or nothing about liturgical reform
and even less about creative architecture. What he does care about,
though, is the financial support of the wealthy planters from the
Delta. Without their support he hasn't a chance in hell of pulling
off his plans for the new parochial schools in Tunica County."

"Yes, they say that before the casinos began to spring up down
there it was the poorest county in the country. Things have im-
proved since, but they still have a long way to go to catch up,"
agreed Cotham.

"One of those planters is D'Arcy Lamar. He's a big, loud man
on the Parish Council who's been against everything I've proposed
from day one. I understand he's still upset about the way the building is shaping up. He knows he's in the minority and that he'll get

nowhere with Sophie, so he's gone straight to Bishop Coltharp. He's been making veiled threats to reduce his pledge, and that got Coltharp's attention.

"It is most important that we not defy or alienate the Bishop. He is a proud man, despite his training as a Benedictine, and is used to being in control. So far he has taken a laissez faire position on the project. But if he suspects that we are fomenting trouble, he is likely to become much more involved, and that will make life difficult for both of us, my friend."

"As though this project isn't tough enough, Tom!" sighed Cotham. Why had no one in architecture school ever alluded to the political side of professional practice? The curriculum had emphasized total immersion in the design studio with a clear implication that if the concept were strong enough, the grateful client would immediately embrace it and reach for his checkbook in a rapture of esthetic ecstasy. With his tendencies toward self-doubt, it had taken Cotham years to disabuse himself of the notion that because this had never been his experience in practice, there must be some serious flaw in the way he worked. He wondered if his mentor, Henry Roper, with his world-famous firm in Philadelphia and his pick of choice projects and sophisticated clients ever had to concern himself with power struggles, turf wars, and fragile egos.

The main course arrived, a basket of ribs accompanied by cole slaw seasoned with hot mustard, baked beans, and more beer. Cellini had visited the Rendezvous with Cotham before and preferred his ribs "wet," while Cotham opted for the trademark "dry" recipe. Like a native, Cellini dug in with gusto using his fingers, pausing only to mutter, "Would you be so kind as to pass the hot sauce?"

They were silent for several minutes as their hands became

covered with the thick, savory goo. Finally Cellini looked up at Cotham, a frown clouding his blue eyes. "Ethan, I've been thinking. I don't have a good feeling about Bishop Hervey Coltharp. We must tread extremely softly at this meeting. In my experience no one is more dangerous than a priest in danger of losing his financing or his power base."

Chapter Six

At the corner of Court Square Cotham paused, as he always did, to pay homage to the most fanciful building in the city, an extraordinary composition of crenelated towers and bulbous Turkish domes known as the Tennessee Club. Founded by a Confederate general, the club headquarters was built in 1890. It had served as a private bastion for the town's railroad barons and bankers, wealthy planters from the Delta, land speculators, and real estate developers until their exodus from Downtown had forced its sale to a prestigious law firm. It was the most obstreperous, cantankerous building Cotham had ever seen, and he loved it as one might an eccentric uncle. One could feel it growling with curmudgeonly charm at those who dared pass by it. As a child, he and his family had been taken to dinner at the Tennessee Club, and he had been entranced by the round dining rooms and the balcony overlooking Court Square where the Maid of Cotton was introduced to the cheering masses at the beginning of each spring's Cotton Carnival.

Cotham reflected on the fact that he had closer relationships with his favorite buildings than with most of the people he knew, a fact that no doubt explained his admittedly small circle of close friends. It was not that he disliked people, he often told himself;

there just were not many whose intelligence and character he deeply respected. There was Pallie, certainly, and his old friend Lew Craig. And perhaps a handful of his clients over the years, the few who understood and appreciated the struggle and aspirations that architecture involved and who had become lasting friends.

He was not particularly proud of this aspect of his personality. He wished it were otherwise, that he made friends quickly and easily, but knew himself well enough to accept that it would never be the case. Cotham had long ago discovered that he was incapable of happily playing the good ole boy game that was so central to success in Memphis society. It had bothered him for years, growing up in the upper middle class enclave in Midtown, at the prep school in the suburbs, and then at the University of Virginia, where his fraternity traditionally maintained a strong Memphis contingent. Running a struggling architectural practice was in many ways simply an extension of this same social web for which he had felt both affection and disgust all his life. While necessity had taught him to play the game, he still winced inwardly every time he caught himself grinning and jabbering about college football with a businessman in the hope that it might lead to a new commission.

Cotham remembered with a shudder that this was precisely what was to be required of him at his meeting with his new prospective clients, Thurston Leroy Quonset and his wife, Roberta.

Jean, his longtime secretary, bookkeeper, and self-appointed mother superior of the office met him as he stepped from the elevator. She looked meaningfully toward the conference room door and then eyed his bow tie with a faint air of disapproval. Although he considered it a perfectly respectable regimental stripe purchased from the Ben Silver shop in Charleston, he knew that Jean believed it made him appear too eccentric. That he held out was a private tribute to his mentor, Henry Roper, the brilliant but courtly radical with whom he had studied at the Princeton School of Architecture, and in whose Philadelphia office he had later worked as an intern. Roper's trademark navy blue bow tie with small white polka dots was a subtle symbol of disaffection from the business establishment and a throwback to the glorious days of the beaux-arts when the bow tie was a trademark of the architect-as-artist. Such subtleties would, of course, be lost on the Quonsets, who were now awaiting his appearance.

Jean reached up and straightened his tie, destroying the intentional assymetry Cotham preferred. "You'll be great!" she whispered. "Now get in there before they decide to leave and go interview that Richard Astor."

Although they had never been close friends, Cotham and Thurston Quonset had gone camping together as members of the same Boy Scout troop which still met in the old Episcopal Church at Peabody and Belvedere Boulevard. As neighbors, they had played football in the large side yard of the imposing Quonset house on Belvedere virtually every fall afternoon until their junior year.

Thurston had been pudgy, indolent, and lacking in athletic ability as a child. In their football games he was forced to play center for both sides, and his exertions often resulted in uncontrollable nosebleeds, even though no one ever bothered to throw a block at him. He was tolerated only because his family owned the best playing field in the neighborhood.

The football ended after Thurston had been bundled off to the Leonidas K. Polk Military Institute in Chattanooga in a desperate attempt to instill in him a sense of discipline. By some miracle he had graduated from Hampden-Sydney College, where a fondness for Jack

Daniels Tennessee Whiskey earned him the nickname "Thirsty Thurston." To Cotham's amazement he went on to earn an MBA from the University of Memphis, became a successful banker, and had recently been named President of the Memphis and Charleston Bank.

"Ethan," Thurston had breathlessly confided over a recent lunch, "I must be living right. My application at the Country Club went through! You and Pallie must be our guests for dinner!" Then he had glanced around the restaurant to be sure he would not be overheard. "And I've even been invited to be a Boll Weevil!" The Boll Weevils, who were supposed to remain anonymous inside their green and gold insect costumes, rode an old green fire truck around town during Cotton Carnival, drinking and crashing the more sedate parties where they gleefully pinched and teased the well-dressed matrons.

"Congratulations, Thurston," Cotham responded. "I realize life hasn't always been easy for you. It must be gratifying to be recognized as a prominent business leader."

"You have no idea, Ethan. You remember what it was like for me when we were kids, always being picked on, having to play permanent center for both sides in our football games? Why, do you know that there were four or five other guys from Memphis who went to Hampden-Sydney along with me? Well, everyone else was invited to pledge the same fraternity, but I wasn't even asked back after the first rush party. But I made up my mind that they weren't going to get rid of old Thurston that easily. So I just kept coming to the parties with the others. I guess the members got tired of shooing me away and eventually I got a bid, too."

Although Cotham had been taller than most of the other pre-pubescent boys in Miss Hutchison's sixth grade dancing class,

Thurston's future wife, Roberta Lee Fontaine, had still towered over him at that unbearable stage of life. He remembered staring straight ahead at her precocious bosom six inches from his nose as they stumbled through the foxtrot. She had seemed oblivious to his ferocious acne, and they had remained friends through the years. Cotham would always remember Roberta as his first love, a fact he had never admitted to her, although he suspected that her interest in him had at one point extended somewhat beyond friendship, as well. The years and her marriage to Thurston had not been entirely kind to Roberta, however. She had developed a double chin and her long face had begun to remind Cotham of the quarter horses she raised on their family farm in Germantown.

By the end of the two-hour meeting with the Quonsets, Cotham was frustrated and exhausted. It had not gotten off to a good start. Thurston was a University of Memphis football fan and launched into a seemingly endless harangue on the biased referees at the past weekend's game against the Ole Miss Rebels. To his dismay the game had been won by Ole Miss 27-0.

"Hot damn, Ethan, I'll bet those refs are all on the Rebel Alumni Council! And if they weren't before the game, they sure as hell are now!" he protested.

Cotham had forced himself to sympathize although he would have been unable to name a single player or coach on either team. There was wondrous irony in the fact that the same Thurston who used to suffer nosebleeds as soon as he stepped onto their neighborhood playing field had evolved into a rabid football fanatic.

Finally the conversation had turned to business as Thurston explained how his new position as bank president brought with it certain expectations that he would begin to move in ever-higher social circles. This would require a suitable venue for entertaining his many new friends and business prospects. For this purpose he had purchased a spectacular lot overlooking the Mississippi River in the new BluffTown development, a gated subdivision on the site of a former warehouse complex south of Downtown where he proposed to build a new house. Thurston, of course, referred to it as a new "home" in the fashion of mortgage bankers and real estate agents, a usage Cotham assiduously avoided. For Cotham a house was a structure, a building. If the design inspired in its occupants a strong sense of place, shelter, and emotional refuge, then a house might earn the right to to be called a home. A house could be built, bought, and sold. A home was a creation of the heart and could not.

The Quonsets' deed carried with it a restriction limiting the minimum area of the house to 4000 square feet with approval of the plans required by the subdivision's own "design review committee" chaired by the developer's wife. When Thurston had allowed the price he had paid, $500,000, to slip into the conversation, he had searched Cotham's face for some sign that he had made an impression. Cotham remained impassive.

Cotham had asked what sort of house the Quonsets had in mind. Roberta brightened and reaching into her voluminous handbag produced a sheath of clippings. Cotham noticed that they came from *Southern Living, Architectural Digest,* and *Southern Accents,* rather than *Architectural Record* or even *Metropolitan Home,* which would have been his own preferences.

"You know how traditional and conservative we are," she began in the mousy little girl's voice that had not changed since the sixth grade. "Thurston and I thought that something sort of, you know, Colonial, would be nice. Of course, that would just be outside, you know, with columns and things on the front. Inside we'd like it to be traditional but contemporary, if you know what I mean. And we want five bedrooms, seven baths, and, like, a three car garage with an automatic door so that when I come home from tennis and it's raining, my hair won't get wet.

"And you know, Ethan, Downtown's not the safest place, even with that big wall they have around the neighborhood. Why, the other day on Front Street, these colored teenagers walked right across in front of our car with their hats on sideways, and they just stared at me, you know the way they do...."

Cotham groaned inwardly as Roberta took the next thirty minutes to catalogue her requirements, accompanied by an extensive dissertation on social criticism centering around the problems caused by "those people." The stylistic requirements of the house were only the start of the difficulties Cotham foresaw. It was beginning to sound like a very expensive project, perhaps a million dollars or more, and he doubted the Quonsets had that kind of money. Even if they did, he was not at all sure that he even wanted the project or that he could work smoothly with Roberta and Thurston over the two years it would take to design and build such a house. At the same time he was acutely aware that it had been six months since he had landed a new project and that this house was currently his liveliest prospect. Cotham quickly made up his mind.

"It sounds stunning," he forced himself to exclaim with an enthusiastic grin. "And the site is superb! Just imagine breakfast on your balcony overlooking the river."

Roberta smiled warmly.

"What sort of budget have you in mind?"

She looked at Thurston and blinked rapidly several times. It was obvious that Thurston controlled the purse strings and that the subject had not arisen between them before. "Well, um, I mean," began Thurston, "what do you think it would cost, Ethan?"

Cotham was not about to be caught in this trap, having learned through experience that often it was better to answer a question other than the one asked. "Let me explain about costs," he began. "There are three factors to consider: the cost of your project, its size, and the quality level of the materials and equipment you select. There's a kind of formula that dictates that you can choose any two of these and the third will be automatically determined."

He continued with examples, explaining how the client shared with the architect the responsibility for the design and cost of the house. Then he launched into an explanation of the stages through which the project would progress, beginning with design, followed by the construction drawings and specifications, the selection of a contractor to build the house, and finally the construction phase. As Cotham wound up his discussion, he could see the Quonsets' eyes begin to glaze over.

Thurston's banking instincts had not yet been entirely numbed, however. "And what sort of a fee are you going to charge us for all this, old man?" he asked.

This was the most critical point of the discussion for the architect, as Cotham well knew. To quote a low fee for a time-intensive custom house, anything less than ten or fifteen percent of the construction cost, would practically guarantee that he would lose money on the project. He was well aware that there were architects in town who would do the job for seven or eight percent by pulling out of their drawing file a similar project completed for another client, making minor modifications to "customize" the design, and then grinding it out on the computer. They would spend the bare minimum of time listening to Roberta or trying to respond to her extensive wish list, and during construction they would frequent the site only when asked.

He would not approach the project in this way. It was crucial to Cotham that such a house be a genuinely creative collaboration between himself and his clients. This was partly practical, for Cotham had learned that in the absence of this kind of bonding the client was likely to turn on the architect the first time something went wrong in the field. And something always went wrong during construction.

Cotham would begin the bonding process by getting to know his clients almost as well as they knew themselves, perhaps better, when it came to understanding how their preferences grew out of their values, their conceits, and their self-images. He would study the site and the zoning requirements, neighboring houses, topography, views, and microclimate. Then would come the rough sketches on yellow tracing paper and the cost estimates that the client would be asked to approve before he moved on to the next step. There would be many meetings and hours of discussions during which the house would slowly materialize in Cotham's mind and then in his drawings and cardboard models.

He would do his best to educate his clients about design and architectural history, gently guiding them and encouraging them to critically examine their preconceptions. He would lavish his own creative energy on the project, his own hopes, and perhaps a few ironic and whimsical details, subtly veiled in the intricacies of the design. Once construction began Cotham knew he would not be able to stay away and that he would probably visit the site two or

89

three times a week and every day at certain critical points. It would become a love affair; when the house was finished, his clients would be astounded and overjoyed. They would share his pride and sense of creative accomplishment, for the result would be authentic and unique, possessing a character that transcended the superficiality of mere style.

His intimate approach to this project would require a higher fee. He knew of architects in Philadelphia and New York whose fees for a custom house were in the twenty percent range, up to $200,000 for a million dollar house. But it would be practically impossible to command such a fee in Memphis, even with sophisticated clients, which the Quonsets were not.

Thurston was awaiting his answer. Cotham sighed inwardly and committed himself. "I can do it for fifteen percent provided that you give me all your requirements on the front end, that you make decisions when they are needed, and that you don't keep changing your mind. If you do that, I'll have to charge you more."

To the Quonsets' credit they had not argued. But then, they had not agreed either, promising to let him know in a day or two if the proposal were agreeable. Following their departure, Cotham felt the familiar ambivalence he had known in so many other interviews with prospective clients. On the one hand he badly needed the work, and there was always the chance that the Quonsets would be good clients, open to new ideas and appreciative of the skills he brought to the project. But the signs were not promising. Neither was secure enough in their own sense of self to engage in an open-ended search for a design solution that would express who they were, as opposed to who they wanted to be. Roberta with her collection of middlebrow magazines had seemed bent on creating a dinosaur, a house based on romantic illusions about the past. Thurston simply wanted a trophy house.

Yet they were hedging on the cost and the fee. To Cotham life seemed too brief to have to sell his talents short in a never-ending series of compromises with clients who had more money than architectural sensitivity, with no compunctions about paying for seven bathrooms with granite vanity tops, Italian plumbing fixtures, and cove lighting, but who drew the line at a reasonable fee for the architect who designed all this. A house often involved as much handholding as it did design, and the thought of trying to act as the Quonset's family therapist depressed him thoroughly. If only he could land a project that would let him show what he was capable of, but without all the accompanying baggage.

The Quonsets finally disappeared into the elevator, and Cotham turned to see Jean waiting for him, a sheaf of papers in her hand, a frown on her face. "Ethan, if you've got a minute we need to talk about the cash flow."

He sighed, but waved her into his cramped private office. It was really little more than a cubbyhole. Over the door, secured by a push-pin, hung a faded quotation from John Ruskin: "Put your work first and you are God's. Put your fee first and you are the Devil's."

The room was only six feet wide and twice as long with a window at one end overlooking Court Square and the southern half of Downtown. The river stretched beyond, curving in a wide gunmetal arc on its ceaseless roll to the Gulf of Mexico. Along the entire length of the office extended a built-in drawing board covered with correspondence and architectural journals—the latter mostly unread. His Macintosh word processor occupied one end of the board. The walls were covered with freehand sketches on tracing paper, his licenses to practice architecture in Tennessee, Mississippi, and Pennsylvania, and his Master of Architecture diploma from Princeton. There was a photograph of Cotham and Henry Roper taken at the Great Pyramid of Giza the night Roper had won the Pritzker Prize, the equivalent of the Nobel Prize for architecture. And there was a portrait of his late wife, Kate, taken in Portofino the summer of the accident. The opposite wall was covered with bookshelves, overflowing with volumes dedicated to his favorite architects and theorists. He thought of them as his old friends: Edward Luytens, Alvar Aalto, Louis Kahn, Frank Furness, Le Corbusier, Frank Lloyd Wright, Bernard Maybeck, Vincent Scully, Brunelleschi, John Soane, and of course, Henry Roper.

"It's going to be tight again this month," Jean began. We haven't gotten the check from St. Mary Magdalene yet, and the consultants are howling. I've gotten three calls this week from Smith and Perkins asking when they'll be paid. I've managed to sweet talk them so far, but I don't know how long I can hold them off. The rent is due tomorrow, and payroll is next Monday. "

"How should we handle it do you think?" asked Cotham wearily. It was all so typical of his practice, a constant battle to keep ahead of the wolves at the door. This was the part of architecture he most despised. He was not a very astute businessman, as he readily admitted to himself. If he were, he would spend less time on design and would seek out jobs like shopping malls and apartment complexes where the high degree of repetition and low design expectations allowed a greater profit margin.

"I think we should start with payroll, of course, but maybe we can string out the rent a bit longer. And we'd better pay the acoustical consultants. They're sixty days past due, and this letter just came. They're waffling on their next site inspection until we send them a check."

"Right, you handle it, Jean. And if Smith and Perkins call back and ask for me, say I've gone trekking in the Himalayas and will be back in a year or two."

"Do you think we'll get the Quonset job, Ethan? A nice fat initial payment would be most welcome right about now."

"I don't know; they were noncommittal. I've known them a long time, but they mentioned they were also going to talk to Astor, and he always quotes a lower fee than we do. The job's more his style too, another modern-but-traditional Colonial trophy house with 'columns and things,' you know."

Jean returned to her stack of payables, and Cotham's mind turned back to the previous night's work. One story below, connected by a spiral stair he had cut through the floor, was the studio. Paul Dole, his senior staff architect, was busy on the telephone, apparently with a mechanical engineer. Cotham overheard him exclaim, "What do you mean you haven't started yet, Mike? You've had those sprinkler submittals for a month already!"

Cotham descended the stair and pulled up a drafting chair next to Paul's desk where a floor plan of the new St. Mary Magdalene Church, now in the sixth month of the fifteen-month construction schedule, was laid out.

"It looks like we've got a glitch with the standpipe," said Paul, hanging up the phone. "The sprinkler sub is saying the fire marshal wants a larger capacity, and the engineer says he sized it to code. Mike has been sitting on the problem for a month. The sub is ready to start putting in the branch piping, but doesn't want to go ahead until the sizing issue is resolved. I don't blame him."

"It sounds as though we need to light another fire under our friend, Mike, the Mechanical Man." Cotham replied. "Why not tell him to call the fire marshal directly and work it out? Tell him he's got until tomorrow and to let us know what he's come up with."

The afternoon wore on. Cotham returned several calls and drafted an e-mail to the contractor at St. Mary Magdalene reminding him that the granite samples were now past due. Just as the sun dipped below the southwest horizon out beyond the Delta, Cotham seized his navy bridge coat and stepped onto the elevator.

For the second time that day he made his way through Court Square. How was he going to pay the rent if the Quonset job failed to materialize? And how were they going to complete the competition entry before the fast-approaching deadline? It had begun to snow, and atop the Hebe fountain a little cap of white crowned the waterbearer's head. But lost in thought, Cotham paid no heed.

Chapter Seven

On some mornings Cotham's timing seemed perfect. He pushed the button for the elevator and immediately the doors parted. With a key he unlocked the access to his floor and pressed number twenty-one. The elevator shot for the top of the Lincoln American Tower, bypassing the other floors like an express train. Twenty seconds later he stepped out into his own little lobby.

The sun was barely over the horizon out past Germantown to the east, and far below him the Downtown streets were still empty. He wondered if the telescope in Pappas' office was still pointed directly at him. For a moment it occurred to him to walk to his window and wave.

Ordinarily Cotham was not an early riser, preferring to arrive in the office around 9:00 a.m. and then work until 6:00 or 7:00 p.m. Today, however, he had been unable to sleep, his mind preoccupied with the Center for Southern Culture. As he fumbled with the coffee pot, he remembered that none of his staff had been told about his meeting with Pappas or about the competition. He would need to call them together and rally the troops for what promised to be an intense three week "charette."

The apocryphal story of the charette known to every architectural student was of the nineteenth century Ecole des Beaux-Arts in Paris, the preeminent school of architecture of the time, where students madly worked until the last hour before a project was due. Because the faculty "jury" was held at a remote location across the city, each student would rent a charette, a wheeled handcart pulled by a porter, into which the presentation drawings and models would be loaded. Since there was never enough time to completely finish, the student would trot alongside the cart as it made its way through the streets madly trying to finish a drawing or glue a roof onto the model while *en charette*.

Would his staff of three, not counting Jean, be able to handle a presentation of this magnitude? Before computers became commonplace in architectural offices, he would have needed three or four additional draftsmen. Now he and Tensing would probably be able to deal with the development of most of the drawings. Then it would be necessary to add by hand the color, trees, people, cars, and the rest of the "entourage," the beaux-arts term for the little touches that gave life to a drawing. The drawings would probably occupy Tensing for several eighteen-hour days. Having an extra intern or two would come in extremely handy, if they could be found on such short notice.

Paul Dole could take charge of the model; he was a meticulous craftsman. But the model could not be started until the design was almost complete. It would take Dole the better part of two weeks working alone to build the handsome model Cotham had in mind, using basswood instead of the usual gray chipboard. That was two weeks they didn't have. A second or third experienced model builder to assist Dole would need to be recruited and standing by to begin as soon as Cotham was satisfied with the design. But where would he find model builders he could count on?

He thought enviously of Richard Astor's stable of a hundred architects and support staff. All Astor had to do was stroll into his drafting room and handpick five or six of the brightest young, energetic employees who would immediately start churning out his presentation for him. They could even afford to be leisurely in their approach since, as Cotham had seen at Pappas' office, Astor enjoyed a head start on the competition. Although Cotham had not been allowed to page through the drawings, from what he had seen it appeared that Astor had already generated his basic concept.

His one chance was that although Astor's presentation would no doubt be beautifully and seductively packaged, it would be seen by the jury as lacking in depth. This was not an unreasonable hope. Having worked for Astor, he knew that his competitor would spend no more time on design than absolutely necessary, preferring to fall back on fashionable clichés gleaned from the pages of *Architectural Record*.

Seth Gerber, the third competitor, was a different animal, however. Gerber was intelligent and creative and labored over his design work as hard as did Cotham. He also maintained a small firm and would be equally pressed by the limitations of time and manpower. He drew well, and his fluid presentation style had become even more polished since leaving Cotham to open his own office. There seemed little doubt that if the jury fielded any knowledge or architectural sophistication, the competition would come down to a battle between Cotham and Gerber.

And what if Cotham won? How could his small team possibly execute the construction documents for a 120,000 square foot complex of buildings and then shepherd it through the two years it would probably require to build? Again he envied Astor; to him monumental commissions were commonplace.

Lately a darker thought had also bubbled up from his reservoir of self-doubts. Might his troubles just be beginning if he managed to win the competition? He did not particularly desire a large or even a medium-sized office. If he won, a permanent staff of fifteen or so, including several experienced licensed architects at Paul's level, would probably be needed. His office was too cramped. He would have to rent more space elsewhere, and it would be the end of his cozy little penthouse in the Lincoln American Tower. Was it hubris that drove him to pursue this competition, as it drove so many designers? Was he about to dangerously overextend himself and his firm only to face the humiliation of losing to a former employer or, worse, to a former employee?

Sighing at the stack of unopened mail from the previous day, he forced himself to focus instead on more immediate concerns, including the problems at St. Mary Magdalene Church. The letter from Bishop Coltharp was troubling. Its tone hinted at some major dissatisfaction involving the design, although the exact nature of the problem remained to be discovered when he and Cellini traveled to Lafayette. The confusion surrounding the sprinkler system stand-pipe was annoying, but fairly routine. It was impossible to get the fire inspectors to commit themselves to all their requirements before construction began so that all the exit signs, extinguishers, annunciators, pumps, dampers, and other complex components of the fire protection system could be fully planned. This was especially true in small towns and rural areas where the fire marshal could be expected to show up unannounced at the site a week before completion with a long list of new requirements. However, there was little Cotham could do. Like most architects, he understood the technical issues of electrical and mechanical systems only at a conceptual level, and found them tedious at best. It was a job for his engineering consultant.

Cotham had to admit as well his anxiety over the Quonset project. It had been three days now since the interview, and he had heard nothing. He shuffled through the mail discarding half of it unopened and putting the bills in a pile for Jean to deal with. On the bottom of the stack lay a light grey envelope. Tearing open the flap, he stared at the neat script on the immaculate Crane note card bearing the monogram RFQ. It was from Roberta. The cursive loops were precisely rounded; every "t" was crossed with precision, and every "i" dotted with a little circle.

Dear Ethan,

Thank you for taking the time to meet with us to discuss the plans for our new home. Thurston and I have given it a great deal of thought, since we realize that this will be one of the most important decisions of our lives.

Although we love your work, there was the question of your fee. After talking to some other architects, it seemed that they were all willing to work for quite a bit less than the figure you mentioned.

We have decided to work with Richard Brisbane Astor. He seems very nice and assured us that he could give us exactly what we want for a very reasonable price.

Ethan, please be assured that this in no way reflects our opinion of your talents. We have the greatest respect for your creative abilities. I guess we are just not that sophisticated.

I know there will be other projects in which you can truly shine. If there is ever anything I can do to help you on one of these, I hope you will not hesitate to let me know.

Fondly,
Roberta

"God damn traitor!" he muttered. He balled the note, fired it toward the trash can, and stalked out of his tiny office. Paul was standing next to Jean's desk, chatting amiably about Christmas shopping. The coffee pot was already empty, and it was barely 8:30 a.m. He glared at her. "Jean, how many times do I have to ask you to keep this damn pot full in the mornings?" he snarled.

Paul stopped mid-sentence and stared. Instantly Cotham regretted his tone, but it was too late. Jean looked wordlessly at him, like an unsuspecting dog kicked by its brutish master. Cotham silently retreated to his office, resisting the urge to slam the door.

It was as though he had been punched in the stomach, the same sense of surprise, pain, resentment, and insult. It was bad enough to be rejected by old friends, but to lose out to Astor! The man was a pretentious hack who specialized in historical pastiche. Then another thought, the old fear, his ever-present companion, elbowed its way into Cotham's consciousness. Perhaps it had nothing to do with fees. People saw him as an outsider. Was he an inflexible purist, a prude? All they wanted was a nice "home," something they could feel comfortable in, designed by a pleasant architect, an affable fellow who could share a bit of gossip or comment on the outcome of the tennis tournament at the Racquet Club. Surely this was not an unreasonable expectation. They didn't care about esoteric design theories, and by going on about these with Thurston and Roberta he had lost the commission. Why hadn't he had the sense to become a lawyer or a banker, instead of a miserable architect? In an explosion of anger and frustration he raised his clenched fist and brought it down hard with all his might on the desktop.

Pain surged through his hand and up his arm, and he stifled a scream. For a moment he thought he might pass out and fought back a wave of nausea. When he looked down at his left hand, the little finger was twisted at an odd angle and was beginning to turn purple at the knuckle.

When Cotham finally returned to the office from the Methodist Hospital emergency room, Jean was waiting for him in silence. As she handed him a cup of coffee, she looked askance at the broken finger in the metal splint, a blue foam rubber pad peeking from beneath the bands of adhesive tape. "Thank you, Jean. Would you please pass the word to everyone to meet in the conference room in about an hour?"

———

Cotham glanced around the table at his staff. No one was smiling, and tension filled the room. Paul sat with arms crossed, staring at the table top. Tensing turned to Jean and under his breath made a lame attempt at a joke. Jean shot him a disapproving glare, and he lapsed into awkward silence.

Cotham raised his bandaged hand. "This, guys, is what happens when you take things too seriously. This morning we lost the Quonset project. They gave it to Richard Brisbane Astor. It angered me, and I lost my temper. I apologize, but I got what I deserved. It hurts like hell."

There were faint smiles of sympathy.

"It may be for the best in one sense. Sure, we need the work, but sitting there in the hospital waiting room for two hours, I had time to reflect a bit. We have enough to keep us going, and they are projects we can be proud of. St. Mary Magdalene is going to turn out well by all appearances. And there's an extremely interesting new prospect I want to tell you about."

He reached into the battered briefcase and retrieved a thick spiral-bound booklet. The staff craned their necks to get a glimpse of the title, "The Center for Southern Culture: Program of Requirements."

"We've been offered the opportunity to enter a design competition for a new building." He paused for effect, noticing that he had the full attention of Paul and Tensing.

"It's an important project, a large and complex building on the river, over 120,000 square feet, and the deadline is less than three weeks away. I've begun sketching already, but I'm concerned about the time crunch. I'm even more concerned about what we will do if we win and have to build the damn thing! I want your opinion as to whether we can pull it off...whether we *should* pull it off. It will mean long hours. We probably don't have enough hands at the moment to do the presentation. And what we do if we should win is, if you want to know the truth, beyond me...."

Tensing stared intently at his computer, a mound of Cotham's charcoal sketches on yellow tracing paper engulfing his workstation. On the screen glowed an embryonic floor plan. Tensing had begun a drawing of one of the curved walls, searching by trial and error for the correct center point and radius of curvature that would approximate Cotham's free-hand original. Obviously frustrated, he glanced over his shoulder with a wry grin and said, "You know, Ethan, some architects draw straight lines for their draftsmen to copy."

Cotham resisted the impulse to sit down at Tensing's side to watch as the drawing materialized. But to do so would not only distract and annoy the intern, it would also reveal more of Cotham's inner feelings than he felt comfortable sharing with others. It seemed important to appear calm and detached, as though there were nothing more routine than the design of the most important work of Memphis architecture in the last seventy-five years. Here at last was Cotham's chance to show what he could achieve. Despite his misgivings about the competition, the Center for Southern Culture was the project of a lifetime. For once, he stood as good a chance as anyone at being selected, without regard to his fee or his political connections. His concept was bold and fit the site beautifully although there was still work to be done on the entry sequence. Tensing turned again. "Pretty cool project, huh, Ethan?" Cotham turned away with a shrug and climbed the spiral stair to his office.

Alone before the window with its sweeping view, he imagined the final appearance of the new structure taking shape on Tensing's computer. Now that they had blocked out the floor plans and cross-sections, he was beginning to fully visualize the massing of the whole in three dimensions. In his imagination he walked completely around the building and inspected it from all sides, critically analyzing its form and proportions. He was dimly aware that there was still something indefinable that was not quite right, but whatever it was lay just beyond his grasp. There would be time to critique the design once Tensing's drawings had been printed. For now it was important that he try his best to maintain a disinterested objectivity. One of the greatest hazards the designer faced was falling in love with his own ideas and losing the ability to ruthlessly criticize his own work.

Jean appeared at his door, wearing her coat and on the way home. "Ethan, Pallie is on line one for you. Didn't you say you were meeting her for an early dinner?"

"Hell!" Cotham muttered, "I forgot all about it. Tell her I'm on my way. And, Jean, tell her to order a Harvey's Bristol Cream while she waits."

———

She was seated next to the window overlooking the row of outdoor tables, all of them as bare as the trees that lined the sidewalk in the early evening darkness. Café Society in Midtown was one of their favorite haunts, the sort of casual but romantic bistro that lent itself to a light impromptu weeknight supper. Pallie took a sip of sherry and watched the tall, slightly limping figure hurrying across the street out of the gloom.

He apologized for keeping her waiting and was relieved to see that she received the words graciously. "I'll be stood up any day as long as it's by work and not some twice-divorced siren who's chasing you.…Why, Ethan, what happened to your hand?" she asked with alarm.

"This has definitely not been my day," he sighed. He pulled Roberta Quonset's crumpled letter from his pocket and handed it to her. The finger throbbed.

She read the note and looked up sharply. "It may be for the best. You've said yourself how a good project takes a client who understands and values design. Roberta and Thurston are nice enough; and I know they're old friends, but they don't have an architectural bone in their body. Think about what a struggle it would be to try to get them to look at things in a new light.

"Besides, how would you be able to design their house and this competition at the same time?"

"The competition will be over in three weeks," he retorted, instantly regretting the dismissive tone. "The only other project we have on the boards is the church, and it's already under construction. We've got to have some new work soon!"

"But you're going to win the competition, Ethan, I know it."

"That's what I'm becoming afraid of," he sighed. "The only thing worse than not enough work is too much of it. If we should win, I have no idea how we would get it all done. I'll be like the dog that caught the car. Schematic design is one thing, but the working drawings would swamp us, not to mention the construction supervision. We would need more staff, including some senior people, and you know how tight the labor market is these days.

"The big offices in town, like Astor, attract the few good young architects with higher pay than the small offices can afford unless, of course, they are motivated by design above all else and don't want to be part of the corporate rat race."

Pallie seemed lost in thought. "Tell me about your relationship with Richard Astor, Ethan. I know you used to work for him."

"Astor is complex. When I came back to Memphis, his new astronomical observatory on the campus of Southwestern at Memphis had just won a *Progressive Architecture* design award, the first architect in town ever to do that. Very prestigious. His work seemed to be on the cutting edge nationally, not just locally, and I naturally wanted to meet him. He had a reputation as avant-garde, charming, and charismatic. He roared around town in an old two-seater '57 Thunderbird and dated local actresses and students from the Art Academy. I used to see him at foreign films at the old Guild Theatre on Poplar dressed in a black turtleneck and I would think, 'There's a real architect. I'll be like him one of these days.'"

"I know about that part," Pallie interrupted. "Did you know that I was one of those actresses? He used to pick me up outside the stage door after I had landed one of the leads in *The Fantastics* at Front Street Theatre. He loved theatre. You know how he likes to quote Shakespeare. And he could play the blues on electric guitar. Quite the Renaissance man."

Cotham was taken aback. He had no idea she and Astor had known each other that long. He began to ask her more, but changed his mind. "I'm not surprised to hear it; there weren't many sweet young things that Astor didn't date at one time or another.

"His office was in Clark Tower out east," Cotham continued, "and even at first that worried me a bit about him. But we hit it off right away. He invited me to lunch at the Memphis Country Club. We shared an Ivy League background—Astor had gone to Cornell—and that made us unusual in Memphis. He knew Henry Roper slightly, although he disapproved of Roper's anti-Modernist sentiments; I had just come from Roper's office in Philly with a nice letter of recommendation in my pocket. I flattered myself that we were kindred spirits.

"He offered me a low-paying job as an intern, but with the understanding that I was to be involved in design, and I immediately accepted. For the first year or so it was grand. I gradually became his personal design assistant. After work he would invite me to his house where we'd stay up half the night sketching, drinking red wine, smoking Cuban cigars, and debating current trends in the profession. Astor is an eclectic today, but back then he was a ferocious Modernist, as was virtually every other architect of his generation. It was more like being called to a religious order than a profession. Gropius, Mies, and Le Corbusier were the high priests, and we were their devoted acolytes. We were firmly convinced of our own enlightenment and of the evils of traditional architecture. We would drink the night away trying to outdo each other in our scathing criticism of what passed for architecture in Memphis. Then he'd pull out his guitar, and it was like sitting at the cross-roads outside Clarksdale when Robert Johnson met the Devil. Most mornings I would drag into the office with a headache.

"Working with him so closely though, I began to realize that while Astor was certainly intelligent his design ability was only average. He was much better at recognizing brilliance in others, and more often than not his own ideas were little more than skillful imitations of work he had seen in the magazines. Like many good leaders, he surrounded himself with people who were brighter than he was.

"Gradually, Astor and I began to drift apart. It began when I first questioned some of his design decisions. Then we disagreed on urban design and city planning theory. Astor was convinced that Downtown Memphis was dead. He was involved in the design of several new suburban apartment and office buildings for Nikos Pappas, who was just becoming active as a developer. On the other hand, having just come from Philadelphia, I had seen how their Center City was being revitalized through historic preservation and with a new generation of interesting buildings designed with their urban context in mind. Henry Roper spoke out against suburban sprawl in his book, *The Tyranny of Modernism,* and I had been strongly influenced by him. I even pasted a bumper sticker on my Volkswagen proclaiming "Midtown is Memphis." I remember one night at Astor's house when after a couple of drinks we got into it. I made some sarcastic references to Modernist clichés and to the marketing slogan that touted the area beyond the perimeter expressway as 'the Center of the Future.' After that, the evening bull sessions ended, and he became decidedly cool toward me.

"My timing was not the best. The economy had begun sliding into a major recession, and Astor's work load took a sharp dive. Several large projects were put on hold by our clients, including a new airport addition in Little Rock I was working on. All over town architects were cutting their staffs, and it became obvious that we were not to be spared. One morning Astor called me into his office and explained that he had reached the conclusion that a personnel reduction was the only choice and that I would be among those to be laid off.

"In retrospect, it was an inevitable business decision, I know. Overnight the firm size plummeted from thirty people to just over fifteen. But given our relationship I took it as a personal and professional rejection, and it caused great bitterness. The other night when we ran into him at the museum, it was our first conversation since that day over twenty years ago."

Pallie sat in silence for several moments. "He did seem fairly cordial," she observed. "Do you think he realizes how much pain his decision caused you?"

"I seriously doubt he gave it much thought, either at the time or later. He has always been too pragmatic for that."

The waiter arrived, and Cotham ordered the grilled salmon for both of them. Outside it had begun to snow lightly, and only a few cars crept down the street. The conversation lagged. Pallie seemed preoccupied, and after several more minutes of silence Cotham finally asked, "What's eating you? Not another premonition, I hope!"

Her gray eyes bored through him, and he remembered Homer's description of the birth of Athena when "Great Olympus quaked fearfully under the might of the flashing-eyed one." Making light of her second sight was not a wise move, and he had added yet another gaffe to the day's dismal record.

But then her expression softened and she replied thoughtfully, "Ethan, I've got an idea. It's probably crazy, and you can tell me so if it is.

"We both know you have a good chance of winning the Center for Southern Culture competition, but you've said you'll have a real problem with the working drawings and construction supervision if you do. You can't just go out and hire another ten or fifteen architects at the drop of a hat, and even if you could, you don't want to have to move out of your office. You're too much the loner and not really comfortable with the prospect of having a larger firm.

"Consider Astor's position. Maybe he does have the inside track with Pappas. But if the jury is impartial, that won't count for much.

I'm sure he's furious to see you and Gerber asked to compete after already having done so much work on the project himself; but if he's as astute as his reputation would suggest, he must be worried as well. Surely he knows that in a fair design competition he's got a good chance of losing to either of you. On the other hand, should he win, getting the project built will be easy. He already has the staff and the resources."

She paused, took a breath, and continued. "I read all the time about architects forming joint ventures to go after large projects. Suppose you were to propose to Astor that the two of you team up. You could do the design, and he could handle the technical side. It increases your odds of winning from one in three to fifty-fifty. From what you've said he has great respect for your design ability, and the two of you used to get along well...."

Cotham stared at her incredulously. He was about to protest, but something in Pallie's manner made him hold his tongue. Instead his gaze shifted to the bare street outside where the snow was falling harder now, whipping past the acorn-shaped globes of the Midtown streetlights. He had to admit that the idea was just the sort of unexpected, creative breakthrough to a problem that he prized in his design work. It might just work, if he could bring himself to approach Astor. That was the main hurdle, whether he could turn his back on the wound to his ego inflicted long ago in order to solve a seemingly intractable dilemma in the present. Of course, Astor might refuse a proposal to collaborate. But then, would he have lost anything by trying?

He turned back toward Pallie and slowly nodded. "I suppose I could see if he would be interested."

As Cotham and Pallie made their way to the car, she took his arm. Beneath the streetlight he brushed the snow from the windshield and then helped her into the front seat, pausing to dust a stray snowflake from her dark hair. As he slid behind the wheel, Pallie snuggled against him.

"Dear Ethan," she whispered, "this too shall pass. Somehow I know it. And I admire your courage. Going to talk to Astor is the right thing to do."

He sighed. "Perhaps you're right. We'll see."

"Ethan," she said, looking up at him, "I've been wanting to try something for a long time." She reached for his glasses, slipping them off and peering into his eyes. "Yes, I thought so. Do you realize what extraordinary eyes you have hiding behind those coke bottle lenses? They're pale blue—like a Viking, or maybe a Welsh poet!" He saw her lips part ever so slightly. She clasped her arms around his neck and pulled him toward her. When he kissed her, she tasted warm and sweet.

"Let's take a drive through the park," she said. "It'll be lovely in the snow."

Overton Park had been transformed. There was no other traffic, and the rapidly thickening blanket of white muffled the soft crunch of the tires. They cruised past the Brooks Museum, its white marble façade indistinct against the snow-covered hillside. Except for the soft glow reflected from the lights of the surrounding city by the hovering clouds, the building would have melted into the landscape.

The road led to the heavily wooded section of the park, where ancient oaks arched overhead, barely visible in the gloom. "It's so beautiful!" Pallie exclaimed. "Can we pull over for just a minute?" Cotham wheeled to the curb and switched off the headlights and the engine. They sat for a moment in the dark, listening to the silence. She flipped on the radio and tuned it to an oldies station—the Drifters were crooning *Goodnight, My Love.*

He felt her warmth against him. She kissed him again, harder than before, pulling him closer.

"Damn stick shift!" he muttered in exasperation, pulling away, turning and gazing out the side window into the shadows.

"What's wrong, Ethan?"

He was silent for a long time. She waited, silent too.

"I'm sorry, Pallie. It's just that…well, it's just that sometimes you make me think of my wife, Kate."

She sighed and turned away. "So that's it. I was afraid it was me.

"Did you know I knew Kate slightly? I remember hearing her play the cello at a Beethoven Club concert. A lovely Schubert trio, as I recall."

"Yes, I remember that concert. It was the Trio in E Flat. She loved Schubert."

"How long has it been now since she died?"

"It will be three years in June," he replied. "June 19th, to be exact."

"How did it happen, Ethan? Weren't you traveling in Europe?"

Again he was silent.

"It might help if you could tell me about it."

"I don't know if I can, Pallie. It still hurts too much."

"Just try. We have all night."

He stared into the old forest. The song was over, the spell broken. He switched off the radio and took a deep breath. "We were sailing along the Riviera, off Portofino—a chartered yacht, just the two of us. Our twentieth wedding anniversary. I was at the helm. Kate never really learned to sail. It was a lovely afternoon with a gentle breeze.

We had a bit of champagne, not much. She was lying with her head in my lap, watching the clouds.

"There were lots of other boats around, other sailors as well as power boats. Off to the port side I saw a big souped-up speedboat coming towards us, still quite far away. No need to do anything except keep an eye on him. He was going quite fast. As he got closer, I could see seven or eight people on board, a man in a yacht cap at the wheel, the women in bikinis, all whooping it up. He was intending to cut across our bow, but I could see it would be close.

"I could have changed course to be safe. All I had to do was come about, and he would have had more than enough room. But I had the right of way, as sailboats always do, and I was within my rights to maintain my heading. So I didn't turn.

"I later found out at the inquiry that they were all drunk. Never even saw us, apparently.

"I was thrown clear by the impact. Not even a bruise. But Kate was gone, along with our boat. She just vanished."

He paused. Gently Pallie took his hand. Finally, in a choked voice, he said, "It was my fault. All my fault. I could have turned."

The mantle of snow was growing deeper and in the dark they were weeping together.

"I've not been able to touch a woman since that day. When I try, all I can see is Kate. I'm sorry, Pallie. I don't expect you to understand...."

———————

Cotham awoke with a start, perspiring, his heart racing. In the dream he stepped onto the express elevator in the lobby of the

Lincoln American Tower, turned the key granting access to his office, and the elevator began to accelerate, the numbers of the passing floors flashing in the tiny window over the door. As the elevator approached the twenty-first floor, however, there was not the familiar deceleration. Instead, its speed increased. In the little window above the door, the number twenty-one flashed and then went blank. A moment later with a deafening crash the walls of the elevator cab were blown apart by an explosion, and to his horror he found himself rocketing skyward through a gaping hole in the roof. Far below him lay the cupola of the Lincoln American Tower, the Main Street Mall, and the rest of Downtown. He was spiraling up and out to the west, toward the river, trapped in the smoking remains of the elevator cab. Then the cab reached the peak of its trajectory and began the long, slow, agonizing plummet toward the churning brown waters of the Mississippi.

Chapter Eight

It was 1:45 as Cotham and Father Cellini wheeled around the corner and cruised past the statue of the Confederate soldier standing guard on the deserted south lawn of the Jefferson County courthouse at the center of Lafayette's town square. Cotham never passed through Lafayette, Mississippi, without being reminded of Saturday afternoons in his youth, returning from some fishing trip with his father to Enid or Grenada Lake.

In his memory it was mid-summer, and the square was crowded with people thronging the sidewalks, jostling each other, window shopping and greeting friends. Those on the sidewalk waved to a never-ending parade of dusty pickup trucks and two-tone sedans that revolved like planets around the courthouse, bound in their orbits by its mass. An insensible sun near its zenith seemed intent upon broiling the procession below. On the courthouse lawn, seeking shelter in the pools of shadow beneath the ancient magnolias, lolled the farmers from the surrounding hill country dressed in faded blue denim overalls and weathered straw hats. Some lounged in twos and threes on the creaking benches while others reclined on the lowered tailgates of their trucks, backed against the curb so as to share the shade. The trucks were piled high with the summer bounty of watermelons and cantaloupes. Occasionally a buyer would appear, perhaps haggling briefly before departing with a paper sack brimming with butter beans or tomatoes.

Cotham and Cellini turned onto the side street off the square that led to the rectory of the Cathedral of the Incarnation. They found a parking space behind a silver Mercedes Benz SUV. On its rear bumper was pasted a sticker emblazoned with the "Bonnie Blue flag" of the Confederacy with its single white star. Next to the entrance a small black metal sign with gold letters discreetly announced, "Catholic Diocese of North Mississippi."

"Ethan, we have a couple of minutes. Maybe we need to go over our plan about how best to handle this meeting," said Cellini.

"Yes, of course, Tom. What's your best guess as to what Bishop Coltharp wants to see us about?"

"That's the problem. We're at a major disadvantage because Coltharp didn't identify the issues in his letter. At least then we could be prepared for the interrogation he's no doubt got planned for us. As it is, we'll have to walk into the bishop's office armed with nothing but our wits and our memory of the project history.

"We should remember that early on Coltharp chose not to participate in the design process. He has left everything to the Building Committee. I've watched you operate, Ethan. You clearly understand the importance, especially on these church projects, of fully involving the client in making the decisions. In my experience these committees are notoriously hard to lead to a consensus. They're usually composed of inexperienced laymen who sometimes think it is up to them to design the building. Without an architect who has his own vision and is willing to stick with it, construction can become a case of the blind leading the blind. You have been quite good at offering a firm guiding hand without becoming autocratic."

"Thanks, Tom. I appreciate your confidence. But we would never have gotten this far without your good counsel. You've got an exhaustive knowledge of architectural and ecclesiastical history, but you've also got practical skills in dealing with people."

They had both tried to walk this fine line, sitting patiently while the committee debated a hundred minute points, often until late into the night. He had found the priest to be a master at allowing the debate to run its course before finally intervening to bring closure. When Cellini took the floor, he would begin by reminding the group of the overall design concept they had previously agreed to. Together, Cotham and Cellini had seen to it that the St. Mary Magdalene committee had, in fact, fully participated in all the important design decisions, ranging from the parking lot layout to the seating plan to the location of the altar.

Cotham remembered one interminable debate centering on the floor finishes in the main worship space. Half the committee, those who placed a high value on the rich musical interaction between choir and organ, had favored following the acoustical consultant's recommendation that the room remain uncarpeted so as to increase the reverberation time of the space. The other half had become focused on the clatter that would result from women walking down the aisles in high-heeled shoes, supposedly disrupting the concentration of those who were in prayer. The argument droned on for over an hour with no sign of resolution. Cellini had finally had enough. He stood and delivered a ten-minute homily pointing out that greetings, gossip, arguments, crying babies, and even the click-clack of high heels were all part of a lively sense of community. It was in the messy vitality of community and not in worshipful silence that the Body of Christ was experienced first hand. His impassioned delivery, combined with his authority as a priest, had won them over, and a decision was quickly reached to eliminate all carpeting from the space.

"As to this meeting," Cellini continued, "I think it will be important to emphasize the collaborative approach we've taken, while bearing in mind that the Bishop's real agenda may be something else entirely. He may or may not be explicit about his real concerns, so we'll need to listen between the lines, so to speak."

They made their way through the side door of the cathedral narthex and took seats next to the aisle in the rear. The morning mass was nearing an end, and the small group of parishioners had begun filing forward, kneeling at the altar rail to receive the Eucharist from the celebrant, a tall black man in white vestments. Cotham was reminded that Coltharp was the first African-American bishop in Mississippi. As the usher reached their pew, Cellini stood and began to move toward the aisle. Cotham remained seated.

"You go ahead, Tom. I'll wait here. I'm not a Catholic, you know—I can't receive communion."

Cellini flushed slightly and abruptly sat down. "I forgot about that, Ethan. Damned popish nonsense. But you're right. This bishop takes a hard line when it comes to refusing to offer communion to non-Catholics. I'm sorry. Come on, let's go wait for him in his office."

The furniture of the reception room was sparse and well-worn. No magazines littered the coffee table, and on the bare white plaster wall hung an icon of the baptism of Christ. They announced themselves to the quiet young woman without makeup who sat at the receptionist's desk.

After a twenty-minute wait she rose. "Bishop Coltharp will see you now. Please follow me."

As they were ushered into the spacious office, Cellini preceding Cotham, the tall black man stood and stepped from behind the heavy antique mahogany desk. He offered Cellini his hand, and Cotham wondered whether Cellini would actually kiss the Bishop's ring. Instead Cellini shook the proffered hand before introducing Cotham. The bishop's handshake was firm and confident.

Bishop Coltharp looked the part. He stood about six feet, but his slim figure and erect military bearing made him seem taller. The hair was black with only a few flecks of gray, and the dark eyes were direct and penetrating. Instead of the white vestments, he now wore a well-tailored black suit over a bright magenta rabat. A silver chain around his neck disappeared into a breast pocket, and Cotham caught a glimpse of the pectoral cross to which it was secured. When he spoke, the voice was deep and liquid. The bishop was evidently a native of Mississippi.

"Welcome, Father Cellini, Mr. Cotham. I appreciate y'all driving down all the way from Memphis, and, of course, Father, you've come even further still, both geographically and in other ways. May I introduce someone to you?" He gestured over Cellini's shoulder. At the rear corner of the office sat a man in a wing-backed arm-chair. They had not noticed him as they entered, and to Cotham it appeared that this had been intentional on the part of Coltharp. What other little surprises were in store for them?

"Gentlemen, this is Mr. D'Arcy Lamar of Lamar, Mississippi. That's over in the Delta, as you may know, Mr. Cotham. D'Arcy is a member of the St. Mary Magdalene Parish Council and one of our most generous benefactors. D'Arcy, this is Father Cellini of Boston and Mr. Cotham, the architect."

Cotham recognized the name. Lamar was a member of one of the oldest, wealthiest families in the Delta. The town had been established by the family sometime in the nineteenth century as an extension of their plantation, which was said to be comprised of hundreds of thousands of acres of the richest farm land in the world. The plantation featured as its centerpiece an antebellum house that was included in *White Pillars,* Frayser Smith's book of exquisite architectural sketches.

It was an odd alliance, the black bishop known for his interest in social activism and this old guard Republican. It was a safe bet that in addition to being fabulously wealthy, Lamar was fabulously conservative. He was a large man in his early sixties, about 6'- 6" tall, dressed in khaki trousers and shirt, lizard skin cowboy boots, and a bolo tie. A cigar protruded from his shirt pocket. On the coffee table next to his chair lay a white Stetson hat and a weathered leather bomber jacket. He acknowledged them in a deep, authoritative bass drawl, "Father, Mr. Cotham." He did not smile.

They took seats in a small semi-circle facing the Bishop, who returned to his chair behind the desk. "Gentlemen," he began, "St. Mary Magdalene Church seems to be moving ahead rather quickly."

Cotham nodded. "If things continue to go according to plans, we should be ready for the dedication in late June."

"Indeed, Mr. Cotham," said Coltharp, glancing at Lamar. "I fear they may be moving too quickly. I have asked you here today because of certain issues that have come to my attention and that cause me concern. As you know, I am bishop to all the people of our diocese. St. Mary Magdalene is in many ways an unusual church in these parts. To begin with, Catholics in north Mississippi are rare.

Scots-Irish Protestants originally settled this part of the country, and we have always been a minority. In addition, St. Mary Magdalene is a parish with an unusually large number of prosperous young professionals and people associated with the University, many of whom are, shall we say, unusually progressive. Mississippi tends to be a traditional place."

Cotham noted no trace of irony in his voice.

"Being progressive, even being liberal, is not necessarily a bad thing, within certain limits. But many of the older parishioners, including some of the major financial contributors, are upset now that they can see what the church will be like. They feel that some of the new ideas it contains go too far, that they have been forgotten in the planning, and that, to be frank, the building will look more like a Protestant church than a Catholic one.

"I want to explore these concerns with you so that I can understand how we got to this point. Mr. Cotham, I believe you have been working with the Building Committee on the design. And I understand that Father Cellini was engaged by the parish to advise on liturgical matters. Is that correct?"

Cellini spoke up. "That's right, Bishop. I was brought in over three years ago before the architect was selected to assist the church in the development of their requirements for the building. As you know, I have a special arrangement with the bishop in Boston that allows me to serve as a sort of roving advisor. I suppose you might refer to me as a carpetbagger," he added with a grin.

"I delivered a series of presentations intended to educate the parish on the evolution of church architecture and the liturgy. These concluded with an exploration of the norms established by the Second Vatican Council and how these might apply to the design of the new building. As I say, this all took place before Mr. Cotham's firm became involved. But I was pleased when the committee selected him, due to his evident understanding of what the parish wanted to accomplish."

"And do I understand, Mr. Cotham, that your religious background is Protestant?" interjected Lamar.

"Not that it has any bearing on your professional judgment, of course," Coltharp added quickly.

Cotham was taken aback. He briefly considered mentioning that in college he had entertained a lively interest in Zen Buddhism, but then thought better of it. Before he made any reply, however, Cellini again took the floor.

"Mr. Cotham's personal background should not be an issue here. As our architect, his role is not to question or influence the theological basis of our architectural requirements, but rather to express them through the medium of design and construction. The only appropriate question is whether or not he has faithfully carried out our instructions."

"Of course. And you have put your finger on the reason for this meeting, Father Cellini." said Coltharp. "How have decisions been made? What instructions were given to Mr. Cotham and by whom?

"Let me give you an example. A question has been raised by Mr. Lamar and some of the other senior members of the parish as to how the decision was made to locate the altar table in the center of the room with no altar rail surrounding it."

"That's right, Bishop," boomed Lamar, suddenly rising to his feet. "And a lot of us don't understand why we have this damn sunken baptismal font in the floor; looks more like a Club Med than a church! When I promised to help build this thing, I thought we was gettin' a real Catholic church with altar railings and statues and candles, not some big shed with a hot tub in the middle! Why, I've seen barns that look more like a church!"

Lamar had become quite red in the face. He was perspiring, and his eyes bulged. Cotham decided that it was not an appropriate time to point out that some historians believed that altar rails dated from medieval times when barns had been used as churches and the railings served as fences to keep the farm animals away from the altar.

"Bishop, Mr. Lamar," Cotham began evenly, "I can assure you that these decisions were not made in a vacuum. In fact, Mr. Lamar is listed as a member of the Building Committee, although I believe it is accurate to say that he has not been able to attend all the meetings, including several in which these very issues were discussed.

"The committee has reviewed and approved every design decision. In the case of the location of the altar we submitted drawings showing a number of alternative locations and seating configurations. The committee debated the pros and cons of each, at length, I might add, before selecting one and directing us to proceed. It has been my understanding that they were duly authorized to do so, and that...."

"Excuse me, Mr. Cotham," interrupted Coltharp, eyeing him coolly. "Regardless of who may have led you to believe that these decisions were appropriate, I believe there have been enough misunderstandings that we need to review the design in some detail before proceeding any further with this project. In addition, I would like to ask that you draft a revised plan that responds to the concerns expressed in this letter."

Coltharp opened the black leather portfolio on his desktop and withdrew a sheet of the same buff-colored stationery bearing the coat of arms that Cotham remembered from the letter written to Cellini.

Dear Mr. Cotham:

Due to growing concerns among key members of the parish of St. Mary Magdalene Church, it has become apparent that certain elements of the design must be revisited before moving ahead. You will please prepare revised drawings with the altar table placed in a traditional position in a sanctuary, separated from the congregation by altar railings. Please notify us as to when these revised plans will be ready for review.

Yours in Christ,
Hervey Coltharp, Bishop, O.B.

Without speaking, Cotham passed the letter to Cellini, who read it rapidly. Then he looked up, glaring at Coltharp, eyes blazing. "Bishop, I implore you to reconsider," Cellini began. "It is much too late to consider a change in the altar location. The entire floor plan is based on its present location, and much of the construction is complete."

But Coltharp rose. "Gentlemen, you must excuse me. I have to prepare my homily for the Christmas Eve midnight service I've been asked to deliver in Memphis. I know I can count on you both to give your most serious consideration to how best to solve this dilemma. We will be counting on you."

Clearly the meeting was at an end. They shook hands all around, and Cellini and Coltharp had turned toward the door when the bishop spoke again. "By the way, Mr. Cotham, I've reached a decision that the construction of St. Mary Magdalene Church will be placed on hold immediately. Will you be so kind as to inform the contractor? I hope this will be a temporary state of affairs."

Lamar wore a look of smug satisfaction, and Cotham pulled the door closed behind them more firmly than would most visitors leaving a bishop's office.

Cotham felt as though he had sustained a second and much harder punch to the stomach than the one delivered by the Quonsets. Inwardly he was reeling, and his knees felt weak. He and Cellini had been scrupulous in their efforts to involve the Building Committee in the design. The decisions that were now being nullified had been made only after many presentations and endless hours of debate, all because of the influence wielded by a blustering, provincial millionaire who had never given five minutes' thought to either theology or architecture. Why was Coltharp even willing to grant Lamar an audience, much less dignify his opinions with an edict of such finality?

To place a project on hold at this stage of construction and to expect a redesign of such sweeping magnitude was unprecedented. It would require untold hours of unbudgeted time, and Coltharp had made no mention of additional fees. He could only imagine the reaction he would get from Sam Ingram, the fiery owner of Ingram Construction Co., when he heard that he was to immediately stop the work of his subcontractors and workers. How was Cotham going to explain to Ingram that he was to cancel the countless orders for everything from structural steel to air conditioning systems to plumbing fixtures, many of which were being specially fabricated for the project? And what about the many items already delivered to the site, awaiting installation?

As they headed for the door, the quiet young receptionist looked up. She was in her twenties, pale, and fragile looking, except for her eyes, which were bright and intelligent. "Excuse me, sir, aren't you Mr. Cotham, the architect for the new St. Mary Magdalene Church?"

Cotham nodded. He was tempted to correct her by adding "former architect."

"I'm Sister Gabriella, and I've heard such wonderful things about what you're doing there. I thought you might like to have this." She handed him a card about the size of a postcard. "It's an icon of Mary Magdalene."

Cotham examined the striking image, painted in the Byzantine style, depicting a brown-skinned woman with luminous black eyes that seemed to stare at the viewer from beyond time and space. She wore a scarlet robe, and in her raised hand she held a single white egg.

"There's a legend about her. Mary was a woman of high social standing, and after the crucifixion she moved to Rome where Tiberius Caesar received her. She described to him Jesus' trial and execution under Pilate. To explain the resurrection she picked up an egg from the dinner table at which they sat. Caesar scoffed saying that a person could no more rise from the dead than the egg in her hand turn red. Immediately, the egg she held did just that."

———

It had begun to rain, and the drive back to Memphis had passed in silence. When Cellini suggested they go somewhere for a drink,

Cotham had offered no resistance. The disappointment they shared was palpable, and Cotham felt defeated and shrouded in a kind of psychic shadow, as though some dark unseen thing had passed overhead.

It was a run-down juke joint, known among the few who had heard of it as The Sharecropper. Located on the fringe of Midtown Memphis in a neighborhood dominated by automotive body shops, plumbing supply houses, and a few warehouses renovated for conversion into artists' studios, the entrance was no more conspicuous than a tick on a dog's ear. A peephole guarded a door that was always locked, and Cotham and Cellini stood in the rain waiting to be admitted.

The peephole flipped open briefly, and after a moment they heard the bolt slide back. They stepped into the darkened interior, thick with smoke and the melancholy aroma of old leather furniture mingled with the sour scent of spilled whiskey. In the far corner at a piano an ancient black woman growled Delta blues in a voice that embraced a thousand cold rainy nights. She wore bedroom slippers and stockings rolled down at the knees. Her face was as grooved and channeled as a sun-parched Delta mudflat.

They took a seat in a booth. The waiter took their orders without a word, Johnny Walker Red for Cellini and George Dickel for Cotham, and disappeared into the blackness. Cotham pointed to a ledge above the door where a dusty, shrunken pack of Camel cigarettes lay.

"The story is that during World War II a paratrooper spent the evening here the night before he was sent overseas. As he was leaving, he reached up and set his cigarettes there, instructing everybody to leave them until he came back from Europe. He never

127

did, and no one has touched them since. That was over sixty years ago."

Cotham rarely drank whiskey, but there was no point ordering a glass of Bordeaux at The Sharecropper. Tonight the Tennessee sour mash tasted heavenly. He lit one of the thin cigars that he sometimes allowed himself when his spirits were either unusually high or low. Cellini looked drawn and somber. His white clerical collar hung open, and there were curious glances from several of the other patrons. Priests were seen less frequently in the bars of Memphis than in Boston.

"You know, Ethan, I'm just an art historian, and I can't imagine what it must be like to be an artist or an architect. You work your heart out, and then it's all put at risk by those who know literally nothing about what it is to make something new, something worthy."

Cotham sat in silence for a long moment. "I'll tell you, Tom, architecture is just about the only thing I really care about. When I was just beginning my own practice, it was the thrill of design; I still love that part of it, although I once calculated that in a typical year I only spend about five weeks actually drawing. The rest of the time is spent writing letters, talking on the phone, visiting the job site, chasing new work, or defending myself against the likes of Coltharp.

"But now that I've been around awhile, the thing that seems to mean the most is giving people a building that adds a little enchantment to their lives. You do that by really listening to them, and trying to understand their hopes and their noblest impulses, as well as their budget. But at a certain point, once you understand the issues, you have to listen to your own heart. That's where the magic comes from, if it comes at all.

"And then you struggle with it, like a fisherman who's hooked a big one down deep but can't manage to reel it in. Finally you wrestle it to the surface and offer your magic to them with the faith that there's something valid, something universal there. That what you've brought forth is as much a part of their hearts as it is your own; that even though they could never have captured it for themselves, they'll recognize it when you hold it up to them.

"It's not about 'bidness,' as Lamar would say, and the Lamars of the world can never grasp that. It's about…," he stopped, unable to find the right words, feeling frustration at his inability to be more articulate.

"Maybe it's about God," said Cellini. "I've often thought that when we say 'God' what we mean is the ultimate source—the source of good ideas in the case of the artist and architect. I suspect that all good ideas come from God.

"You mention the ability to listen, Ethan, and I agree that for an architect that ability is crucial. You don't have the same luxury a painter has, the freedom to make something extremely personal, something so idiosyncratic that it has meaning only for the artist himself. Architects design for others; they build using other peoples' money, and so their art must be meaningful to others. The architect must have empathy for his client and for the people who will experience his creation. I once heard a Holocaust scholar say that evil is simply the absence of empathy."

"And what of the Lamars, those who cannot, or will not, allow the good idea from God to become a reality because of their own fears, prejudices or limited vision?" Cotham asked, trying to keep the bitterness out of his voice.

"I am reminded of Christ in the desert, challenged by Satan." replied Cellini.

"And Coltharp, what about him?"

"Coltharp is not really interested in design. Based on other things he has said, he doesn't really care about where the altar or the font are placed. What he does care about, though, is funding for his parochial schools initiative in Tunica. I've heard that Lamar is making a major contribution to his plans, as well as to St. Mary Magdalene. It doesn't take a historian of church politics to know that bishops listen very carefully to major financial contributors."

As they rose to leave, Cotham stepped across the tiny room to the piano. He took a five dollar bill from his wallet, leaned over and said something to the pianist that Cellini could not make out, handing her the bill as he did so.

"And God bless you too, baby," she beamed. "Say, where you been, anyhow? Mamie Dell been missin' you. You come back an' bring yo' Reverend friend, you heah?"

They stepped out into the rain. The night seemed to have grown very dark. As the door was barred behind them, they could hear the husky voice down-shifting into the *Beale Street Blues,* "I'd rather be there than any place I know...."

Chapter Nine

Gotham had asked Jean to call Astor's office to make the appointment, but he had given her no hint of the subject of the meeting. He ordinarily favored a tweed sport coat, but today he wore an immaculate gray business suit, a white shirt with French cuffs, shiny black cap-toe shoes and a black and orange striped Princeton tie. He knew Astor would be dressed to the nines, and he did not want to venture into his rival's camp at a psychological or sartorial disadvantage.

Astor's office was no longer in the suburbs. It now occupied an old office building on Union Avenue, a few blocks south of the Lincoln American Tower. It was ironic, given his past convictions concerning the premature death of Downtown, that Astor had belatedly decided to join the migration of businesses back to the inner city. In order to create a new double height lobby, part of the floor above had been removed. Two new upper stories had been added to accommodate the growth of what was now the largest architectural firm in the city. One entire wall of the lobby was covered with framed licenses to practice architecture in virtually every state in the Union, and on another hung framed photographs of the firm's completed buildings, an impressive thirty-year portfolio. Cotham noted, however, that as the years had gone by and the quantity of projects had increased, their quality had steadily declined. There had been no more *Progressive Architecture* design awards since the one for the observatory at Southwestern. Above the photographs, three-foot high backlit Helvetica letters announced, "Astor Architects." A monumental concrete staircase spiraled to the mezzanine floor above. At its base, ensconced in a beautifully detailed white oak cubicle with a charcoal gray granite top, sat a stunning receptionist with long red hair and green eyes. She wore a bright red blazer over a low-cut black stretch top. Freckles covered her upper chest, and in each of her earlobes danced three or four earrings, no two of which appeared to match. On the desktop a little placard was inscribed "Ashley."

"May I help you, sir?" The barely discernible twang hinted of origins in rural West Tennessee not quite erased by her modeling school curriculum, Cotham speculated.

"Ethan Cotham to see Richard Astor," he snapped. Was there an unintended military formality to his tone, as though he were a lowly lieutenant requesting an audience with an admiral? He would need to make an effort to seem more relaxed and confident. It was important that he approach Astor as an equal.

"Yessir, I'll let Mr. Astor know you're here...uh, what was your name again?"

He sighed in exasperation. "C-o-t-h-a-m," he spelled out the name for her with exaggerated care, "the 'h' is silent."

As he was shown down a corridor separated from a large drafting room by a glass partition, a man passed him walking in the opposite direction. It took a moment for Cotham to recognize Charlie Griswold, now one of the firm's partners. Griswold had worked his way up since he and Cotham had both been interns. He was bald now and had developed a paunch, but the weak chin and averted gaze had not changed.

"Morning, Charlie," Cotham said without stopping. It was the first time they had spoken to each other since the day Cotham had been laid off by Astor.

Griswold looked shocked. "Ethan!" he managed to gasp, "What are you doing here?" As Cotham was directed into a conference room, he glimpsed Griswold, reflected in the glass partition, still standing immobile in the corridor, his jaw hanging limply.

On the wall was displayed a vintage Gibson electric guitar next to a framed photograph of Astor and a grinning B.B. King, their arms around each other, taken on Beale Street. Ten minutes later Astor appeared. He stepped into the conference room, pulled the door closed, and offered Cotham his hand. His smile was not reflected in his eyes. "It's good to see you, Ethan," he said simply.

They chatted amiably for five minutes. Cotham inquired about Astor's son, Josh, now a successful musician, whom he remembered as a precocious little boy of about six who had loved to draw. Astor, in turn, asked about Pallie. Cotham briefly considered an allusion to her role in *The Fantastics* as a way of letting Astor know that Pallie had shared something of their prior relationship, but then thought better of the idea.

Enough small talk, Cotham decided. "Richard, I know it must strike you as unusual for me to come to see you like this, so let me get right to the point. You've no doubt heard that we've been asked by Nikos Pappas to enter the design competition for his Center for Southern Culture. That's what I'd like to discuss."

Astor's face was a mask, utterly devoid of expression.

"Let me be frank. I think my team may have a good shot at winning. It all depends on who the jury is, of course, but we've had some success in recent AIA competitions, and I know Downtown as well as anyone. I don't think Pappas would have asked me if he didn't see us as a serious contender.

"As you know, I have a small office. I like it like that way and have no particular desire to grow any bigger. But I recognize that if my team wins, we will have a big problem on our hands with the construction documents and administration." Here he paused. He was coming to the tricky part, and there was no alternative but to lay down his cards.

"We both know you've got the inside track with Pappas. Your firm could, of course, do a first rate job with one hand tied behind your back. You've got the large staff, the experience, and the necessary resources. Or, perhaps I should say, most of the resources….

"What you don't have, and we might as well be honest about it, is the kind of first rate design talent it will take to win, again assuming that the jury is competent." Astor sat up straighter. He looked as though he had been slapped.

"We used to work together quite well," Cotham continued. "Why not give it another try on the competition? We could structure a joint venture with my firm taking the lead in design and yours taking the lead with the working drawings. We could divide up the construction supervision."

Astor stood up. He walked around the conference table past Cotham to the opposite side of the room. Cotham swiveled around in his chair. On the wall hung a framed certificate, the *Progressive Architecture* Honor Award Astor had won. "Ever seen one of these, Ethan?" His tone was acidic. "No, I don't expect you have. There weren't many of them given out."

"I won one of only eight PA awards given in the entire nation that year. I won it by myself with just two draftsmen to help. I was thirty. No one else in town has managed to do that since.

"Nice try, Ethan. I must admit I'm surprised you've got the balls to propose such a thing. 'Chok'd with ambition of the meaner sort,' that's you. It would be a quick ticket to success, I suppose. An easy way to enhance your little portfolio.

"Let me tell you something. We do the best design work in town. The fact that we're not generally recognized for it is due to one thing and one thing only. If the damned Postmodernists hadn't set architecture back seventy-five years, and if the Modern movement hadn't been derailed by a bunch of yuppie dilettante critics who've never built anything in their lives, we would still be winning national awards!

"I've been designing for Nikos Pappas for over twenty-five years, and this is the thanks I get. He wants to be trendy, to bring in some new blood, or maybe he just wants to keep me on my toes, so he invites in a couple of whippersnappers like you and Gerber. Hell, Gerber's barely finished his first house remodeling, and *you*...."

Cotham was now standing as well. He felt a peculiar mixture of anger and sympathy for Astor. "I'm sorry to have wasted your time, Richard," he interrupted. "I truly believed there might be something in the idea for us both. I wish you luck in the competition."

Cotham turned his back and strode out of the conference room.

Back at his office as Cotham prepared for the meeting of his staff he had called for 3:00, he thought over the disastrous meeting with Astor. The worst part was that Astor had apparently perceived his offer as an attempt to jump on the winning bandwagon. Cotham knew this was not the case and how much Cotham would have contributed to the team. But he had little doubt that Astor's version of the conversation, when he shared it with his partners, would be quite different. Cotham would be portrayed as the arrogant and opportunistic former intern who had forgotten where he had gotten his start, a charge that Griswold and the others would be only too willing to believe.

His main reaction to Astor's stinging rejection, however, was a strengthened determination to prevail in the competition. To win under these new circumstances would be an especially sweet vindication. Not only would it attest to his design ability, but it would also help put to rest once and for all his unresolved feelings about the way his former employer had treated him. The problem of how to get the project built remained, of course, but he would worry about that later if he won. He wished he felt less drained by the confrontation with Astor but shrugged it off as a slight loss of resilience, one more inevitable nuisance of aging. He would try to leave the office a little early to work out on the treadmill at the University Club.

He ran through a mental list of the tasks that lay ahead. Even though he had a beginning concept, the design for the Center of Southern Culture was far from complete, and he still had the vague sense that something essential was missing. There were photographs and sketches to be made at the site, capturing the best views up and down the river and back toward the bluffs. The extensive program of requirements would have to be studied so that the sizes and relationships of the spaces would be committed to memory before he plunged into the details of the floor plans. The building code requirements would have to be researched, but fortunately he could delegate the demanding task to Paul Dole, who virtually knew the code by heart already.

He had to plan the presentation, of course. There were drawings to prepare, beginning with the basic floor plans, cross sections, and elevations of the exteriors. There were also the perspective renderings, which would carry more weight with a jury composed of laymen. These served to give a better feel for what the structure would actually look like when seen with the river as a backdrop and how it would feel to stand inside the major rooms.

Cotham would have to decide on the style of each drawing. Should they be precise "hard-line" drawings, giving the impression that every detail had been thought out and resolved and that the project was eminently constructable? Or should they be sketchier, perhaps drawn in freehand on yellow tracing paper with exquisite colors and shading intended to evoke a poetic sense of the artistic power of the concept? The former would be more likely to inspire confidence among the pragmatic business and construction types who would no doubt be represented on the jury. The latter would appeal to the other architects, assuming there were any, who would know that no project of this size could have been completely worked out in the short amount of time allotted for the competition.

Finally there was the model, undoubtedly the most important component of the entire presentation. Everyone, including businessmen, housewives, contractors, developers, and architects, loved the three-dimensional materiality of a model. Cotham knew of commercial model builders he could hire for the project, but he had found that their work tended to be unpleasantly realistic, reminiscent of the HO scale electric train layout he and his father had once built in their attic. The best architectural models were more abstract, unlike models built by hobbyists. In these no attempt was made to replicate the wood clapboard, shingle roofs, or bushes around the foundations of pristine cottages, not to mention the brown strands of cotton intended to suggest wisps of smoke from their chimneys. The only way to get a model of the sort that Cotham favored was for his team to build it themselves.

In the end the jury had to fall passionately in love with the architect's vision. The businessmen would go to the bottom line first, the estimated cost. But they, as well as the other architects on the jury, would also have to be moved by the elegance of the concept, its creativity, and its emotional impact. For a knowledge-able few, such as Pappas himself, the cost and the concept would be equally important. He could not afford to appeal exclusively to either group if he expected to win.

Cotham gathered his small staff around the conference table and shared his plan with them, making assignments. Any redesign of St. Mary Magdalene Church to deal with Bishop Coltharp's objections would have to wait. Tensing was to continue developing the floor plans under Cotham's direction before moving on to the sections. Paul was assigned the code research, site photography, and development of the site plan along with Cotham, who would guide the design concept.

Once the plans and sections were fixed Cotham and Tensing would begin work on the elevations while Paul began construction of the base of the model. By the time Paul was ready to begin on the model of the building, the elevations should be complete. Finally,

Tensing would "render" the drawings, adding color, people, trees, and cars, while Cotham worked on the perspectives.

Jean was assigned the thankless job of fending off interruptions from the routine onslaught of manufacturer's representatives, life insurance salesmen, and financial planners who called and dropped in unannounced on architects at all hours of the day. She was to weave a cocoon of isolation for the three architects, keeping them supplied with coffee, sandwiches, tracing paper, chipboard, Prismacolor pencils, scalpel-like Exacto knives, Elmer's glue, firewood, and CDs of Schubert and Beethoven—with perhaps an occasional "Rolling Stones" thrown into the mix. Cotham also assigned her to find a surplus canvas army cot to be placed in his office. There would be no time to return home to sleep.

Cotham did his best to prepare his crew for the fifteen long days and nights that lay ahead, reassuring them that there was no need to worry about St. Mary Magdalene and wishing that he felt the same way. Initially they would all work twelve-hour days, but Cotham made it clear that the schedule was likely to be extended as the deadline approached.

As the meeting broke up, Paul and Tensing headed off to the studio, talking animatedly. There was an electricity in the air that reminded them all of being back in architecture school. Jean began calling army surplus stores on Summer Avenue, and Cotham sat down at the telephone. He dialed the number in Philadelphia from memory.

He was relieved when after a few minutes' wait he heard Henry Roper's familiar professorial voice on the line. "Ethan, it's so good to hear from you! How are things away down South in Dixie?"

Despite Roper's lofty reputation as one of the greatest living architects, Cotham was immediately put at ease by the genuine warmth the man exuded. "Henry, it's damned good to hear your voice! I'm surprised to catch you in Philly. I thought you'd be in Istanbul working on the mosque."

"I wish it were so," replied Roper, "but the Imam is having trouble with some of his more conservative colleagues. We've finished the working drawings, but so far they haven't given us the go-ahead for construction."

Roper's preliminary design of what was to be the largest mosque in Turkey had recently merited a cover story in *Architectural Record* magazine. The building was generating an international debate focusing on its immense crystalline dome illuminated from within by laser beams and surrounded by elegant titanium minarets. The forms were traditional, and one could readily see allusions to the nearby Suleiman Mosque, but the structure and materials were thoroughly high-tech. Many critics viewed the design as an affirmation by the more progressive elements of Islam that it was possible to accommodate both the modern and the traditional at the same time.

They chatted on amiably with Roper giving no indication that he had anything better to do than talk all day. Cotham knew this to be far from the case, and so he came to the point. He described the CSC project, its lofty social aspirations, the riverfront site, and the emphasis on seismic design required in the competition program.

"What I think we need, Henry, is the best structural engineer in the country for seismic design. If anyone knows who that is, you do. Aren't earthquakes a major issue in western Turkey?"

"You're right about that, Ethan. You'll probably recall the seven-pointer that hit there two years ago. The total collapse of many of the new apartment buildings contributed to a massive death toll. Since then the government has gotten serious about code reforms and we've had to design the mosque to withstand that sort of quake with only minor damage. We're using August Hardegen. He knows his stuff, if you can put up with his Prussian drill sergeant personality."

Hardegen. Of course. Cotham had once heard him deliver a lecture, in which he had lambasted the architectural profession for its preoccupation with fashion rather than the visual expression of underlying structural principles. He had a reputation as something of a tyrant, but as an engineer, he was without peer.

Cotham thanked Roper profusely and hung up. He missed working with Roper in his old messy office in the non-descript office building in Center City with its spectacular view overlooking Rittenhouse Square. For some reason, he thought back to the day the telephone had rung and Roper had been informed that Constance Claiborne, heiress to one of the great Newport, Rhode Island, fortunes, had swept unannounced into town and hoped to come by the office in fifteen minutes to discuss the selection of the architect for the proposed Claiborne Library. Roper had looked around the office in dismay at the piles of tracing paper, the fragments of chipboard study models moldering on drafting tables supported by wooden sawhorses, and the old tuna fish cans bulging with cigarette butts. The place looked like a dung heap, and one of the most elegant women in the world was to be calling in a quarter hour. Roper had bellowed for Cotham, the junior intern, handed him a five-dollar bill, and instructed him to sprint around the corner to Woolworth's. "Quick, Ethan, bring back as many of those big old glass ashtrays as you can carry! While you're doing that, we'll get rid of these damned tuna cans." It was Roper's one concession to Claiborne; and, of course, he had lost the job to the polished and persuasive I.M. Pei.

Cotham had been happy there, surrounded by some of the brightest young architects of his generation, recent graduates of the best architecture schools in the country like Penn, Princeton, MIT, and Harvard. All of them seemed to worship Roper. To be invited to join him at the drafting board discussing the problem at hand while he drew great swooping lines with a stub of charcoal on yellow tracing paper was as close to heaven as a mortal architect could aspire to. Although Cotham had fallen under the spell for a while, it was this deification of the master that eventually led him to resign. Instinctively he had understood that his task must be to absorb what Roper offered but then to make it his own, reinterpreting some parts and discarding others.

When he had finally worked up the courage to tell Roper of his decision to leave, the master had responded warmly, encouraging Cotham to do what he had to do and offering his assistance. What a contrast there would be in his departure from Astor's firm a couple of years later.

When Cotham was finally able to reach August Hardegen two days later after leaving several voice-mail messages in which he shamelessly dropped Roper's name, the gruff voice was not encouraging. "I'm very busy with other projects, Mr. Cotham. How big did you say this Center for Southern Culture is? And it's where? In Memphis, Tennessee? Is that anywhere near Nashville? I think I was in Nashville once just after the war."

Having lived in the North, Cotham was no longer surprised

when Northerners displayed an unapologetic ignorance of geography west of the Appalachians, and he was determined not to let Hardegen intimidate him.

"It's on the Mississippi River, you say?" the engineer continued. "Isn't that near the location of that huge earthquake back in the early 1800s? Hell of a place to put a building, I'd say! Whose bright idea was that?"

"It's not the only building on the river, Dr. Hardegen. We've got a whole city here. It's been here since 1819," Cotham stated dryly. He heard a reluctant chuckle on the other end.

"Very well, Mr. Cotham. It sounds like an interesting project. I'll check the airline schedules. We must lose no time!"

———

The sun was sinking fast over the Arkansas horizon as Hardegen and Cotham strolled along the banks of the Mississippi at the foot of Beale Street. The site selected for the CSC was at the edge of the surging, brown torrent, already prodigious in width even though hundreds of miles remained in its tireless roll to the Gulf of Mexico. Out in the channel, giant whirlpools boiled. An entire tree, its trunk some four or five feet in diameter, swept downstream like a splintered pencil. High above, a flock of geese drifted silently in the same direction, their cries masked by the muted roar of the Father of Waters.

Despite his eighty years Hardegen carried himself with military rigidity. When he spoke, it was with a touch of a German accent, each word enunciated with precision. "From an engineering perspective, it's one of the last places on earth a sane man would want to place an important building," he growled. "And yet, the view is unparalleled, I must admit.

"If you are serious about siting your project here, Mr. Cotham, we must contend with three different problems." His manner was that of a statics professor addressing a class of young engineers.

"First, the river bank must be stabilized so that the current will not undercut the foundations. That will no doubt mean a rather massive reinforcement using concrete revetments.

"Secondly, we will have to consider the rise and fall of the river in the context of a one hundred year flood. I understand the fluctuation can be as high as forty or fifty feet. The Corps of Engineers must approve the design of the embankment or quay, and they are, I regret, notoriously inflexible when it comes to making changes along navigable waterways and in flood-prone areas.

"Thirdly, there is the issue of seismic stability. In my opinion, the risk of a major earthquake in Memphis is real. You are assigned a very high risk classification by the Uniform Building Code—quite appropriate given your location so close to the New Madrid Fault, one of the most active and potentially dangerous seismic areas in the country. The new International Code is even more stringent and requires us to design for the 'maximum credible event.'"

"And what exactly is meant by that?" asked Cotham. "It sounds quite ominous."

"It is bureaucratic jargon. What it means is that no one knows the real statistical probability of a major quake in Memphis. What is certain, however, is that to design this building to withstand the kind of cataclysmic event that apparently took place in 1811 will result in a very substantial cost increase compared to normal construction. I hope your client is prepared for this.

"If one can believe the eyewitness accounts, the series of earth-quakes that hit this region almost two hundred years ago would have been strong enough to severely damage much of Downtown Memphis had the epicenter been further downstream. To make matters worse, the geology of this site makes it the least stable part of the city. Atop those bluffs," Hardegen turned and pointed up the steep slope immediately above them, "things are at least a little better. The substrata are mostly wind-blown alluvial silts, or loess, as they are known. Not the best for foundations, but superior to the river's edge. Down here the subsurface is just sand and clay. No one really knows what could happen, but one researcher at your University of Memphis has written a paper predicting that in a severe earthquake the entire river bank, as well as Mud Island, could liquefy and be washed away downstream.

"As an objective outsider, I must conclude that so far you have been extremely fortunate."

They turned again and gazed at the large offshore sandbar known as Mud Island. The name, peculiar and picturesque as it was, described its geological composition perfectly. The island had been built up by the mighty river and was now the site of an imposing complex of reinforced concrete walls upon which sat a museum and outdoor amphitheater. Its most popular feature was a scale model of the lower Mississippi, complete with topographic contours and running water that tourists loved to stride along like giants covering miles at every pace.

"So what would you recommend for the seismic design?" asked Cotham.

"I would need to study the matter in more depth, of course," replied Hardegen, "but my first instinct would be to adopt a two-fold approach. First, we must do what we can to lessen the transfer of lateral seismic movements to the foundations. That suggests some form of base isolation pads below the footings that will, in effect, allow the ground to vibrate back and forth at a high frequency without taking the foundations with it. This is similar to the approach used by Frank Lloyd Wright for his Imperial Hotel in Tokyo, which in 1922 did, in fact, survive a major quake while many other structures collapsed. Wright employed a large number of individual concrete 'stilts' to penetrate below an unstable stratum of mud in order to bear on stronger soil, supporting the floor slab 'like the fingers of a waiter supporting a tray of drinks,' as he put it. In recent years we have used Teflon for the isolators. This we have proposed at your friend Roper's mosque in Istanbul where we discovered it to be a more economical approach than a totally rigid frame.

"There is no way to achieve complete separation of the footings, of course. So, in order to resist the large lateral forces that are transmitted to the building in a major earthquake, we must also shape the structure so that its geometry provides an inherent stability and resistance to deformation.

"Architects should know that the seismic stability of their buildings is related to their geometry. A triangle built of skeletal members, wood or steel, for instance, is an inherently stable form. Its geometry resists deformation under loading in a way that a parallelogram composed of the same members does not. Similarly, both Pliny the Elder and Galileo knew that a fragile hen's egg possesses prodigious strength when pressure is applied at its ends. Geometry has everything to do with how the structure will behave in an earthquake, as we have discovered through forensic analysis of buildings that have actually withstood major events."

They returned to Cotham's car parked a short distance north on the cobblestone quay where steamboats once docked and where slave auctions had been held. At high water the entire paved surface would be inundated. Hardegen maneuvered a bit unsteadily across the protruding stones. Cotham watched his own step carefully; this was the sort of situation in which his injured leg could sometimes fail him. One former military officer could often spot another. He estimated that Hardegen must have been in his late twenties during the Second World War. Had he been in Germany? And if so, on whose side had he fought?

The radio came to life as he switched on the ignition, and the first movement of the *Pathétique* Symphony flooded the car. Hardegen listened in silence as the tires bumped over the cobblestones. "Tell me, Mr. Cotham," remarked the engineer, "don't you find Tchaikovsky's emotionalism rather tiresome compared to the dignity and restraint of Brahms?"

It had been only a little past nine o'clock when Cotham dropped Hardegen off at the Northwest terminal beneath the champagne glass-shaped concrete vaults of the Memphis airport. He returned to the office; as he crossed the darkened Court Square, he gazed admiringly up at the floodlit spire of the Lincoln American Tower.

He sat down at his drawing board, leaned back, and stared at the charcoal sketches that now covered the walls. There was still something missing in the floor plans; he might as well admit it to himself. But what? The sinuous curves of the walls were pleasing enough, and there was a successful counterpoint created by the play of the curves against the straight walls of the east façade. It was not an esthetic issue. He turned the program over in his mind; were all the required spaces accounted for? Were the relationships among them correct?

He tried a few new sketches, then tore the paper off the roll and started to draw all over again. He experimented with a few small doodle-like "bubble diagrams" hoping the change of scale might jog loose whatever it was that was eluding him. He lit a fire in the corner fireplace and turned on his new recording of English plainsong. By midnight, however, it was apparent that a breakthrough was not to be, at least not tonight.

He reread the letter from Pappas that had arrived earlier in the day announcing the members of the competition jury. Pappas himself was the chairman—no surprise there. There was panther-like Lucretia Silvetti, Director of the Brooks Art Museum, and Judge Leroy D'Aloisious Freeman, President of the Memphis chapter of the NAACP. The Chairman of the Art Department of Rhodes College, Diehl Halliburton, was the fourth member. These struck him as largely neutral with respect to his own chances, although, of course, one could never tell about Lucretia. Halliburton he knew only slightly, although his reputation as a knowledgeable art historian who had written a well-researched book on Memphis architecture seemed to bode well for an informed evaluation of the entries. He had never met Freeman, who had earned a reputation as an even-handed jurist and dedicated civil rights activist, although his architectural credentials, if any, were a mystery.

The fifth and final member of the jury was none other than Roberta Quonset. His heart sank when he read her name. Surely Roberta would side with Astor having so recently chosen him over

Cotham to design her own house. He was going into the competition with a twenty percent handicap on the front end.

He was growing tired. As his mind wandered, he glanced at the Memphis Heritage calendar pinned to the wall with its photograph of the old Napoleon Hill mansion. In the twenties the impressive Second Empire extravaganza that had loomed over the corner of Third and Madison had been demolished to make way for the Sterick Building, which was to be known as the city's tallest structure for the next four decades. The Sterick Building bore a striking resemblance to Eliel Saarinen's losing entry in the Chicago Tribune competition in which a reactionary conservatism had triumphed over progressive Modernism. The thought brought him back to reality. According to the calendar, exactly a week and a day remained until the deadline for the Center for Southern Culture competition.

Chapter Ten

I t had been unusually cold in Memphis since Christmas with temperatures in the low 30s, but overnight a warm front had pushed its way up from the Gulf of Mexico. As the warm moist air blanketed the icy water of the Mississippi, fog settled over the river. From the top of the Lincoln American Tower, it looked as though the river had been replaced by a fleet of battleship-gray clouds blockading the city. Even the Hernando Desoto Bridge was reduced to a faint outline like a spider's web shrouded in gauze.

The fog had seeped through the windows and into Cotham's spirit as well. With only five days remaining until the deadline he was exhausted and sick of the CSC competition. His team was barely keeping to their schedule. On the wall of the studio a five-foot long sheet of tracing paper showed the sequence of overlapping tasks graphed against a calendar. A vertical red line indicated the current date, and it could be seen at a glance that the floor plans were lagging behind.

Cotham was at fault. The floor plan was, as Le Corbusier put it, "the generator" of the sections and elevations. The plan came first; everything else followed. He had been grappling with the floor plan for the better part of a week in an attempt to identify that elusive missing element. The struggle had dominated his waking hours, and he knew from experience that his unconscious mind was now involved as well. He dreaded the nightly attempt to fall asleep on the army cot in the corner of his office. He had half expected to awake in the middle of the night with the elusive solution suddenly apparent and had begun keeping a sketchpad next to the cot so as to be prepared in this eventuality. In a departure from his natural inclinations, he would rise as soon as the first rays of sun fell across his tiny office, throw on the jeans and sweatshirt from the night before, shave in the men's room two floors below, and then rush back up to the drawing board. Seizing a fat felt-tip pen, he would hurriedly sketch the floor plan from memory, hoping that some new insight might have bubbled to the surface of consciousness as he slept.

After several attempts it became obvious that once more he had failed to produce a breakthrough. He took the elevator down to the Yellow Rose Cafe on the ground floor, which began serving at 7:00. He bought a copy of *The Commercial Appeal* at a newsstand outside on the Main Street Mall and selected a table next to the window where he could watch the city begin to stir. He ordered a breakfast of scrambled eggs, grits, sausage, biscuits, and coffee. It did nothing for his elevated cholesterol count, but the hot food eased his frustration and exhaustion. He felt a welcome jolt of renewed hope and energy.

Then it was back up to the office, where Tensing had arrived. Seated together at Tensing's computer station to inspect the progress of the previous evening, Cotham suggested a few minor revisions. "I like what you've done with the entrance to the plaza; making the steps wider is more welcoming. But remember that we'll have to have a ramp to one side and handrails every eight or ten feet. Better check the code on that. Besides, you've got the registration exam coming up, don't you? You'll be glad if you know that code backward and forward."

Paul was at his desk by 8:45, later than usual, and apologized. "Couldn't find my keys anywhere this morning," he explained wearily. "Finally I noticed Rascal kind of grinning at me. Only dog I've ever seen who can grin. But it gave me an idea, so I went and stuck my head in his doghouse and damned if my keys weren't lying right there on his mattress. Couldn't figure out what a dog would want with my keys; but then when I got to the car, there he was waiting to ride along with me." Cotham glanced at the bushy red tail protruding from beneath the drawing table.

"Well, if he can drive, maybe we should see if he can draw too," said Cotham. "We could use an extra paw around here."

On the corkboard above his layout table Paul had secured a series of photographs of the CSC site. Several had been taped together to create a 180 degree panoramic view of the river from south to north. Another panorama looking east showed the bluffs crowned by the tall buildings of the central Downtown core to the north and a row of antique brick warehouses south of Beale Street.

The views were a critical part of Cotham's design concept. The axis of Beale Street, which intersected Riverside Drive, was the obvious orientation for the buildings. But Cotham remembered the lesson he had learned on a visit to the MIT campus to see the famous dormitory on the Charles River designed by the Finnish architect Alvar Aalto. Aalto had realized that on a river, the long views upstream and downstream were more dramatic than the shorter views across to the opposite bank. His plan for the dormitory, a series of sinuous, serpent-like curves, allowed each room to capture the longer views.

Cotham's plan for the CSC was organized about a central paved plaza on axis with Beale Street so as to acknowledge the grid of the city and to create a direct link to the historic Main Street of black Memphis. As one moved west along Beale descending the bluff, the plaza opened directly ahead. Along both sides of the plaza were arranged the museum, theatre, classrooms, and art galleries. The view across the river was intentionally blocked, however, by the mass of the main building, the concert hall. Upon entering the lobby of the concert hall, the visitor turned, descended a flight of steps, moved through a narrowed passageway, and then emerged into the main hall. Here a surprise awaited. The ceiling soared, and at the far end of the room a great wall of glass afforded a breathtaking view of the river looking almost directly downstream. The glass was to be placed at the very edge of the riverbank so that only the rushing water was visible in the foreground. The view would be identical to the one afforded from the bow of a towboat lumbering down the river with nothing but water stretching away toward the old Harrahan Bridge in the distance.

The glass wall was not only the most dramatic part of the concept; it was the most technically challenging as well. Cotham envisioned a sixty-foot high curtainwall that could be automatically opened so that on balmy spring and autumn evenings the hall would become an outdoor amphitheater with the audience in direct contact with the river. This would require a sophisticated, computerized network of motorized panels and high-tech gaskets to insure that the wall remained watertight when closed and that it could withstand the winds that scoured the riverfront.

It was the shaping of the concert hall that continued to elude him. The space had to be large enough to accommodate fifteen hundred seats, a large stage, and the myriad dressing rooms, green room, loading dock, stage manager's office, storage spaces, and other "back of house" requirements the public would never see. In addition, it had to provide a reverberation time in the range of two and a half seconds without echoes. This meant that the finishes of the floor, walls, and ceiling must be carefully considered with acoustically absorptive materials on some surfaces and reflective ones elsewhere. Of equal importance for the acoustics was the shaping of the room which had to be such that the focusing of reflected sound waves would be avoided. Further complicating the problem were the structural considerations relating to seismic stability. Cotham was acutely aware that unless he was able to hit upon a scheme that integrated all these concerns in the very near future, the completion of the plans by the deadline would be in jeopardy.

He and Paul talked for a few minutes longer, Cotham satisfying himself that Paul had done his usual painstaking job of researching the building code requirements. Then he climbed the spiral stair back to his office to resume his studies of the floor plan. Behind him he heard an indignant Paul shouting at Rascal to bring back his copy of the *International Building Code.*

———

Cotham glanced at his watch suddenly aware that outside it had grown quite dark and that the floodlights that illuminated the spire of the Lincoln American Tower reflected through the windows. It would be another late night *en charette;* if he were to keep his efficiency high, he needed a break. A workout at the University Club followed by a hot shower and a light supper would lift his spirits and fortify him for the hours ahead.

He did not particularly enjoy the thirty-minute run on the treadmill, but it always cleared his head in much the same way as did the meditation he had learned as a student of Zen and that he still practiced on occasion. For what seemed like the first time in days he was able to forget about the CSC and the approaching deadline. Once into the hot shower he closed his eyes, concentrated on his breathing, and emptied his mind, mentally repeating the mantra he had been given by the Buddhist monk whom he had sought out as his spiritual adviser in college.

He had stood there in peace for perhaps five minutes, the hot water streaming over him, when he saw it. Floating in front of his closed eyes was a woman in a scarlet cloak, her dark brown eyes staring at him. It was Mary Magdalene from the prayer card he had been given by the Bishop's receptionist. In her left hand she held an egg, her right forefinger pointing at it.

Cotham snapped back into full alertness. That was it. An egg! Hadn't Hardegen cited it as an example of the inherent strength provided by geometry? His floor plans for the concert hall already contained a series of curved walls, but the design was based on esthetics alone. Here was a sound structural basis for his intuitions. With only minor modifications the floor plan could be made to resemble an egg. Surely the change would increase the building's ability to resist lateral seismic thrusts in the same way the curved shell of the egg resisted crushing. The curves could be kept flat enough to avoid acoustical focusing and still direct the eye to the stage and the view of the river beyond.

In the grill Cotham ordered a hamburger. He hesitated, decided he had earned a small treat, and addressed the waiter, "and make it with French fries." As he waited for his meal to arrive, he doodled on the paper napkin, redrawing the floor plan for the hundredth time. This time he saw the familiar plan with new eyes. The allusion to the egg would work. He had experienced similar design breakthroughs before. Without exception they occurred only after a prolonged period of searching. When they did come, it was often during a period of quiet when he had temporarily set the task aside in frustration not knowing where to turn next. There was always the same feeling of relief, accompanied by gratitude and the realization that he could not really claim credit. It had come to him from somewhere beyond his conscious self. Was this what theologians meant when they referred to "grace?" He thought about what his friend Tom Cellini had said about God as the source of good ideas. He had done nothing to merit a reward, he decided, resolutely setting aside the French fries.

———————

With twelve hours left before the 9 a.m. competition deadline everyone's batteries were running low. They were cutting it close.

The drawings were being plotted. One by one they inched out of the printer, and Tensing expertly cut them loose from the roll of paper. He then scurried to his desk to double check for printing errors. It would still be a couple of hours until all sixteen sheets of plans, sections, and elevations were ready to be hand-colored and mounted on foam-core boards.

In one corner of the studio, Paul had established his model-building shop. The base was done. It was an elegant thing built up of thin layers of birch veneer over which he had applied a coat of clear sealer. The site was at the center of the three by four foot base, framed by the bluffs on one side and the edge of the river on the other. He was now creating the buildings using an Exacto knife and a metal straightedge to cut the delicate pieces to a perfect fit. It was as demanding as surgery. Cotham kept his distance, fighting the temptation to stand over Paul's shoulder.

Along the other side of the studio, they had set up five temporary drawing boards made of wood doors resting on sawhorses that were now occupied by "Tensing's Troopers." Tensing had appeared with them in tow that morning, four fresh-faced undergraduate architectural students from the University of Memphis commandeered without bothering to seek Cotham's permission. Each of the Troopers, as he had christened the students, had been assigned a drawing to pochè—to add color by hand. As they worked, they chattered merrily among themselves. Someone had replaced Cotham's beloved Schubert with rap on the CD player, and the atmosphere now resembled a studio in architecture school with all its frenetic activity and hectic enthusiasm.

At the fifth board sat Pallie coloring madly as she and the young oriental woman in jeans at the neighboring board discussed the politics of abortion rights. Pallie had insisted that a degree in architecture was hardly required to wield a Prismacolor pencil, and Cotham had gratefully accepted her offer to join the charette. Jean bustled about forcing coffee, sandwiches and doughnuts on them and offering encouragement.

Cotham would have liked to work alongside the younger people, but he had noted that his presence had a slightly chilling effect on the general air of merriment and that a respectful silence fell over the students when he passed by inspecting their work.

Besides, it was too late now to make any design changes, and there was nothing more he could contribute. The point was to finish.

He resigned himself to completing his perspective alone in his private cubbyhole upstairs. For the previous five hundred years since the perfection of linear perspective by Filippo Brunelleschi during the Renaissance, architects had used an elaborate graphic system to generate the illusion of depth by combining and projecting the floor plan and section. Renaissance artists and architects became so adept at the technique that it was possible to fool the eye into confusing a painted scene with a real one. In one famous demonstration Brunelleschi had created a trompe l'oeil perspective painting of a street scene in Florence, including a mirror that reflected the clouds and birds in the sky. Standing at the same spot where Brunelleschi had painted the scene and using a hand-held mirror to compare the painted image with the real one, an observer was said to be unable to distinguish the perfectly executed perspective from the real view of the street.

The computer had taken the laborious projections and calculations, if not the requirements for artistic interpretation, out of the composition of perspectives. By combining the floor plan, sections, and elevations, Tensing had easily generated a diagram of the essential elements of the interior of the concert hall. With a click of his mouse the diagram, known as a wire-frame, had come scrolling out of the plotter on 24" x 36" paper, the size of the finished drawing.

Cotham had taped the computer diagram down to his drawing board and laid tracing paper over it. Using a felt-tip pen he began tracing the main elements of the room: the curving walls, the stage and wall of windows at one end, the seats and aisles. He drew quickly and in freehand so that the rigid mechanical quality of the wire frame melted away. He then removed the computer diagram, leaving only the sketch on his board. Next he began to add the details: the exposed roof structure, lighting fixtures, a band on stage and a few people in the audience for scale, the sweep of the river, and the bridge in the distance. At last he forced himself to put down the pen and walk away, so as to regain a sense of objectivity when he returned later to complete the drawing.

At 1:00 a.m. the studio was still a beehive. Cotham grabbed a left-over chicken salad sandwich and a mug of coffee and made the rounds of the studio. He was pleased. The pochè of several of the drawings was now complete, and they were ready for mounting. Pallie had taken it upon herself to add trees, a towboat, and a number of happy concertgoers to the front elevation of the hall. They were drawn skillfully with a light touch that did not upstage the architecture, and Cotham was reminded that she had studied briefly at the Academy of Art before opting for the theatre. He glanced at her and smiled.

He paused at the desk of Lisa, one of the Troopers, an attractive young black woman. He explained how to accurately cast the sun's shadow on the site plan. Assuming the sun to be at an angle of forty-five degrees above the horizon, the length of the shadow cast on the ground was equal to the height of the building. He suggested that the shadow be rendered in blue-violet, rather than black or gray, and that the shadow increase in density as it approached the mass of the building. It was a technique he had admired in Impressionist paintings for lending an air of atmospheric realism to the drawing. She seemed skeptical but began the pochè as he had instructed, laying down the color in a light wash at first, then gradually building it up. She held it out for Cotham's inspection, and he nodded approval.

Suddenly a great hue and cry erupted from the far corner of the studio. Startled, Cotham tried to make out the source somewhere in the vicinity of Paul Dole's model factory. Something was thrashing about below the worktable, and he heard a thud and a muffled curse. A drafting stool overturned with a metallic crash, followed by a furry blur as Rascal shot out from under a table. A red-faced Dole followed him. "Stop him!" he cried. "The damn dog's got the whole frickin' museum!"

General pandemonium ensued as a posse converged on Rascal, who had taken refuge beneath Tensing's board. Between his outstretched front paws he held the delicate wooden model of the building that would complete the east side of the plaza. Just as Tensing grasped his collar there came a loud crunch. Everyone froze in horror, and Cotham was reminded of the old films in which the buildings of Tokyo were laid waste by some gigantic prehistoric reptile. Paul carefully pried open Rascal's jaws and extricated the museum, mournfully holding up the crumpled remains. Rascal looked nonplused and yawned.

With only hours remaining until the deadline, there was no question of starting over on the museum wing. "Give it to me," Pallie briskly demanded. She took the ruins from Paul and turned toward the rest of the model. "Paul, you finish up the concert hall, and I'll take care of this. Don't worry; there's still plenty of time!" She pulled a drafting stool up to the model base. "Lisa, hand me an Exacto knife and a bottle of Elmer's glue," she barked like a surgeon in an emergency room.

Cotham bent over her shoulder to examine the extent of the damage. "You know, Ethan, this model is too stark. It could use a few trees. And I know exactly where they should go."

"I think I know what you mean," he replied. "Give me fifteen minutes. Do we still have that flashlight that used to be around here?"

The Main Street Mall was utterly deserted. Bundled in his old navy coat, a beat-up felt fedora pulled low over his forehead, Cotham hurried across the parking lot to Front Street and Confederate Park. The solitary statue of Jefferson Davis stood brooding in the predawn darkness as alone and desolate as in the days following Appomattox. At the southwest corner of the park beside the anachronistic World War I howitzer that guarded the river approaches to the city a steep stone staircase wound down the face of the bluff. At the bottom Cotham stepped onto the tracks of the Illinois Central Railroad's main line.

He flipped on the flashlight and gingerly picked his way down the tracks, bent over, scrutinizing the edge of the roadbed. After a half-hour of searching in the dark along the tracks, he found what he was after. As he made his way back across Front Street, he gazed up at the lights shining from the two top floors of the otherwise blacked-out Lincoln American Tower. The dark mass of the tower was now very slightly silhouetted against the eastern sky, and Cotham realized that the dawn would soon be upon them.

The spotlight caught him unaware, and in the blinding glare he stumbled on the curb and almost lost his balance. "Hold it right there!" The command was sharp, metallic. A figure was approaching him out of the light. "Sir, I need you to step over to the car and place your hands on the hood where I can see them, please." The figure drew closer, and Cotham could see that the young black cop wore an anxious expression. He was wrapped in a black leather jacket and carried a long black nightstick.

"Good evening, Officer. Chilly tonight, isn't it?" he replied with nonchalance, stepping obediently over to the MPD cruiser parked at the curb. The cop was shining his flashlight in Cotham's face. He stepped closer, no doubt sniffing for the odor of alcohol.

"It's a little late for a stroll isn't it, sir?" he dropped the beam of the flashlight down the length of Cotham's figure. Cotham looked down at the bunch of brown weeds protruding from both side pockets of his bridge coat. His trousers were covered with beggar's-lice.

"Sir, I need to ask you to remove those plant materials from your pockets and place them on the hood. Please move very slowly. And then I need some identification." The cop's hand tightened imperceptibly around the nightstick.

Cotham understood. An unshaven middle-aged man in an ancient overcoat and hat, stumbling along in the middle of the night in Downtown Memphis, his pockets stuffed with weeds, must look to the cop like some over-the-hill pothead, AWOL from the Union Mission on Poplar. He was probably about to spend the next twelve hours in the Shelby County Criminal Justice Center, locked in a cell with some DUI case or worse. He would miss the deadline and would have to call Jean to come bail him out.

"Officer, please let me explain about these, er, plant materials. My name is Ethan Cotham, and I'm an architect. Look, my office is right up there, at the very top of that building. You can see the lights. These weeds are not what you think. You see, we're working on a model...."

"What do you mean? What are you doing to her?"

"No, no, not that kind of model. It's an architectural model of a building! Look, I don't have my wallet with me, but it's up there in the office. Just come with me and I'll show you." The young cop was obviously trying to decide what to do. He was probably considering calling for back-up from the vice squad to crash an all-night orgy where a bunch of old hippie perverts enveloped in clouds of marijuana were having their way with innocent young victims.

As Cotham descended the spiral stair to the studio with the policeman following closely on his heels, he could sense that the animation that had filled the room earlier in the evening had vaporized. In its place a general lassitude enveloped the studio, the result of almost twenty-four hours without rest. Tensing looked up, and Cotham saw his eyes grow wide, the fatigue replaced by curiosity.

A horrible thought suddenly occurred to him. What if one of the staff, one of the Troopers perhaps, or even Tensing, had lit up a joint while they worked? He had seen it happen more than once in architecture school during the wee hours of a charette.

The cop looked around suspiciously. Cotham cleared his throat. "Excuse me, everyone, but I'd like to introduce Officer Dajuan Wilson. It seems we both enjoy Confederate Park at four in the morning. Tensing, would you mind getting Officer Wilson a hot cup of coffee? Are there any of those doughnuts left?" He noticed the cop's eyes brighten. "And, Pallie, I wonder if you'd be so kind as to run upstairs to my office and bring my wallet down. I think it's in my briefcase.

"Now, Officer, if you'll step this way, I'll show you the model we're working on."

Ten minutes later having escorted the apologetic officer back to the elevator lobby, Cotham returned to the studio. Still wearing his coat, he produced the two bouquets of brown weeds and presented them to Pallie. "Sweets for the sweet," he smiled, wryly. "Who would have thought you could find Perkins weed growing in

Memphis in the middle of the winter! Just like along the Schuylkill River in Philly although the railroads of Memphis are apparently better protected by the gendarmes."

There was hardly an intern architect in Philadelphia who had not been dispatched to the banks of the river that divided Center City from West Philadelphia in search of the prickly little plants that grew in profusion along the tracks. When tied together in bundles, they made perfect trees for architectural models, as had been drummed into the heads of generations of Penn Architecture students by the legendary Dean of the Graduate School of Fine Arts, Holmes Perkins. Over the years, the use of Perkins weed had become synonymous with the practice of architecture in Philadelphia.

Cotham took stock of their progress. The model was virtually completed. Pallie had patched together the museum; and as he watched, she punched a tiny hole in the wood base with a pushpin. Applying a drop of Elmer's to a small bunch of Perkins weed, she planted it in the hole next to the battered roof so that the branches overhung, neatly obscuring the tooth-marked dent.

The drawings had been mounted on boards and stood propped against the walls. Seen together they made an impressive collection, and he was suddenly filled with pride and gratitude for his little staff. With drawings like this they might actually stand a chance of winning the competition. Then he remembered the unfinished perspective on his own board upstairs.

"Heads up, everybody, I think we've about got it. I'm going to stay and finish the perspective, but the rest of you need to call it a night. I can't tell you how much I appreciate your good work. The presentation is strong—simple, but compelling. I can't think of a thing we could change if we had more time. Except that next time we pull a charette, Paul needs to bring a bone for Rascal to chew on instead of the model."

———————

Morning sunlight streamed through the windows of the silent office as Cotham placed the finishing touches on the perspective. He had added a few human forms in the foreground to give both animation and scale, keeping the figures abstract so as not to compete with the building. He knew that no matter how extraordinary the appearance of a work of architecture, the most ordinary pedestrian could easily upstage it. This was the reason that people rarely appeared in the photographs of buildings that filled the professional journals.

Finally he added the shade and shadow, the *chiaroscuro* used by artists since the early Renaissance to produce a final illusion of reality and lend heightened drama. He often had to explain to his clients that architecture was fundamentally an art and that drawing lay at its heart. He had never known a talented architect who did not love to draw. The power to visualize the unbuilt structure and then convincingly render it with a few deft strokes of a pencil on paper so that others could see it too struck many as magical, akin to sorcery. For Cotham it was as natural as whistling a tune, although to draw well required constant practice, planning, judgment, and knowing when to stop. Overworking had spoiled many a good drawing, and he did not want that to happen with his perspective.

He stood and backed away from the board in order to give it his "ten foot test." It was from this distance that the jury would probably view his perspective, and it was crucial that the balance of light and shadow be effective from that distance. In hindsight, were he to start the drawing over, Cotham could list at least a dozen changes that would improve it. But he decided that it was finished; it was as good as he could make it given the time constraints under which he had to work. He stepped back to the board and scrawled the initials "E. C." in the lower right corner of the drawing.

As he did so, he paused, suddenly aware of the pure joy he took in this part of his profession. He was dog-tired, beat to the socks; but as he stood over the drawing board in his little office high above the still-sleeping city, he could not imagine doing anything else with his life. He had created something that had never existed before, a new reality that had power and presence, regardless of whether he would ever step inside it. At one level that didn't even matter. Few people had ever experienced the thrill of making something truly new, and it was an integral part of his life's work. As he considered this, the mists that had enveloped him since the trip to Lafayette parted a bit. He realized to his surprise that regardless of what lay ahead, despite the fatigue and the pressure, on this sunny morning he was as happy as he was ever likely to be. He glanced up to the card pinned to the wall above the drawing board where the icon of Mary Magdalene pointed to the egg and stared silently back at him.

Chapter Eleven

Personal animosity between people of similar background in Memphis society seemed to be no reason for them not to socialize. And so it happened that on the evening of February 14th with a cold rain falling, Cotham, Pallie, and Roberta Quonset found themselves ensconced at a tiny table in the ballroom of the Capleville Country Club.

This unwritten rule explained how Pallie had been invited to a party hosted by Lucretia Silvetti, the director of the Brooks Art Museum, and why she had accepted after having confirmed that Cotham would serve as her escort. Ever since Pallie's comments about the Giuliani painting at the Brooks Museum opening, Cotham had been aware of the tension between Pallie and Lucretia. Was the conflict really about him, Cotham wondered, instead of esthetics? Then the day after the opening Roberta had called Pallie explaining that her husband, Thurston, would be unable to attend and asking if she might possibly accompany them.

"It would have been rude not to say yes," Pallie explained to Cotham when he had objected that the Quonsets were the last people with whom he had a desire to spend his free time. "I understand, Ethan," she had assured him. "You feel betrayed by people you thought were your friends." But at length he had agreed. After all, as Pallie pointed out, Roberta was a member of the CSC jury. It would do no harm to court her a bit, and he might be able to pick up some hint about the jury's prolonged deliberations, which were still in progress.

The Cotton Carnival, or Carnival Memphis as it was technically known now that cotton was no longer king in Memphis, did not officially begin until the spring. Most of the secret societies, however, threw small unofficial preseason parties before this. It was to celebrate Valentine's Day that Lucretia Silvetti, newly crowned Queen of the Krewe of Thebes, had invited Pallie, Cotham, the Quonsets, and a large group of others to be her guests at the Capleville Country Club.

As Lucretia explained, with its deliciously tawdry history of raunchy bacchanals it was the perfect spot for an evening of slumming. The Capleville Country Club was little more than a derelict roadhouse. Located just across the Mississippi line on Highway 78, it was only a thirty-minute drive from Midtown Memphis. In the fifties it had been infamous for its back room where the losers of the high-stakes craps games sometimes had to beg their friends for a ride home, having thrown their car keys on the table in a show of bravado, only to lose the family sedan on the next roll. When Cotham was in his teens, the place had been a favorite venue for Memphis high school fraternity parties, notably the annual "Seven Sins" ball. These days it was largely forgotten, its foundations crumbling, its forlorn sign rusted and overgrown with kudzu vines so that one could hardly make out the faded martini glasses and champagne bubbles.

It was an indication of Thebes' high rank in the Carnival

pecking order that no one attached any significance to the location. It would never have occurred to the matrons who presided over the lower order societies, Rameses or Khufu for instance, to throw a party in Capleville. For them it might have provided an uncomfortably strong reminder of their own roots. For the Thebans, however, it provided an amusing break from the gala events usually held at the Hunt and Polo Club, the Memphis Country Club, or some stately house on Belvedere or East Parkway. Its allure was made all the more irresistible by the rumor that the great Konrad Klaxon had been lured out of retirement to provide the evening's entertainment.

Klaxon was probably over seventy now. He looked younger, however, until one got close enough to see his eyes; then he looked closer to a hard ninety. His heyday had come in 1956 when his hit single, "Cat Daddy," rode the Top 40 charts all summer. It was followed by "Squeeze Me, Mama" and "Jelly Roll," which established him as the preeminent star of the rockabilly genre. Then had come the scandal involving Klaxon's alleged membership in a coven of self-styled witches presided over by his half-sister, Doreen. Veins bulging with booze and heroin, they had been arrested in a raid aboard Klaxon's houseboat on Sardis Lake.

These days Klaxon was retired, spending most of his time in seclusion on his farm outside Byhalia, Mississippi, where he careened through the woods on his Kawasaki dirt bike. He played the piano for his own solace, and it was said that of late he had turned his formidable artistic skills to a mastery of Beethoven's sonatas. To anyone familiar with his pounding but supple renditions of boogie-woogie and rhythm and blues classics this seemed well within the realm of the possible, if not the probable.

Cotham surveyed the vaulted log ceiling of the ballroom festooned with red balloons and crepe paper. Around the perimeter,
ensconced in little circles of candlelight, men in tuxedos chatted
with women in cocktail dresses. Others circulated from table to table
like butterflies in a flower garden, sampling the conversation before
fluttering away to the next blossom of light. Their table adjoined a
low stage flanked by flat plywood columns painted to resemble those
at the temple of Karnak. A baby grand piano stood vacant nearby as
the North Mississippi Allstars waded into the hard-driving "Snake
in My Bush." Couples began to take to the dance floor.

Pallie and Roberta seemed to be thoroughly enjoying themselves.
They surveyed the crowd, picking out old acquaintances from Miss
Hutchison's School. Cotham, on the other hand, was preoccupied.
It was unnerving to sit at the same table with an old friend who had
rejected him for the design of her house and who was now sitting in
judgment of his entry in the CSC competition. Although this was
the first time he had seen her since the disastrous interview in his
office, Roberta had made no reference to either project during the
trip to Capleville. Cotham found this odd but decided that to bring
up either subject would create an even more awkward situation.
With Cotham at the wheel of Pallie's old Mercedes and Roberta in
the back seat, the conversation had been lighthearted with more
than one pointed observation by the women concerning Lucretia's
guest list and the Machiavellian motives behind each invitation.

It had been almost six weeks now since the deadline for the
competition with no word from the jury and no indication of when
a decision might be forthcoming. Cotham and his staff had turned
to the only other work they had, the redesign of St. Mary Magdalene
Church to comply with Bishop Coltharp's instructions. A series of

extended telephone conversations with Fr. Tom Cellini had prompted a flurry of e-mailed sketches back and forth between Memphis and Boston. An appointment for a presentation had been made with the bishop at his office in Lafayette. It was to be in a week, and Cellini would be flying down to attend. "It's a long shot, Ethan—I agree," commented Cellini after receiving Cotham's proposed solution to the problem of the altar's position. "If he fires us, I can always go back to my old parish as a priest. What's your alternative career?"

The band stopped, and the leader stepped to the microphone. "And now, ladies and gent'mums, here is what you been waitin' on. Come out of retirement especially for the Krewe of Thebes, the great Konrad Klaxon!"

A few long moments passed, and the bandleader looked nervously to the wing of the stage. "Here he is, folks, all the way from Byhalia. Let's give him a big hand!"

The figure that emerged from behind the column of the Temple of Karnak was no more than five feet in height, much smaller in person than Cotham had imagined. He was dressed in a bright red satin jumpsuit. Long gray hair pulled back in a ponytail framed a chalk-white face, the countenance of a cadaver yanked from a coffin. He made no acknowledgment of the audience and with obvious difficulty, whether due to age and infirmity or to alcohol and drugs it was impossible to tell, shuffled to the piano. He looked as though he might go into cardiac arrest at any moment.

The transformation was instantaneous. The long white fingers leapt for the keyboard like striking rattlesnakes, and the old piano exploded into "Johnny B. Goode." The crowd yelled, and couples made for the dance floor. A group of spectators began to gather around the piano, and Cotham found their little table surrounded. He and Pallie stood in order to see. No more than five feet away directly across the baby grand, Klaxon was playing with wild abandon. The fingers danced maniacally; the torso leaned and swayed, but the face remained utterly impassive, the eyes staring straight ahead as opaque and lifeless as lumps of clay. Cotham wondered if he were watching a zombie, a dead body animated by some infernal imp.

Klaxon began to improvise, working seamlessly from one rockabilly standard to another in a formidable display of artistry. At one point Cotham was amazed to hear the recurring theme of Schubert's *Trout* Quintet woven into the midst of "Your Cheatin' Heart." At length Klaxon took a break. To wild applause he made for the stage wing, reaching urgently for the bulge in his hip pocket as he disappeared into the shadows.

The crowd around their table dissipated, and the Allstars quickly reclaimed the stage. The music was deafening; the tabletop vibrated to the throb of the base guitar, and conversation became impossible. Cotham caught Pallie's eye and raised an eyebrow as if to say, "How much longer should we stay?"

Instead of responding, Pallie broke off her attempted conversation with Roberta and looked sharply past his shoulder. Simultaneously he became aware that the hairs on the back of his neck were standing on end. Someone was behind him. He turned and caught his breath. Leaning over his shoulder not three inches away were two very round, very white breasts, barely concealed by the low-cut neckline of a black sequined dress. He glanced quickly up into the smiling face of Lucretia Silvetti dressed as Cleopatra, a golden cobra rearing on her forehead.

Cotham stumbled to his feet. He saw Lucretia mouthing

greetings to Pallie and Roberta above the din. Then he felt her hand take his. He was being dragged toward the dance floor.

Cotham was not much of a dancer. Since the hostess was obviously honoring him, however, he resolved to give it a try. They moved into the midst of the throng, and Cotham commenced to move his feet in an odd way attempting to keep time with the beat. He had to admit that Lucretia was a beautiful woman. She was slim and lithe, a fine dancer, and there was a lascivious quality to the way she moved her hips. He was finding it hard to keep his eyes off her and as a result had already bumped into a man dancing next to him.

The song ended, but now the band launched into a steamy rendition of "Unchained Melody." They were hemmed in on all sides by other couples, and there was no possibility of escape. Lucretia stepped closer, and once more he had the panicky sensation of being cornered by a panther. She smiled and actually licked her lips as they began a slow box step. He was aware of her belly and thighs pressed tightly against him, and he vehemently hoped that they were obscured from Pallie and Roberta's view. So far not a word of conversation had passed between them. He felt compelled to say something and was about to utter some lame architectural witticism about the plywood columns from the Temple of Karnak when he was stopped by a blood-curdling howl rising above the music, a sort of weird, high-pitched wail. It became rapidly louder, and the band stopped. A siren was shrieking just outside the building. Was the Capleville Country Club on fire?

Without warning the pair of front doors to the ballroom burst open, and a frigid blast of air from the desolate cotton fields surrounding the club flooded the room. Through the doors was visible a fire engine parked at the curb, lights flashing, the siren dying away.

But this was no ordinary fire truck; it was painted a bright green with green flashing lights. Instead of firefighters dismounting from its running boards, there was a swarm of large two-legged insects. It was the Boll Weevils.

The crowd parted as they pushed their way into the ballroom. There were about a dozen of them, all wearing green capes. Their heads were completely ensconced in oversized golden helmets, each with a long proboscis protruding between the eyes. It was impossible to tell their identity, though they wore numbers as if they were members of some hallucinatory football team. Some were weaving unsteadily, especially Number Four, who tripped on the steps and crashed against the door jamb, crumpling his proboscis at an acute angle. Several were tossing silver coins to the guests while others were attempting to pinch the most dignified of the ladies, eliciting squeals of protest. Number Five had pulled out a high-powered water gun and was firing indiscriminately into the crowd. Next to Cotham a well-dressed matron exclaimed, "My word, they're shooting beer at us! How absolutely vulgar!"

The Boll Weevils made for the stage in what was beginning to look like a planned operation. The piano was mounted on casters and was being rapidly rolled down the dance floor toward the doors. Cotham noticed a flash of scarlet among the green capes. Konrad Klaxon was teetering along behind the rolling piano. Crouched over the keyboard, he was breaking into "That's Alright, Mama" as he stumbled along in pursuit. It took only a few moments for the procession to reach the fire truck. The Weevils hoisted the piano on their shoulders and with a great heave thrust it onto the bed of the truck. Then they lifted the squirming Klaxon and set him down at the keyboard.

Number Four jumped into the cab, and the engine roared to life. Off drove the truck, gravel flying from beneath the wheels, siren wailing, while Klaxon pounded at the piano with demonic fury. The truck began to circle the clubhouse, the other Weevils chasing wildly in its wake. One of them, swifter than his fellows, managed to leap onto the running board. But the truck veered sharply, and he landed in a heap in the parking lot.

The entire crowd had now spilled out of the little building. They watched in mock horror as the truck made another pass by the front doors, spraying gravel as it accelerated. Whistles, rebel yells, and applause accompanied the spectacle. Number Four waved wildly from the cab, his proboscis flapping in the open window. In the back, Klaxon was having difficulty maintaining his footing on the curves as the piano careened from side to side. The other Boll Weevils had now fallen far behind, and several had collapsed in a mound of green from their exertions. As they passed a flask around, each in turn wedged it into a hole in his helmet, tilting his head back in order to take a deep pull.

Suddenly there came a squeal of brakes followed by a loud crash. At the far side of the parking lot the truck sat immobilized, its flashing lights reflecting on the dark trunks of the trees and the clumps of newly blossomed yellow forsythia. In front of the hood a geyser of water shot thirty feet into the air, the droplets sparkling in the green pulse of light. The truck had evidently struck and decapitated a fire hydrant.

There was no movement in either the cab or the bed of the truck where the splintered piano hung precariously over one side. The rest of the crowd, struck dumb, stood frozen, except for Cotham, who sprinted toward the wreck.

He saw Klaxon pulling himself to his feet and staring around in a daze, apparently unscathed. As Cotham climbed up to the cab, something crunched beneath his feet. He realized the ground around the truck was littered with little slabs of white. It took him a moment to recognize them as piano keys. The driver's door had been sprung open by the impact, and he could see Number Four slumped over the wheel. Cotham leaned in and switched off the ignition. Directly in front of the driver's seat gaped a hole in the windshield through which the top of the Boll Weevil helmet protruded. The broken proboscis bobbed forlornly in the downpour from the ruptured fire hydrant. Cotham took Number Four by the shoulders and gently pulled him back into his seat. As he did so, the driver's head popped out of the helmet. The helmet remained stuck in the broken windshield where it had undoubtedly helped save the driver from a fractured skull. An overpowering reek of alcohol filled the cab. Then with a low groan "Thirsty" Thurston Quonset opened his eyes. He looked dully at Cotham and grinned. "Hey, Ethan, how 'bout them Rebels?"

The crowd was running toward them. Just ahead of the throng a green Mercedes Benz sedan roared across the parking lot and skidded to a stop beside the fire truck. Cotham grabbed the helmet and pulled hard. It came free in a miniature shower of glass shards, and Cotham hastily jammed Thurston's head back into it. "Come on, old boy. We've got to get you out of here fast or else there'll be hell to pay. The Mississippi Highway Patrol frowns on middle-aged party animals from Memphis destroying public property!"

He half-dragged Thurston out of the cab by his green cape, pushed him into the back seat of the car, and piled in beside him. As he did so, he caught a glimpse of Pallie at the wheel with

Roberta next to her, their faces like masks in the green lights. As the crowd gathered around hoping to catch a glimpse of an unhelmeted Number Four through the back window, Pallie gunned the engine; the Mercedes leapt forward. It paused at the entrance to the highway and then roared away up Highway 78 into the darkness toward Memphis.

Chapter Twelve

Cotham was worried about how Bishop Hervey Coltharp would receive his redesign of St. Mary Magdalene Church. The solution was clever, but its deceptive simplicity belied the hours spent pursuing other ideas that had ultimately led nowhere. Tensing was well aware of the effort it had required. To him had fallen the task of drawing the myriad of options Cotham had generated only to see them end up crumpled in the wastebasket. Most of their time since the CSC deadline passed had been spent in the search for a way to accommodate Coltharp without utterly destroying the original design of the church.

The difficulty lay in the fact that the building was well under construction, and Coltharp's instructions to revise the floor plans to provide an altar table placed in a traditional setting, separated from the congregation by altar railings, would wreak havoc with the structure. Moving a wall was one thing when it involved only the erasure of a few lines on a drawing. At this stage, however, it was a monumental task that affected not only the walls but the foundations and the roof as well.

Now that a solution was at last in sight, Cotham was holding forth on the problem. "You see, Tensing, a well-designed building forms what Louis Sullivan referred to as an 'organic whole,' by which he referred to the esthetic relationships among the parts. We can't just blithely change one part of an organic form without altering the entire composition. In our case, moving the walls would fundamentally change the relationship between the altar platform and the seating. It would, as we've discovered, destroy the underlying order of the floor plan. Not only that, it would also involve a significant increase in the project cost. Owners may not care much about organic relationships, but they hate change orders.

"For every problem there are likely to exist multiple solutions of varying complexity. For some mysterious reason, however, the complex solutions are usually the most obvious. It's easy to focus on the difficulties they pose and throw up one's hands in dismay concluding that the problem is insoluble."

"So how do you find a simpler solution that works?" asked Tensing.

"There is a way. You've heard it called 'right brained thinking.' It involves a re-examination of the problem and then a challenging of our assumptions. The assumptions are where the difficulty so often lies. We assume that certain parts of the design equation are fixed and then spend our time trying to work around them. They either become insurmountable obstacles or the means for circumventing them becomes so complicated that we instinctively believe that they are impractical."

"I know what you mean, Ethan. It's like sometimes I'm my own worst enemy," replied Tensing. "I thought it was just me. I guess I'm not the only one. But what about the real geniuses?"

"The geniuses don't get off the hook any easier than the rest of us," replied Cotham. "The design of the dome for the Cathedral of

Florence during the Renaissance is a good example. The proposed
height and diameter were so immense that the complexity of the
'centering,' or scaffolding, required to hold the masonry in place
during erection would have taxed the limits of engineering technology. The cost of erecting it would be astronomical, and the time
required was unacceptable. Brunelleschi, however, refused to give
up and eventually found a way around the problem. Rather than
focusing on how to build the centering, he broke out of the box.
His design avoided centering altogether by concealing an ingenious
system of self-supporting devices inside the dome.

"Frank Lloyd Wright's solution to the siting of the Kauffman
House is another famous case in point. The rocky site had been
carved in half by a stream, creating two steep, apparently unbuild-
able banks with a rushing torrent in the canyon between. The client,
who had insisted on a view of the water, kept wondering which
side his architect would choose. But Wright refused to be bound
by the obvious choices, deciding instead to build directly over the
stream, and in the end the house was christened *Falling Water*.

"Let's hope that on a modest scale we've been able to make a
similar leap beyond the obvious. We'll find out soon enough when
we present the idea to Coltharp. I'm sure D'Arcy Lamar will be
there too and...."

He was interrupted by Jean's voice on the intercom. "Ethan,
you have a call on line one. It's Mr. Pappas."

He felt his pulse accelerate. He had not spoken with Pappas
since the start of the competition, and clients usually conveyed bad
news through the mail, preferring to call when the news was good.

"OK, I'll take it upstairs." He sprinted up the spiral stair and
grabbed the phone.

"Ethan? This is Nikos Pappas." Cotham tried to read the tone, but the voice was controlled and even. "I'm calling as Chairman of the Board of the Center for Southern Culture. As you know, we've been deliberating over the competition entries for some time now. Frankly, it has taken longer than I expected to reach a consensus."

Cotham worked to control his breathing.

"I have some good news for you although I want to say on the front end that our jury was not unanimous in its decision. But we have declared your entry to be the winner of the competition—on two conditions. I'll come back to that in a moment. For now, though, let me congratulate you on your design. We were all quite taken with it, especially the powerful views of the river it frames and your creative approach to the seismic issues."

Cotham felt suddenly lightheaded. Not a day had passed since the deadline that he had not anxiously speculated on the jury's deliberations. This could be, at last, the affirmation he had longed for, the recognition that he had what it took to visualize and organize a large, complex program on a demanding site. It could be a new day for his humble little practice!

Cotham fought to keep the exhilaration out of his voice. "That's wonderful news, Nikos! I feel honored. Please convey my thanks to the jury."

"We will be sending a press release to *The Commercial Appeal,* and so you can probably expect a call from a reporter," Pappas continued. "I expect they will be interested in writing a major story about your design.

"Before you get too excited, however, I do want to say something about the jury's concerns. First, we are all concerned about the cost. While we like the plans very much, this project will have to be built within a budget. We are still in the process of determining exactly how much we can afford. Several principal donors have already signed on, and we anticipate a major fund-raising campaign. Just how successful we will be remains to be seen. The Board wants to ask you if you will agree to modify the design as necessary to meet our budget."

This was unexpected. No budget had been established in the guidelines, and it was highly irregular for a competitive commission to be awarded based on conditions imposed after the fact. To promise that the project could be modified to meet an unknown figure would be impossible.

"In the first place, Nikos," explained Cotham, "if there's a budget it should have been established on the front end. An architect designs very differently when he knows a maximum cost must be met. To develop the budget after the fact and hope it will fit the design is naïve in the extreme. And then to penalize the architect if he does not match it is hardly fair. What I can agree to do, if we have a budget problem, is to work with you to reduce the size of the project, perhaps by dividing it into phases."

There was a long silence on the other end.

"What else?" asked Cotham. "You mentioned two conditions."

"That is correct," replied Pappas, "Secondly, there was a feeling among some of the members that while the organization of the plan is excellent, the outward appearance of the buildings may be a bit too, how should I say, *contemporary*, given the focus of the Center on the traditions of the South. Some of the jury thought that a more traditional vocabulary might be appropriate to the site and to our mission. There was not complete agreement on this, however, and so the jury would like to ask that you agree to submit the plans to the Memphis

Board of Design Review. The idea is to get an objective opinion."

"You mean the jury would prefer something like Tara from *Gone with the Wind?* Maybe a white-columned veranda?" He knew he sounded bitter, but this was too much.

"Ethan, I would urge you not to become defensive," replied Pappas soothingly. "This is a major civic project, as you know, and it's important that the people of Memphis be able to relate to it. We feel sure the Board of Design Review will approve it with no difficulty. We just want to be able to say that we've taken the proper steps to assure ourselves that the design is truly timeless and that it will blend in with the rest of Downtown."

"There was nothing in the competition rules about this either, Nikos. If the jury's decision were not final, that should have been made clear on the front end. As far as the Board of Design Review is concerned, you should know their reputation—at least among architects. Richard Astor has developed the board into his own private fiefdom. The group is made up of housewives, dentists, and radical preservationists who think the only good building is an old building. They think Astor's word is law. If I won, it means he lost; and Astor will never agree to approve my design if he has the power to reject it."

"Ethan, I know how you feel. But the jury discussed this at great length, and our decision is contingent on these conditions. If you don't feel you can accept them, then we'll have to award the commission to our second choice."

"And may I ask who that would be?"

"I don't suppose there's anything wrong with my sharing that with you although I'd appreciate it if you'd keep this between us. As I've already said, the jury was not unanimous, and there was some strong support for the runner-up, Richard Astor. His plan was thoroughly competent and very well organized. But it lacked flair. To be frank it was a little ordinary. The consensus was that Gerber's ideas were too far out in left field, very trendy, if you know what I mean, but lacking in depth. Your design, on the other hand, seemed progressive and creative without being too radical."

Cotham paused to reflect on the situation. Despite his anger he could recognize that to withdraw based on principle would be futile. If he fought and lost, the project would go to Astor. But if he resigned, the result would be the same. There was always the chance that his design could clear both hurdles if he could bring himself to jump obediently through the hoops. It was maddening, but it was the only sensible course.

"Very well, Nikos. You may tell your jury that I will play by the new rules," Cotham said with resignation.

"I'm happy to hear it, Ethan," Pappas replied with genuine enthusiasm. "We'll see if we can still get on the Design Review agenda for the upcoming monthly meeting. I'll get back to you after I've spoken to Astor. He hasn't heard of our decision yet, but I will call him now. I'm sure he will be very fair and objective. Once we get their approval we can deal with the cost issue."

———

As twilight fell, Cotham gazed over the great expanse of the river and the Arkansas flood plain. In the fading light, the warm gold band that was the Mississippi at sunset had been transmuted to the cold blue-gray of stainless steel. Behind him to the east the purple curtain of night was being rapidly drawn across the city.

He reflected on the telephone call he had received an hour

earlier from Gertrude Philpot, the real estate editor of *The Commercial Appeal.* She planned to run a large spread on the competition the following morning featuring his winning entry. She had been cordial without a trace of the caustic wit for which she was known. His answers to her questions had been taken down carefully word for word, and it appeared that there might be numerous direct quotations included in the write-up. She had arranged to have him send over copies of the drawings and a photograph of the model. Cotham had to admit that he was pleased.

It was time to call it a day. He had invited Pallie to dinner, looking forward to surprising her with the news; he was due to pick her up in an hour. There was just time to run by the University Club for a workout on the treadmill followed by a shower.

The telephone rang as he was about to step into the elevator.

"Ethan? Richard Astor. I thought maybe I'd still find you at the office."

Cotham was instantly on guard. Astor was the last person on earth from whom he would have expected a call. "Hello, Richard. What can I do for you?"

"I just called to say congratulations. I hear you won the CSC competition. Pappas called me earlier." Astor's voice was cool, neutral. He sounded neither pleased nor displeased.

"Yes, that's right." Cotham was not going to adopt a cordial tone before he knew what was on Astor's mind.

"I'd like to run an idea past you, Ethan. The CSC will be a pretty big undertaking as you know. When you came to see me suggesting that we collaborate on the competition, you mentioned that you were shorthanded. We've got a pretty big staff, and we could help you out. I'd like to take you up on your suggestion that we work together."

Cotham was taken aback. Was this the same Astor who had so arrogantly dismissed him as an upstart? Was his former employer coming to him with hat in hand asking for work? Astor must feel humiliated, and to make such a suggestion indicated a certain vulnerability that Cotham found attractive despite the old wounds. But he quickly reminded himself that it could also be indicative of a callous insensitivity on Astor's part, a pragmatic willingness to do whatever it took to get a piece of the action.

It was true that he did not have the staff to complete the construction documents, and he faced a major problem in that respect. But what would it be like working with Astor should he accept the proposal? Would there not always be an unspoken resentment between them? He could imagine the jockeying to see who would control the development of the design and who would take credit for the completed building.

"I'm sorry, Richard. I do sincerely appreciate the offer. But I don't think it would work out. You gave me your answer that day in your office."

There was a pause. "I hope you're making the right decision, Ethan. As they say, 'there's many a slip twixt cup and lip.' I understand that the plans will have to be passed by the Board of Design Review. They can be unpredictable, you know."

Was Astor voicing a veiled threat? "I suppose I'll have to take my chances," Cotham replied. "I do appreciate the call, though. Listen, I'm going to have to ask you to excuse me, Richard. I was just walking out the door to pick up Pallie."

"Yes, of course. Tell her hello for me. Goodbye, Ethan." The line went dead.

That night he had the dream again. He was riding the Lincoln American Tower's express elevator to his office, but it refused to stop at his floor. Instead it continued to accelerate, the G-forces seeming to double his weight as he gripped the handrails, helpless and terrified. Then came the flash of the explosion as the elevator cab ripped through the roof, and he was spiraling up into the sky, tumbling end over end. Finally he reached the peak of the trajectory and began the long, silent fall toward the dark river.

What did the dream mean he wondered? Was his practice getting dangerously out of control? He thought of the old maxim that one should be careful what he wished for in case his prayers were answered.

———————

The next morning's *Commercial Appeal* proclaimed him a hero. "Architect Cotham Selected to Design New Center for Southern Culture" shouted the headline at the bottom of page one. "Memphis architect Ethan Cotham has been declared the winner of a competition to select the design for the proposed Center for Southern Culture," the lead ran. The article went on to mention the other competitors, naming Astor as the runner-up. The "prestigious" commission had been awarded to Cotham based on the "boldness" of his concept, combined with "a singular understanding of and sensitivity to the historic site on the banks of the Mississippi." The jury was also "impressed by Cotham's ingenious solution to the challenges posed by the requirement that the buildings withstand a major earthquake." It continued, mentioning the Teflon base isolation pads that supported the footings. There was even a color photograph of the model. All in all it was a glowing piece, and Cotham immediately dashed off a note to Gertrude Philpot thanking her for her generosity and accuracy. *So this is fame,* he mused to himself, reflecting that he did not at all object to the sensation.

———————

The old Jefferson County courthouse on the square in Lafayette, Mississippi, was wreathed in a white mist of flowering pear trees as Cotham and Cellini passed beneath the unblinking gaze of the Confederate statue, erect and vigilant on perpetual guard duty. Parked in front of the cathedral annex was the silver Mercedes Benz SUV with the Bonnie Blue flag bumper sticker, and Cotham groaned inwardly.

After a short wait the soft-spoken young woman who had given Cotham the icon of St. Mary Magdalene led them down the hall toward the office of Bishop Hervey Coltharp. The bishop stood as they entered, smiling and extending his hand. "Father Cellini, Mr. Cotham, welcome back to Lafayette. It's good to see you again." Like other north Mississippi natives, he accented the second syllable of the town's name, rhyming it with "hay."

He gestured toward the tall, heavy-set man who stood at one of the armchairs in front of his desk. "And you remember D'Arcy Lamar, I'm sure? Mr. Lamar has been telling me about his fund-raising drive for the Catholic schools in Tunica County. It seems we are making excellent progress." They shook the beefy hand of the unsmiling Lamar, who was dressed as before in khakis and cowboy boots.

"Mornin'," he grunted. Clearly Lamar would have preferred

spending his morning steering a tractor across one of his hundred-acre soybean fields.

At Coltharp's invitation Cotham laid the large black leather drawing portfolio on the conference table and withdrew the first of several presentation boards upon which were mounted the floor plans of St. Mary Magdalene Church. He set the board on one of the easels that stood in a semi-circle about the table.

"We are looking forward to seeing how you've solved the problem of the altar platform, Mr. Cotham," said Coltharp. "I realize, by the way, that what we've asked you to do is not easy." Was there a slight note of sympathy in his voice?

Pointing to the floor plan, Cotham launched into the presentation he and Cellini had rehearsed. "Bishop, as you'll recall from our last meeting, the original plan placed the altar platform here in the midst of the worship space surrounded by pews on three sides, as recommended by the Second Vatican Council guidelines. You then directed us to revise the drawings to provide a more traditional arrangement in which the altar table is located at the end of the room separated by a railing." Cotham was careful to maintain eye contact with the bishop, throwing only a cursory glance toward Lamar.

"Father Cellini and I have studied the problem at some length. We have, I believe, hit upon a solution that addresses your concerns, but also addresses the requirements of Vatican II as well as the instructions received from the Building Committee." He set three more boards on the easels. They too were floor plans all showing the same enclosing walls of the building, unchanged from the original drawing. "It occurred to us after trying a number of approaches that there is no reason the altar platform has to be a raised concrete floor slab fixed in a single location. Imagine the platform instead as a series of nine wooden boxes, each some three steps high, that can be moved around the worship space and arranged in various ways as needed for different kinds of services. They can even be removed altogether. These drawings illustrate the possibilities."

Cotham pointed to the first of the new drawings. "Here we have the altar pushed against the end wall to create a very traditional arrangement. The seats are lined up in conventional rows facing the altar with a central aisle dividing them into two groups. Recessed sockets in the stair treads support a removable altar railing."

The next drawing showed the raised platform floating in the space at the opposite end of the room. "This second alternative moves the platform into the middle of the space for a more contemporary service. Chairs surround it on all four sides, and the altar rail has been completely removed so as to offer no symbolic barrier between the clergy and the people.

"Finally," he said, pointing to the last board, "We see the platform removed from the space entirely. The chairs are placed in storage so that the room can be used for a different sort of function, a dance or a reception, perhaps.

"This concept requires that the seating be changed from pews to moveable chairs. The chairs stack on top of each other to reduce the space needed for storage. Not only can they be arranged in many different ways, it's only necessary to use the number needed so that for a small service there are not a large number of empty seats.

"There's one more idea I'd like to propose. I will be the first to admit that it is not original; it's borrowed from the Finnish architect Alvar Aalto whom I've always admired. Everyone has had the experience of being the first to arrive for a meeting and taking a seat at the rear so as not to be the center of attention. As others arrive, the seats in the front are usually the last to be taken. If the house is not full, the celebrant or the speaker finds himself addressing several rows of empty seats with the congregation or audience beyond. Why not make the seats closest to the front the most likely to be filled by making them the most comfortable? Suppose the front one-third of the chairs are well padded, with arms. Next come a group of unpadded armchairs. And finally, placed at the back of the room, are several rows of bare wooden chairs without arms or cushions. These would tend to be taken by latecomers while the first to arrive would be attracted to the more comfortable seats at the front.

"So, Bishop, to summarize our solution to the problem you've asked us to address, the altar platform is moveable, as is the seating. As the need arises for different types of services, as different priests come and go, or as there are changes in the liturgy over the years, the church has a built-in flexibility that allows it to accommodate change."

Cotham paused and watched Coltharp as he leaned forward, studying the drawings.

"Oh, and one more thing," Cotham added as though the idea had just struck him, "There will be a significant cost savings compared to our earlier plan with a fixed concrete platform and pews. We've estimated that as much as ten to twenty thousand dollars could be freed up by this approach."

Cellini, who had been sitting quietly watching Coltharp and Lamar to gauge their reactions as Cotham spoke, added in a quiet voice, "That extra money could do a world of good in the Tunica Schools, Bishop."

Coltharp turned toward Lamar but said nothing. Cotham permitted himself a glance at Lamar. The big man's face had grown quite red, and he gripped the arms of his chair. Above his khaki shirt collar a vein in his thick neck stood out like a cord.

For a few moments the room was silent. Then Lamar exploded. "Bishop, I reckon the reason I'm here is that I represent the people of our parish. Not these Northern liberals who been coming down here from Illinois or Massachusetts or God knows where to retire, mind you, but the ordinary people who've been the backbone of the church all their lives. Farmers, railroad men, folks who know what it means to work for a living. I'm here to tell you this intellectual nonsense about altars that go slidin' all over the place won't fly with these people. The very idea of parties in the sanctuary! And what about the pews? Did you hear 'em say we ain't having any, just chairs? What kinda church hasn't got pews? I'm tellin' you fellers, maybe that's how they do it in Boston, Father, but this here's Mississippi, and down here we have pews in our churches!"

Now all eyes shifted to Bishop Coltharp. Coltharp stood and moved closer to the easel and pointed to the floor plan. "Mr. Cotham, do I understand that this moveable platform of yours could be set up like a traditional church against the wall with an altar rail and rows of seats all facing the same way?"

"That's correct, Bishop," replied Cotham. "You would not be able to tell that it's moveable simply by looking at it."

"I must say the chairs strike me as a very practical idea, D'Arcy, particularly for a small service when we wouldn't want rows of empty seats like we would have with pews. You know, I was in Chartres Cathedral a couple of years ago and was surprised to see that they don't have any pews there, just some little wooden chairs

195

they set up when they need them. The rest of the time it's just one big open room. Father Cellini, don't they have both chairs and pews in the cathedral in Memphis?"

"They do, Bishop. It was part of the recent restoration there, and everyone seems to find the flexibility very useful."

"And you're saying that this plan is actually less expensive than the one we had before?" asked Coltharp directing his gaze at Cotham, his voice rising ever so slightly.

Cotham nodded. "We believe that to be the case, Bishop. Instead of a concrete floor structure supporting the platform, this plan would use all wood construction to reduce the weight and make it easier to move the modules. The wood framing is also less expensive than concrete."

Coltharp turned to Lamar. "D'Arcy, I appreciate your position. I know that new ideas are hard for many people to get used to. But our church is not only the guardian of tradition. Christianity began as a new way of looking at God's world. We forget that it was originally a radical movement; and I believe that if it is to survive, it must change with the times. Indeed, we should have the courage to 'make all things new,' as the Gospel urges us to do. I am beginning to see the power of architecture to accomplish this.

"I had not thought of it in this way before. But as Mr. Cotham points out, there is no reason the arrangement of the altar and seating cannot be a very traditional one when desired. At other times, however, I am coming to believe that there are significant advantages to the flexibility this plan offers." Lamar stared at Coltharp, his eyes bulging.

"Mr. Cotham, I'm going to authorize the resumption of construction at St. Mary Magdalene based on making the changes you have presented to us. I appreciate your patience and your willingness to work with us on these revisions. And, D'Arcy, I want to use the money we're saving for our Tunica schools program. In fact, I'd be honored if you would allow the Diocese to set it aside as a special gift in your name, in recognition of all you've done to help make the fundraising a success."

Chapter Thirteen

New shoots of grass sparkled in the morning sunlight. The oaks in the grove below St. Mary Magdalene Church were dazzling in their delicate mantle of fresh growth, and a chartreuse halo seemed to envelop them. Redbud and Japanese magnolia trees dotted the slopes of the hillside, and the dogwoods at the edge of the grove were heavy with buds. Around the building scurried a small army of construction workers. Masons, carpenters, electricians, and plumbers unloaded trucks laden with multicolored pallets of brick, gleaming sheet metal for fabrication into ducts and flashing, steel and cast iron piping. A concrete truck, its mixer drum slowly rotating, waited, a long rubber hose snaking toward the entry plaza where the wooden formwork stood ready to receive the fresh concrete. From inside the church came the staccato blasts of a jackhammer, and Cotham guessed that the demolition of the concrete altar platform was under way.

The swarm of activity combined with the freshness of the countryside on this sunny spring morning cheered him immensely. The splint had finally been removed from his broken finger, which was still stiff but no longer throbbed. His only complaint (and it was a minor one) was the old leg wound from Vietnam that caused him to limp slightly as he made his way across the unfinished plaza. He reflected that he should be grateful that the slug had missed the artery and that he still had a leg on which to limp.

He was early for the meeting with the Building Committee, and it would be an opportune time to pay an unannounced visit to the trailer that served as Ingram Construction's field office. To a casual observer the scene was chaotic, but Cotham recognized the underlying order. Every aspect of a project of this magnitude had been choreographed in advance, laid out on the eight-foot long critical path flow chart displayed on the wall of the office. Sam Ingram, the general contractor, could be blunt, even caustic, but he knew construction and cared about quality, unlike some of the other contractors Cotham had encountered. He had campaigned on Ingram's behalf when it came time to select a firm to build the church, advising the Building Committee to forego the bidding process in favor of selection through interviews and negotiations. While bidding was a necessary evil on public projects where the lowest cost was the first consideration, Cotham had argued that it was an inappropriate way to select the builder of a work of architecture where quality was as important as cost.

Ingram was one of an elite group of contractors who could grasp not only the specific instructions contained in the architect's drawings, but also the larger design intent that lay behind them. From a single detail in the drawings, he could infer the correct approach to similar conditions. Because his cost proposals reflected this understanding, he was seldom the low bidder; but he would stick with his negotiated price rather than looking for opportunities to increase it through change orders once construction began. So far the only change order had involved the redesign of the altar platform, and the result had been a handsome credit to the Owner's account.

When Cotham had passed along Bishop Coltharp's order to stop work on the project, Ingram had ripped the cigar out of his mouth, snarled a curse, and stormed out of the field office, slamming the door so that the entire trailer shook. Cotham did not blame him. It was a difficult position for a contractor who had already entered into agreements for everything from structural steel to toilet partitions, electrical wiring, mechanical equipment, doors, windows, fire sprinklers, and hardware. In order to land the job, Cotham had pressured and cajoled Ingram to submit his best price and to commit to an overall time schedule. When construction had been halted, Ingram had been forced to tell his subcontractors to find other work until it resumed. Now that Coltharp had given the order to begin again, many of them would want additional compensation for the lost time, and some might no longer be available having committed to other projects.

Cotham recognized the two figures in the fire engine red hard-hats striding toward him as Ingram and his superintendent, Don Childers. Ingram was chomping on an unlit cigar. "Ethan, you'd better get out of here," Ingram boomed," before the elephants get you!"

Cotham was taken aback. He must have misunderstood. "What did you say, Sam?"

As they shook hands, Cotham noted the twinkle in Ingram's eye and Childers' sheepish grin. "Mornin', Mr. Ethan."

"Go ahead, Childers, tell the architect what you do in your spare time. Ethan, step over here and look at this sorry excuse for a truck my superintendent drags onto my jobsite."

Mystified, Cotham followed them to the gravel parking area

where a dust-covered Dodge Ram pick-up waited. In the back had been thrown a bale of hay. The cab was littered with discarded Big Mac wrappers, and on the dashboard a plastic sculpture of the Blessed Virgin Mary surveyed the world through a cracked windshield. Ingram pointed to the right rear fender of the truck, which bore a sizeable dent.

"Go ahead, Don, tell Mr. Cotham how you came to get that dent in your otherwise pristine vehicle."

Childers squirmed. He pulled a pack of Winstons from his shirt pocket and lit one up. "Well, you see, it was like this. Every year about this time there's this traveling carnival that passes through. You know, a little midway with some rides for the kids, some of them booths where you pay to throw rings over bottles, some freaks, that sort of stuff. They usually set up in a pasture outside Byhalia, and I like to go to the strip show they have. No harm in just lookin', it seems to me.

"Well, I went last night, and this year they had this here elephant. Not in the strip show. I mean they had him chained outside the tent. When the carnival first gets to town, they have this parade down Main Street with the elephant in front and one of the strippers rides him. He was a big ol' bull, and he kinda seemed restless to me; but I didn't think much of it. So I parked my truck outside the tent along with everybody else. I bought my ticket from Larry Jenkins, this ol' boy I know who always gets a part time job helpin' out at the carnival, and went on inside.

"Well, the show is just getting to the good part, if you know what I mean, when Larry comes running into the tent looking for me and saying something about the elephant, about how I'd best come outside with him.

"So I did, and there's this bull elephant standing over my truck eatin' on this bale of hay, holding it in his trunk. Well, I was taking that hay home to feed my livestock. I keep a couple of cows and some goats around the house; I always have. It reminds me of growin' up in Panola County. Anyway, I didn't figure my hay oughta be that elephant's salad so I start yelling and clapping my hands and telling him to shoo.

"I must've said the wrong thing, though, 'cause he lets out with this kind of screech, or whatever you call that noise elephants make when they're riled up, and he takes a big step towards me. He looked real mean, and I started thinking he was out to trample me. Well, just about that time, Larry comes running up with this big bucket of soapy water he must've been using to wash down the strippers' stage, and damn if he don't throw that soapy water right in the elephant's face.

"That elephant let out another screech, and he yanks at his chain. Then he throwed down my bale of hay, turns around, and sort of shuffles away. But before he leaves he gives my truck this big kick with his hind leg. Put this here dent in it, I swear to God."

Ingram pulled the cigar out of his mouth and eyed Childers. "And what did your insurance company say when you called in a claim?"

Childers grinned. "I'll tell you the truth, Mr. Sam, I ain't going to report it. I figure how many people can say they got a truck what's been kicked in by an elephant? I've decided to keep it as a conversation piece."

———————

Ingram and Cotham strolled into the church. As they passed from one space to another, Cotham cast a critical eye on the workmanship, pointing out a poorly raked mortar joint, an incorrectly aligned light fixture, and a door that had been hung swinging in the wrong direction. He questioned the contractor about the planned sequence of construction as a way of judging how closely Ingram was monitoring the process. Ingram answered his questions promptly and with assurance.

"Sam, we've got some minor glitches, but that's only to be expected. Overall you're doing a fine job here. And I haven't had a chance to thank you for the way you got this project started up again." For the most part Ingram had been successful in his summons for the subcontractors to return to the job although it appeared that the plumber, who had taken on another large project, might have to be replaced.

"I'll admit I had to twist some arms," Ingram replied. "And the new plumber is going to charge half-again what we had in the original budget. Says he'll have to work overtime to keep to the schedule. You know I'll have to have a change order for that. The bishop needs to understand that he can't just send everybody home at the drop of a hat and expect them to come back at his pleasure without asking for more money."

"I understand that, Sam," Cotham replied, "but is there any way we can wait a little while to hit him with the bad news? Things seem to be back on track for the moment, but it wouldn't take much to derail them again."

Ingram hesitated. "You know, Ethan, we needed this job and you put in a good word for us to the selection committee. I appreciated that. I guess we could wait until the end and then see about the plumber. Maybe it won't take him as much overtime as he seems to think."

———

A folding table had been set up in the nave for the meeting of the Arts and Furnishings Subcommittee, and at Cotham's request Childers had ordered all the workers out of the space. Without the cacophony of the jackhammer the great room now seemed supernally calm; although in its midst where the concrete altar platform had stood, there was now a gaping hole that would have to be patched and then covered with oak flooring.

The committee, whom Cotham knew from the innumerable meetings in which he had presented his early design ideas, took their seats around the table. They included Sophie Leland, the Building Committee chair; two perky young housewives; the balding, myopic, executive director of Catholic Charities; a retired mechanical engineer; and a matronly interior decorator, Clarissa Avent. They were now craning their necks gazing at the plaster ceiling high overhead where a twenty by twenty foot area had been painted midnight blue. Stenciled over the blue was a field of gold stars. He watched their expressions carefully, noting the mixture of smiles and frowns as well as several blank looks of perplexity. Clarissa Avent was among those who were not smiling. Cotham sighed. It promised to be a challenging discussion.

"Okay, folks, let's try to get started," announced the ever-efficient Sophie, glancing at her watch. We're here to discuss the decoration of the nave and to hear Mr. Cotham's ideas. Ethan, it's all yours."

Cotham stood and smiled. "Good morning. I know you are as happy as I am to see St. Mary Magdalene under construction again. As you know, today's agenda is our proposal for the decoration of the ceiling. Directly above you I have ordered the painters to apply a sample for your review.

"The idea is based on historical precedent, the ceilings of the spectacular Byzantine chapels in Ravenna and later medieval churches such as the Saint Chapelle in Paris, which I'm sure some of you have visited." He gestured toward the table where several large tomes on the history of art and architecture lay open, the color photographs marked with scraps of paper.

"In these ancient churches the ceiling of the worship space was seen as a metaphor for heaven. In their pre-Copernican world view, heaven was the uppermost tier of the universe, the middle tier was earth, and the lowermost was hell. While we, of course, no longer share this pre-scientific view in which the earth was the center of the universe, I believe that the ceiling can still serve as a striking and appropriate metaphor for the natural world.

"At first glance the stars may appear to be placed at random, but for those of you who may be astronomically inclined a closer examination will show that we have depicted the constellations Gemini and Orion. This is just the first step in recreating the entire winter sky as it appears at the midnight mass on Christmas Eve, the defining moment in the Christian calendar."

There was a stirring among the committee members as several turned and shared brief whispered comments with those seated next to them. Cotham continued with his presentation.

"The stars are made using real twenty-three carat Florentine gold leaf which, I'm told, is only one molecule thick. It's applied with a sort of liquid glue, using a burnishing process. Metallic leaf is more expensive than gold-colored paint, which oxidizes and turns brown after a few years. Unlike paint, gold leaf will retain its brightness for fifty years or more."

He paused while the faces around the table looked back and forth at each other. Cotham patiently awaited their comments.

"Well, if no one else wants to start, I will," spoke up Clarissa Avent, standing and eyeing the committee members one at a time with an air of authority. "I have to be honest. As you know, this is my field." Now she stared directly at Cotham. "You asked us what we think. I think it's just too busy."

Cotham groaned inwardly. There was nothing more difficult than a client with a little knowledge of architecture and design.

"As you know, Mr. Cotham, I work with interiors all the time, and I find that the simplest ideas are usually the best. I'm a firm believer that 'less is more.'"

"Yes, I'm familiar with that aphorism, Clarissa," Cotham replied evenly. "Mies van der Rohe, the German Modernist architect, was famous for his minimalist design where every detail was stripped down to its barest, most direct expression. But there's another side to that argument that holds 'less is a bore.' To me there is a place for decoration and symbolism, especially in a church where we are dealing with the spiritual. We need symbols as a kind of window into the inexpressible." He looked around the table at the others.

"I like the stars," the executive director meekly offered, "but won't the dark ceiling make the room seem smaller?"

"Actually," responded Cotham, "there are many studies of visual perception that show that there's an optical illusion at work here. Dark walls and ceilings actually make a room seem larger. Dark colors recede, you see. Since the dark surface appears to be further away, the brain reads the size of the space as larger. It runs counter to our intuition perhaps, but perception is a tricky business."

"I am sure an off-white ceiling will make the room seem much larger," insisted Clarissa. "We'll get tired of all those stars, and then it'll be too late to change them. Take my word for it, we'll be making a mistake. Besides, it seems so *modern.*"

Cotham sensed that he had gone too far in refuting her argument and had caused her to lose face.

"It's really a very conservative approach, when you think about it," Sophie noted soothingly. "Just look at these photographs, at how far it goes back, all the way to the early church. I just wish we could afford to have these gorgeous mosaics."

"I don't know, Sophie, I've just never seen anything like this before," ventured one of the housewives, an attractive young brunette in a hunter-green tennis warm-up suit. "I think I agree with Clarissa. She used a beautiful warm ivory, 'Khalua and Cream,' when she decorated our living room, and we've never gotten tired of it. And you can do so much more with a neutral color."

"Sandy's right," chimed in the other housewife. The two were obviously friends and had been whispering to each other throughout the meeting. "I'm on the altar guild and we have to think about flowers and the colors of the vestments and altar cloths at all the different liturgical seasons."

"We all need to remember," Sophie pointed out in a reasoned tone, "that we have engaged an architect to design this building. We are paying him to make these kinds of esthetic recommendations, including colors and finishes. It's certainly the committee's role to advise and consent; but when it comes to design, it is not the place of us non-professionals to challenge his concepts."

Bless her, thought Cotham, who had held back for fear of alienating the group. How could he make them see that his recommendation was not simply based on a personal preference for one color over another but rather had grown out of the countless design decisions made already? His proposal for the ceiling was a way of reinforcing an astronomical theme that was already established. It included the entire orientation of the nave as well as the round window in the south gable through which the shaft of sunlight would stream at noon.

"I must say I disagree, Sophie," retorted Clarissa. "We're not talking about the design of the building here. No one questions Mr. Cotham's judgment when it comes to the design of the roof or the walls. That's what architects do. But when it comes to colors, our opinion is as valid as his. Why, I've taken entire courses on furniture and even the history of wallpaper design. I may not have much to contribute to the church, but when it comes to colors...."

"Yes, and Clarissa has such beautiful taste," added the housewife in the warm-up suit. Clarissa beamed.

"Perhaps," said the retired engineer in a weary voice, "we should take a vote."

Cotham's heart sank. He knew that in a committee meeting where a bold decision was needed votes were to be avoided whenever possible. The result would surely be that the safest, least imaginative alternative would win.

"Perhaps rather than voting," offered Sophie, "we could discuss the matter a bit more in hopes of arriving at a consensus."

"I really have to be going or I'll be late for tennis," said the woman in the warm-up suit. "Everyone has had a say. What's wrong with a vote?"

"Yes, otherwise we'll be here all day!" chirped her friend.

"I agree, let's vote," added Clarissa hastily, sensing the shift in momentum.

"Very well," sighed Sophie, "all in favor of the blue ceiling and the stars, say 'aye.'"

"Aye," said the executive director, blinking nervously as he looked around the table.

"Aye," added Sophie.

"All in favor of a neutral color."

"Aye," said everyone else but Sophie. Clarissa's voice overshadowed the others with a tone of deep conviction.

"Very well then," pronounced Sophie with reluctance. "The decision is to go with the neutral color. Perhaps Clarissa could make some suggestions at our next meeting. Is that all right with you, Ethan?"

"Of course," Cotham replied, determined to maintain a show of nonchalance. Clarissa met his gaze with a polite smile, but beneath it the hard glint of victory blazed in her eyes.

"Any further comments, anyone?" asked Sophie. She was clearly embarrassed for Cotham. "Ethan?"

Cotham choked down the temptation to observe that once more the good had triumphed over the best. Instead, however, he rose and looked around the table.

"Thank you all for your input," he forced himself to reply. "I know it will be a splendid building that we will all be proud of."

Cotham retreated toward the security of his old Rover. Gone was the sense of tranquility that had begun his day. How many times had he heard that plaintive lament that spelled the instantaneous death of an idea, "I've just never seen anything like that before!"

Blocking his path was Childers' parked pickup truck. As Cotham passed, he suddenly turned and gave it a hard kick in the fender in the middle of the dent left by the elephant.

Chapter Fourteen

The disastrous meeting of the Board of Design Review in which Cotham's winning design for the CSC was rejected took place the next day. Following his defiant speech and the vote, Cotham made his way out of the library, past the dried-up reflecting pool with its headless sculpture, and turned up Front Street toward his office. He was still reeling from Evelyn Penobscot's parting words, which had struck him like a blunt instrument, "I can tell you that there was near-unanimous agreement that the CSC plans as drawn are unacceptable. I suppose you'll just have to start over, won't you?"

At the corner of Madison Avenue, despondent and lost in thought, instead of waiting for the light to change he stepped off the curb. With a screech of brakes and an ear shattering blast from an air horn, a FedEx delivery truck sped by, missing him by inches. At the last moment a hand grasped his arm and pulled him to safety.

Cotham scrambled back to the curb, looking around sheepishly like a man awaking from a dream, with Roberta Quonset gripping his arm. "Ethan, you were almost killed! I've been following you, trying to catch up. What happened in there was inexcusable.

"Come on, we have to talk."

Together they walked down Main Street. After a couple of blocks

Cotham felt his pulse rate returning to normal. He took several deep breaths. They chose the diagonal path that crossed Court Square past the Hebe statue. The fountain was running once more now that the oaks were leafing out and the daffodils were in bloom. The water-bearer poured an unending stream from her upraised urn into the basin. A little boy stood at the stone parapet exclaiming at the glint of pennies, nickels, and dimes that shone beneath the surface like brown and silver carp. A weather-beaten old man in the overalls of a farmer, perhaps the boy's grandfather, sat on a nearby bench lobbing popcorn to the greedy pigeons that swarmed around him.

"You know, Roberta," Cotham mused, looking around the square, "most of these buildings hold memories for me. It's like a family reunion with a roomful of ancient relatives, all talking at once. Each of them can recount events, large and small, that have shaped my life."

He nodded toward the Exchange Building. "I remember the Phil A. Halle clothing store off the lobby and the cotton trading room on the mezzanine with the mosaic bull and bear design in the floor. The building stood there vacant for most of the seventies and eighties until they converted it to a warren of tiny apartments. That grand, two-story ballroom on the top floor is now an exercise spa and laundry room. It reminds me of the phrase coined by the Pentagon during the Vietnam War—'in order to save the village it was necessary to destroy it.'"

Roberta smiled. "I used to go to parties in that ballroom. So did you. I used to look for you across the dance floor and try to find some excuse for us to talk. I thought you were quite handsome, you know. You were taller than most of the other boys, too. And you seemed to like me."

"Well, of course I did, Roberta," he fumbled.

"Ethan," she interrupted, "enough nostalgia. Aren't we avoiding the subject? Do you understand what happened in that meeting?"

He hesitated. "Well, if I'm not mistaken, I just lost the biggest commission I'll ever have," he replied, surprised at the resentment in his voice. He could hardly believe it. First the church building committee and now the Design Review Board had given thumbs down to his work. Worse, though, were the self-doubts about his own judgment that he could not bring himself to acknowledge to Roberta. Once again he had spoken his mind, accusing the Board of censorship, when he should have kept his thoughts to himself. Would he never master the art of diplomacy?

"Perhaps that remains to be seen. But that's only the tip of the iceberg, Ethan. I'm going to put it to you bluntly. Do you realize Richard Astor has been out to get you ever since you won that competition?" Despite the heat of the day Cotham felt a chill. "What happened in there was a carefully planned ambush. Poor little Evelyn Penobscot, the executive director, is just his mouth-piece—he's the chairman and her job depends on him. And he has poisoned her against you—we've all heard him. But none of us are architects, so no one challenges him. Richard scripted every word of her attack on your plans."

"Richard knows you better than you may think," she continued, "including the issues that are most likely to incense you—to provoke you into a tirade against the Board. This is his revenge. Just think of the envy, humiliation, and resentment he must feel at having lost the competition."

"My God, Roberta," Cotham gasped. "It never occurred to me. But it makes perfect sense. Now that I think about Penobscot's comments, they did sound more like an architect than a preservationist. And you don't even know about the call I got from Astor just after Pappas announced that I'd won. Astor wanted us to work together—the very thing I had suggested to him at the start of the competition. Astor turned me down then; and so when I refused his offer of assistance, it must have been the ultimate insult. Yes, I've fallen into his trap. What an idiot I've been.

"And now my old friend, my first love, has come to my defense. And I thought you had rejected me when you picked Astor to design your house."

"Ethan," she replied in amazement, "whatever do you mean 'your first love?'"

"I could never bring myself to tell you how deeply in love with you I was. Why, on our first real date I was trembling all over, miserable and exhilarated at the same time. We were just sixteen. I couldn't think of anyone but you.

"I'll never forget your sorority formal at the old Clearpool. You wore a black velvet dress. I knew I would make a fool of myself on the dance floor, and you'd never want to see me again. And when I came to the door to pick you up, your father actually frisked me to see if I was hiding a bottle of whiskey. I didn't drink, but I was petrified that he would find the package of Trojans my older brother had slipped to me as I was leaving home!"

"How I wish I had known how you felt," she said. "I adored you too, Ethan. I always have...."

She took his arm, and they made their way back toward the Main Street Mall in silence, Cotham lost in thought. He was at once amazed and oppressed by Astor's machinations, deeply touched by Roberta's loyalty, and flooded by guilt at his readiness to believe she had betrayed him. Ahead of them stood the shining white Lincoln American Tower and its dark, hulking Romanesque neighbor, the old Rhodes Jennings Department Store, rotten at its core, and now in the terminal stages of demolition by neglect. The contrast in the buildings was as striking as the difference between Astor and Roberta.

"Just look at those glorious cast iron arches and columns, almost rusted through in spots," observed Cotham. "And those plywood panels where there used to be huge plate glass windows are like the eyes of a blind man. What a pity."

"You know, Ethan, sometimes I think your best friends are buildings instead of people."

"Perhaps you're right," he conceded. "They're easier for me to understand. They're more straightforward, solid and dependable, and they never stab you in the back."

"Look—right over here was the old Beasley, Jones & Ragland Building. My father bought me my first suit there. And just down the street was Gerber's Department Store."

"Oh, my, yes," Roberta, replied. "Where the Gerber's Tearoom was; it overlooked Confederate Park and the river. My mother and aunt never missed lunch there when they came Downtown to shop."

"And now we have a Sleep Inn motel instead; that's progress for you," he said. "At least that project put the Design Review Board to the test. Do you remember how the Board opposed the design at first on the grounds that the wrought-iron balconies were more appropriate to the Vieux Carré in New Orleans than to Memphis? It also objected to the fact that the building turned its back on Main Street in favor of a parking lot and that the pink synthetic stucco façades belonged in the suburbs, not Downtown. It was a courageous stand based on well-founded arguments.

"When the developers threatened to abandon the project though, the Board backed down under pressure from the Chamber of Commerce, according to rumors. Eventually the Board agreed to allow the stucco if the wrought iron was eliminated and a front door was added on Main Street. That was all before you became a member, of course, Roberta," he added diplomatically.

"So, Ethan, I gather you don't think much of the Design Review Board," Roberta observed, "to put it mildly. But you must admit that they've saved a few handsome old buildings from demolition. Without us there'd have been a lot more outrages like the loss of the Cossitt Library and the old Gerber's."

"I'd be the first to agree that the destruction of the library was a travesty. And I'll grant you that the Board was initially founded with the best of intentions. They helped make people aware of historic architecture. And it began to dawn on my generation of young architects that much of the corporate architecture of the time was inhumane, banal, and anti-urban. There was a sort of revolt against Modernism, and we began to see cities and suburban subdivisions, and even entire new communities, enact design review legislation. As time went by, design review agencies accumulated political clout. Before long developers and dentists and housewives, no offense, Roberta, had gained the power to reject architects' designs, even when their clients, who were footing the bill, were satisfied.

"Why, I have a mind to write the mayor and tell him I want to serve on a new citizens' board that will review the work of all the dentists in town!"

"So, if it were up to you, you'd abolish all design review?"

"Well, I'll admit I've seen some good come from it in other places, particularly when the boards include design professionals and educated laymen. But I believe we pay a price for the good they do. Like all artistic censorship, the result is a chilling effect on creativity.

"But shouldn't citizens have something to say about what gets built? It's our city after all," she countered. "Look at all the awful modern buildings that threaten our great cities—like that horrible Pompidou Center right in the heart of Paris, the one with all the pipes and ducts on the outside."

"Look, Roberta, it's an old story, the shock of the new. You mention Paris. One of the most infamous cases involved the Eiffel Tower. When it went up in 1889, a great hue and cry arose from the Paris intelligentsia. In a city dominated by conservative mid-rise masonry architecture, they strenuously objected to its height and to its revolutionary use of cast iron, a vulgar material associated with bridges, railroad stations, and factories. It narrowly escaped demolition under the pressure to conform to the artistic preconceptions of the public."

"I don't understand you, Ethan. You make speeches about the evils of design review and about us shortsighted preservationists, but then you talk about old buildings with the greatest affection, comparing them to members of your family. You agree that the old Cossitt Library should never have been torn down and replaced by a modern box. You admit that the Design Review Board has done some good. You chose a historic landmark for your office. And yet when you designed the CSC, you made no attempt to follow historic prescedent."

"I suppose it sounds inconsistent," he replied. "Sure the preservation movement has done much good. I'm not against preservation—I'm against the design police. Most of the great buildings of history are recognized at least in part because they represented radical departures from the prevailing architectural norms of their day. It's as true for the first Gothic cathedrals as for the first skyscrapers. Would the façade of Chartres have been approved by a design review committee? Why, the two towers don't even match. The original tower was Romanesque and the other, designed much later, is Gothic. The later one was *modern,* for God's sake!

"Here's my point. When preservation becomes official policy, it can help save landmarks; but it inevitably exerts a chilling effect on architectural creativity. And after today it seems pretty clear that some preservationists are less motivated by love of the past than by fear of the future and in some cases the advancement of their own careers."

"There's not much love lost between you and Richard Astor is there, Ethan? What happened? Didn't you once work for him?"

Cotham was silent.

"Ethan, I know you were hurt by our decision to hire Richard to design our house. If it's any comfort, I can tell you that he has been difficult to deal with. He can be very autocratic, and things have gotten pretty tense between us."

"Yes, well, that's between you and Astor, of course. I've really got to get back to the office," he said, glancing at his watch. "It was awfully good to see you again, Roberta. Thank you for what you said in the meeting and for all the rest."

He wondered whether to offer her a little kiss, but after a moment's hesitation, settled for an awkward one-armed hug instead. Then he turned away.

"Ethan," she called after him. "There's one other thing I want to say to you. You know you haven't heard the last of today's meeting. The city fathers are very conservative people, and they're gun-shy when it comes to modern buildings on prominent downtown sites. They don't understand about design competitions or artistic integrity. The involvement by Design Review was necessary for political reasons as well as for Richard's own agenda. Pappas needs the Board's blessing to reassure the City Council, so that they'll make the site available.

"You might as well recognize that your position in refusing to redesign jeopardizes the CSC. When Pappas gets wind of your little speech at the meeting, he's going to be plenty upset. Richard Astor will see to it that he gets a transcript, of course. Can you afford to lose this project? Isn't there some way you could agree to at least a token effort at making a few changes?"

Chapter Fifteen

Roberta had been right. Nikos Pappas' face was dark with anger as he waved Cotham into one of the Knoll armchairs at the mahogany conference table overlooking East Memphis. From where Cotham sat, the hollow-eyed sculpture of Poseidon appeared to be aiming the trident directly at his heart. Had Pappas intentionally directed him to this chair where the wrathful god could skewer him?

Pappas had carefully removed the red carnation from his boutonniere as though it might be wilted by what he had to say. He placed it in an Alvar Aalto crystal vase and then launched into a restrained but bitter tirade. Cotham listened respectfully for a while. But he had anticipated Pappas' main points, and after a while his mind began to wander as he gazed toward the horizon. In the direction of Downtown the distant towers had vanished into the greenish gray cloudbank of an approaching squall sweeping towards them from somewhere out west beyond the river. As he contemplated the threatening sculpture of Poseidon, it had come to him. The god of the sea was also known as "the earth-shaker," the god of the earthquake. Was there a relationship between Pappas' insistence on seismic design for the CSC and his acquisition of this stunning piece of ancient art?

A flash of lightning inside a dark cloud brought him back. Pappas was still chewing him out, and Cotham found himself at the center of another storm raging inside Pappas' private art gallery amidst the serenity of the Corots and Monets. "...and the report goes on to say that you wouldn't even explain your ideas to them; that instead you lectured them about trying to redesign your building! And, of course, you had to refer to them as a censor board. Honestly, Ethan, I gave you credit for better judgment. Don't you know that whatever you think about their opinions the Design Review Board carries political clout in this town? How the hell are we supposed to raise money for this project when it's been disapproved by them? Why, the city council is likely to turn us down on our request for the site! This report is very damaging to this project, not to mention your own reputation. You've made your bed, Ethan, and now I'm afraid you're going to have to lie in it.

"Our own Board met last night to review the situation and will be meeting again as soon as you and I finish this discussion. I'll be frank. There is a strong sentiment among several members to reject your design for the CSC in favor of Astor's runner-up entry. They feel that because it's more traditional it'll be easier to raise money for construction, and there is, of course, no question of Astor's concept being approved by Design Review."

No, I shouldn't think so, Cotham thought to himself. With an effort he forced himself to remain silent, having learned the hard way during his first billet as an ensign aboard a destroyer that the only way to weather a dressing down by an angry superior was to maintain a respectful silence.

"I'll admit there was also some discussion about Astor's role in influencing the staff recommendation. Some of our Board seems to agree with you that he should have gone on record as recusing himself. In the end, though, it was decided that we are to instruct you to redesign the project to comply with at least some of the recommendations of Design Review. We don't expect you to start over—just to adjust some of the details, like the roof for instance or perhaps adding some red brick just to show that we have considered their input. I need to give them your answer."

Outside, the visibility had dropped to zero, and the building was enveloped in a dark green cloud as though it stood at the bottom of the sea. Cotham felt he was drowning. Blowing rain pelted the windows, and sheets of water ran down the plate glass.

"And what if I agree and it's rejected a second time?" asked Cotham. "Before the competition I suggested to Astor that we collaborate, but he turned me down flat. Then after the winner was announced, he called me to try to get a piece of the action. When I rejected him, he decided to use his power as head of Design Review against me. Nikos, don't you see that this isn't about design? It's about power, about who calls the shots, about wounded egos, and revenge.

"I'm sorry, but I won't redesign. Your own jury selected my submission, and they'll get that or nothing. You could have made your selection contingent on the approval of Design Review in the first place. You could have simply hired Astor to design your project instead of holding a competition. But since you didn't, you have no right to change the rules after the fact."

Pappas looked more hurt than angry. "Ethan, I'm truly sorry to hear you take this position, although I suppose I understand at some level. Your profession seems to be unique. You architects think of yourselves as artists, not businessmen, and that has been your downfall. I regret that if this is your final decision we will have to ask for your resignation as our architect. The Board will be very sorry to hear it, but the consensus was clear."

Cotham stood and faced Pappas. "You may tell the Board, Nikos, that I refused to redesign and that I also refused to resign. I won't make it easy for them. They will have to fire me."

With a sharp thwack the tiny black missile rebounded off the white-painted wall of the little room and hurtled toward him four inches off the floor and five feet to his right. Cotham lunged, his extended arm only half-cocked. The racket barely caught the ball and sent it heading for the side wall at half its original speed where it careened on a diagonal and nicked the front wall before dying in the opposite corner, a lucky shot.

"Seven–eight," he announced breathing hard, stepping with one foot into the service box and glancing back at his opponent bouncing on the balls of his feet in the opposite court, racket raised at the ready. Cotham threw the ball into the air and smashed it overhead as hard as he could toward the front wall. It would require a high return executed before the ball reached the side wall, but his lithe opponent stepped forward and took it on the volley, driving it straight and hard back toward the front wall. It was a perfect shot, parallel to the side wall, and Cotham never got within two feet of the rebound.

Now it was his turn to receive, and his opponent lobbed a slow, lazy shot toward the rear left corner, to Cotham's backhand side. Cotham stepped back and let the ball bounce off the back wall and down onto the floor. Sluggish, it rose no more than an inch, but he scooped under it and sent it flying toward the right front corner. His opponent had anticipated this, however, and was already charging toward the front wall. He met the ball hard, three feet away from the front wall, blocking Cotham's view as he did so. On a guess Cotham moved right only to see the ball come crashing toward the left. Desperately he swerved, just managing to reach it with his backhand. It was not a strong shot, however, and the hollow boom left no doubt that he had struck the tin, the low metal baseboard that extended across the bottom of the front wall.

"Game!" gasped his opponent with unconcealed relief.

Cotham grinned ruefully and extended his hand toward the man who stood dripping with perspiration in the middle of the small, harshly lit white cell. "Well-played, for an elderly gentleman."

"Age and cunning will prevail over youth and skill any day," replied the tall, thin man dressed in whites, his longish gray hair restrained by a white headband. Cotham, who preferred individual sports to team efforts, had been playing squash with Llewellyn Craig, his oldest friend, for at least thirty years, although it had been a month since their last match. It showed in their heavy breathing. For the last hour, however, no thought of Pappas had crossed his mind. Instead he had attacked the innocent little black ball as though the entire CSC project and the Design Review Board were packed into its tiny hollow core. He felt drained and exhausted but curiously at peace. The winner of these squash matches never seemed to matter afterwards, and the next time they played neither would remember the outcome of today's game.

"Should I call 911?" asked Pallie Pelham from her seat in the spectator's area behind the thick plate glass rear wall of the court as

Cotham and Craig stooped through the three-foot high door.

"Can I buy you two a beer?" asked Craig. "I gather Ethan's been through quite a ringer today."

"Sounds nice, Lew," she replied. "Why don't you guys shower, and I'll meet you on the terrace overlooking the tennis courts?"

———————

It was growing dark, and the tennis court lights were slowly blossoming to full brightness. A men's doubles match was in progress. Amos, the headwaiter, appeared in his starched white jacket with a silver tray of drinks. The three old friends talked quietly, effortlessly, unselfconsciously. For once Cotham was too engrossed in the simple pleasure of conversation to step outside himself as he usually did. How good it was to simply say what came into his mind without first analyzing how it might be taken by his listeners or worrying that he might sound too serious.

The rubico tennis courts at the University Club were in top shape as usual—as immaculately groomed as Lew Craig. Craig had changed into his seersucker suit, perfectly proper for the first week following Memorial Day, a convention that was hard-wired into his patrician brain. His navy blue tie sported a pattern of miniature cotton bolls. With his bushy mustache and sad eyes, the genteel attorney reminded Cotham of a romantic poet or a Confederate cavalry officer. No one who did not know him would have guessed that he had marched with Martin Luther King in the sixties and had been briefly jailed during a demonstration in Selma, Alabama. A few years earlier, Craig had sponsored the first black member to be admitted to the University Club, Judge Leroy D'Aloisious Freeman.

Beyond the courts, the eastern sky was almost dark, and a full moon was rising, the scent of honeysuckle heavy in the night air. Pallie sat motionless, watching the moon, and for a moment she seemed far away, as though her companions had ceased to exist. Whenever she lapsed into one of these trance-like states, Cotham was reminded of some ancient priestess, the Delphic Pythia perched on a tripod over a cleft in the floor of a temple, inhaling hallucinogenic vapors and uttering cryptic prophecies. Craig seemed to notice as well. After only a moment, however, she returned from wherever she had been. She gazed at them a bit uncertainly. Cotham took a sip of Bordeaux and extracted one of his rare cigars from the pocket of his gray pin cord suit. It was usually a sign that something had gone either very well or very badly for him.

"Two hours ago," he began, matter-of-factly, "I lost the biggest job of my life. Nikos Pappas wanted me to start over on the CSC design, and I told him no. When I left, I knew that I would either go throw myself off the Hernando Desoto Bridge or meet Lew on the squash court. Fortunately he saved me, and not for the first time, I might add. Who else would have walked out of his office at 3:00, no questions asked?"

"I knew the moment I picked up the phone," replied Craig, "that you weren't yourself. It was clear that something had happened."

When he finished recounting the scene in Pappas' office and Roberta's account of Astor's role in the sabotage of his plans, there was silence. Pallie looked pale, and Cotham wondered if somehow she had known in advance what he was going to tell them.

"Ethan, Lew," Pallie began, "I wouldn't mention this to just anyone. But for a moment I saw it all…. I saw how all this is going to come out in the end. I don't know how, and now it's gone like a dream I can't remember."

She shivered. "I can tell you this. The CSC project is not over yet, Ethan. I don't know how it's going to turn out, but I'm sure of one thing. It is not over yet."

"I don't understand you architects," Craig said in a gentle voice. "The insults and injury you put up with. As a group you are bright enough to have been lawyers or doctors—professionals who are highly paid and seldom second-guessed. I can't imagine one of my clients trying to tell me how to present evidence in court or how to structure an argument. You have to suffer the abuse of people like Pappas, and you keep coming back for more. I think they know they can get away with it and take advantage of you."

"It's funny you should mention coming back for more, Lew, because I'm seriously thinking that maybe I should hang it up. I put everything I had into this CSC competition, as Pallie well knows since she stayed up all night helping us finish the model. I accepted the rules they laid out on face value. It never occurred to me that there would be more hoops to jump through if I won."

"And what would you do with yourself if you did give up architecture?" queried Craig. "You're too old to get into law school, and you're not ruthless enough to make it in real estate or the cotton business."

"Well, I suppose I could turn pro and go on the squash circuit." Craig rolled his eyes. "Or maybe archaeology; I could be perfectly content trudging across Attica with a sketchbook, shovel, and toothbrush."

"It's certainly unfair, the way you've been treated," agreed Pallie, "but I'm more surprised to hear Pappas' position than I am to hear that Richard Astor was behind it. Did I ever tell you about how

Astor got the idea for his famous observatory, the one that put him on the map when it was published in *Progressive Architecture* back in the seventies?

"We were dating some back then. I was studying art history in addition to my acting and was working on a paper about the early, unbuilt works of Eero Saarinen. One night after we had been to a movie at the Guild he took me to see his office, no doubt with seduction on his mind. I remember that it was freezing, but he had the top down on his Thunderbird. We had a glass of brandy to warm up, and he began showing me his sketches for the observatory that were pinned up in the studio. As far as he knew, I was totally ignorant of architecture so I'm sure it never occurred to him that I might know what I was looking at. The observatory for Southwestern at Memphis was an outright copy of one of Saarinen's projects, an obscure building in New Jersey that was never constructed. I had run across the drawings in a copy of *Perspecta,* the Yale architecture journal, purely by chance a few days before, so I recognized it. I've never said anything to him about it, but I've never forgotten it, either."

"I'll be damned!" exclaimed Cotham. "That could explain a lot, including why he was never able to reach that same level again. I'm amazed that he was never found out. Architects generally know each other's work too well to be able to get away with outright plagiarism of someone like Saarinen."

"Perhaps he realized how lucky he had been," Pallie offered, "and was smart enough not to try it again."

Craig apparently had not forgotten Cotham's earlier comment. "It would be a great loss for this city if Ethan Cotham were to give up architecture," he said, looking at Pallie, "not to mention what a threat it would be to the science of archaeology." He turned back to Cotham. "Ethan, I've been sitting here thinking. There might be a way to fight back. Who would you say are the best architects in the country these days?"

Cotham paused. It was a question he and other architects took seriously; it was often difficult to separate the truly gifted from those with the best publicists, since the press tended to hold up certain stars for worship by the masses.

"Well, not everyone would agree, of course, but for my money there are two or three. There's Mario Bughatti in Milan. His work is undeniably fresh, iconoclastic, and very self-confident. His new airport is stunning. But he's still young for an architect, only forty-five or so, and it may be premature to say whether he has staying power.

"Paul Howe in San Francisco is probably the current media favorite; you're as likely to read about him in *People* magazine as in *Architectural Record*. It seems he can do no wrong as far as landing big international commissions, and people love those sinuous glass skins. They're designed using aerospace computers, a field Howe has practically invented single-handedly. And his underground mausoleum in Hamburg is pretty amazing.

"For me, the third would be Henry Roper in Philadelphia, although he's seen by many as a dangerous radical for daring to challenge the hide-bound historic preservation establishment. Roper tries to make the point that you don't honor a historic building by copying it, a point that's lost on the general public."

"That doesn't matter. Would the CSC Board recognize his name?"

"I feel sure that some of them would," replied Cotham, "His photograph was on the cover of *Time* magazine a couple of years ago."

"Good. And don't I remember your telling me that Lucretia Silvetti and Leroy Freeman are members of the jury that picked you as the winner of the competition?"

———————

Three days later Cotham was seated at his desk grinding out a letter he had been avoiding writing to Sam Ingram, the cigar-chomping general contractor for St. Mary Magdalene Church. It was a difficult letter to write, having as its purpose his ruling that the quality of the architectural woodwork failed to meet the standards spelled out in the specifications. It was an esthetic judgment based on years of experience, one he was sure the building committee would support, although he was aware that many other architects would be less exacting. Not only was it important that he find a way to express his thoughts as objectively as possible; it was equally critical that he do so without alienating Ingram. He valued their relationship and was conscious of the tenuous state of affairs that had existed since he had been obliged to issue the stop work order on the project at the direction of Bishop Coltharp. Cotham had begun the letter by sincerely praising the work of Don Childers, but was now wondering whether this might be mistaken by Ingram as a transparent attempt to soften the blow. Perhaps it was better to be direct and to the point.

His train of thought was interrupted by the buzz of the telephone intercom followed by Jean's voice. "Ethan, you have a call from Ms. Silvetti of the Brooks Museum. On line two."

"Good morning, Ethan," came the throaty greeting, "Rescued any more inebriated Boll Weevils lately?"

"Hello, Lucretia. No, I've decided to give up Valentine's dances at Mississippi roadhouses. They're bad for my heart."

"That's a shame. You were the hero of my little soiree. You know, I'd really like to find out who it was driving that fire truck. Of course, I have my theory."

"Yes, and I imagine the Highway Patrol would like to know as well. Tell me. Did your insurance cover the flattened fire plug?"

"Now, Ethan, let's not dwell on unpleasantness." Lucretia paused. "Oh, well, since you're obviously not in the mood for gossip, I thought you'd be interested to hear, unofficially, of course, that the CSC Board met again last night to discuss your competition entry. The Board was divided. Some of us felt that it might be premature to overrule the jury's decision much less to accept your resignation. And there was concern about what sort of story old Gertrude Philpot might run in the *C.A.* when she heard that the town's newest architectural hero had been sacked.

"But really, Ethan, don't you think you overreacted a bit in telling poor old Nikos Pappas that we'd have to fire you? He was very upset."

Cotham said nothing, and after a moment she pressed on.

"As you know, Roberta Quonset is a member of our jury. For some reason that I find hard to fathom she took up for you. She argued that you did not receive a fair shake from Design Review. I hadn't realized before that she is also a member of their committee. Then Judge Freeman suggested that we get a second outside opinion about your design. We debated inviting a disinterested third party, an out-of-town expert, you might say, to review the three entries and advise us. In the end after much discussion that's what we've decided to do. We will be showing all three of the entries to our expert, who will then make a recommendation to the Board about whether to retain you as our architect."

"I must admit that's a creative approach, Lucretia. And I don't suppose it's been lost on you that whatever this outside expert says the Board can avoid the political heat that comes with making their own decision. It means that everything hangs on his particular point of view. Do you mind if I ask who has been selected?"

"Oh, I really shouldn't answer that, Ethan. It's all very hush-hush. Nikos is afraid the press will get wind of the dissension on the Board over the winner.

"But I suppose I could give you a little hint since you're such a dear friend. Are you familiar with Henry Roper, the old iconoclast from Philadelphia? He's due to meet with us tomorrow."

Chapter Sixteen

Above the double front doors of the Lincoln American Tower, the bas-relief figure of a portly man clad in a Roman toga gazed in perpetual tranquility over the Main Street Mall. He smiled benevolently and gestured toward an idealized classical landscape of chastity and decorum in the background. Cotham recognized it as a self-portrait of Colonel Bucksnort, the hypocritical censor who had commissioned the building. As his effigy stood guard over the public morality, the real Bucksnort had frolicked in an altogether different garden of earthly delights at the top of his tower.

"Evening, Mr. Ethan," croaked the building's ancient janitor holding open the door for Cotham, whose arms were filled with an assortment of Styrofoam boxes.

"Good evening, Jesse. You're here late tonight."

"Yessir, we got air conditioning problems again, and I got to stay as long as the repair men are here. They got the guts of the chiller laid out on the roof, and it looks like it'll be real late before they get it all put back together. It was up in the eighties today though. Soon be ninety, so we got to have it running."

"That's a relief," replied Cotham, "I thought maybe you were here looking for the ghost of Colonel Bucksnort. You haven't seen him molesting any more sweet young things in the alley, have you?"

"Nossir, why, I 'spect it's been over fifty years since I run across him and his secretary up against that wall. Even old Bucksnort bound to be beyond that by now."

The old janitor eyed Cotham. "You workin' late too, look like."

"Yes. I'll be up on twenty-one for a while, myself. Got a contractor on my case. Come up for some coffee later on if you feel like it."

"I may just do that, Mr. Ethan. Thank you, sir."

———————

Cotham stuffed the remains of his dinner into the paper sack and sat back with a Styrofoam cup of coffee and a last stub of cornbread, his feet propped on his desk. Through the open window the soft, warm breeze of early June carried a hint of roses, and he idly wondered who in the midst of Downtown Memphis had cultivated a rose garden. It made him think of the evenings when as a senior in high school he had enrolled in the drawing class at the Academy of Art in Overton Park. He had been infatuated with one of the other students. Her name was Mollie, and after class they would stroll together through the shadows of the park until they reached the deserted pavilion with its rose-entwined trellis. What was Mollie's last name anyhow? He couldn't remember.

On the tack board over his drawing table next to the icon of Mary Magdalene hung one of his early charcoal sketches of the Center for Southern Culture. He had saved it because it contained the first seed of the idea that ultimately became the basis for his floor plan. Gazing at it, Cotham felt extraordinarily alone and on an impulse picked up the telephone and began to dial Pallie's number. Then he looked again at the pile of drawings in front of him, sighed, and hung up.

There was really no way he could postpone the inevitable any longer. A serious glitch had developed at St. Mary Magdalene, and the shop drawings had arrived from Don Childers via FedEx the day before with an urgent note requesting his help. Apparently it had occurred to no one, including Cotham, his engineers, or Childers, that there was insufficient headroom in the office wings to accommodate the steel beams, the air conditioning ductwork, and the sprinkler piping. By the time the pipes were run below the ducts, only a little over seven feet would remain. It was clearly not enough; at least twelve more inches were needed. The fact that the structure was already in place and that the ductwork was fabricated and ready for installation meant that the solution would have to involve the sprinkler piping. But where to run it if not in the space below the ducts, just above the suspended lay-in ceiling?

Cotham unfolded the first of the large sheets and began to examine the maze of sprinkler pipes. If only the ducts could somehow be raised. If only the structure were a system of open trusses instead of solid steel beams, then the piping could be run through them above the ductwork.

He tried to remember his classes in structures from years ago. Wasn't there something called the "neutral axis" in a beam, a zone where the opposing forces cancelled each other out and where, at least in theory, the stress became zero? What if the crew cut holes in the steel beams in that area and then ran the sprinkler pipes through the openings? That would allow the ceiling to be hung directly below the ducts. He quickly did the calculation. Yes, a ceiling height of at least eight feet might just be maintained that way.

Slowly Cotham became aware of a vague but uncomfortable feeling that he was being watched. He looked up from the drawings. It had grown quite dark, and just outside the open window, apparently attracted by the light, a huge, lime green moth with round yellow wing markings was fluttering about. It was trying to get in. But there was something else too. The faint aroma of roses had been replaced by another fragrance. What was it? Magnolias? That was odd; it was too early for magnolias to be in bloom. With a start he realized that he was not alone; someone was standing behind him looking over his shoulder.

"Burning the midnight oil again, I see. I'm impressed."

Cotham whirled around, momentarily losing his balance and almost teetering off the drafting stool. It was Lucretia Silvetti. "My God, Lucretia! How the hell did you get in here?" he gasped.

"I hope you don't mind my letting myself in, Ethan, but I have a little something for you. Tonight's a special occasion, or haven't you heard?" She reached into her large black canvas purse and retrieved a bottle of champagne.

He had to admit she looked striking. Her dark hair had been swept up. She wore a filmy green blouse beneath the tailored black suit, and her dark eyes regarded him frankly.

"Aren't you going to ask me to sit down? And perhaps you'd be a gentleman and pop this cork for me; I always manage to send it flying off in the wrong direction." Pulling up another drafting stool, she sat down a foot away from him and crossed her legs, rather slowly it seemed to Cotham, so that he received a fleeting glimpse of thigh beneath the short skirt. She was not wearing stockings.

She extracted two crystal glasses from the bag.

"Maybe you should tell me what's going on here, Lucretia. Did you fly in the open window like this luna moth?" The fabulous green creature had now found its way to the top of his drafting lamp where it sat motionless watching him through its bright black compound eyes. Its antennae quivered.

He was both annoyed and intrigued by the interruption, and it was with some relief that he put aside the shop drawings and examined the elegant label. It was a Moet Chandon. Lucretia smiled as he gently pried the cork loose. A deep thunk was followed by a hiss as he obediently filled both of the fluted glasses.

"You were quite the topic of discussion at the CSC Board meeting. I just came from there and thought you might be interested in hearing about it first hand. I'm sure you'll be getting an official call from Nikos in the morning."

Cotham raised an eyebrow but said nothing.

"Have you ever met Henry Roper? Well, he really is the most charming man. I was expecting some egotistical intellectual, but he was gentle and polite, quite professorial. His buildings are so crisp and elegant that I was surprised to see that his suit was rumpled, and his long white hair looked like he had just gotten out of bed. His old blue polka-dot bow tie looked as if he'd been wearing it every day for twenty years. I felt sorry for him until I looked closely at his eyes. I don't think I've ever seen eyes like that before. They were like lasers.

"We had all the competition boards set up on easels for him to inspect. Seth Gerber's, Richard Astor's, and, of course, yours. There were no names on any of them so he would have had no way of knowing whose entry he was looking at. He only had a few minutes to study each one, but he just plunged in, moving from one easel to the next very briskly like a general inspecting his troops. One would have thought he had already spent days studying them."

Cotham tried to look slightly bored hoping to conceal the fact that he was hanging on every word.

"One thing that impressed me was that he always had something good to say before he made any negative comments. He began with Gerber's. He remarked on its energy, how the building seemed to be reaching out toward the river. But then he said something about how it was perhaps too aggressive and lacked any sense of repose. He pointed out some features that he called 'trendy,' something about the use of the isosceles triangle in plan being a recent cliché. 'A little too cute,' he commented at one point.

"When he came to Astor's boards, he seemed to be impressed and immediately remarked on the beautifully colored renderings. 'Like something from the Ecole des Beaux-Arts,' I remember his saying. He went on to point out its symmetry and formality and compared it to some of McKim, Mead and White's work. But then he commented that it seemed to be a project from another time, as though Memphis had not changed since 1900. I think his phrase was 'the re-creation of a past that never was.'"

Cotham was momentarily startled. Hadn't he used a similar phrase in his speech before the Design Review Board? Perhaps he had heard it from Roper in the first place, and it had spontaneously spilled out of his memory banks. Did Lucretia have any idea about his past association with Roper?

"Then," she continued, "he asked rhetorically whether neoclassicism was an appropriate vocabulary for our time. He digressed a bit to talk about the 1893 Columbian Exposition in Chicago and the 'deathly purity' of the buildings. He cautioned Memphis about looking to the past to express its future.

"After he finished with Astor's entry, he came to yours. Shall I tell you what he had to say about it?" Lucretia paused and took a sip of champagne. "Ethan, I don't know how you work in this hot little office. Don't they provide any air conditioning?" She reached up and casually unfastened the top button of the translucent green blouse. From its perch on the drafting lamp, the luna moth eyed them.

"You know, Ethan, I don't think you realize that you are a very attractive man. You doubt yourself too much." She extended her hand and placed it over his. "And you have such long, thin fingers, the hands of an artist."

Lucretia turned and followed his gaze to a distant point somewhere beyond her left shoulder where the sketch of the Center for Southern Culture hung pinned to the wall.

"Ever the architect, I see," she sighed in resignation. "Very well. If I tell you what Roper said, what do I get in return?" The tone was both mocking and seductive.

Cotham thought for a moment. On one hand he was well aware that he was being manipulated. On the other, he very much wanted to hear the outcome of Roper's critique, and the process entailed in eliciting the information, while dangerous, was by no means entirely unpleasant.

He looked her in the eye with what he hoped was a rakish expression. "I promise I'll make it worth your while."

"You'd better," she replied.

"Roper stood looking at your drawings for a long time without saying a word. He examined the elevations and then walked back to the floor plans. He frowned and cleared his throat before he finally turned back to face us. We were all sitting around the conference table, and some of us were taking notes. I think he said, rather quietly, 'This submission is very good.' No, actually, now that I think about it, what he said was, 'This submission is in a different league from the others.' He said that while the other entries had merit, they lacked inner conviction and tended to play it safe. He mentioned 'boldness,' 'assurance,' and something about 'architectural vision.'

"He did say it was not perfect and that some of the spaces seemed rather hastily, almost sketchily, conceived as though the architect was impatient with the necessity of working out the merely functional details. But he assured us that these could easily be refined with more time. 'What I see here,' I think he said, 'is a statement about a city that draws spiritual life from its site on the banks of the greatest river on the continent. In the siting of these buildings, particularly in the orientation of their principal visual axis downstream, the natural and the man-made are unified.' He said your plans showed the kind of thinking about monumental architecture that has almost disappeared in our culture. That we are incapable of humbling ourselves in the presence of the natural world on the one hand or of celebrating our nobler instincts on the other, and so our cities are built in a spiritual vacuum dedicated only to the pursuit of money and convenience.

"In the end he said, and I think I remember his wording exactly, 'Ladies and gentlemen, I can say with conviction that you will be making a huge mistake if you do not select this project as the winner of your competition.'"

Cotham swallowed with an odd gurgle.

"After that the meeting wound up very quickly. Nikos Pappas made a last ditch attempt to gain support for Astor's scheme, but Roberta and I made it clear that we supported you. Then Judge Freeman and Professor Halliburton hopped on the bandwagon, repeating some of Roper's observations as though they had been the first to offer them. There was obviously no need for a vote, and it was agreed by consensus to reinstate you as our architect. No redesign will be required, and Nikos thinks that Roper's stamp of approval will satisfy the politicians. Nikos was dreading having to tell Astor, I suppose, and was also less than pleased that he had lost face by not having backed your scheme more enthusiastically. As a kind of concession prize, he suggested that Astor be named to the CSC Board, and everyone quickly agreed. It was a painless way to restore equilibrium. So, Ethan, my dear, let me be the first to congratulate you."

She reminded Cotham of some exotic raven perched there on the drafting stool, the shimmering black plumage relieved only by the green of the filmy blouse. There was a hypnotic quality in the way she looked at him. He was beginning to feel paralyzed, immobilized by those predatory dark eyes. Slowly she reached for another button of the blouse, and it fell partially open. In one fluid movement she slipped off the stool and her arms encircled his neck. The room was enveloped in the scent of magnolias, and the night seemed to stream through the open windows, wrapping him in a humid blanket. Out of the corner of his eye he glimpsed a blur of green and yellow as the moth took flight. Lucretia's lips grew closer as she pressed against him, and he felt his will power evaporating.

"Knock, knock. Mr. Ethan? Anybody still here? I hope that coffee pot is still on." The wizened janitor stood at the door surveying the office in obvious surprise. Lucretia hastily backed away.

"Uh, oh. Sorry, Mr. Ethan, I didn't know you had company. I'll be getting back down to check on those air conditioning repairs. Those monkeys had better be finishing up by now. It's been a long night—for some of us, anyhow."

They listened in silence as the shuffling footsteps faded down the stairwell. Lucretia smiled ruefully at him.

"Lucretia," he began lamely, "you know that I find you attractive, extremely attractive, but…."

There was passion in her dark eyes and something else as well. The spell was broken, but the game was not quite over yet.

"Ethan," she interrupted, "I do want to make one thing clear to you. I don't want to enmesh you in some clumsy, embarrassing relationship. I don't want to be tied down any more than you do. As far as I'm concerned, our little celebration of your success never happened. You can rely on my discretion. I promise."

He looked at her, feeling a mixture of gratitude and even affection, oddly mixed with a twinge of something more sinister. Whether it was regret that the moment had passed or self-reproach over his vulnerability to her carefully orchestrated advances, he was unable to sort out for the moment. He took her hand.

"Thank you, Lucretia, for bringing me the news about the competition. You've made my night, and in more ways than one."

"You're quite welcome, Ethan. There is one more little thing, though. I believe you promised you'd make the visit worth my while. In one sense you already have. But there's something else. I'm in the art business, and I've just spent an evening with an architect who may soon be justly famous as the designer of one of the most important new buildings in the country."

She pointed toward the wall over the drawing board at the smudged floor plan on yellow tracing paper secured by pushpins, rustling gently in the breeze. "I want to buy that charcoal sketch from you for our permanent collection."

"I'm sorry, Lucretia, but I really couldn't consider selling it." He saw the flash of disappointment in her eyes, but before she could reply he unpinned the sketch, carefully rolled it, and slipped a rubber band over the end. "But I will give it to you. Here, please accept it with my compliments. Perhaps it should even belong in your private collection."

Chapter Seventeen

Cotham felt a surge of pride as he leafed through the completed working drawings of the CSC, sheet after sheet of floor plans, sections, elevations, schedules, and details—all fully dimensioned and covered with abbreviations and symbols, the enigmatic runes of construction. They showed how to fit together the pieces of the building into a structure that would not collapse under its own weight or allow rainwater to leak onto the valuable artifacts preserved within its walls. An entire sheet was devoted to details showing the flashing of the masonry parapet walls. Another addressed light fixtures and electrical circuits with every switch and receptacle located. Still others bore diagrams of the steel columns and beams hidden in the walls, floors, and ceilings. There they would silently resist the inexorable tug of gravity, the unpredictable lateral loads imposed by the fierce winds that could sweep across the Mississippi River or perhaps the infinitely more sinister jolts of an unexpected earthquake.

In the Middle Ages the secrets of geometry and mathematics the plans contained would have been jealously guarded by the guild system. Today the computer held the key to their making. Now as then, however, it was the creative minds of the architect and engineer that encoded order, beauty, and meaning into what would otherwise be simply a set of technical instructions.

Six sheets of engineering drawings were devoted to the foundations alone. Prepared by August Hardegen, they showed the base isolation pads below grade upon which the concrete footings rested. Like great Teflon-coated frying pans they had been selected for their slippery surface. In the event of a quake the footings could slide back and forth across the surface of the pads, absorbing the punishing seismic shocks that would otherwise threaten to collapse the huge egg-shaped cage of steel that rested upon them.

The summer had developed into a frantic ordeal as Cotham and his staff, augmented by Tensing's Troopers, had labored to refine the schematic drawings into construction documents in which nothing could be left to the imagination. The organization of the effort had fallen to Paul Dole, who had risen to the occasion with stoicism and a Teutonic attention to detail. Dole had growled at his charges with increasing frequency as the seemingly endless effort dragged on. He had even cursed under his breath when he discovered that a detail had been incorrectly referenced to the wrong floor plan or that an intern had omitted one of the two hundred odd doors. It was the largest job any of them had ever undertaken, and now that summer was at an end the strain was showing.

Despite Dole's impatience, Cotham knew that the Troopers had performed heroically. He had cajoled them into giving up their summer vacations to labor in his little sweat shop, promising that under Dole's stern tutelage they would come away with an understanding of how to put a building together. Somehow they had seemed caught up in the romance of working fifty and sixty hour weeks that often extended late into the nights, only to be relieved by an occasional pizza break at the dilapidated deli at the corner of Main and Monroe.

When the evening's work was finally done, they would break out cold bottles of Rolling Rock beer from the office refrigerator. Some would lounge on top of the drawing tables. They would listen to Tensing tell stories of growing up in India, where he and his eight brothers and sisters slept on the roof, their only shelter a parasol of stars. With Rascal dozing under his desk, Paul would go on about his favorite art films from the fifties and sixties, waxing eloquently over Liv Ullmann in *Persona* or Marcello Mastroianni in *La Dolce Vita*. The young Troopers had heard of none of these; and it was doubtful they would ever see any for themselves, but they enjoyed listening to the normally phlegmatic Dole whose well-hidden artistic passions were revealed through his love of film.

Sometimes even Cotham would allow himself to be persuaded to talk of his navy days, which the Troopers saw as impossibly glamorous, although it was rare that he touched on his tour as captain of the swift boat in Vietnam. They listened as though he were describing the Trojan War, so distant was that awful time from their own. *Have they ever thought to connect that experience with my limp?* he wondered.

The ceremonial groundbreaking had been set for the week before Labor Day ten days away, although they were behind schedule; and the final cost estimate had not even been started. Cotham had insisted that the structural drawings be complete before releasing the documents to the estimators. He was increasingly concerned about the cost of Hardegen's exotic seismic design and well aware that the usual rules of thumb were likely to prove useless in determining the cost of such a unique approach. For an accurate determination of costs a full "takeoff" would be required, pricing each component individually. This could only be done using a complete set of structural drawings.

The $30 million budget sounded generous enough until one divided it by the area of the building. That yielded a cost of $250 per square foot, an adequate but far from luxurious target for a high-quality civic project with a unique set of requirements and very few repetitive elements. Unlike an office building in which every floor was virtually identical, the CSC was comprised of a series of one-of-a-kind spaces. This, combined with the special construction demands that resulted from its seismic design and its riverfront site where space for construction staging was severely limited, could well result in a cost that exceeded the budget.

It was a difficult dilemma. Ordinarily a client established the budget with the architect's input before the building was designed. The probable cost was based on research into the cost of similar projects, adjusted for the local economy. But there were few valid prototypes for the CSC and none that had been built to withstand a cataclysmic earthquake. The architect could only deal with the resulting unknowns by advising the client to factor a contingency into the budget in hopes that it would prove adequate for the thousands of decisions that were as yet unmade. Inexperienced clients often resisted this, and many thought that planning a building should be like shopping for a new car. One simply decided on the make and model and added the cost of the optional accessories to the base price. The architect had only to design and deliver the final product with the pre-established price tag. There was only one problem. This particular building on this site with these special requirements had never been built before and would never be duplicated. There was no past history on which to base estimates and only approximations of the individual components of labor and material.

———————

Cotham, attired in his rumpled seersucker suit and polka dot bow tie, surveyed the crowd of Center for Southern Culture Board members and dignitaries assembled on the gaily festooned dais that had been hastily constructed for the groundbreaking ceremony at the foot of Beale Street overlooking the river. Seated to his left was Pallie, Cotham's guest, who was whispering something to Roberta Quonset. Next to Roberta sat Thurston, sunburned from yesterday's exhibition football game between the University of Memphis Tigers and the Mississippi State Bulldogs. To Thurston's left was Mayor Ramos Sanchez, Memphis' first Hispanic chief executive. A Democrat and a product of the San Antonio housing projects, he was now in his third term. Nikos Pappas had been strategically placed between Mayor Sanchez and the Republican mayor of Shelby County, Billy Earl Tyler. Sanchez wore a dark green Armani suit, while Tyler was dressed in banker's blue pinstripes. The contrast between the wardrobes of the progressive city mayor and the conservative county mayor symbolized to Cotham the differences in the two men. The thinly veiled animosity that characterized their personal relationship seemed to mirror the racial and economic polarization that so often pitted the inner city against the suburbs.

On Cotham's right sat Professor Diehl Halliburton followed by Judge Leroy D'Aloisious Freeman, both members of the competition jury. Next came Richard Astor, the newest member of the Board. Cotham wondered if Astor would speak to him should their paths cross. Was Astor making a point of looking straight ahead toward the river rather than turning in Cotham's direction?

Next to Astor sat the only person Cotham did not recognize, a small middle-aged man dressed in an ill-fitting brown suit. Astor turned and said something to the man who nodded. Finally, at the end of the row vested in full ecclesiastical splendor including cape and miter, the admirable profile of his aquiline nose presented to Cotham, sat white-haired Bishop Leonidas Crenshaw of the Church of God in Christ, a major backer of the ecumenical CSC.

The ceremony was opened by the Germantown High School Glee Club. Two dozen fresh-faced teenagers attired in navy blue blazers, white shirts, and khaki trousers and skirts, mounted the dais and performed a complex arrangement of *The Battle Hymn of the Republic*. Mayor Sanchez sat with his eyes closed, and it was difficult to tell whether he was praying or napping. Next came the invocation delivered by Brother Amherst Edwards, Pastor of Greater Hernando Community Fellowship, a forty-acre megachurch complex on Interstate 55, ten miles south of the Mississippi state line. The menacing, over-scaled colossus was known by local wags as "Six Flags Over Jesus."

"Lord, we just ask you to help heal this troubled city and this troubled land. And we beseech you to just show us the way of Jesus and His Merciful Goodness. And Lord, we just want to thank you for this fine new building we are startin' here today...."

At last the rambling prayer drew to a close. With military precision the Mount Moriah Tabernacle Full Gospel choir, resplendent in gold robes, stormed the dais like an army of the Lord, occupying the high ground and ready to do battle with the forces of darkness. The choir began slowly with a dignified rendition of *Oh, for a Closer*

Walk with Thee. Suddenly the staccato roll of a drum broke into the stately hymn. A bass electric guitar pounced on the syncopated drumbeat. The dais vibrated as the choir plunged into a spiritual, clapping, swaying and weaving in unison.

Wade in the water
Wade in the water, children
Wade in the water
God's a-going to trouble the water.

Fifty yards beyond, the Mississippi churned past, and it seemed that at any moment the thick brown waves might part like the Red Sea itself. Suddenly Mayor Sanchez was on his feet, seemingly awakened by the hubbub, clapping and grinning. Not to be outdone, Mayor Tyler and the other dignitaries stood as well. The assembled crowd of perhaps a hundred began to join in; and soon the entire throng, including the Bishop and the Germantown Glee Club, were clapping and swaying in unison on the banks of the mighty river beneath the merciless sun of the last days of summer.

The honor of the actual groundbreaking had fallen to Mayor Tyler. Carrying a gold-painted shovel, he made his way with great solemnity down the steps to a patch of crabgrass cleared in the midst of the audience. Placing a foot on the blade, he attempted to push the shovel into the earth, hard-packed after a summer of near-drought across the Mid-South.

"Hell, this ground is hard as a rock!" The angry voice boomed out over the huge loudspeakers that flanked the dais. The crowd tittered with embarrassment. The mayor, whose face suddenly resembled the purple of the bishop's cape, clutched the lapel microphone he wore. "Why didn't somebody tell me this damn thing was on?" he exclaimed, his voice exploding over the gathering, this time provoking gales of unrestrained laughter.

Cotham turned to Pallie, grinning. But her expression brought him up short. She had grown pale, gazing silently, a look of distant horror in her eyes, at the pathetic little divot the bishop had at last managed to excavate with his golden shovel. In desperation she grasped his wrist so tightly that her nails felt like the claws of a terrified animal.

"What is it?" he asked in alarm unable to detect anything amiss. The crowd was still smiling, and the mayor had even joined in, good-naturedly acknowledging his gaffe. Pallie was silent and continued to stare at the little hole in the ground. He suddenly realized that she was caught in the grips of a vision and could neither hear him nor see the smiling crowd. Then he felt her body go limp as though the thing that held her enthralled had passed, and with his help she sagged into her chair.

Cotham heard his name called over the loudspeaker. Nikos Pappas, a bright red carnation in his lapel, had assumed the podium and was smiling beatifically in his direction. Cotham was being introduced as the architect of the new Center for Southern Culture, the winner of a "tightly contested" competition, whose "visionary" plans had captured the imagination of the jury. He smiled and nodded, but Pappas was already moving ahead with his list of introductions. Next to him, Pallie was stirring and looking around, disoriented as though she had just awakened from a drugged sleep.

"A project of this magnitude and complexity," Pappas was saying, "brings special challenges during the construction process. The Board is aware of its responsibility to ensure that this extraordinary under-taking proceeds in an orderly fashion and that it will be completed on time and on budget. So it also gives me pleasure to introduce the newest member of our design and construction team, Colonel Sidney Sigler of St. Louis, who will serve as our construction manager."

As Pappas looked toward the end of the row of dignitaries, the man in the brown suit next to Astor rose and moved briskly to the podium. Pappas appeared surprised. The others he had introduced had kept their seat, but he graciously stepped aside to allow Sigler to approach.

"Thank you, Mr. Pappas," he said, standing slightly on tiptoe in order to reach the microphone. "All of us at Sigler Associates are honored to be a part of this outstanding project that will mean so much to the City of Memphis. A significant challenge lies ahead of us. We have an extremely tight budget and schedule. The architec-tural drawings, as imaginative as they are in this case, will require interpretation, and there may even be opportunities for cost savings not previously identified. These matters are our job. My associates and I thank Mr. Pappas and the Board for their confidence. Now that ground has been so ably broken for us by Mayor Tyler," he paused for a few chuckles from the audience, "we will continue the job using slightly heavier equipment...."

"Er, thank you, Colonel," interposed Pappas, stepping forward at Sigler's elbow, "We are all anxious to get under way, I know. And now, it is my pleasure to introduce our other guests of honor."

Cotham sat immobile, confused and taken aback, momentarily forgetting Pallie, whose grip on his arm had lessened. A construc-tion manager? It was the first he had heard of any such arrangement. Who was this Sigler anyway? Did Pappas say St. Louis? What did this mean for his role as architect? And what about the man's allusions to the drawings requiring interpretation and opportunities for cost savings not previously identified? Sigler had reluctantly taken his seat, and Astor was smiling and saying something apparently of a congratulatory nature to him.

Cotham looked more closely. Sigler was perhaps fifty, thin and wiry in build, with gray hair cropped in a military-style buzz cut. His brown shoes were perfectly shined, but his suit was cheap, judging from the shine of the cloth. His tie bore an unpleasantly realistic floral pattern. His face was tanned, and the eyes, although intelligent, were somewhat closely spaced. The overall impression was of a rather bright rodent, a squirrel, perhaps.

The proceedings having at last reached their conclusion, the honored guests stood and began to file toward the steps. Cotham moved with them, Pallie clinging to his arm. Several, including Mayor Sanchez, spoke cordially to him, "Beautiful plans, Ethan, we can't wait to see the work get started." Others acknowledged him with a friendly nod from further away. Once he almost caught Astor's eye, but Astor looked away and disappeared into a mass of gold choir robes.

"Well, Pallie, I'd have thought Ethan should have given the speech, wouldn't you?" They turned to see Lucretia Silvetti, stunning in a black straw hat with an enormous brim. "He's certainly the one who could tell this crowd a thing or two about this project! Who was that peculiar little man anyway?" She had addressed Pallie, but it was Cotham whom she fixed with her dark eyes. It was the first time he had seen her since her nocturnal visit to his office.

Pallie smiled weakly and murmured some pleasantry, still holding Cotham's arm. "Pallie's feeling a little under the weather,

Lucretia. I think I'd better find her some shade."

"Certainly. I do hope you feel better, Pallie. Perhaps we should have lunch some day. I've missed seeing you at the museum lately." Lucretia smiled sweetly as they moved away across the dusty field toward the impromptu parking area cordoned off for the ground-breaking.

"Let's wait a moment, Ethan," said Pallie, breaking her silence at last, "Could we walk over by the riverbank?"

Despite the ninety-degree temperature, a refreshing layer of cool air hovered over the red clay bank where they stood looking down into the thick sepia froth. "What is it, Pallie?" he asked gently, hugging her in what he hoped was a reassuring manner. "I know you saw something back there that nobody else could see."

"I'm afraid to tell you, Ethan. It's probably silly, anyway. Too much sun and one too many glasses of wine last night. I didn't sleep well, and I think I must be exhausted. It was nice of Nikos to acknowledge you as the architect. Who was the last client to do that?"

"Don't try to change the subject. I know that whatever it was, it wasn't simple indigestion. Who knows whether there's anything to this second sight or whatever you call it, but you'll probably feel better if you don't keep it bottled up."

"Oh, Ethan, it was so quick, I hardly remember myself. But I was looking out over the river, watching the poor mayor trying to turn up the ground. Suddenly things went black for just a moment. Then I could see again, but everything had taken on a red cast as though a dust storm had coated the whole landscape with a layer of silt. The sun had turned red; and when I looked at the river, it was red too. Out in the river were great, jagged black shapes being swept downstream. And around them were flecks of silver, like shiny leaves floating in the red water."

They were both silent for a moment. When he looked down at her, he saw that she was weeping.

Chapter Eighteen

"Sigler Associates," proclaimed the firm profile on its website, "was created in 1990 by Lieutenant Colonel Sidney Sigler, U. S. Army (Ret.), in order to provide quality consulting Engineering and Construction Management services to an international clientele. Colonel Sigler is a graduate of The Citadel in Charleston, SC. After a distinguished career highlighted by service in Vietnam where he was awarded the Bronze Star, Colonel Sigler decided to turn his experience gained in the U.S. Army Engineers to service in the private sector.

"As an advisor to the State of Kuwait he was instrumental in rebuilding that nation's ravaged infrastructure following the first Gulf War. Since returning home to his native St. Louis, Colonel Sigler has served as Construction Manager for a number of significant projects, including additions to casinos in Tunica, Mississippi, and Atlantic City, New Jersey, as well as new Wal-Mart stores in Maryland and Arkansas.

"Sigler Associates pledges to complete projects on time and on budget, serving as the Owner's Representative and managing the work of architects, engineers, and general contractors to assure clients of construction quality and maximum value for each construction dollar."

Cotham had read enough. He snapped his laptop closed and dialed the number for Pappas Investment Corporation. The wait was short.

"Ethan, good morning," Pappas greeted him cheerfully. "I was hoping you'd call. I thought the groundbreaking was a huge success, didn't you? I just finished reading the coverage in *The Commercial Appeal*. Have you seen it yet? They give you a nice mention, and thankfully there's no reference to the mayor's excavation skills."

"Yes, Nikos," Cotham replied, trying to keep the irritation out of his voice, "I thought it went very well. But who the hell is this Sigler character, and why was I not told you were planning to hire a construction manager?"

"Ah, Sigler...I apologize, Ethan. I truly meant to bring this up with you before. But with all the time I've had to spend organizing the ceremony and making sure the funding is in place and that our Board is fully supportive of the decision to move into construction, I just didn't get around to it.

"There is no cause for alarm, I assure you. The Board has formed a new construction task force to oversee the details of the project, and it met for the first time last week. We've asked Richard Astor to chair the group, and he recommended the construction manager approach. We all agreed that given the tight budget it makes sense. In fact, Astor assures me that it will actually make your job easier. You won't have to worry about the contractor's payments, change orders, or time schedule. Sigler will take charge of all that, and you'll be freed up to pay more attention to maintaining the quality of the design."

"Nikos, I must point out that our agreement makes no mention of the CM approach. This will require a fundamental change in our working relationship. Does your task force understand that our contract calls for us to act as your representative and to carry out the other traditional duties of the architect? Do they understand that without the power to approve the contractor's draws we, in effect, lose control over the quality of the work?"

"I really don't think it's as bad as all that," replied Pappas soothingly. "We will continue to rely upon your advice and judgment. By the way, Ethan, I've been looking over this new cost estimate you've submitted. Do you really think it will take $30 million to build this project?"

"Well, as you know, Nikos, I did not put the estimate together myself," Cotham replied. Years of experience in attempting to predict the outcome of bids had long ago convinced Cotham that it was an exercise in soothsaying best delegated to specialists. "We hired an independent estimator, a firm I've worked with many times before. But I believe it's a fair number."

"Then you'll be interested to hear," continued Pappas, "that Sigler Associates has proposed a contract for only $27.5 million. Plus they say they can do the work in fifteen months instead of the eighteen you've been suggesting."

"That's a very good price and a very fast pace, Nikos. I assume that he proposes to build from the plans as drawn?"

"To be honest, I've not discussed that with him. We're leaving a lot of the technical details to Richard Astor. You see, Ethan, we're not construction experts, and quite frankly some of the board members are concerned that a $30 million project is quite large for an office the size of yours. Others are concerned about the resources it will take to oversee fifteen to eighteen months of construction. We feel that the experience and resources of a large firm like Sigler's will be as much a help to you as to us. We've asked our attorney to draw up a short amendment to your contract. I'll be sending a copy over to you this afternoon as a matter of fact."

"And what is in this amendment, if I may I ask?"

"Oh, just the usual boilerplate clarifying the relationship between the CM and the architect. We'll be looking to Sigler Associates to review the plans and then give us a guaranteed maximum price for the work and a firm time schedule. Look it over, Ethan, I'm sure you won't have a problem with it. But let me be clear; the Board has made up its mind that this is in the best interest of the project. Now, if you'll excuse me, I've got a long distance call holding. Let's get together to talk about this in more detail in the next day or so. In the meantime I'll send you the papers to look over. Goodbye, Ethan."

———

Cotham detested meetings with lawyers; but if there were no way he could avoid one, he wanted Llewellyn Craig at his side. In the one and only lawsuit Cotham had ever had to file against a client, Craig had decimated the opposition through his mastery of the intricacies of the AIA contract.

He looked around the table in the now familiar main conference room of Pappas Investment Corporation. Nikos Pappas was seated at the head of the table. Across from Cotham and Craig sat Sigler, tanned and wiry, with a fresh crew cut. Next to him Bethel Malone, the Pappas attorney, a gigantic man in a rumpled suit and braces with a huge flowery silk handkerchief overflowing his breast pocket, dwarfed the diminutive construction manager. At the opposite end sat Richard Astor. In his gray Italian suit and Hermès tie he was the picture of elegance.

Spread out on the table before them lay multiple copies of the contracts, some with passages highlighted in yellow. Judging from these and the half-filled porcelain coffee cups around the table, Cotham had the distinct impression that they were joining a meeting that had begun before their arrival.

Cotham was introduced to Sigler as he and Craig were ushered in. Sigler's handshake was firm enough; but when Cotham instinctively attempted to look him in the eye, Sigler had looked slightly askance toward the vicinity of Cotham's right ear.

"Gentlemen," Malone began, glancing across the table, "let's see if this dog won't hunt. You've had an opportunity to review the proposed agreement between Pappas Investments and Sigler Associates, as well as the changes to the contract between Pappas and Mr. Cotham. I'm suggesting these changes be made to provide for Colonel Sigler's role as construction manager.

"Quite simply, what we are suggesting is that Colonel Sigler's firm assume some of the tasks previously assigned to Mr. Cotham with respect to monitoring the quality of the work. In addition, Sigler will be responsible for coordination of the work, completion of the job on schedule, and guaranteeing to the owner that the cost will not exceed the maximum price. That's it in a nutshell. What do you think?"

Craig shuffled through his papers for a moment before removing his horned rim reading glasses and addressing Malone. "Bethel, Mr. Cotham is, I believe, quite willing to have certain authority delegated to a construction manager, with no change in his fee, of course, and with the understanding that the project will be built as designed by

Mr. Cotham's firm. In addition, it will need to be clearly understood that Mr. Cotham can assume no liability for any errors or omissions by Colonel Sigler's firm."

"That would seem fair," replied Malone. "Anything else we should consider?"

"Well, there is, of course, the issue of the value engineering," spoke up Astor from the end of the table. "Colonel Sigler and I have reviewed the plans rather closely and have developed a list of possible changes in the documents. We do not believe these have any significant impact on the design, but in the aggregate they appear to save as much as $2.5 million. In fact, Colonel Sigler has already agreed to guarantee a price of about $27.5 million and to begin construction within a week of signing his contract."

So, thought Cotham, *the changes have come from my colleague, Astor.* "And may I be allowed to see this list?" Cotham asked, eyeing Pappas.

"Certainly, Ethan," Pappas replied, smiling warmly, "we not only want you to see it; we value your input. Let me assure you that no one is trying to alter your design in any significant way."

"It could be that the word 'significant' is significant in itself," observed Craig dryly. "Perhaps you have a copy of this list with you?"

"Gentlemen, perhaps I can save us all some time," spoke up Sigler. His voice was surprisingly high-pitched, and he spoke with the earthy accent Cotham identified with the blue-collar areas of Midwestern cities. "The list includes a number of relatively minor suggestions, such as adding additional approved products to the specifications, the use of PVC instead of cast iron piping, a different masonry manufacturer who offers a brick that is virtually identical to Mr. Cotham's selection, and so forth. The lion's share of the potential savings, however, is in a single area.

"We believe that the building is over-designed from a seismic viewpoint. There has not been a major earthquake in the Memphis area in over two hundred years, and my research indicates that geologists are by no means in agreement as to the level of risk that exists. If Mr. Cotham's special base isolation pads were removed from the foundation design, I believe we could be talking about a cost reduction of a million dollars. That, combined with certain other associated changes, accounts for most of the $2.5 million we could save."

"And what kind of 'associated changes' might you be referring to?" Cotham asked, unable to suppress the acidity in his voice. He again attempted eye-contact with Sigler, who instead fixed his gaze at a point on the wall over Cotham's shoulder. Somehow he doubted that Sigler was admiring the Corot that hung there.

"We believe that the egg-shaped main auditorium space is unduly expensive," said Astor. "If this room could be reshaped to a more conventional form such as a rectangle, the framing, the finishes, the seating layout, virtually everything, becomes much more regular and therefore more economical."

"Construction time would be reduced as well," piped up Sigler.

Cotham thought of Mary Magdalene holding the red egg and confronting the emperor of the Roman Empire. "Gentlemen, it appears that before this conversation proceeds further we must have an understanding." He looked around the table before focusing on Astor. "I am not opposed to finding more cost-effective ways to build this project, and I welcome Colonel Sigler's input. I know that he is accustomed to building other projects, such as shopping centers and department stores, where cost is the primary consideration. That is not necessarily the case here though. And we are not going to redesign this project. We will not change the shape of the most important space in the entire complex.

"This room is not shaped like an egg because I'm partial to poultry. It has nothing to do with my personal preferences. The form is inherent in the desire to make a room that embraces the audience and the performers while at the same time providing resistance to seismic forces. Its unique geometry grows out of these requirements and has nothing to do with taste. We are not going to redesign it. Do I make myself clear?"

The group was silent for a moment. Sigler, his eyes narrowed to slits, shot a surreptitious glance toward Astor's end of the table before turning toward Cotham.

"Really, Mr. Cotham," Sigler said with no hint of emotion, "there's no need to react defensively. We're all on the same side here. We are simply trying to point out to the owner that there may be some cost savings that haven't been identified so far and that should be considered."

"Then let's stop wasting time and move on to the next item on your list," retorted Cotham.

"Very well," replied Sigler. "As I mentioned, we feel that the base isolation pads may not be necessary. They are an extremely expensive part of the design. No other buildings in Memphis, as far as I am aware, are constructed using this approach. These structures are more common to the West Coast or Japan where experience, not theory, demonstrates the seismic risks to be higher. Your Dr. Hardegen is a well-known engineer, Mr. Cotham, but he has a reputation as a theoretician, an Ivy League professor. Has he built anything in this area before?"

"I'm not here to defend my engineering consultants, Colonel Sigler. I chose Hardegen for precisely the reason you mention. Here in the vicinity of the New Madrid Fault we are dealing with a risk that, thank God, has not been demonstrated by experience in modern times. That does not mean there is no risk. Hardegen is on the cutting edge of seismic design theory, and his solutions are sound. He has worked as the engineer on major projects in the areas you mention for architects like Henry Roper, who only use the best consultants." At the mention of Roper's name, Cotham noticed a shadow cross Astor's face. "I will agree to remove the base isolators only if I'm instructed to do so directly by the owner."

"And in that event," Craig interjected, "we would need full indemnification holding the architect and consultants harmless for any seismic-related damages. That would presumably transfer the liability to Sigler Associates since the idea is yours, Colonel. Would that be agreeable?" In his velvet-smooth voice Craig might have been asking Sigler to pass the cucumber sandwiches.

"Lew, we're getting a bit off the subject here, don't you think?" Bethel Malone had been listening impassively, but at the mention of the word "liability" he seemed to stir like a dozing crocodile. "I'm sure the owner is going to need some time to consider the cost-benefit relationships surrounding these, what do you call them, base plates. In the meantime, why don't we just move on down the value-engineering list? Didn't I hear something earlier, Colonel, about the possibility of changing the color of the brick slightly?"

An hour later they had agreed to a dozen minor changes, totaling a half-million dollars or so. Having already chosen his battles,

Cotham had made an effort to adopt a conciliatory attitude regarding other changes that would have little effect on his vision for the building. The brick coloration would now have more orange and although he had spent considerable time at the masonry supplier's warehouse before finding exactly the right shade of cherry red, he decided not to protest. And he had voiced no objections when Sigler proposed the listing of three additional manufacturers who were to be allowed to bid on hardware, plus an additional bidder for glass.

More significantly, a closer examination of Sigler's costs had turned up an interesting item, previously overlooked, in the form of a $1 million contingency. Sigler had explained that because the proposed contract was capped by a guaranteed maximum price, the contingency was needed as protection against unexpected increases in the cost of labor and materials. Cotham had been tempted to add, "or a shoddy estimate," but had managed to hold his tongue. In the end, Nikos Pappas ended his long silence and put his foot down.

"Colonel Sigler," Pappas had intoned solemnly, "we invited your firm to make a proposal for the construction management of this project on the recommendation of Mr. Astor based on your assurances of bringing in the CSC on time and on budget. We don't have $30 million to spend, and your confidence that you could build it for $27.5 million in fifteen months was naturally very attractive to us. But we do not intend to redesign the project at this late date. We made it clear to the architects from the first that seismic design was an underlying practical and philosophical concern. In response, Mr. Cotham engaged one of the foremost experts in the world to serve as his structural consultant. I agree with him that we should not back away from a concept that has been used successfully in other parts of the world where earthquakes are a concern.

"These minor value-engineering adjustments are all well and good. No one seems to have any problem with them, and they will save us some money. But if you cannot guarantee that you can build this project as designed for the amount you have quoted, then I will recommend that we scrap this CM approach and put the whole project out to bid instead. I have a feeling that there are some other big firms out there who would jump at the chance to build our project for $27.5 million or maybe even less."

Sigler was scribbling on a yellow legal pad. Then he tapped a long series of numbers into his pocket calculator. Finally he looked up and glanced around the table.

"Very well, Mr. Pappas. If you will sign the contract we've submitted, and if we can begin work immediately incorporating the other value-engineering items we've just identified, we have a deal."

"Including the full seismic design and with no changes in the design of the auditorium?" asked Pappas.

"Yes. We'll find a way to include those without an increase in the cost."

———

Craig waved Cotham to a seat at his regularly reserved table near the rear of the Little Tea Shop on Monroe. Cotham ordered a plate of turnip greens while Craig settled on the chicken salad and tomato aspic. Both orders arrived with huge baskets of hot cornbread, the best in the city. Around them in the intimate little restaurant huddled prominent lawyers, several war-horses from the large bank around the corner, and the remains of the old Front Street cotton establishment. Coriolanus Godshaw, a former four-term mayor and now a circuit court judge, presided over his table of six, including two city councilmen and a Downtown developer. Here and there, the pastels of seersuckers, pincords, and poplins blossomed like pale flowers amidst the solemn field of gray and navy bankers' garb. A stranger would have been mystified at the high-spirited greetings and gossip freely traded from one table to the next.

"I suppose," began Cotham, speaking quietly, "I should be relieved that Pappas finally drew the line with Sigler and Astor. He could have just as easily told us to spend the next six months redesigning. But even though I'm ready to get started on construction, I have to tell you, Lew, I'm feeling uneasy about it. "

"You're going to have to watch Sigler," replied Craig. "Pappas put him in a difficult position. He has agreed to build this project for less than the budget but without being allowed to remove all your special seismic features or reshape your main auditorium. I'll be surprised if he doesn't look for some way to wiggle out of that box. Otherwise he could stand to lose a lot of money if the cost runs over his guaranteed maximum price."

"You're right, Lew. And it doesn't make me feel any better that he's apparently got Astor in his court. There's no love lost between Astor and me, and I feel sure Astor's been active behind the scenes. First, this Sigler appears out of nowhere, and then the two of them begin suggesting that we cut the heart out of the design. Nothing, of course, would please Astor more that seeing our concept watered down."

"Except, perhaps, seeing it not get built at all," observed Craig, thoughtfully buttering a piece of cornbread.

"You know, Lew, what I like about you is your total lack of cynicism. You always look on the bright side.

"By the way, I've been meaning to ask you about an amazing coincidence."

"And what would that be?" asked Craig, innocently.

"The fact that one night you ask me to name the best architects in the world and three days later I hear that one of them, Henry Roper, is coming to town to meet with the CSC Board about my project. Doesn't that strike you as odd? Then add to that the fact that Lucretia Silvetti drops in on me out of the blue to tell me about it."

"And you're still alive to tell the tale? She's a man-eater, you know."

"Didn't you and Lucretia have something going a couple of years ago?" Cotham's question was purely rhetorical; he was well aware that the affair had nearly cost Craig his marriage.

"Let's just say that Lucretia and I reached an understanding," Craig replied. "She watches my back, and I feed her a dainty morsel from time to time. We belong to a little mutual admiration society, a purely pragmatic, symbiotic arrangement, highly civilized and fairly effective."

Chapter Nineteen

The Quonsets' gardener had arranged the flowers carefully with a studied lack of symmetry, artfully alternating fall colors of gold, bronze, and red in the manicured border. He was intent on his work and only looked up at the last moment to the sound of crunching gravel as the old Rover rattled past along the gracefully curving driveway and pulled up to the front porch. He was unused to seeing anything but the latest model Lexus or BMW arrive at the home of his affluent employer and watched with some curiosity as the man with the scarred face and hawkish nose emerged and stood for a moment appraising the French Provincial architecture. The gardener noticed that he shook his head slightly before he headed for the front door, and that despite his erect bearing he limped slightly.

The morning was still slightly chilly even though the clear sky promised temperatures climbing into the eighties later in the day. Roberta Quonset wore a tennis warm-up suit. She ushered Cotham through the entry hall into the den where a bar made from a red London telephone call box stood in the corner. Beyond the den a screened porch festooned with hanging ferns overlooked an immaculate lawn carpeted in zoysia grass. On the wall he noticed the Quonset coat of arms.

Next to the coat of arms hung a black and white photograph of a house, and Cotham paused to look more closely. It appeared to be a two-story wood-frame farmhouse sited in a grove of trees. From the narrow width of the siding and the chaste detailing of the taut clapboard skin, he guessed that it dated to the mid-nineteenth century. A wide porch wrapped across the front and around the side. He found the austere beauty of the proportions and the utter lack of pretension compelling.

"That's our old family place in Smith County near Nashville," explained Roberta. It was torn down about ten years ago by a developer, and I hear there's a subdivision there now. My grandfather grew up in that house. It was built by his grandfather who was one of the first pioneers to settle in Middle Tennessee."

An elderly black woman dressed in a light gray uniform served coffee on a silver tray. The coffee was weak for Cotham's taste.

"I do appreciate your driving all the way out to East Memphis, Ethan. I know how you feel about leaving your beloved Midtown. When was the last time you ventured beyond the Parkways, anyhow?"

Cotham smiled. "I expect it was the last time I met with our friend Nikos Pappas about the Center for Southern Culture. I'll go most anywhere for an interesting project."

"I expect you're awfully busy on the CSC. I was so happy to get all that unpleasant design review behind us. We are all excited to be moving ahead with construction at last."

"And I want you to know, Roberta, that I appreciate your support. I understand from Lucretia that you backed me at that board meeting when my fate hung in the balance."

"It's Lucretia you should thank, you know. After Henry Roper's critique it was she who really picked up on his comments and stood up to Nikos. Frankly I was shocked. I never thought of Lucretia as the type to take a stand on principle."

Was there a touch of irony in Roberta's tone? Cotham felt it wise to turn the conversation in another direction. "How's the design for your new house at BluffTown coming along?"

"Actually," Roberta replied," that's why I asked you to drop by." Her demeanor was suddenly more somber. "It's not moving ahead like we had hoped. We've met with Richard Astor several times and he keeps promising to show us some ideas, but so far we've seen nothing. He seems to be very busy, and the last couple of times I've called he's been in meetings. When the call is returned, it's not Richard, but one of his young assistants. Frankly, Ethan, I don't think we made a very good decision to hire him. I had already begun to suspect it, but after the disgraceful way he allowed you to be treated at that Design Review meeting, I really began to have doubts.

"You know, I was very impressed by the way you stood up to them, although there was nothing I could do at the time. Richard has the staff and the rest of the committee in his vest pocket. I'm sure it's no secret to you that you made some enemies on the Design Review Board; they are used to doing the lecturing, not being on the receiving end. But then you may have made a friend or two as well.

"That brings me to the reason for this meeting. We've sent Richard a check along with a note telling him we want to engage someone else. Thurston and I have been talking, and we'd like to ask you to design our new home after all. I wouldn't blame you if you turned us down, but Richard is just too busy and too full of himself. Besides, we owe you a debt. You'll never know how much it meant to us the way you rescued Thurston from that ridiculous Boll Weevil fire truck. His career at the bank could have been ruined if it had gotten out that he was the driver. We should have come to you in the first place, and I do hope you'll consider being our architect."

———————

The air was choked with reddish dust and diesel fumes. Two yellow Caterpillar dozers lumbered about the yawning excavation like huge mutant ants in a subterranean hive. Cotham was suddenly reminded of an old sci-fi movie, *Them,* that as a ten year old had given him nightmares for months afterwards.

A doublewide job trailer stood next to the growing pit, its exterior emblazoned with "Sigler Associates" in three-foot high letters, the dot over the first "i" made using a small silver oak leaf, the badge of rank of a Lieutenant Colonel. Along the bank had been erected a corrugated steel cofferdam reinforced with heavy timbers to ensure that the deepening cavern remained free of water as the ever-fluctuating river rose and fell. Ton after ton of silt had been removed already, undoing in tiny measure a million years of inexorable efforts by the river to relocate substantial portions of Missouri, Illinois, and Iowa downstream to Tennessee. The Mississippi riverfront had once served as Memphis' city dump, and in the first days of digging they had encountered several strata of passing archeological interest. These consisted of the detritus of several centuries, including hundreds of hand-blown patent medicine bottles, automobile tires, a couple of rusted pistols, and countless shards of pottery and china. There was even the hulk of a steamboat, the name *Miss Matilda* etched into the encrusted brass of the bell that had once hung on the bridge. A few feet deeper in the muck had been found a Civil War canon ball and innumerable granite stones brought as ballast aboard the steamboats that docked in Memphis only to be pitched overboard as they took on the compensating weight of cotton bales. Deeper still had been encountered a layer of Chickasaw and Choctaw pottery fragments interspersed by a few arrowheads.

The University of Memphis' Archeology Department had insisted that all artifacts, no matter how commonplace, be meticulously retrieved and catalogued. This process, however, had not been factored into the elaborate critical path schedule that plastered the walls inside the trailer.

As a consequence of the archaeological survey, the work was already a month behind schedule, even though only six weeks had passed since the groundbreaking ceremony. Since it was possible that an early onset of winter rains and freezing temperatures could delay the installation of the footings until spring, it was critical that this part of the work be completed before Thanksgiving. Sigler had fumed and ranted to no avail as day after day the U. of M. graduate students in their rubber boots and baseball caps waded about amidst his excavations. With their sieves, cameras, and notebooks, they paused frequently to pry some piece of nineteenth century household ephemera from the silt. A China cup or broken bottle would be handled as gingerly as though it were a fabulous jade scarab embedded in the dust of the Valley of the Kings. At last it appeared that the sedimentary layers of silt and clay had been penetrated, giving way to a thick, featureless, primeval ooze, silent and unmarred by all traces of human habitation.

The construction crew had been doubled up to expedite excavation for the footings, and work was proceeding from dawn until dusk six days a week in a frenzied attempt to catch up. Sigler himself was spending more and more time on the site, and now Cotham spotted him standing at the edge of the pit in a white hard hat, gesticulating to the superintendent. Cotham hung back a few feet so as not to interrupt what was obviously a tirade. From where he stood he could see the rush of crimson spreading up Sigler's neck from below the collar of his shirt until it reached his hairline. It continued to rise like a column of mercury on a morning in August, still visible beneath the man's crew cut until it was enveloped beneath his helmet. On the back of the hard hat was stenciled "The Colonel."

"...and you tell those sonsabitches that if they don't have that steel on the site by 0800 tomorrow I'll fire their asses. Do they think that just because they're the only suppliers in town I won't do it? By God, I've got ten others I can call up at the drop of a frigging hat!"

"Yessir, Colonel, I'll do my best...."

"Your best, hell! You have that steel here tomorrow, George, or you'll be out on the street along with those lousy bastards!"

He turned away abruptly and almost walked into Cotham. "Jesus, where did you come from?" Sigler exclaimed. His face was as red as the dust that coated the pickup trucks parked in a tight little cluster around the trailer.

"Good morning, Sid," said Cotham evenly. "Everything going all right?" Ever since it had been called to Cotham's attention by the superintendent that Sigler insisted upon being addressed by his military rank, Cotham had made it a point to call him by his first name.

Sigler glared with unconcealed hostility. "This is a hard hat job, Ethan. We need to get you one if you're going to wander around on the site like this."

"Certainly, I understand. But I'm not wandering around, Sid, I'm checking on the work. I'm the architect, you know."

"Listen, you may be the architect, but I'm running this job. There's more to construction than sitting in an air-conditioned office drawing fancy plans. If it was up to me, that AIA contract of yours would have gotten thrown out long ago. I don't need some Ivy League intellectual looking over my shoulder and telling me how to pour foundations on the Mississippi! Hell, I was in the Corps building levees along this river back when you Princeton boys were sitting out the Vietnam War in Toronto!"

"And while you were building those levees in Missouri," replied Cotham evenly, "I was drawing fire on a swift boat in the Mekong Delta."

Sigler seemed momentarily at a loss for words. He looked sharply at Cotham and then wheeled around, barking over his shoulder, "Come on, let's see if there's an extra hard hat in this trailer."

———————

Paul Dole was angry, and this surprised and concerned Cotham. Dole was usually the most taciturn of individuals. In all the years Cotham had known him he could remember only one other occasion when Dole had raised his voice, when his dog almost devoured his model of the CSC.

"We're being swamped with Requests for Information, Ethan, and nine out of ten of them are bogus. Here, look at this one. Sigler's asking for more information on the finishes for the door hardware. They haven't even completed digging for the foundations, and they're bugging me about the doorknobs! Here's another. This one wants a drawing showing where the site enclosure fence should go. Hell, we don't care, as long as it keeps tourists out. But now I've got to fill out a form explaining why it's not our problem.

"And we've just gotten a change order request for a two month time extension because of those kids from the U. of M. digging for arrowheads. Sigler claims it's disrupted their schedule. He's claiming—you'll love this—that they lost two months even though the students were on site only for one month! Ethan, the guy's a piece of work."

"He's obviously scared to death," mused Cotham, "that he won't be able to finish on time. Their contract carries a penalty of $10,000 a day if they're late. It's clearly an onerous burden; but Pappas insisted, and Sigler had to agree or be made to look like he didn't trust his own schedule projections. And, of course, they must be sweating the cost as well, since they boxed themselves into doing the job for so much less than we originally budgeted.

"So they're playing the old game of 'blame the architect,'" observed Dole bitterly. Every time they can find the least little hole in our drawings or specs they plan to capitalize on it to increase the cost and extend the time."

Cotham stepped to one of the southeast-facing windows of the office. From the top of the Lincoln American Tower the view was virtually unobstructed, and his eye followed the Main Street Mall south to the red and yellow upright sign of the Orpheum Theatre that anchored the corner of Beale. From there it was only three blocks west and down the bluff to the sinuous curve of Riverside Drive where the column of dust boiled into the ethereal blue of the October sky. Over the tops of the lower buildings that lined Front Street, he could make out the bulldozers, intermittently visible through the dust only to be swallowed up again after a few seconds.

"Sounds like it could be a tough job, Paul. Let's just hope any holes in those drawings are pinpricks."

Cotham recalled his earlier comment to Dole as he read the memorandum from Sigler Associates.

To: Ethan Cotham, Architect
From: Col. Sidney Sigler, P.E.
Subject: Procedures

The following procedures shall be implemented immediately with respect to the Center for Southern Culture:

1. *Meetings to review the progress of the work shall be held on the first and third Monday of each month at the construction site. Any objections to the quality of work in progress during the past two-week period shall be brought to the attention of the Construction Manager by the Architect at such meetings. Failure to point out deficiencies in the work shall be taken as approval of said work.*
2. *The Architect shall notify the Construction Manager in writing at least 48 hours prior to conducting site inspections.*
3. *Correspondence to the Owner from the Architect concerning the quality of the work shall be forwarded through the Construction Manager.*

Cotham had to read the memorandum twice to make sure he was not imagining its contents. He was unsure which was more outrageous, the condescending bureaucratic language that smacked of military communications from superiors to their subordinates or the content itself. The responsibilities of architects during the construction of a large project were well established. Sigler's memo was a blatant attempt to corral Cotham and limit his authority to monitor the work of the contractor and to watch for lapses in quality or deviations from the drawings. It was an intolerable infringement on his turf.

"Jean," he called through the open door, "could you help me with a letter? I don't want to send this by e-mail." Stepping into his cubbyhole of an office a moment later, Jean peered at him over her reading glasses. It was unusual for Cotham to ask her to take dictation, but she sat down, a legal pad on her knee, and waited.

Two can play this game thought Cotham to himself, calling up countless dry official naval communications he had written and received.

Dear Col. Sigler:

With regard to your recent memo:

1. Procedures are established in the contracts between the Owner, the Architect, and the Construction Manager and are not subject to unilateral modification by your office. We reserve the right to point out deficiencies in the work at any time.

2. The architect is to be afforded access to the site whenever work is in progress. We will not give advance notice of site inspections.

3. The Architect is the Owner's representative, charged with keeping the Owner informed of the progress and quality of the work. We will communicate directly with the Owner.

Sincerely,
Ethan Cotham, Architect

It was extraordinary how much better he felt. As soon as he had sent Jean off to transcribe the letter, however, he began to have doubts. Was he being too thin-skinned and too impetuous? Would it be wiser just to ignore Sigler's demands and choose a different battle? No, he told himself, this was a test by a bully. If he backed down, it would only lead to other more serious challenges to his rightful authority.

Five minutes later Jean handed him the crisp white sheet printed on his letterhead. He scanned it hastily and then snapped, "Very well. Send it by courier. I want it there within the hour."

Chapter Twenty

Cotham had to admit he had reached a dead end. He had read the Quonsets' program of requirements through until he knew every luxurious Jacuzzi, wet bar, granite counter top, and wine cellar by heart. He could diagram in his sleep the three guest bedrooms, each with its own bathroom, the master bedroom suite with the separate dressing area the size of his own entire bedroom, the three-car garage, the swimming pool with bathhouse, and the solarium.

The problem did not lie with the site, certainly one of the most dramatic in the city. Perched at the leading edge of the third Chickasaw Bluff, it offered an unobstructed view across Riverside Drive to the magnificent expanse of the Mississippi. It must have been the same view that greeted Hernando Desoto and his band of explorers when they first beheld the great river almost five hundred years earlier.

The problem could only be described as a spiritual one. Cotham was immediately aware of this anachronistic way of defining it. As Cellini had pointed out, the spiritual had become largely irrelevant to most architects these days unless one were designing a religious building. In fact, it was an increasingly irrelevant term in that context as well, now that so many churches were being replaced by theaters and country clubs masquerading as worship spaces euphemistically known as "family life centers."

There was something about the Quonsets' requirements that offended him. It read like a spoiled child's Christmas list. Perhaps it was its emphasis on bigness. Or maybe it was the requirement that the house fit the "English style," which, of course, was not a style at all. What was it about this preoccupation with style? For the newly rich, of which there seemed to be a great many these days, the French chateau and the English country house with their popular associations with an idyllic agrarian past were generally the fantasies of choice.

Were the Quonsets trying to impress him with their requirements? Surely not. He had known both Thurston and Roberta too long. There had been too many afternoon football games, dancing classes, and sorority formals. Surely they did not think they could fool him into thinking they were to the manor born. Apparently he was their accomplice, their trusted confidante, the means to the end of making a statement to the larger community. Thurston's fellow bankers and Roberta's tennis league had fallen for the quarter horses and the luxury cars, and now they would be awed by the palatial house Cotham was to design.

Why couldn't more of his clients find the inspiration for their houses in something of substance? Take Nikos Pappas for instance. He felt an increasing admiration for this wealthy, self-made man who had not lost touch with his roots in the Pinch district and who was willing to spend a substantial portion of his own fortune to build a project that would contribute to the larger community. Other than Roberta's position on a couple of boards, what was there of the authentic or the selfless in the Quonsets' life? Football? A seven-figure net worth? Membership in "the Country Club" or a Cotton Carnival society? As far as Cotham could tell, these were the sole sources from which the Quonsets' identity was derived. It was no wonder that their architectural vision was as limited as the other accoutrements of their wealthy but shallow existence.

In frustration he threw down his pencil. He glanced up at the icon of St. Mary Magdalene above his desk gazing back at him in serenity. He desperately envied her tranquil existence and the inner peace that radiated from those dark eyes.

Fifteen minutes later he was at the wheel of the Rover roaring past Southhaven along I-55 toward St. Mary Magdalene Church. He took the exit onto the two-lane highway that wove through the hills and past ravines choked with the kudzu that transformed ordinary pine trees and utility poles into the crenelated walls and towers of some fabulous Green Knight's castle. Cotham always held his breath as he rounded the bend where he knew the first glimpse of the bell tower awaited him.

The project was nearing completion at last, and the small cross atop the tower had been installed since his last visit. Rising above the distant tree line where the hardwoods were now flecked with the red and yellow of October, the tower's lonely silhouette recalled the hills of Umbria. The broad entry plaza had at last been paved so that instead of traipsing across a sea of mud on a temporary boardwalk it was now possible to follow the intended approach across the open expanse. The route led past the disk of granite inlaid into the paving where the Easter fire would be kindled to the covered ambulatory that in turn led to the main entrance. Cellini had insisted that for symbolic reasons there should be only a single main entrance, and Cotham had readily agreed. The wisdom of the decision was clear as he stepped through the door and under the broad cast-stone lintel inscribed simply, "I am the Way."

He strode through the narthex and into the nave where the water of the baptismal font gurgled softly as it trickled over the stone lip and flowed down into the broad pool recessed into the floor. As it neared completion, the room had taken on a primeval quality that derived from the preponderance of space, light, and water, the most elemental of the architect's tools. He wondered if others would feel it as well, or whether he was simply projecting his own desires into this place that he had made.

He noted that the painters had finished the ceiling and that the scaffolding had at last been removed. Had he been right to argue for the midnight-blue ceiling covered with stars instead of the safer off-white selected by the committee? Perhaps he had been wrong and less had been more. The question was quickly followed by a flash of annoyance at his lack of self-confidence and never-ending questioning of his own judgment. Of course the missing stars would have been a stunning addition to the space.

Don Childers was standing with a small group of workmen in the tower chapel. As Cotham approached, he could see that the group was preoccupied by something on the floor; several of them hunkered down in a circle like the farmers they had once been. Childers looked up.

"Hey, Mr. Ethan. We got ourselves a mystery here!"

"Good morning, Don. Morning, gentlemen. What's up? No more elephants, I hope."

Childers stepped aside and pointed to a puddle of dark, viscous liquid congealed on the concrete slab. "This here's really weird, Mr. Ethan. Every day for the past week we been gettin' this stuff dripping down from the ceiling. We clean it up, and the next day it's back again. Looks like motor oil, but we ain't got no machinery up in this tower."

Cotham looked closely at the puddle. In fact, it did have the thick sheen of motor oil or antifreeze, although it lacked the green tint of the latter. He looked up. Once the Tabernacle containing the consecrated host was installed, the chapel would become one of the most important places in the church, a fact that had led Cotham to design the room with its unusual dimensions. It was small in plan, only fifteen feet square, but above them the ceiling soared to a height of sixty feet. Palladio would never have approved of such extreme proportions, but Cotham had sought a special effect.

The walls were punctuated by small randomly placed square windows, each deeply recessed into the thick wall. Now that the sun had risen halfway to its zenith, a single narrow shaft of light sliced across the space through one of the windows. On the opposite side of the tower the light, scattered and diffused by the rough plaster wall, softly illuminated the space. Which poet had observed that the sun never knew how great it was until it shone on the wall of a building?

He could see no source for the oil, no dark stains on the walls or ceiling. "Have you had anyone up there on a ladder, Don?"

"Nossir, no ladder of mine will reach to the top of this little room of yours. I got a man-lift, but it won't fit in the door. Maybe we need to call the fire department. We've been up on the roof and in the attic looking for busted pipes. Didn't find nothin' unusual, unless you count them ol' hornets buzzing around under the eaves.

"You know, Mr. Ethan, when I first looked at the plans for this tower, I thought it was the craziest thing I ever seen. But I got to hand it to you; it's real neat the way the sun comes in each of them little windows, one at a time. Why, by afternoon, it'll be comin' in the other side, and just before sunset the whole room will turn orange."

Cotham turned back to the puddle on the floor. He crouched down once more, perplexed. Then on an impulse he extended his arm, coating his fingertip with the ooze and tentatively sniffed it. Then he licked the finger. Childers watched him in silence. Architects were strange people. Suppose it was some sort of poison?

Cotham slowly stood. "Don, what you need isn't the fire department. You need a beekeeper. This stuff is honey, and I'll bet those wasps you saw were actually bees. They must have a hive somewhere up in the belfry."

———————

As he rolled out the sketches on the Quonsets' dining room table, Roberta gave an audible sigh of pleasure. It was a handsome drawing, Cotham admitted to himself, executed in colored pencil in a soft freehand style. The concept was loosely based on "Windsor," a famous Mississippi antebellum mansion. One could almost smell the honeysuckle. As he walked Roberta and Thurston through the floor plans explaining the layout of one extravagant room after another, he was afraid she might swoon with pleasure. He had taken pains to include every detail mentioned in the program. There was Roberta's private dressing suite and bath with its sunken travertine tub and bidet. Outside by the pool terrace was Thurston's small practice putting green. In the den the large-format television screen was ingeniously concealed behind book-matched retractable mahogany paneling. A motorized dumbwaiter that would have made Thomas Jefferson envious rose from the basement wine cellar to a niche in the wall of the butler's pantry.

"It's simply splendid!" she gushed. "Oh, Ethan, I so admire creative talent like yours. What a gift you have!"

Throughout Cotham's presentation Thurston had been strangely silent. He took a rather large sip, perhaps it was a gulp, from his glass of Groth Vineyards 1985 Reserve Cabernet Sauvignon and cleared his throat. "Well, Ethan, I agree that this is a beautiful design, all right. It certainly appears that you've worked in everything we asked for." He shot Roberta a glance. "I suppose you have some idea of the cost?"

As a young architect, this had been the moment Cotham had come to dread. Somehow he had let himself believe that he was responsible for working miracles when it came to the cost of construction. Through the years he had experimented with a variety of strategies to cope with the sticker shock that inevitably greeted any initial discussion of cost. But when it came down to the damage his plans would inflict on his clients' bank balance, there was, in the end, no substitute for cold, clinical, forthrightness.

"I have to tell you, Thurston, this is not an inexpensive project. To begin with it's quite large, about 5000 square feet, 6000 when you add the garage. Then we have to factor in the many special features. With so many bathrooms and high quality plumbing fixtures, the nice materials, the pool, landscaping, and so forth, we're probably talking about somewhere around $300 or $400 per square foot. It could even be more, of course, since we haven't begun the working drawings, and there are still many decisions to be made."

Thurston had gone pale. He stared at Roberta, his eyes bulging slightly. Then he turned back to Cotham. "My God, Ethan, that's 2.4 million dollars! And possibly more, you say? That's out of the question!"

"Really, Ethan," interjected Roberta, "we had no idea what we were asking for would be so expensive. And I was so excited…." Tears welled in her eyes, the enthusiasm of five minutes earlier rudely dashed and supplanted by despair.

"Roberta, Thurston, please remember that you didn't give me a budget; you only told me what you wanted. If you want a two million dollar house, you shouldn't be surprised to hear that it'll cost two million."

"Well then, what do we do now? We can't go ahead with this, that's for sure. It's way too much!" exclaimed Thurston. Cotham thought he detected an accusatory tone. Were they one step away from blaming him?

Cotham stood and walked to the bay window, seemingly contemplating the sprinkler's graceful oscillations back and forth across the manicured zoysia lawn. They had asked him what to do, but were they prepared to hear the answer? He turned to his clients, still sitting stunned on the leather Chesterfield sofa.

"Let me ask you a difficult question. What would you be willing to give up? To put it bluntly, the reason this house costs so much is that it's a palace. No one with grown children really needs three guest bedrooms, each with its own bathroom. There are plenty of entire houses that would fit into this master bedroom. You don't own three cars, so it's unclear to me why you need a garage the size of an airplane hanger. And why do you need a two story Greek-revival portico? You are Thurston and Roberta, not Rhett and Scarlet, and that's nothing to be ashamed of. Why not let me design a house that reflects who you really are, not some ostentatious anachronism with an inflated mortgage?"

Silence. Roberta, blinking back tears, turned to Thurston. Thurston stared at the floor, apparently counting the knots in the antique Shiraz rug. Finally he looked up at her.

"This house was your idea, Dear. Architecture goes right over my head, and I really don't care what it's like as long as I can have my little study. But I do care about our portfolio. If you and Ethan can agree on something that doesn't bankrupt me, you can build any damn thing you want. Now if you'll excuse me, I'm urgently needed on the golf course."

As Thurston abruptly departed, Roberta brightened a bit. "I'm sorry, Ethan. Thurston's right; this house has been my idea all along. We need something new, something fresh in our lives, and I thought maybe this could be it. It seemed like an adventure to move Downtown, and I love the thought of being on the river. I think Thurston would like it more than he realizes, and with his new position…." She paused.

"Suppose we were to do as you say—start with who we are. How would we do that? Don't we need to tell you what style we prefer?"

Cotham sighed. Perhaps the public's preoccupation with styles was inevitable in a society influenced by the hype of the real estate industry and where the study of art and architecture was the province of a few specialists. Most people could not conceive of the possibility that an architect might design from the inside out, as well as from the outside in, never pausing to consult a history text.

"Let me show you something, Roberta. Something you may have forgotten about." He motioned toward the den, and she followed him. Cotham stopped in front of the bar and pointed toward the photograph of the white clapboard farmhouse with the wide porch nestled in the grove of trees.

"Here is a house that has the quality I'm talking about— *authenticity,* one of the the rarest and most precious commodities in the world. Look at its simple elegance, the way it's been fitted to the land, the way the materials were selected from what was at hand and then shaped by craftsmen who loved and understood wood. Look at the porch. It's not about 'curb appeal.' It's there to provide shelter, a place to sit and talk with a friend on a summer night. That's why your family grew to love it. This is what a house should be about, not hot tubs and three-car garages."

Roberta was gazing at the photograph; and as he finished, the tears filled her eyes once more. "Oh, Ethan, you sound just like my grandfather. He loved this place so; I think when he had to sell it and they tore it down it was just more than he could bear. We used to sit on that porch in the swing and eat grapes and listen to his stories of growing up in Middle Tennessee. Some nights he would read Greek myths or maybe a modern novel aloud to us. *The Grapes of Wrath* was one of our favorites. There were railroad tracks nearby, and we could hear the steam engine coming a long way off, not even as loud as the katydids at first. Then the katydids would be drowned out as the train rumbled past, and we'd sit and listen to the noise fade away into the distance. Everything would go dead still for a minute or two, and then those darned katydids would start their singing again. I'd forgotten all about that."

"It seems to me," offered Cotham, "that architecture can be a resonator for those kinds of memories. If it has authenticity, that is. But it must grow out of a real time and place, out of who we really are, like your grandfather's house."

"And you think our new house could be like that for Thurston and me?"

Cotham picked up the roll of drawings he had presented earlier and walked to the counter of the bar where he unrolled the front elevation. Then he extracted a fat black felt-tip pen from his pocket.

"Here, let me show you. First, let's get rid of this ridiculous portico and substitute a real front porch." Like a surgeon laying open the belly of a fat man, he drew the pen across the façade. Roberta gasped at the violence of the act as though she expected the drawing to bleed. More heavy black lines followed in quick succession until a modest one-story porch had been overlaid on the delicate colored pencil of the original drawing. As Cotham added deep shadows in its recesses, the porch took on a three-dimensional character and seemed to jump from the paper.

"Next, let's amputate the garage wing and substitute a two-car porte cochere, maybe connect it to the house by a little breezeway. Now we'll lower the roofline several feet. You can live without twelve-foot ceilings, can't you? And we'll put Thurston's study in the attic with his own little dormer window overlooking the river." The marker flew across the page as he spoke. "And now that the massing has been reduced, let's increase the scale of the windows and the chimney and arrange them asymmetrically so as to provide a touch of complexity. There."

He held up the sketch for her to see. Instead of a grandiose manor house suited to the insatiable appetites of a dot-com multi-millionaire, there now remained an unpretentious but charming clapboard structure. In its overall proportions and inviting sense of shelter, it bore a distinct resemblance to the Middle Tennessee farmhouse in the photograph. But in its asymmetry and over-scaled fenestration, it possessed individuality, an insouciant confidence that could only be called *modern*.

Roberta stared. Then she slowly began to smile. "Oh, Ethan, it's lovely. It's so…friendly! All it needs is a weather vane like the one granddaddy had on his roof. We used to watch it spin just before a big thunderstorm rolled in…."

"Then you shall have one." With several quick, short strokes, Cotham added a weather vane to the peak of the gable. Roberta smiled.

"And what, may I ask, is that funny looking blob with legs on the top?"

Cotham smiled. "That, of course, would be a boll weevil."

Chapter Twenty-One

Although the structure was far from complete, under the constant badgering and bullying of Sigler the CSC project had seen enormous progress. As recently as Christmas, there had been little more to greet the layman's eye than a gaping hole in the riverbank. Now only six months after the groundbreaking, anyone could, with only a little effort, imagine the completed buildings rising from the ooze. There was an air of austere dignity to the unadorned concrete walls and the spaces they enclosed. When viewed from the top of the bluffs above Riverside Drive, one could read the intricate organization of solid and void, courtyard and concert hall, as clearly as a floor plan on a sheet of white vellum.

This was Cotham's favorite vantage point; and whenever he paid a visit to the site, he first stood on the bluff top to view the progress against the backdrop of the river. Standing here alone, he sometimes allowed himself to admit his pride in this accomplishment. It was the culmination of his career, the opportunity he had awaited for over thirty years of eking out a living. He had invested everything he had learned through those years in the design. All his technical skill and esthetic sensibilities had been demanded, and he had risen to the challenge. It was a good building. It might even turn out to be a building of importance, one that would be published, that would win design awards. More important, the Center for Southern Culture promised to make a real difference in Memphis' tortured history, helping to heal old wounds and to reconcile black and white people. It was a noble cause, one that he believed in. In the moments when Cotham reflected on this achievement, his chronic doubts about his choice of a profession vanished, and he knew that he was meant to be an architect.

After the bluff top the second best view was from the opposite bank of the river, from the midst of a soybean field at the end of a tiny dirt track reachable only by an old bridge just downstream from the heart of the city. It was a remarkable thing to stand in the middle of that field at twilight, surrounded by thousands of acres of the richest farmland in the world, gazing across the greatest river in North America toward the city on the bluffs. With the lights of its office towers reflected in the waves, Memphis might as well be the Emerald City of Oz. Before the light faded away to dusky purple, the concrete walls of the CSC were transformed by the last rays of the sinking sun into golden parapets reared above the flood plain, guarding the gates of the city.

From his observation post at the pinnacle of the Lincoln American Tower, where he kept a powerful pair of old navy binoculars on the windowsill, Cotham could keep a watchful eye on the site without leaving the office. The magnified view was much the same as from the bluff top, and it had become his ritual upon arriving at the office each morning to check the progress of the previous day's construction activities, like a sea captain inspecting the horizon from the bridge.

The progress to date had not been a pleasure cruise, however, although an uneasy truce seemed to have been established with Sigler. Cotham had tried to patch things up after the flap provoked by Sigler's inflammatory memo and Cotham's defiant response and had been on the lookout for opportunities to compliment the quality of the work.

As to Sigler's demand that Cotham provide advance notice of his inspections, Cotham had simply chosen to ignore the order, making it a point to visit the site at least once a week with no warning. There was little anyone could do to stop this, he reasoned, and it was an effective way of reminding the construction manager of the architect's time-honored duty to keep a close watch on the progress of the work. Cotham had ignored as well Sigler's decree that correspondence with the owner be routed through Sigler, addressing many memos directly to Pappas.

There had been much to write about, and Cotham fully expected the truce to be shortlived. As a result of the archeological work, the project was still a month behind by Sigler's own estimates, and Cotham had begun to suspect that the truth was closer to two months, an opinion he had shared with Pappas. Once the structural steel had arrived the progress of the work had appeared to accelerate, but new problems had quickly become apparent.

One frigid January morning Cotham had watched as a forty-foot long wide-flange beam had been swung into place atop a column. A daring steelworker straddled its end like a cowboy, suspended sixty feet in the air, as the crane slowly lowered the beam into position. The man held a large mallet and a foot-long bolt in his gloved hand while the crane positioned the beam two or three inches from the exact point of connection to the column. He began tapping at the steel with the mallet, coaxing it into its final position so that the pre-drilled holes would align, and he could bolt the two giant pieces together. Instead, after a few moments he looked down at the crane operator in exasperation and gave a thumbs-down signal. When the operator hesitated, he repeated the signal, this time gesturing in obvious frustration and irritation. The crane lowered him, and he stepped to the ground near Cotham, dark anger in his sunburned face.

"That's the fourth piece in two days that don't fit. Damned if I'm gonna keep bein' waved around up there in this wind like a worm on a fishhook trying to connect holes when they're a half inch apart!"

That incident had prompted an e-mail memo to Sigler with a copy to Hardegen. An hour later Cotham had received a blistering retort in which Sigler blamed errors in the shop drawings that had failed to be detected during Hardegen's review prior to fabrication. A careful check by Paul Dole was required to determine that the shop drawings had, in fact, contained no error and that the fault lay at the fabrication plant. Rather than have the steel returned to the plant, an option that could cause weeks of delay, a decision was made by Sigler to field-drill new holes. Cotham, worried that the result could be a weakened connection, decided to hold his tongue in deference to Sigler's responsibility for what the contract termed the "means and methods" of construction. It was a gray area at best, but the incident had been documented.

Paul Dole knocked at Cotham's door, and Cotham waved him in. Dole was looking even grayer than usual of late. He sat down with a sigh and produced a sheet of paper bearing the silver oak leaf of the all too familiar Sigler letterhead. Cotham had assigned Dole to the day-to-day oversight of the job, and the strain was beginning to show.

"You won't believe this latest memo, Ethan. Now they want us to tell them what color to use to field-prime the steel of the lobby skylights. I don't give a rat's ass, as long as it's primed. We've already called out the final color, the charcoal gray, and the primer will never show once we're finished. It's a little thing, I know, but I've got a pile of stuff like this on my desk. We get two or three new questions every day and I hardly have time to get to the job site any more."

Cotham had seen the daily crop of memos demanding that the architects produce additional data on the most minute aspects of the drawings and specifications. There were now over a hundred of these, and it had become impossible to keep up with them. At every monthly progress meeting the first item on the agenda had become a spurious list of unanswered questions and information allegedly missing from the construction documents.

"Let me handle this one, Paul. Why don't you go on down and have a look at the rainwater they left standing in the concert hall yesterday? Looks like it's a foot deep. Take the specs, and if you need to, read them the passage about dewatering in the 'Temporary Facilities' section. And have a look at the bolts on the new roof beams; if they keep field drilling holes, we're going to have to get Hardegen himself down for an inspection. I'm starting to worry. Every time a new hole goes in, those moment connections get a little weaker."

"OK, Ethan," Dole replied. "But what I can't quite figure out is that standing water. It hasn't rained in a week."

Cotham poured another cup of the oily black Community Coffee from New Orleans, the office standard that Jean bought by the case in Midtown. He leaned back in his chair so that he could just see through his doorway to Jean's desk. He was surprised to see her chair empty. Now that he thought about it, he had not seen her all morning.

Jean could hardly remain unaware of the tension that had begun to pervade the firm. She had antennae as sensitive as a radio telescope. No nuance escaped her; and since she was responsible for the filing, she must surely be reading Sigler's unending stream of memos. She was too discreet to question such technical communications directly, but she would have found a way to let Paul know that she knew what he was up against. Jean offered a badly needed dose of warmth to the beleaguered little band of architects. If Tensing broke up with his girlfriend, she would bring him a plate of cookies as consolation. If Cotham were experiencing one of his irascible moods, she generally knew enough to stay out of his way; he suspected that she had suggested to Pallie on more than one occasion that an evening at the theatre or a movie might be in order to distract him from the private demons that had hovered around him since the beginning of the CSC project. But there were times when not even Jean could soothe his ragged nerves. A few days before, Cotham had let loose at Sigler's tactics, venting his frustration at some length in a rare outward display of anger.

"That Little Napoleon is going to push me too far!" he stormed.

"Ethan, maybe you're worrying too much about all this," she had offered in an attempt to mollify him.

He had glared at her. "Dammit, Jean, it's my *job* to worry!" Since then she had been keeping a low profile.

"Paul," he called over the intercom, "Have you seen Jean this morning?"

"Nope," came the reply from the downstairs studio, "I was here at eight, and I noticed the answering machine was still on. She's usually here before I am."

He heard the elevator doors open around the corner. Perhaps it was finally Jean.

"Good morning, Ethan. I didn't see anyone out front so I just wandered on back."

It took him a moment to recognize Roberta Quonset. She had undergone some sort of transformation. Instead of the matronly flowered dresses she favored, she was wearing a striking tailored gray flannel suit over a grayish purple blouse. Her hair seemed much lighter, almost blond, although he was unable to remember its precise original color. It was cut shorter. She seemed even taller than usual and looked almost striking, a term that he would have never thought to apply to her in all the years they had known each other. It took Cotham a moment to remember that they had an 11:00 appointment, and he glanced at his watch. It was two minutes past. Again he wondered where Jean was. She would have reminded him of the meeting in time to have the latest drawings of the Quonset house spread out in the conference room.

"Roberta!" he exclaimed, rising to greet her. "Excuse me, I didn't realize the time." She extended her hand, a confident, business-like greeting that he would not have expected from her.

"Let's sit down in the conference room. How about some coffee?"

"Thank you, Ethan. Black, please." Even her voice was changed. The too-cute little girl's chirp was replaced by a low, well-modulated tonality.

But there was no more coffee in the pot. He had taken the last cup himself, and Jean was not there to make more. "Tensing!" he called down the spiral stair trying to suppress the irritation he felt. "Help! Can you find the latest Quonset drawings and make us a pot of coffee? We're short-handed up here, and Mrs. Quonset is in the conference room for a meeting! And make it fast!"

"Sorry, Roberta, we're a little disorganized this morning. Tensing will be up with the drawings and coffee in just a moment."

"That's perfectly all right, Ethan. In fact, there's something else I want to talk to you about before we discuss the plans. I need your advice—your professional advice and your advice as a friend."

"Of course," he replied. "Anything I can do…."

"When you urged us to design a house that would express who we really are, that somehow struck a chord with me. I began thinking about your notion of authenticity and about who I really am. To be frank I realized that I've never bothered to ask that before. It's an old story, very boring really. For the last twenty years, my life has been about Thurston and our children. Now that he's done so well at the bank and Caitlin and Michael are out on their own, I can think about myself. It's a new feeling and one that I still haven't gotten used to. But it doesn't seem to want to go away.

"Did you know that I majored in art at Vanderbilt? I actually thought seriously about a career in interior design until Thurston came along and, then we just got swept up in the young-married scene, he corporate ladder, the children, the carpools, and all the rest.

"I think now that it must have first begun to stir that day at the Design Review meeting when you lectured us about censorship and refusing to settle for the good instead of the best. I remember feeling disturbed, restless, and I had trouble sleeping that night. And then later when you were sketching over your first drawing, talking with so much conviction about how we could express ourselves in our new house, something came back to me that I had not thought about in years. I had forgotten how excited I used to get about art, about how I could lose myself for hours on end in the painting studio. And then we had our Board meeting with that Mr. Roper from Philadelphia, and I was so impressed with his sincerity and his clarity, with the way he is committed to the life of the mind and to how deeply he cares about what he does.

"To be honest, Ethan, neither Thurston nor I much care about what we are doing with our lives. Oh, we get along fine, don't misunderstand me. He's content to make money and be on the social circuit. He likes having me around to go with him to football games and dinner parties, but that's about all we seem to have in common. I waste my time playing tennis or puttering around in the garden or going to endless committee meetings. But if the truth be known, I don't really care about any of it. I find myself thinking back to my college days, to the excitement of beginning a new painting or sculpture, of taking a risk and not knowing how it will turn out.

"So I've been thinking about myself again for the first time, it seems, since I got married; and I've gotten this crazy idea that I want to try out on you. I'm hoping it may not be too late to make a new start, to discover who I really am and maybe have a life that's more worth living."

She reached into an elegant black Kate Spade purse that looked as though it could have been designed at the Bauhaus and pulled out the bulletin of the University of Memphis.

"Ethan, you've known me since we were in grade school. I've heard you say the U. of M. has a good program. I want you to tell me, honestly, if you think it's too late for me to think about going back to school in architecture. "

––––––––––

Roberta had left following a long discussion. After recovering from his initial astonishment, Cotham had tried to lay out for her the pros and cons of taking up a profession in middle age that would require years of study and internship before she could hope to receive her first small commission. There had been a time when he might have enthusiastically encouraged her willingness to take such a risk. But he realized as he listened to her that he was deeply fatigued, perhaps approaching the point of burnout, and that he could not recommend without reservation the road he himself had chosen.

He had tried to be balanced, remembering the moments of exhilaration when a design breakthrough finally occurred after days and nights of frustration. But perhaps in retrospect he had been too discouraging, focusing too much on the downside of what he did. Had he overemphasized the tiresome business aspects of running a struggling practice that seemed to consume the majority of his time? Certainly no profession was perfect. Perhaps the isolated design epiphany and the satisfaction he felt when he visited the CSC or St. Mary Magdalene Church were not an excessive price to pay for the stress of duking it out with the likes of Sidney Sigler.

He had pointed out to Roberta that his was not the only possible career path for an architect. Indeed a small one-man design office was probably the most difficult route he could have chosen. He had often wondered what would have happened had he chosen to remain in Roper's office in Philadelphia. Perhaps he would now be in charge of some high profile project in some exotic locale, a project that would be published internationally to great acclaim. He could be spending most of his time on design, leaving the timesheets, rent, and the payroll to the Wharton MBAs who ran that side of Roper's practice.

In the end Roberta had seemed confused and ambivalent. He felt sorry about that, but it was better to get used to the conflicting emotions now if one were really serious about architecture. He reflected that it was not unjustified to have mixed feelings given the unrealistic expectations of some clients, the occasionally ruthless competition with other architects, and the shenanigans of some contractors. His was a rough and tumble profession.

Cotham had heard it observed as a sign of intelligence to be able to simultaneously sustain two mutually contradictory ideas or emotions. By that definition he must indeed be a genius. His work had brought him much joy but considerable pain as well, and he often vacillated from exhilaration to despair in the course of the same day.

He had tried to end the conversation with Roberta on a positive note offering to serve as a reference should she decide to make application to the U. of M., and she had thanked him profusely. He had kissed her cheek as she left in an unexpected rush of affection for this old friend who had displayed more courage than he would have guessed possible. He wondered if he would be able to do the same in her shoes.

It was 3:00 that afternoon when Jean finally reported for work. Cotham was hunting and pecking his way through a memo to Sigler and did not look up as she stood in the door. Beside the computer lay a fan of paint color samples open to the pinks and lavenders.

He had selected the colors based on their names as well as their delicate feminine hues, hoping that the ones he had selected might nettle even an esthetically challenged army engineer. He desperately wished he could be present as the hardboiled colonel read the names aloud to his painting subcontractor. He finished the memo and reread it to himself:

MEMORANDUM
To: Sidney Sigler
From: Ethan Cotham
Subject: Primer Colors

In response to your Request for Information No. 107 with respect to the primer paint color to be used for the framing of the lobby skylights, please refer to the Section 09900 of the Specifications. This indicates that three coats of Sherwin-Williams primer are to be applied before the finish coats. In order to visually confirm that all three coats have been applied, a different color shall be used for each as follows:

1st coat: "Ballerina"
2nd coat: "Bridesmaid Pink"
3rd coat: "Blush"

Jean, still standing in the open door, finally cleared her throat. "Well, I guess you thought I'd deserted the ship, Captain Cotham."

He looked up. "So there you are, Jean. No, I know you too well for that. But we're lucky Roberta Quonset hasn't filed suit against us after she drank the coffee Tensing had to make." It was a trivial jab, and Cotham instantly regretted the remark.

"Actually, I think you'll be interested in how I've spent my day," Jean replied with a conspiratorial air, ignoring Cotham's dig. Without waiting for an invitation she sat down and opened her well-worn leather satchel. Cotham fully expected to see several unopened cans of cat food tumble out. He knew she routinely picked these up during her lunch hour to take home for her two Siamese cats, Elvis and Priscilla. Instead she extricated a sheath of handwritten notes.

"Ethan, this Sigler is taking a toll on us all. You're short and irritable. Poor Paul is beside himself and told me the other day that he's seriously thinking of looking for work in another office. Tensing doesn't really know all that's going on, but he senses the change from the days when we were one little happy family. It's become like a war-zone around here, and I'm afraid to open the next letter. We're all terrified that we're about to be sued or fired or both.

"I first considered assassination, but it's not very subtle and not as satisfying as certain other options. So I decided instead to do a little research into the Colonel's dim, dark past. It's really quite amazing what you can find out about people by a couple of phone calls, a trip to the library, and an hour on the Internet."

She flipped through her notes. "I began with his military record. As it happens, my sister's brother is an Army JAG Corps officer and has access to case histories of past disciplinary hearings. It's all a matter of public record if you know where to look. I asked him to run a check on Sigler, and he called back within the hour. I was able to find out a good bit about him. He enlisted as a private and worked his way up in the Corps of Engineers. Interestingly, he helped build the Hernando Desoto Bridge here in Memphis. His career was fairly unremarkable until he got in over his head. Ethan, the Colonel was allowed to take early retirement from the army under the threat of a dishonorable discharge. I gather that there were financial irregularities discovered in his unit's supply department, including allegations of misappropriation of funds. There was no conviction due to a lack of sufficient evidence, but there was enough of a shadow cast to make it clear that he'd never be promoted to full colonel and that his military career was effectively over.

"That was in 1989. I couldn't find much more about him or his company for the next seven years except that he was listed as a licensed engineer and that Sigler Associates was registered as a general contractor in a dozen different states. They seem to have built several shopping centers in the Baltimore suburbs during that period.

"Then he made the news big time." Jean unfolded a photocopy of a newspaper article dated January, 1996. At the top of the page was the masthead of the *Baltimore Sun*.

"You can read the details yourself, but the gist of it is that in '96 he was sued by HRS for defects in the construction of a new shopping mall in Columbia, Maryland. I gather they're a huge east coast developer. HRS alleged that Sigler Associates had intentionally left some of the reinforcing out of the concrete in order to reduce costs and that they had falsified the testing lab's reports in order to cover it up. Sigler countersued, charging that the engineering drawings were vague and incomplete and that they had been unable to keep to their time schedule.

"The developer claimed they had borne the expense of tearing out and replacing the bad concrete and that the resulting delays had cost them ten million dollars. Apparently the case dragged on for over three years before it finally went to the jury. They deliberated for two days before returning a verdict against Sigler. He was found guilty of fraud and gross negligence, and the developer was awarded a huge judgment. Sigler was also found guilty of unprofessional conduct by the Maryland registration board, and his engineer's license was revoked. According to the article, he was forced to file bankruptcy. That's all I could find, except that he's been duly licensed in Tennessee since '98."

"Whew," exclaimed Cotham, "so I haven't been imagining that there's something funny about the Colonel, after all." He paused, lost in thought. Cotham believed in the advantages of trying to think like his adversaries, and the alarming possibilities were becoming apparent. Sigler's most obvious problem on the CSC was that he had allowed himself to be maneuvered by Pappas into agreeing to a guaranteed maximum price that was too low. In that scenario Sigler could end up paying for any additional labor and material costs out of his own pocket. But perhaps that was not the full extent of his difficulty. The contract also contained a penalty clause for the construction manager. Sigler had exactly 540 days, some eighteen months, to achieve completion of the work. If the CSC was not open for business by the deadline, he faced a penalty of $10,000 a day for every additional day required to complete the job. Either of these eventualities on a project of this size could threaten to bankrupt even a large construction company, and both errors together could prove catastrophic.

If Sigler believed he faced either difficulty, his obvious course of action, the one he had apparently employed in Baltimore, was to cast doubt on the completeness or accuracy of the construction documents. The architect and engineer could always complain to the owner about such spurious allegations, and Cotham had considered taking his concerns about Sigler directly to Pappas. But since most owners were inexperienced in construction matters, few were inclined to take sides in a dispute involving the intricacies of the construction industry. If Cotham forced the issue, Pappas would be unable to readily distinguish between legitimate requests for additional information and those issued as a form of harassment and as ammunition for a future legal battle over costs and delays. A more likely result would be that the owner would begin to wonder about the architect's ability to manage the work or about the completeness of the original construction documents. An unscrupulous contractor or construction manager bent on exploiting a breakdown in the relationship between the owner and the architect could then drive this wedge deeper. It was for these reasons that Cotham had decided to leave Pappas out of the dispute as long as possible or until a legal conflict began to appear inevitable.

Sigler's strategy was becoming quite clear. If a convincing case could be made in court that Sigler's failure to meet deadlines or to keep the project within the budget was due to shortcomings in Cotham's performance, then the financial penalties might be avoided. It would require the sort of major lawsuit at the end of the job that Jean's article described, a legal nightmare in which all parties— owner, contractor, and architect—sued and countersued each other. But from the point of view of a besieged contractor, the sums involved might well justify such action. For the contractor, or in this case the construction manager, to prevail, the first requirement would be an airtight paper trail that would convince a jury that the architect had been the source of problems from day one. In light of the Baltimore case, the endless stream of accusatory memos from Sigler was beginning to resemble an attempt to create just such a trail.

Cotham knew what Lew Craig would advise—reply in kind making sure that no accusation from Sigler went unanswered. While Cotham agreed with the wisdom of this approach, to do so would further reduce Paul Dole from a talented field architect to a petty bureaucrat. Dole was plainly becoming exasperated and unhappy; Cotham didn't need Jean to point out the obvious. Paul was a loyal and longtime employee, but even loyalty had its limits; other firms were always eager to hire away a senior technical architect.

If Sigler really had gotten himself into this predicament on the CSC, there was a second possible strategy. It was one that carried infinitely greater risks if discovered, but that might avoid a legal battle if it remained undetected. This was to intentionally disregard the architect's drawings, partially or even completely omitting some expensive or complicated component of the design in order to reduce the cost or the time required for completion. Since the architect was not obligated to make exhaustive or detailed inspections at the site and was not authorized to require completed work to be uncovered without reasonable cause to suspect a defect, the chances of successfully covering up some such shortcut were probably quite good. If an unscrupulous construction manager could keep the defects concealed until after the one-year warranty period had expired, they might never come to light.

Cotham suddenly remembered that his secretary was sitting in respectful silence awaiting his instructions. "It's like this, Jean," he explained. "If Sigler underbid the CSC in order to get the job, perhaps underestimating the time as well, then he could be planning to try his Baltimore strategy on us. That would explain a lot, the general lack of cooperation, the attempts to discourage us from visiting the site without advance notice, and the flood of memos finding fault with our documents. The question, of course, is where exactly he's cutting corners, if he is. The memos could be just a small part of his plan. Using them alone he'd never be able to convince anyone that he's due a lot more money. But he could well be planning something larger, some major departure from the drawings that he thinks he can get away with. We've already caught him ignoring the steel shop drawings, but that seems more like carelessness. It shouldn't have cost any more to drill the holes correctly in the first place. If he does have something big up his sleeve, either he hasn't reached that point in the construction sequence yet, or we just haven't found any evidence of what he's been up to.

"You'd better share what you've dug up with Paul. And here, send this memo to the Colonel; let's not miss a chance to brighten his day." She took the memo from him, rose, and headed for her desk. Cotham hesitated, then stepped to his door. She turned.

"And Jean, thank you…."

Then he walked to the southwest corner window of the little office. He picked up the heavy binoculars from the windowsill and squinted into the winter sun, already sinking swiftly toward the horizon. He could see the steel roof beams of the CSC rising above the concrete walls, their elegant linear geometry silhouetted against the flashing surface of the river like a jeweler's engravings on a sheet of silver foil.

Chapter Twenty-Two

The morning sky was the color of an iron skillet, and an icy wind scoured Court Square. It was still a half-hour before dawn, and Cotham was alone as he shuffled past the Hebe fountain, head bent in concentration. The bare branches of the old oaks creaked in the wind like the joints of the arthritics who later in the day would sit bundled in dark overcoats on the benches throwing peanuts to the squirrels. Cotham felt old and tired, too. He had been unable to sleep for most of the night, his mind feverishly reviewing the plans of the CSC. When he had finally dozed off, it was only to be awakened by some frightful dream he could no longer remember but which still haunted his unconscious.

Disgusted and anxious, he had arisen, dressed, and driven to the office in the dark. As he stepped into the elevator, he remembered the dream. It was the recurring nightmare of the elevator exploding through the roof of the Lincoln American Tower. As the G-forces increased and the floor numbers clicked past, he was momentarily unsure whether he was waking or still dreaming. Perhaps this time the elevator would really bypass his floor and keep accelerating. It was with a sense of relief that he stepped into the dark little foyer of his office.

He made a pot of coffee and then retrieved the record set of CSC plans from the stick file in the studio. He hauled them up the stair to his office, unrolled them on his drawing table, and began to flip through the sheets. He tried to think like Sigler. If he were under severe pressure and wanted to leave something out, something big and expensive, something that would be difficult to detect, what would it be? He stopped himself. Was he overreacting? Had the article from the Baltimore paper made him paranoid?

There was after all no direct evidence of any such devious intent on Sigler's part. His bullying and defensive behavior could be explained in any number of other ways. Cotham had known other mid-level military officers, bitter and disillusioned about being passed over for promotion, who had degenerated into petty tyrants.

On the wall Mary Magdalene gazed at him with black eyes from somewhere beyond the frame of the icon, the egg held aloft before the pagan emperor. He realized that his mind was wandering.

He walked over to the window and raised the binoculars. The sun was probably above the horizon by now, although it was impossible to say because of the cloud cover that hung low and sullen over the city. A towboat loaded with mounds of coal was making its way downstream, its own power augmented by the sweep of the current. The captain had turned his rudder hard to starboard, swinging the bow toward the west bank so that the tow slid diagonally under the three old bridges. As it cleared the piers of the bridges, the captain put the rudder amidships and with smoke belching from the twin stacks powered straight ahead into the wide bend.

Cotham swung the binoculars back toward the construction site. The steel trusses gleamed dully above the gray of the concrete walls. All was quiet, and the place had the same eerie quality of desolation he had felt at the ruins of the ancient Greek and Roman sites he once explored as a student. He glanced at his watch. It was 6:40 a.m., and the first shift of workers would be arriving soon. As he continued to scan the buildings, he noted a subtle change in the atmosphere. The flat, lifeless forms seemed to be taking on a three-dimensionality they had lacked a moment before. He dropped the binoculars and glanced to the east where a shaft of sunlight had plunged through the cloudbank. It was drifting across the bluffs like the beam of a giant klieg light.

He looked again through the binoculars. The walls of the CSC were now casting sharp shadows, and it was possible to read the volumes and masses contrasted with the voids of the spaces they enclosed. The spaces were dark, filled to the brim with shadows in the low raking light. But what was that flash of light in the darkness? Cotham checked the focus and swept the binoculars back across the egg-shaped concert hall just as a beam of sunlight illuminated the site. The interior of the great room was shining in the sun as though it were made of burnished sheet metal. It was unbelievable, but it could mean only one thing. His heart sank.

Cotham gunned the Rover down the still-deserted Second Street past the Peabody Hotel, the roar of its worn-out muffler reverberating between the stone façades that lined the street. He swerved right on to Beale Street. At the corner of Wagner Place where Beale began its plunge down the bluffs, he pulled over and switched on his emergency flashers. Above him a bridge carrying the Illinois Central main line, the vital rail link between Chicago and New Orleans, spanned Beale. At the south side of the bridge stood the darkened hulk of a renovated late nineteenth-century brick warehouse. It was deserted, having contained a succession of failed restaurants, now forlornly awaiting the next brave entrepreneur. At the base of the trestle a flight of concrete stairs rose from the street to the tracks. Cotham bounded up the steps. He had to be certain of what he had seen from his office window.

Directly below his vantage point on the bluff top just across Riverside Drive sprawled the Center for Southern Culture. He glanced down the tracks where a distant headlight glimmered. A moment later the prolonged blast of an air horn reverberated along the bluffs. Amtrak's pale reincarnation of the legendary *City of New Orleans,* late again, was rumbling into town.

The sun had again disappeared into the soggy mass of stratus cloud, its milky light coating the riverscape in shades of gray and ochre. But he was close enough now to see the CSC clearly, even without the earlier play of light and shadow. It was unbelievable. The great oval room, the centerpiece of his creation, the main concert hall of the Center for Southern Culture, stood half full of water.

Cotham descended the stairs, suddenly engulfed in a cataract of white noise. The ground shook and what little light had found its way into the recesses beneath the trestle was obliterated as the *City* passed overhead. He hardly noticed as his brain raced through the possibilities. He and Hardegen had insisted on soil borings before they began the design of the foundations. The test results had shown no ground water, no hidden springs, no hydrostatic pressure. The elevation of the slab was set well above the one hundred-year flood stage of the river. What was the river stage at present he wondered? Damn! He should have noticed the level of water along the bank from the bluff top. He thought back to the beginning of the working drawings. Soil borings were not infallible and so to be safe he had specified that the below-grade foundation walls and the underside of the floor slab be waterproofed with a heavyweight bituminous coating. The joints where the walls met the floor slab were supposed to have been detailed with steel waterstops embedded in the concrete to prevent the penetration of moisture. Had he missed something? He had not personally checked every single detail, relying on Paul Dole, and it was entirely possible that some oversight had crept into the drawings. He shuddered at the thought. One such innocent omission could land an architect in a multi-million dollar lawsuit.

There were a limited number of possibilities for the source of the water, and he began to mentally eliminate each in turn. Rainwater seemed the most likely since there was as yet no roof in place, only an open gridiron of structural steel. Had it rained in the last few days? He could not remember any big storm, although it was certainly possible that one might have rolled in during the night from across the river drenching Downtown but missing the rest of the city. He had lain awake most of the night, however; and he always kept a bedroom window open. He had heard no distant thunder. He crossed the street to the parked car, noticing that the pavement seemed dry. Even if it had rained, the contractor should have pumps on-site to remove rainwater; and except in the event of a flash flood there should be no reason for any significant accumulation.

If the plumbing supply lines had already been installed, and he could not recall whether they had been, there was always a possibility of a leak there. But the large volume of water he had observed standing in the concert hall would have required the rupture of a major water main. Surely a Memphis Light, Gas and Water crew would have been on the scene by now.

The only other possibility seemed to be groundwater under

hydrostatic pressure seeping in from outside the foundations from either an uncharted underground spring or from the river itself. But if so, how could it have penetrated the waterproofing?

It was a Saturday morning, and traffic was light. The few cars that trickled into Downtown still had their headlights burning. Cotham turned onto Riverside Drive and then almost immediately turned again into the site. He glanced at his watch. It was 7:30, and there were now several pickup trucks and vans parked next to the chain-link fence that surrounded the buildings. He grabbed the hardhat he had begun carrying in the back seat and headed for the open gate.

A man he did not know stood by the gate, arms crossed, eyeing him with unconcealed hostility. The guard was a giant, much taller than Cotham and much heavier. His eyes, gouged into the chiseled, weather-beaten features, were cold. He wore a camouflaged army field jacket and a white hardhat. He looked like a military policeman.

Cotham ignored him, striding briskly toward the gate. The giant stepped forward blocking his path.

"Please state your name and business, sir," the voice was metallic, toneless, a Midwestern accent.

"My name is Cotham. I'm the architect."

"I'm sorry, sir, you can't come in. This site has been declared off-limits to all personnel not employed by Sigler Associates."

"And who might you be?" Cotham demanded.

"Please back away from the gate, sir. The Colonel has given me orders to secure this site, and that's what I intend to do."

"Where is Sigler? Is he here? Tell him the architect wants to talk to him."

The big man stepped forward, unbuttoning the jacket. He brushed it aside, and Cotham saw the brown leather holster on the web belt. It was the same vintage flap-type holster embossed with the letters U.S. that he had once worn as Officer of the Deck, and he knew that it would contain a Colt .45 automatic.

"At ease, Manasco, I'll handle this." The voice came from behind him.

Cotham turned to see Sigler advancing toward them dressed in a long army officer's overcoat that somehow made him seem even smaller. His face was drawn and pale, but his eyes flashed. He was smoking a cigarette, which he dropped at Cotham's feet, stubbing it out in the gravel with the toe of a freshly polished Wellington boot. Then he exhaled a lungful of smoke, not quite in Cotham's face.

"What's the meaning of this, Sidney?" Cotham snapped. "This gorilla has just told me the site is 'off-limits.'"

"Manasco is simply following orders, Ethan. The site is off-limits…temporarily. We have a safety problem, and we can't have outsiders roaming around until it's resolved; our insurance company insists on it."

"What kind of safety problem?"

"I'm really not at liberty to discuss it at this time, Ethan. But I must ask you to defer to my authority as construction manager with responsibility for site safety. I would not want you to be endangered in any way."

"You know as well as I do that the architect is not an outsider. Our contract, as well as yours, is quite specific. We are entitled to full access to the site whenever the work is in progress."

"Ethan, I don't give a damn about your contract. And besides, the work is not in progress, as you can see. We are devoting our full resources to dealing with our safety concerns. Please be good enough to leave. Manasco…."

The gorilla reached out as if to take Cotham's arm, but Cotham stepped back out of reach. "Very well, Colonel, I'll leave. But I'll be back, and I'll not be denied access to this site."

Cotham turned and walked away. To his left a white van stood waiting to be unloaded. Its double rear doors were standing open, and he glanced inside. The van was filled with a dozen or so machines of some sort. He looked more closely. Each consisted of a steel cylinder painted a bright yellow out of which emerged a pair of large black hoses like those carried on a fire department pumper truck. It took him a moment to recognize them. They were heavy-duty portable pumps similar to those a warship would carry for emergency use if it were in danger of sinking.

Chapter Twenty-Three

As soon as Cotham reached his office, he summoned Paul Dole, who as usual was working on a Saturday morning, directing him to bring the CSC drawings to the conference room. Together they quickly turned to the foundation details. The water stops and waterproofing membrane were clearly drawn and noted, and Cotham experienced an enormous sense of relief. It now appeared that the water penetration, whatever the source, was not caused by an oversight on his part. Dole was silent for a moment.

"You remember, Ethan, we first noticed water standing inside a couple of days ago. I asked George, the superintendent, about it. He said it must be rainwater and that they'd take care of it right away. It looks now as if we were seeing the tip of the iceberg.

"Suppose I take a second and call the weather bureau." He looked up the number, listened to the recording, and then hung up.

"The National Weather Service has recorded zero rainfall in the last twenty-four hours. It's not rainwater, Ethan. The water has got to be coming from somewhere else—penetrating through the walls or slab, I'd say."

"OK, Paul, call Light, Gas and Water and ask them if there's been any report of a broken water main in the area. And, Paul, do you know whether the plumbing lines have been installed yet?"

"Yep, as a matter of fact I discussed that with George the other day. They plan to core drill through the walls for the lines next week. But it's not done yet."

Cotham picked up the phone and dialed Pappas' number. There was a limit to how much could be worked out between the architect and the contractor without involving the owner, and that line had apparently been crossed in the most flagrant manner. While Cotham still knew no more about the cause of the problem, the important thing was that Pappas hear about it first from the architect along with assurance that the architect was committed to helping find a solution.

"Mr. Pappas' office, Kimberly speaking."

"Kimberly, this is Ethan Cotham. Is Nikos there, please? It's quite important."

"I'm sorry, Mr. Cotham, but Mr. Pappas is out of the country. He's in Greece until next week. He said he didn't want to be bothered with business, and we don't even know where he's staying. He may be calling in for his messages, but I don't know when that might be. Is there anyone else who could help you?"

"Damn!" exclaimed Cotham in exasperation. "Okay, thanks. If he calls, please tell him to get in touch with me immediately."

Paul Dole stuck his head around the corner. "LG&W says no reports of water main problems anywhere Downtown this morning."

Cotham nodded. *Now what*, he asked himself. To do nothing was out of the question, but he had to be careful about appearing to exceed his authority. And Pappas had appointed no one to act in his absence.

He hesitated a moment longer and then dialed the number for

the Brooks Museum. Perhaps he would be lucky enough to catch her on a Saturday.

It only took a few moments for Lucretia Silvetti to take the call.

"Hello, Lucretia. Listen, something's come up at the CSC. Pappas is out of the country, and I need your help as a member of the board."

She seemed to sense the urgency in his voice; and when she responded, there was none of the flirting he had dreaded.

"Of course, Ethan. You know you can rely on me. What is it you need?"

Cotham hastily explained the crisis. He was candid about having no explanation of the cause for the veritable lake lapping at the walls inside the concert hall.

"Lucretia, I want to get August Hardegen, our structural engineer, down here from Philadelphia. Whatever is causing this problem, it probably involves the foundations. That's his area more than it is mine. It's an unbudgeted expense, but frankly I don't know where else to turn."

"I understand," she replied. "Call him. I'll tell Nikos I gave you the OK. But, Ethan, if you are being barred from the site, what good will it do to have Mr. Hardegen here?"

"I have an idea about that, Lucretia. But it might be better for you to be able to say you knew nothing about it in case anything goes wrong."

"Very well, Ethan, have it your way. Call me back if there's anything to report."

"It's a deal." He paused. "Lucretia, I guess this means I owe you another favor...."

"Yes, Ethan, it does. And this time you're going to have to pay up!"

He dialed the 212-area code followed by the number for Hardegen's office. The phone rang and rang. Great, he thought, the old guy's in Berlin working on the new Reichstag or something.

"Hardegen here," came the deep voice with the German accent. He sounded peeved that someone had had the audacity to call him on a weekend and that he had been trapped into taking the call himself.

"August, this is Ethan Cotham in Memphis. We've got a problem at the CSC. How fast can you get down here?"

————

It was well after dark when Hardegen appeared outside the Northwest baggage pickup area where Cotham and Pallie sat waiting at the curb. He was carrying a small, old-fashioned leather valise. Cotham threw it into the trunk where it landed with a metallic clink on a large black canvas duffel bag. They headed west on I-240 toward Downtown, and Cotham briefed Hardegen.

"Ordinarily in a situation like this we would simply inform the contractor that we want to inspect the site. That won't work given the reception I received this morning. There is something seriously wrong, August, but we're not going to get to the bottom of it in the conventional fashion. Here's what I have in mind...."

They were beginning the long descent down Riverside Drive toward the CSC site as Cotham finished outlining his plan. The river loomed directly before them, stretching away toward the northern horizon, a highway of black onyx nearly invisible in the moonless night. They could sense, rather than see, its massive, indifferent presence suggested by the illuminated twin arches of the Hernando Desoto Bridge in the distance. Instead of turning left into the site, however, Cotham turned right onto Beale Street. He slowed long enough to verify what he had been sure of already—that the gates in the high chain link fence that enclosed the project were closed. They drove beneath the railroad trestle, up the bluffs, and turned south onto Main Street.

At the Orpheum Theatre the umpteenth performance of the touring version of *Cats* had just let out, and the remnants of the crowd were dispersing beneath the garish lights of the marquee and evaporating into the shadows. Cotham, Pallie, and Hardegen continued down South Main Street past rows of anonymous three- and four-story loft buildings. They passed the former flophouse where Martin Luther King's assassin, standing in a bathtub at a rear-facing window, had drawn a bead on the balcony of the Lorraine Motel. At Calhoun Street opposite Central Station Cotham pulled the Rover to the curb, and they climbed out beneath the neon sign of the Arcade Cafe. The Arcade was one of the few Downtown establishments still open at 10:30 on a Saturday night where one could find a kitchen in operation. They were in luck; a sign announced that "Memphis' oldest restaurant" would be open late for a weekend arts festival organized by the South Main Street merchants' association.

They took a seat in a booth, its ancient vinyl patched with duct tape, the Formica tabletop festooned in a pattern resembling orange and green amoebae. Cotham tried in vain to identify some detail that might have changed in the years since he had first sat here with his father. For a moment he was ten years old again, his suitcase under the table, feeling the pangs of homesickness mixed with excitement at the prospect of a summer spent with his cousins.

He and his father each ordered a grilled cheese sandwich. Then they sat and watched the big clock on the façade of the station through the plate glass windows. Finally it was time to walk across the street and board the brown and orange *Panama Limited* streamliner that would whisk him away to that exotic realm of skyscrapers known as Chicago.

Hardegen seemed wide-awake and garrulous despite the hour. He ordered a "Great Balls of Fire" sandwich and launched into an account of the ongoing trial of Little Ralphie Scarpino, the Philadelphia mob boss. Cotham called for the "Mystery Train" sandwich, while Pallie settled for black coffee. Cotham was grateful for Hardegen's cheerful monologue; it helped dispel the air of tension that was becoming increasingly palpable. Pallie seemed nervous as well. She sat quiet and erect next to him. When he had told her about the morning's encounter with Sigler and his unorthodox plan for gaining access to the site, she had insisted on coming along. He had resisted, but in the end agreed that it might be helpful to have a lookout posted while he and Hardegen made their investigation.

When the Arcade closed at midnight, Cotham paid the check while Hardegen inspected the glass case unaccountably containing a sculpture of Elvis, a ukulele, and a tiny plastic camel. They drove back down Beale Street to Wagner Place, which ran along the top of the bluff. Cotham pulled into the far side of the empty parking lot away from the streetlights. He opened the trunk and unzipped the duffel bag, handing out black nylon windbreakers and dark navy surplus watch caps to the little party. Then he shouldered the bag and motioned to them to follow.

The gravel of the railroad bed crunched softly as they stepped across the tracks and headed down the face of the bluff, the incline slippery with wet grass. At the edge of Riverside Drive they paused in the shadows behind a magnolia while a solitary car approached. It was a police cruiser; it seemed to slow, but then accelerated. They waited until its taillights disappeared around the bend; then with Cotham in the lead they quickly crossed to Tom Lee Park at the river's edge.

They found themselves about a hundred yards south of the CSC site in the midst of an open expanse of meadow. There was no cover here except the blackness, and Cotham gestured to keep moving forward toward the river past the solitary obelisk dedicated to the memory of Tom Lee, "a very worthy negro," who in 1925 saved the lives of thirty-two passengers aboard the sinking steamboat *Norman*.

At the edge of the park the clay bank was reinforced by stone riprap that dropped away twenty feet or so to the water. With their eyes at last accustomed to the darkness they could make out a narrow strip of rocks and gravel at the waterline. The river was low; Cotham could remember the previous spring when no more than five or ten feet of riprap peeped above the surface. He clambered down the bank and then turned to help Pallie descend. Hardegen half slid, half rolled down the bank after her, landing in the shallow water. He was breathing heavily. "Mein Gott!" he muttered irritably. "This is work for a younger man!"

"Very well," Cotham hissed, "we have to move along the bank until we come to the concrete terrace that steps down into the water. The chain link fence runs along the top of the steps. But if we keep to the water's edge, we can work our way past it and around to the gates on the east side. They may be unlocked, but I doubt it. If they are, we go in. If not, we'll come back to the edge of the water and find a suitable spot to make our own gate."

From Tom Lee Park it was impossible to see the three figures threading their way along the river's edge, occasionally wading knee-deep when the strip of gravel disappeared. It took only five minutes or so to reach the broad, curving concrete steps that formed the edge of a small man-made peninsula jutting into the river. The steps disappeared into the water; and at their top Cotham, Hardegen, and Pallie could see the southwest corner of the fence. Crouching, they made their way around the perimeter until they had rounded the curve to the north side. Cotham cautiously climbed to the top step and peered over.

Fifty yards away he could see the gates and nearby the white Sigler Associates job trailer. Through the window in the door shone a glimmer of light. He retrieved a small pair of Nikon binoculars from his windbreaker and focused. The interior of the trailer was illuminated by what looked like a drafting lamp. Sitting with his back to the window, a man was bent over a layout table studying a roll of drawings.

He eased back down the steps and turned to Pallie and Hardegen.

"Bad luck. Someone's in the trailer. I don't think we'd better chance the gate."

They moved back in the direction they had come, stopping again after about fifty feet. Directly above was the corner of the fence; they had reached the opposite side of the site from the trailer, their backs to the river. Cotham dropped the duffel bag, unzipped it, and rummaged around inside. He handed a long black Maglite flashlight to Hardegen and gave the binoculars and a small pocket flashlight with a red lens to Pallie.

"Pallie, we need you to go back to the north side where you can keep an eye on the trailer. Stay below the top of the steps. If anyone leaves the trailer flash the light once in our direction. After we're through the fence, we'll give you one flash every time we move to a new spot. If anything unexpected happens, slip away along the water and keep going north until you get to the cobblestones. Don't go back to the car. Catch a cab home, and we'll contact you there."

"Ethan," she whispered, "I assume this is the kind of thing they don't teach in architecture school. What if you get caught? I can see the headlines now, 'Architect Breaks into Own Building.'"

"Get going, Pallie!" he whispered urgently, and her slim figure disappeared into the gloom.

Cotham reached into the duffel bag once more, extricating a long scissors-like pair of bolt cutters. He slithered up the steps to the fence, and Hardegen could hear the soft clinking of metal.

"Okay, August, we're in! Come on up."

The hole in the fence was small, and Hardegen grunted as he dragged himself through with the duffel bag. "Mein Gott!" he grumbled, as the bag momentarily snagged the fence.

Ten feet away the gently curving outer wall of the concert hall loomed above them. The concrete wall had not yet been completely backfilled with earth, and an open trench some five feet deep lay at its base. They crept forward and slid down into the trench amid a tiny avalanche of gravel. Hardegen flipped on the flashlight. The face of the wall extending up to grade level was covered with bituminous waterproofing. That was as it should be. Cotham knew that the finished floor level inside was several feet below grade at this point. Should the river overflow its banks, a statistically unlikely but not impossible occurrence, the waterproofing was all that would prevent the interior from flooding. But the thick black coating would just as well serve to keep water in, Cotham reasoned. He had no way of knowing the depth of the water he had observed inside the concert hall and wondered if the surface was somewhere above them.

"You will note that the bottom of this trench is dry," observed Hardegen as though he were delivering a lecture on engineering forensics. "That means the water is either penetrating underground at a lower level or that it is finding its way in at some other location."

"We might as well make our first probe here. Hold the light, August."

Hardegen nodded. From the duffel bag Cotham pulled a small army surplus folding shovel of the sort used to excavate foxholes.

"You know, Ethan, they issued us little shovels very much like this in the Wermacht. I became quite fond of mine one winter in Belgium. I'm sure it saved my life more than once."

As Cotham dug, he tried to position himself facing in Pallie's direction beyond the fence in the darkness that separated them from the black river. He pointed the Maglite and pushed the button once sending a brief beam in her general direction to mark their position. There was no reply, and he wondered if she had seen the signal.

After ten minutes, panting with exertion, he whispered, "I feel it!" Hardegen directed the flashlight into the hole, and Cotham began scraping carefully at the bottom. The edge of something curved, gray and faintly shiny showed at his feet.

"There it is, the top of the Teflon pad, just where it should be," whispered Hardegen. "The seismic base isolation pads are spaced ten feet on center beneath the building."

They examined the exposed section of wall above the pad. "The wall seems sound," said Hardegen. "No cracks that I can see."

"Right," replied Cotham. "Let's refill this hole and check another spot." He glanced at the luminous dial of his watch. It was almost 1:00. Although he was dripping with perspiration from tension and the effort of digging, his feet were wet and freezing from wading in the river. He glanced in Pallie's direction and flashed his light to signal to her that they were moving. In response there was only blackness.

They scurried along the wall like rats until they reached the northwest corner where they resumed digging. A sharp clang broke the silence as the flashlight slipped out of Hardegen's grip and tumbled into the hole striking the shovel. They froze, watching in vain for Pallie's danger signal. For a full five minutes they sat perfectly still. Finally Cotham nodded and they resumed work, more slowly and carefully this time.

Cotham dug another hole and found another Teflon pad. Again the wall above showed no signs of holes or cracks. They moved around the corner and stopped ten feet further along. Another hole, another pad. No cracking. No water in sight.

They moved further around the perimeter until they approached the northeast corner. Cotham peered over the lip of the trench. He could see the job trailer about thirty yards away. Light still bathed the interior. This was not a good place to be. Should they forget to stay hunched over in the ditch anyone leaving the trailer would have an unobstructed view of the interlopers. All seemed quiet, however. Whoever was in the trailer was likely preoccupied with the drawings and not inclined to venture forth into the cold night without provocation.

They began to dig again. They were down about four feet when Hardegen tapped Cotham's shoulder, shaking his head. He shone the light into the hole as Cotham probed several feet in each direction with the tip of his shovel.

"It is not here!" Hardegen hissed. "There should be a pad at all the corners, and there is not one here. We're already a foot below the depth of the others. Ethan, they've left the damned seismic isolator out completely."

"Give me the light!" whispered Cotham. Shielding the beam with his free hand, he moved the beam slowly along the wall. Suddenly he stopped. A trickle of water ran down the face of the waterproofing forming a little pool at their feet. As he stepped back and looked around, he noticed the disturbed soil where they had been digging. It was soaked as though by a hard rain. Yet a couple of feet higher up at the surface of the trench, the earth was dry, almost dusty.

With the sharp tip of the shovel Cotham gently peeled back the waterproofing membrane at the point where the trickle issued from the wall. As he did so, the volume of water increased. With a rasping sound he scraped the shovel over the coating and peeled back more of the membrane, exposing the source. An open crack ran diagonally across the surface of the exposed concrete, an ugly, jagged, black breach in the fabric of the foundation. The crack was wide enough to insert a pencil. Where he had scraped away the protective membrane, water was now pouring out, and the bottom of the trench was quickly becoming filled with mud.

"Mein Gott," Hardegen breathed, "this is how the water got in. The ground water must have risen under hydostatic pressure and flooded the interior through this crack. Then it receded, and now the water is pouring back out. But what has caused this crack? I wonder...."

He held the flashlight close against the face of the wall so that the beam penetrated into the gap. When he looked back at Cotham, the old man's eyes were cold in the faint gleam.

"Look here, Ethan. What do you see inside this wall?"

As Cotham bent down, his face scraped Hardegen's chin, rough and bristly with a day's growth of beard. He peered into the recesses of the wall at a point where the outpouring of water was less.

"All I can see is concrete," he whispered mystified.

"Exactly! That is the point, my friend. Only concrete. There is no steel! We should be able to see number ten steel bars every twelve inches. The bastards have left out the reinforcing, too! We must try to determine the extent of the omission. Let's dig again ten feet further along where the next isolation pad should be."

To do so would take them even closer to the trailer, but there was no sign of movement inside it as they crawled through the deepening mud. Cotham dug once more until they came to another crack. A glance into the fracture followed by another five minutes of digging confirmed the worst; there was neither steel in the wall nor a seismic isolator below it. Based on what they had seen, it appeared likely that the cracks continued around some considerable part of the perimeter and that all, or a sizeable portion, of the reinforcing steel and pads had been left out.

"It is clear now what has happened," exclaimed Hardegen, his voice hard with anger and louder than it should be. "The hydrostatic pressure from the saturated soil just below the surface, probably from the river, had sufficient pressure to create strong lateral bending forces. With no steel in the wall to resist the tension, the wall cracked and the waterproofing membrane was breached. It is outrageous! Never have I seen such gross incompetence and even…."

From behind them came the metallic rattle of a door latch and a flash of light from the interior of the job trailer. Someone was standing in the open doorway, silhouetted against a glare of florescent light from within. It was a large man, and he was coming down the steps with a flashlight. The trailer rebounded slightly on its shock absorbers as he transferred his weight to the ground. Behind him came a smaller man in a long coat. Cotham and Hardegen were close enough to smell the stale cigarette smoke that issued from the trailer.

Cotham glanced back toward the river and saw the quick flash of red light low against the ground. He looked back toward the men, now advancing toward them. Had they seen it too? Probably not. The larger man was looking straight toward the spot where Cotham and Hardegen huddled in the trench up to their knees in water. He recognized the man's bear-like gait, the army field jacket, and the white hard-hat. It was Manasco, and in the light that spilled from the open door he could see that he was still wearing his army pistol. Then he heard the smaller figure say, "I'm sure I heard a voice. It sounded close. Let's check the trench around the wall." It was Sigler.

All they could do was remain motionless in the trench. The gate squeaked as it swung open, and they listened to the approaching footsteps on the gravel. They had perhaps another thirty seconds until they would be staring up into the beam of Manasco's flashlight and probably into the barrel of his Colt .45 as well.

Cotham forced himself to summon every ounce of righteous indignation. If discovery was inevitable, it was better to seize the offensive by standing up now and angrily demanding an explanation for what they had discovered. He began to get to his knees.

The noise came from outside the fence, a half-stifled, high-pitched sob. Manasco and Sigler stopped and turned in the direction of the sound. Manasco's flashlight swept across the fence, first to the left toward the river and then back to the right toward the gate. Nothing.

Now a sort of gurgle followed by a squish, like someone walking in wet tennis shoes, came from beyond the chain-link enclosure. Cotham saw a small, slim figure at the gate, staggering toward Sigler and Manasco out of the night. The beam of their flashlight swept the perimeter again and stopped abruptly, illuminating a woman in a black windbreaker, dripping with water. Her dark hair protruding from beneath the watch cap was smeared with mud, and her pale features were frozen in a mask of desperation. Sigler and Manasco ran toward her as Pallie collapsed to her knees at their feet.

Cotham started to bound out of the trench and rush to her aid, but an iron grip clamped onto his arm as Hardegen jerked him back down out of sight. Sigler was bending over Pallie no more than twenty feet away.

"Who are you? What happened? What are you doing at this construction site?" Sigler's voice was cold, accusatory.

Pallie looked dazed by the beam of the flashlight mercilessly directed into her eyes by Manasco but managed to pull herself to her feet. "I'm...I'm the second mate of a towboat, the *Nancy Sturgis* out of Paducah. We're on our way home from Vicksburg. I was out on the bow fixing our port running light; it had burned out."

She paused, shivering. "We must have hit something in the water, a big tree or something...I don't know, I couldn't see three feet in front of me. It's foggy out there. The whole deck lurched; the next thing I knew I was in the water and the boat was heading away up river. I yelled, but no one could hear me. So I started swimming for shore. I almost didn't make it…the current swept me all the way back down here before I could make it in to the bank." Her knees seemed to give way again, and she almost fell.

"What happened to your life jacket?" demanded Sigler.

Huddled in the ditch, Cotham winced. It was a logical question. No experienced Mississippi River towboat deckhand would venture on deck in the middle of the night without a life jacket. The Hernando Desoto Bridge was a long way upstream, perhaps a mile. It would be an incredibly long, cold swim, although the swift current would have reduced the time required to drift down to the CSC. Would Sigler buy her story?

"I must be an idiot. I left my life vest inside the cabin; it's a calm night, and I didn't plan to be up on deck more than two or three minutes. I'll never do that again! Christ, I'm freezing. You guys wouldn't have a cup of coffee, would you?"

Sigler hesitated, apparently thinking over her explanation. Pallie's only hope was that these two were complete landlubbers. Thank God her bedraggled watch cap lent an air of nautical authenticity to her outfit.

"Come on, Manasco, let's get her in the trailer and warm her up," growled Sigler.

Peeping over the rim of the ditch, Cotham watched as the three figures climbed the steps, and the door slammed behind them. Should he intervene? Pallie seemed to have convinced Sigler. Perhaps they would give her coffee and dry clothes and let her call a cab. Sigler might be a crooked construction manager, but he was an army officer after all. Cotham decided she knew what she was doing.

It had taken courage and presence of mind for her to intentionally douse herself in the river on a night like this.

Wordlessly, he and Hardegen crammed the shovel and flashlight into the duffel bag. Crouching, they retraced their path along the wall moving as quickly as they dared without stumbling over each other. They squirmed through the hole in the fence, pulled the duffel bag through, and headed back south along the riverbank.

About fifty yards downstream they paused and looked back. The CSC towered above them, illuminated by the city lights in a dull orange glow. Directly above the walls, the Big Dipper tipped toward the horizon as though to empty a soup of stars into the great concrete basin of the concert hall.

They continued along the bank for most of the length of Tom Lee Park before finally climbing up and heading back across the park toward Riverside Drive. By now the street was utterly deserted, and they clambered up the bluff to a gap between the renovated warehouses of Beale Street Landing and Landry's Restaurant. From there it was only a block's walk down Wagner Place to where the Rover stood waiting, although their sodden, freezing clothing and the state of exhaustion produced by almost two hours of digging made the short trek seem endless.

Cotham turned the car down Beale to the intersection of Riverside. From there they could see the white job trailer. The lights inside were off. Where had Sigler taken Pallie? And what might he do if he began to question the truth of her improbable account?

Chapter Twenty-Four

Cotham and Hardegen huddled in silence at the curb surveying Pallie's darkened house on Central Avenue. Neither said very much; they were too exhausted. Cotham had rung the bell repeatedly until it became obvious that Pallie had not returned from the CSC. Then he returned to the car. Neither of the men was ready to speculate on their next move.

Hardegen chewed the earpiece of his glasses while Cotham kept a convulsive grip on the wheel. The heater was running full blast to counteract the chill of their wet clothing, and the windows had fogged over so that the profile of the handsome Italianate structure was reduced to a dark blur.

A flash of headlights illuminated the interior of the Rover as a yellow cab pulled into the driveway. They watched as the passenger emerged wearing a long overcoat and climbed slowly up the front porch steps. It was Sigler!

The cab backed out of the driveway, and in its headlights the figure on the porch turned to face the street. No, by God, it was Pallie, draped in Sigler's army coat.

"Once he decided I was a legitimate drowned rat, Colonel Sigler was quite the gentleman," said Pallie with a wan smile. Her gray eyes were quickly regaining their flash of green. She was ensconced in a heavy terry cloth bathrobe in one of the twin wing-backed chairs flanking the fireplace of her living room. Cotham had hastily built a fire, and he and Hardegen leaned toward its warmth. All three sipped brandy from Waterford crystal glasses. The sky outside still contained no hint of an approaching dawn.

"They gave me some coffee, and he wrapped me up in his coat. Then they insisted on driving me to the Peabody to get a room. I made them drop me off, waited in the lobby a few minutes, and then caught a cab.

"It was a good thing you two cleared out as fast as you did. Before we left the trailer they walked around the perimeter of the buildings with their flashlights. I was afraid they'd notice the hole in the fence, but they came back to the trailer after about five minutes. They seemed satisfied that nothing was amiss."

"Ethan, my flight leaves at 7:00," said Hardegen, "and I've done all I can for the present. I am beginning to dry out and have only my old man's rheumatism to worry about.

"You, however, must lose no time letting your clients know what we have discovered. The structural implications are profound. I will recommend that construction be stopped immediately and not resumed until the deficiencies are corrected. That will be no small undertaking. It will delay completion by many months and will, I fear, prove to be exorbitant in cost. It must be done, however. The integrity of the structure has already been gravely affected, and certainly its seismic resistance is nonexistent. You must issue a Stop Work Order, the sooner the better."

It was no use trying to sleep any longer. Cotham glanced at the alarm clock: 5:35 a.m. He had been only half asleep, and for only an hour or two at most. But in his half-conscious state he was drafting the Stop Work Order already; he might as well get the real thing done so a courier could deliver it to Sigler Associates as early as possible. Then he remembered that it was Sunday morning. He would hand-deliver it himself if he had to; it was important that it not be said he had slept late or delayed in any way.

He was so stiff and sore he could hardly pull himself out of bed. What must poor old Hardegen feel like? And what about Pallie? Was there any truth to the old wives' tale that one could come down with pneumonia from an icy bath like the one she had taken to protect him?

He parked in the loading zone at the base of the Lincoln American Tower; no one would be around for hours on a Sunday. A warm front had pushed through during the night, and it appeared that it was going to be one of those peculiar winter days in Memphis when the temperature soared into the high fifties. The air was very still, and in the early morning light a low ceiling of yellowish cloud obscured the sky.

He made a pot of coffee, flipped on one of his favorite Schubert CDs, and sat down at the computer to begin the Stop Work Order. Outside his window the clouds smothered the sleeping city in a blanket of ochre. Nothing seemed to move while Cotham, lost in a search for the right phrase, paused at the keyboard. Then he resumed hunting and pecking.

The phone startled him. It was Pallie.

"Ethan! I tried to reach you at home. Can you feel it?"

"Pallie, it's six o'clock. What are you doing up? You should be tucked in bed with a hot water bottle after what you've been through...."

"No, Ethan, I'm serious! Can't you feel it? It's so odd...something in the air. There's something coming. I think you should go home, Ethan—better yet, come here. You should definitely leave now, I think!"

In front of him the words on the computer screen dissolved into meaningless gibberish, then went blank. He muttered a curse as he realized he had not saved the last half-hour's worth of typing. The lights blinked off and then after a moment came back on. Then they blinked off again for good.

"Pallie, are you there?" The phone was dead. What was going on?

Cotham fumbled for his mug of coffee. In the half-light of dawn tiny waves were rippling across the surface of the liquid as though a large truck were lumbering by. But he was on the 21st floor of a skyscraper, and there were no trucks outside. Then he heard the noise. At first he thought it was the wind. It had something of the sound of an approaching rain squall at sea. But it was not the wind. It contained a sort of tormented groaning, full of a grief and anger that he had never heard in the wind.

A jolt hit the building like a surprise blow from a hidden assailant. He could feel the floor tilt, and a cascade of pencils, tracing paper, the coffee mug, and the telephone went bounding off his drawing board onto the floor. A window shattered in the outer office. It was as though something monstrous had grabbed the

Lincoln American Tower and was shaking it in its jaws. Absurdly, Cotham had a momentary vision of King Kong atop the Empire State Building. The old building pitched and yawed, and he imagined that he could hear the steel columns and beams screaming in protest. A series of two or three sustained jolts were followed by an eerie quiet. Somewhere a woman was sobbing in terror.

Cotham sat still, immobilized, waiting for another shock to hit. When it did not, he rushed to the window. The shards of broken glass that littered the floor crunched under his feet. At first the view seemed normal. The buildings surrounding Court Square immediately below him appeared to be intact. But there were no lights burning as far as he could see across the city, and an odor of natural gas permeated the still air. All was unnaturally quiet, and far away dogs were beginning to howl.

Cotham looked toward the CSC site, but the entire southwest quadrant of Downtown was obscured by a pall of dust. He seized the binoculars from the floor where they lay among the broken glass and aimed them at the CSC, but could see nothing through the dust. Cotham knew that an aftershock could hit at any moment and sprinted for the elevator. Then he stopped short. Instead, he lunged for the single fire stair and bounded down the first of the twenty-one flights. The woman, wherever she was, had stopped sobbing, and he met no one else in the stairwell. After long minutes at top speed he at last reached the lobby and burst onto the Main Street Mall gasping for breath. There was no one on the street, but he could hear sirens as fire trucks roared out of the station at Front and Union. Around him lay shattered fragments of white terra cotta mixed with splinters of broken glass. Other than that though, all seemed normal for a Sunday morning. He could see no collapsed structures, no fires.

Cotham rounded the corner into Court Square. Across the park he could see a small knot of people gathered outside one of the condominiums. They were wearing pajamas and looked about in stunned silence, but he could see no evidence of injuries or panic.

He ran to his Rover parked in the loading zone. Where the windshield had been lay a chunk of the Lincoln American Tower's terra cotta cornice the size of a bowling ball. Cotham opened the door, heaved the terra cotta out, and started the engine. He backed the car around and with a squeal of tires gunned past the Tennessee Club, swerving to avoid a few shattered red clay roof tiles littering the pavement.

He roared down Second, pausing briefly at each intersection where the disabled traffic lights stared blindly down at the deserted street. Outside the Peabody Hotel a ragged cluster of fire engines stood along Union, their lights flashing. On the rear of one of the pumper trucks was pasted a bumper sticker, "Jesus to the Rescue." Although there was no sign of smoke or structural damage, a throng of guests was beginning to gather on the sidewalk.

As he sped further south, he began to see more damage. He wrenched the car around the corner onto Beale and headed west toward the river. Through the hole in the windshield, his eyes watering in the wind, he could see that broken glass, bricks, and tile littered the sidewalks. The concrete plinth at the corner of Beale and Main was cracked and no longer supported the sculpture of a youthful Elvis. Looking closer, he saw Elvis lying face down at its base, bravely refusing to let go of his guitar.

The first sign of major damage awaited him at the corner of Main Street. On his left stood the Orpheum Theatre where not eight hours earlier twenty-five hundred souls had packed the house.

The north façade of the main auditorium along Beale between Main and Front Street was simply gone. It was as though he were looking at an architectural section cut through the structure. Inside he could clearly see the tiers of balconies, the red-upholstered seats, and the sparkle of gold leaf. A crystal chandelier swung from the ceiling like a pendulum. It reminded Cotham of a photograph he had seen of a house hit by a tornado, the wall torn open to reveal a bathroom with towels still hanging peacefully on their rods, toothpaste and brushes placidly protruding from an unbroken glass on the countertop.

On the next block the high-rise concrete apartment tower at Front and Beale had been ripped open like a tree struck by lightning. A vertical crack extended its entire height although so far, at least, the wall had not collapsed. As he neared the river, the damage became worse. Where Number One Beale Street, the vacant restaurant, had occupied the old warehouse on the corner of Wagner Place, there was only a large pile of brick rubble. Mangled steel columns and splintered heavy-timber floor joists protruded out of the wreckage. Only one partially intact wall remained standing. The building looked as though it had sustained a direct hit by high explosives and was a total loss. Had anyone been inside? Probably not, he decided, unless perhaps some unfortunate homeless person had taken up residence.

The railroad trestle across Beale was sagging, but had not collapsed. Had it only been twenty-four hours since he stood at this same spot watching the *City of New Orleans* lumber past? Did the *City* run on Sundays? He could not remember. If so, it could rumble into town at any moment, unaware of the earthquake. There—he had given the disaster a name. It had finally happened, as all the crazy geologists had predicted. But now it was over, and he was still alive. And as far as he could tell, there had been no loss of life. It could have been much worse.

Cotham jerked the car to the curb. He sprinted up the steps next to the trestle, bracing himself for the view from the bluff. He was prepared for it to be bad, but not for the scene that lay before him.

The bluff itself had simply disappeared. It seemed to have collapsed inward upon itself, and a yawning cavern of red earth dropped straight from the edge of the railroad to where Riverside Drive had been. The remains of the paving lay in heaps, broken and buckled. Entire sections of asphalt, a yellow line running through some of them, lay at crazy angles overlapping each other like a losing poker hand flung down in disgust. He could see no vehicles among the debris and sighed in momentary relief. Then he forced himself to look beyond to the CSC. The cloud of dust that had obscured the site was slowly clearing, and he could make out a short section of concrete wall. It seemed to lean at an odd cant. The river foamed and crashed against the banks. Amid the whitecaps and the spray he could see dozens of malevolent whirlpools engorged with tree trunks and debris.

Something in the familiar landscape was missing, and it took a moment to realize that all three of the old bridges were gone. Their stone piers, as well as the steel spans they had supported, had disappeared without a trace.

He remembered the *City of New Orleans*. How could he warn it of the damaged trestle? He glanced down the tracks, relieved to see no approaching headlight in the distance. He looked around for something to use to fashion a barricade. In the pile of restaurant debris on the far side of the trestle he spied a half-buried wooden table. A couple of captain's chairs lay overturned next to it. Cotham climbed carefully into the rubble across piles of brick and broken joists. He pulled the table and chairs out and stumbled back to the stair. Leaving the chairs he dragged the table back up to the tracks. How long did it take to stop a passenger train traveling up a grade at twenty miles per hour?

The trestle looked solid enough to support his weight, even though the steel rails were buckled like strands of baling wire. He shouldered the table and carried it across the bridge and then down the railroad another hundred yards, finally setting it down in the center of the tracks. Then he jogged back and retrieved the chairs, placing them atop the table like a waiter at closing time. Hopefully the arrangement would send an effective, if bizarre, message to any unsuspecting engineer. It was the best he could do under the circumstances.

He made his way back down the stair and began picking his way across the remains of Riverside Drive to the CSC site. The dust seemed to be clearing. As Cotham drew closer, the extent of the catastrophe became apparent. Where the walls of the CSC had loomed against the night sky a few hours earlier, only ruins remained. The portion of wall he had seen from the bluff top was one of only two or three sections that remained standing. The rest of the site had been effectively leveled, and he was reminded of the ancient sanctuary of Apollo on Delos where an earthquake had decimated the holiest site in the Aegean.

No longer did Sigler's chain link fence separate Cotham from his devastated creation. The concrete promontory that had extended out into the river was largely gone, and an angry current roiled over whole sections of wall that had been uprooted and flung into the waves. The water had taken on a dark reddish cast, and a thick coat of red clay coated the concrete fragments. Here and there among the concrete, jagged sections of dark steel beams protruded from the water like obstacles set up to deter an amphibious assault. Now and then the powerful current shifted one of the beams with a mournful groan.

Cotham turned back toward the city. Just above the bluffs a red sun shone dully through the haze, and he remembered Pallie's vision at the groundbreaking. In it the river and the sun had both turned red, and there had been black things in the water.

Then he saw the other man, a small figure, standing at the edge of Riverside Drive near the site of the now vanished job trailer. He was staring at the uprooted foundations of the corner of the concert hall near the spot where Cotham and Hardegen had dug their final inspection hole. Red ooze clogged the cracks that extended from top to bottom of the canted walls. It was Sigler, and he was staring at the exposed footings where the seismic isolator pads should have been visible but were not.

Had the Colonel still been working in the trailer when the quake struck? Without acknowledging Cotham's presence he turned and picked his way through the rubble, up the hillside toward Beale Street. Cotham watched him a moment then looked back out over the churning river where the whirlpools were beginning to subside. They still spewed forth clouds of mist, but now, in the reddish light of the rising sun a rainbow hung over the Mississippi.

Chapter Twenty-Five

Early the next morning Inspector Dan Crews of the Tennessee Department of Transportation and R.P. Shaw, his Arkansas counterpart, made their way along the Hernando Desoto Bridge, which carried I-40 across the Mississippi at Memphis. At each girder they stopped and inspected the structure for signs of damage, taking photographs and making careful notes. Only a year before, the bridge had been reinforced to increase its ability to withstand an earthquake, and so far the inspectors had found no damage other than superficial cracking of the pavement.

The bridge had been closed since the previous morning's earthquake, and a massive traffic jam stretched for miles in both directions along I-40. Some motorists had spent the last twenty-four hours fuming in their vehicles. Tempers were frayed, and Crews and Shaw had weathered a series of abusive comments as they skirted the traffic jam in their truck.

Crews looked up from his work, allowing his gaze to follow the sweep of the river to the south. A mile or so downstream a queue of a dozen towboats stood motionless, their great engines holding them against the current in hopes that the Coast Guard would soon allow the resumption of normal operations. This seemed doubtful to him, however. Just ahead of the boats, protruding from the surface, he could make out a few jagged remains of the steel trusses that had spanned between the abutments of the old bridges and that now lay buried in mud on the river bottom. From a distance the blue steel sheen of the river was tranquil with no other hint of the twisted wreckage massed below the surface. "Ol' man river just keeps rolling along," he commented.

The inspectors were surprised to see the white pickup truck parked in mid-span just ahead. "It's empty. Don't much like the looks of this," said Crews as he approached the driver's side. "It says Sigler Associates on the door—ever heard of them?"

"Aren't they the contractors for that new building that was going up on Riverside Drive?" answered Shaw. "Look, you can see what's left of it from here, on the river bank just below the bluff—where that big pile of concrete is."

Crews opened the unlocked door. A sheet of paper lay on the driver's seat. He unfolded it and scanned the contents. Shaw could see that it was written with a ballpoint pen in a shaky hand.

I always wondered what it takes to drive someone to commit suicide. Now I know. It won't be long before some engineer thinks to inspect the foundations. When he does, he'll see that they don't match the plans—some of the base isolators are missing. The reinforcing steel, too. It's all about money, of course. I guess it always is. There was no way we could afford the foundations as they were designed. It was my decision to leave them out, but Richard Astor was in on it, too. The SOB told me not to worry; there hadn't been an earthquake in Memphis in two hundred years. And if there was ever another one, we'd

*both be long gone. I know that I'm a disgrace to my uniform
and to all the people I care about. Please tell my wife how much
I love her.*

I'm sorry,
Sidney Sigler

It was not until the following afternoon that a fisherman near Tunica, Mississippi, snagged his line on a pile of brush half-submerged at the edge of a sandbar. When he waded over to free the lure, the reflection of something metallic flashed from beneath a log. That was when he found the body. Pinned to the man's silt-encrusted sweater were the silver oak leaves of a Lieutenant Colonel.

That same afternoon a pair of police detectives knocked at the door of Richard Astor's handsome townhouse.

Cotham's first thought when he heard the news was of Jean's discovery that Sigler had helped build the bridge from which he had leapt to his death. Pallie was distraught to hear of Sigler's death, reminding Cotham that the Colonel had treated her decently when he believed her to have fallen overboard from the towboat.

"I could have done something, Ethan," she sobbed. "I should have understood about the silver leaves floating in the river. It's all so clear to me now—why couldn't I have seen it sooner?"

The City and County mayors issued a proclamation establishing a curfew and a state of emergency. Monday was declared a holiday in order to facilitate the inspection and repair of all public facilities, including ruptures in a number of Downtown gas and water mains. It was announced that both Riverside Drive and Mud Island would be closed indefinitely. The bluff-top condominiums and the luxurious houses of BluffTown, all wondrously spared despite the collapse of large sections of the bluff slightly further north, were evacuated pending studies of the stability of the remaining bluffs.

Miraculously, and due principally to the timing of the quake early on a Sunday morning, no lives were lost, although several elderly residents of Downtown and one guest at the Peabody were hospitalized for shock and possible heart attacks. The *City of New Orleans,* rolling nonchalantly into town about 7:00, late as usual, had been alerted to the danger of the severely damaged Beale Street trestle by an impromptu barricade erected on the tracks by some anonymous citizen, probably saving hundreds of lives.

A joint task force of local engineers and professors at the Center for Earthquake Research and Information at the University of Memphis was appointed by the mayors to evaluate the seismic requirements of the local building code and to recommend changes. The local Construction Code Enforcement officials and the Tennessee Board of Architectural and Engineering Examiners announced that an investigation would be conducted into the design and construction of the foundations of the CSC. Both Cotham and Hardegen, as well as Sigler Associates' Vice-President and their Superintendent, received subpoenas to testify.

The river at Memphis remained closed to commercial traffic for the better part of a month while the Corps of Engineers dredged the channel and cleared away the debris from the fallen bridges and the CSC buildings. They took soundings and reported that the bottom of the river opposite Beale Street had sunk some ten feet lower than the rest of the channel.

It appeared that the epicenter of the quake, which had been measured at 6.1 on the Richter Scale, was below an Arkansas soybean field ten miles to the west of the city and that most of the shock had dissipated before reaching the core of Downtown. In Midtown and the eastern suburbs damage had been minimal and life continued at its normal leisurely pace. In the public and private schools, the earthquake drills, forgotten since the great quake predicted for 1990 had failed to materialize, were reinstituted. Teachers were once more instructed how to mark the foreheads of the dead with a black X using the felt tip markers issued in their earthquake preparedness kits.

Nikos Pappas had been sitting in his hotel room on the Aegean island of Santorini watching CNN when he heard the news of a major earthquake in Memphis, Tennessee. The broadcast had included footage shot by Action News 5 at the site of the ruined CSC, and the reporter was interviewing a local structural engineer who had been called out by the City to assist in the emergency survey of damaged buildings. The engineer had alluded to the well-publicized seismic design of the Center and had pointed out the exposed footings amidst the ruins where the seismic isolator pads seemed to be missing.

Pappas had taken the next flight home and had called a meeting of the CSC Board for Wednesday morning at his office. When Cotham was requested to attend, he immediately telephoned Hardegen to ask him to be present as well. As he hung up, Cotham remembered the sculpture of Poseidon, the earth-shaker, standing with poised trident in Pappas' conference room.

Chapter Twenty-Six

The warm sun of an early spring morning beamed benevolently down on the procession as it wound its way up the hillside below St. Mary Magdalene Church. With Pallie at his side Cotham threaded his way between the ranks of the Knights of Columbus. The Knights stood at attention, glorious in full dress uniform, complete with plumed cocked hats and glittering swords, lining the walkway leading to the main entrance.

Despite the jubilant air, Cotham could not suppress his anxiety. He was acutely aware of a hundred details that were not as they should be. He had still not forgiven himself for not taking a stronger stand about the color of the ceiling of the nave. Despite repeated adjustments the baptismal font pump was still far too noisy, and only the day before he had discovered an entire corridor wall that had received only a single coat of paint. He was particularly embarrassed by an awkward intersection in the wood trim above the front entrance that he had failed to notice until it was too late to correct. Surely everyone in the procession would be staring at it and wondering why the architect had not done his job. And there had been an exasperating series of problems with the operation of the hardware requiring several items to be replaced at the last minute.

On one of his inspection visits the bishop had even been unable to open the front door.

Several yards ahead of them in the procession a heavy-set figure turned and glanced in Cotham's direction. It was D'Arcy Lamar, the wealthy planter from the Delta. Cotham tried to read the big man's expression: hostility, disdain, or merely indifference? Abruptly Lamar turned his back.

The procession halted as the bishop reached the doors, which stood closed. Through the glass the interior was dark. Flanked by a squad of acolytes and visiting clergy arrayed in gold vestments, the bishop stepped to a microphone and began the service for the consecration of a new church. Cotham glanced to his side and caught the eye of Father Thomas Cellini, vested in scarlet, who favored him with the slightest of smiles.

The bishop then called for the key to the doors, and Cotham stepped forward. Leaning into the microphone he spoke the words scripted for him by Cellini. "Bishop Coltharp, as the architect for St. Mary Magdalene Church, I present you with the keys to your new building."

The bishop smiled. "Thank you, Mr. Cotham. The church is truly beautiful. You should be very proud, indeed," he said, too quietly to be heard over the microphone.

Cotham nodded, his attention focused instead on the spot above the bishop's head where the awkward trim detail proclaimed his incompetence.

Next Coltharp called for the plans. Out of the crowd stepped Sam Ingram accompanied by a sheepish Don Childers, dressed in a shiny new blue suit.

"Bishop Coltharp, as the contractor for St. Mary Magdalene

Church, we present you with the plans for your new building."

Then Coltharp turned toward the door. He inserted the key and tugged on the bronze handle, then turned and frowned. He tried again, fumbling with the lock. Cotham felt a surge of panic as an alarmed Childers moved forward to help. But the bishop merely smiled and pushed gently on the door which swung open. It had never been locked.

As the procession filed into the narthex and then the nave, the lights came up. They passed the baptismal font where the water flowed and gurgled with a musical note, although Cotham could hear a faint mechanical hum in the background.

The people began taking seats on either side of the center aisle. The new pipe organ broke into the "Ode to Joy" from Beethoven's Ninth Symphony as the acolytes, clergy, choir, and finally the bishop marched up the steps to the altar platform near the center of the room. The bishop took his seat in the new cathedra, the large chair designed by Cotham that symbolized his office.

As the last of the procession filled the nave, the organ fell silent. Bishop Coltharp stood and issued a blessing followed by a prayer. Then with the help of several acolytes he anointed the top of the altar table with oil, spreading the viscous amber liquid lovingly over the surface until the oak glistened. Cotham sat scanning the ceiling, asking himself for the hundredth time how he had failed to notice that one of the rows of recessed ceiling lights was not properly aligned with the supply air diffusers.

The bishop returned to his seat and the organ resumed, this time playing a lilting tune that Cotham did not recognize. From the side door entered a trio of young girls, perhaps twelve or thirteen years old, dressed in short, gauzy tunics that would not have looked out of place in the court of Herod the Great. Each carried in her arms a great silver platter of incense, which slowly suffused the room with an exotic fragrance as the dancers pirouetted in a hypnotic and frankly sensual ballet. Pallie nudged him, and he looked down into her deep gray eyes sparkling with little flecks of emerald light. She gazed back, an oddly archaic smile on her lips, as though she were reliving some long-forgotten ancient rite.

The dance completed, the bishop stood once more. "Before we begin our celebration of the Holy Eucharist, I want to say a few words about the making of this beautiful new house of worship. Until I began working with Sophie Leland of our dedicated Building Committee; D'Arcy Lamar of the Parish Council; Father Thomas Cellini, our erudite liturgical advisor; and of course, our talented team of contractors, I had no idea of all that is involved in the construction of such a building."

Cotham's heart sank. How naïve of him to have dared to hope that he and his colleagues might merit a brief word of recognition.

"But there is something else I want to share," continued Coltharp, "and another who deserves special recognition. This experience has afforded me a second liberal education. It has given me a new appreciation for the art of architecture. And I want to ask our architect, Mr. Ethan Cotham, to stand."

Caught off guard, it took Cotham a moment to react. Slowly he rose, remembering to button his coat and suck in his gut as the nave erupted into applause. He looked around at the people, old and young, most of whom he would never know, smiling and clapping for him. Next to Pallie, Sophie Leland rose to her feet, applauding with enthusiasm, and was quickly joined by the rest of the assembly. Several rows behind them he saw Thurston, Roberta,

Lew Craig, and Lucretia, all standing together. Genuine joy shone in their faces, and he felt tears welling up in his eyes. It appeared he did have friends, after all. His work had not gone entirely unnoticed. Surely he was not going to be asked to make some sort of speech....

"This has not, I suspect, been an easy project for Mr. Cotham, and I know that our prayers are with him and his friends following the recent tragedy in Memphis," resumed the bishop as Cotham, greatly relieved, took his seat.

"He has been asked to accommodate many different needs. St. Mary Magdalene is a diverse parish, and we do not all necessarily agree on what a church should be. But as we look around us now, it is apparent that he has given us all something we could not have dreamt possible. Yes, he designed this place in response to our requirements. But I believe he went beyond that, far beyond. I believe that God was guiding Mr. Cotham's hand as he drew our plans. As Father Cellini puts it, all good ideas come from God. I see now that Mr. Cotham has been God's instrument. For that I say, thanks be to God."

"Thanks be to God," repeated the congregation in unison as Pallie squeezed Cotham's arm.

The mass proceeded with the Lord's Prayer, followed by the consecration of the bread and wine. The visiting clergy arranged themselves about the base of the altar platform, and lines of communicants formed in front of each. When it came their turn, Pallie and Ethan rose and made their way to the line headed by Cellini. As non-Catholics they knew they were not entitled to receive the Elements and that the priest would instead bestow a blessing. D'Arcy Lamar stood next to them. Lamar leaned over.

He put his large head next to Cotham's ear. He smelled of cigars.

"Mr. Cotham," he said under his breath, "we've had our differences. But you're a fine architect, and it's been a privilege to work with you. We all owe you a great deal.

"Hell, I'll even admit these chairs you picked out are a lot more comfortable than pews."

Before Cotham could reply Lamar had resumed his place in line. They moved forward until it was their turn to receive Cellini's blessing. Pallie stepped to the side, and Cotham moved forward beside her, facing Cellini.

Cellini looked Cotham in the eye and then took a small piece of brown bread from the wooden bowl he held, placing it in Cotham's hands.

"The Body of Christ," he murmured. Cotham hesitated.

"Take it, Ethan," said the priest, and Cotham obeyed.

Out of the corner of his eye he could see the bishop watching. But as Cellini raised the chalice, Coltharp turned and looked away.

"The Blood of Christ," murmured Cellini, and Cotham raised the brown pottery goblet to his lips. The wine was ordinary communion fare. But for a moment it seemed to have been transformed, and Cotham imagined he could detect elegant notes of moist earth and cedar. It could almost have been a fine Bordeaux.

About the Author

James Williamson is an award-winning architect. A Fellow of the American Institute of Architects, his buildings have been published internationally. He is a graduate of Rhodes College and the University of Pennsylvania, where he was a student of architect Louis Kahn. He has taught at Yale, Penn, Rhodes, and the University of Memphis. Williamson lives in Memphis, Tennessee, with his wife. *The Architect* is his first novel.

Breinigsville, PA USA
03 February 2011
254800BV00001B/11/P